D0174176

BUTCHER'S ROAD

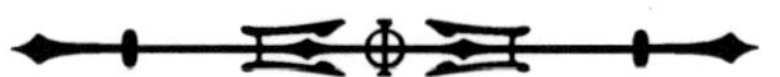

Also by Lee Thomas available from Lethe Press

The Dust of Wonderland
(Lambda Literary Award winner)

The German
(Lambda Literary Award winner)

Like Light for Flies

BUTCHER'S ROAD

Lee Thomas

Lethe Press
Maple Shade, New Jersey

Butcher's Road

Published in 2014 by Lethe Press, Inc.
118 Heritage Avenue, Maple Shade, NJ 08052 USA
lethepressbooks.com / lethepress@aol.com
ISBN: 978-1-59021-470-1 / 1-59021-470-6
e-ISBN: 978-1-59021-515-9 / 1-59021-515-x

Set in Caslon, New Orleans, and New Orleans Engraved.
Interior design: Alex Jeffers.
Cover design: Matt Cresswell.

LIBRARY OF CONGRESS CATALOGING-IN-PUBLICATION DATA
Thomas, Lee, 1965-
Butcher's road / Lee Thomas.
pages ; cm
ISBN 978-1-59021-470-1 (pbk. : alk. paper) -- ISBN 1-59021-470-6 (pbk. : alk.
paper)
1. Criminals--Illinois--Chicago--Fiction. 2. Criminals--Louisiana--New
Orleans--Fiction. 3. Noir fiction. I. Title.
PS3620.H6317B88 2014
813'.6--dc23

2014006083

For Jim Moore, a gentle giant
whose talent, good nature, and optimism I admire more than I can say.

And John Perry, as always.

Author's Note

I enjoy research and have done a considerable amount of it to give this story some meat. Not only do I want a novel to accurately convey the period in which it is set, but I also don't want to hear about all the stuff I got wrong from readers. That noted, this is a work of fiction, and I'm sure I got stuff wrong. Things have been tweaked. Rules have been broken. Regardless, I hope you'll enjoy the story, and if you do find errors, please let me know. Future editions will benefit from your observations. Thanks ahead of time.

—LT

They used to tell me I was building a dream, and so I followed the mob,
When there was earth to plow, or guns to bear, I was always there right on the job.
They used to tell me I was building a dream, with peace and glory ahead,
Why should I be standing in line, just waiting for bread?
—"Brother, Can You Spare a Dime," by Yip Harburg and Jay Gorney

He who allows oppression shares the crime.
—Desiderius Erasmus

Part One

Chicago
November 1932

Chapter 1
Far from Home

Butch Cardinal stood in a rundown house in Chicago's Southside, enduring a tedious and one-sided conversation with a man who would be dead in less than seven minutes. Since entering the ugly room with its stained and peeling lime green wallpaper, Butch had heard about sports, politics (both local and national), and the weather, which had taken a turn to the snowy earlier that evening. Normally Butch was an easygoing guy, even gregarious when the situation called for it, but this one didn't. The talker was Lonnie Musante, a short and slender man with big ears, skin as white as milk and a single lopsided tooth that rose and fell like a guillotine behind the mushy curtains of his lips. He was an ugly little man, but Butch had seen worse in his day. Much worse.

Before settling in Chicago he'd scraped by doing wrestling exhibitions and strong man acts on the vaudeville and carny circuits. On those stages and in those tents, in the trucks and train cars, he'd interacted with variations of humanity: the pinheads and dwarves; living skeletons, all transparent skin and knobby bone; bloated and hirsute women; men with afflictions Butch could hardly describe. The most profoundly disturbing character he could remember was the geek, Despero. He was one-armed and had fashioned a set of teeth from tin. He kept them polished and they shone through his curtain of wild hair as he stalked whatever unfortunate creature—usually a chicken—the show's captain chose to toss into his ring. With only one arm, Despero had taken to kicking and stomping his chickens into a daze before shooting out his bone-thin arm and grasping them by the necks. Then he'd smile his cold-tin smile and commence the atrocity his audience had paid to witness.

Butch preferred the work in Chicago, even though it was miles from the life he'd once lived—a life of real money and arenas and respect.

He'd been sent to Musante's on business, a simple transaction that should have taken no more time than a handshake or a yawn, but the creep wouldn't put a sock in it and finish up their business so the polite smile Butch had affixed to his mouth was growing tighter by the second.

"Why don't you hand over that package now?" Butch asked.

"Don't you never ask why?" Musante replied. The man stomped from one side of the room to the other as he spoke. He acted nervous, like he was expecting Butch to pull something. "I mean, you're muscle for Moran."

"I don't work for Moran," Butch said. He remained at his place by the door, hands in the pockets of his wool overcoat.

"You work for Powell, and Powell works for Moran, so you work for Moran."

"Never met the man."

"What the frosty fuck difference does that make? You think you only work for the people you know? You that much of a knucklehead?" Musante asked. He paused, waiting for an answer from Butch, who chose to remain silent. "Nah," Musante continued, "you ain't that much of a knucklehead. Even the things you don't wanna know, you know. In this town you either work for the Italians or the Bug. Now me, I work for Impelliteri and that's a straight line to Nitti, to Capone, but you're tied up in the Bug's crew, so don't you never wonder why Powell would send you over here to make a pick up?"

Butch let his smile loosen a bit as he silently wished Powell had sent him over to crack the blabbermouth's skull. It would have been quicker and the pain would have been on the other side of the conversation, but he knew better than to get rough with the member of a competing syndicate without orders. He left the real thug work, the blood work, to men who had sewn themselves deep into the gangland quilt. Butch wasn't one of them. To his mind, he was a bouncer at Powell's club, and the other duties—the errands, roughing up the occasional deadbeat—were just part of the job description. He didn't need any trouble so he wouldn't start any.

"I don't ask questions," Butch replied, "makes life easier."

"And longer, *sometimes*," Musante said. He cackled out a laugh with an ample spray of spit. Then the man chewed a bit, saying nothing but crushing his lips together. He returned to pacing. "But see, I do ask questions, even if no one's around to hear me but the roaches."

"That so?" Butch asked.

"Figure people don't ask questions 'cause they're afraid of the answers, right?" Musante said. "Their daddy or their boss or their priest or their senator tells 'em a thing is a thing, and they lap that up like starving kittens, because otherwise they got to find their own supper. They gotta think for themselves is what I'm saying, and that takes guts, which most feeblos ain't got."

"Look, Musante, I don't have all night. We can talk philosophical some other time."

"That's the thing, Butchy." Musante's eyes narrowed and his lips clamped down so tight his nose and chin nearly met. "Ain't likely to be another time. I got to asking myself about this particular situation and do you know what answer I came up with?"

"How about you just give me the package, and I'll show myself out?"

"Hold your horses," Musante said as if scolding a child.

Butch clenched his fists in the pockets. His patience was running out of him like a stream of piss after a hard night of drinking. He checked the grandfather clock in the corner of the room; its walnut cabinet was chipped and scratched. The glass face was cracked over filigreed hands that put the time at nine minutes past seven. Butch had come in as the weathered device was chiming the hour.

"You used to be somebody," Musante said. "Used to be a big deal on the wrestling circuit. Heard you used to be the best there was, except for Simm."

And he was a crooked pile of horseshit, Butch thought.

"But you ain't somebody anymore," Musante said. "Fallen good and far, ain't ya? Powell probably brought you in because he saw you in your glory days and thought he'd like having you around. Thing is, you don't belong in this game. You might be tough enough. Might be shrewd enough. But you don't belong here. You didn't grow up on our streets, and you don't have any threads tying you to anyone, least of all Moran and his syndicate."

"Musante, you've got three seconds to give me something besides your lip. Then I'm putting your lights out. I'll tell Powell you held out on me. He can decide what to do about it."

The aged man kept stomping across the floor, wholly unaffected by the threat. "Like I said, I got to thinking about this situation, and I got to wondering what Marco Impelliteri could possibly give the Bug. They say we got an all's-quiet, and that's a fine thing, but that don't mean we're working together."

"Just give me the package, Musante."

"And it's not like Marco is going to be sending a token of his gratitude to the Bug. We Italians aren't exactly known for our peace offerings, so what kind of gift is Marco sending? Why are you here, in the house of a Southsider? Why you, a thug for the Northside Bug?"

"Been asking myself that very thing for the last ten minutes," Butch said, snidely.

"Me, I understand," Musante said. "I been around too long. I'm tired of the rackets, and the rackets are tired of me. I'm an old man and I'd be in the dirt soon enough even if they weren't going to… Even if things were different. Besides, I get a few drinks in me and I talk. Never used to, but these days these loose lips can't stop a wagging once they get wet."

"I'm guessing you had a few before I got here?"

"More than three," Musante said. This busted the guy up, and he let fly another spit-drenched cackle. "Kills the pain."

"I'm just here to pick up a package, Musante," Butch said. "Give me the damned thing and I'll be on my way. I didn't mean what I said about bustin' your head."

"Yeah," Musante said. "I figured that. Saw that clear as day two seconds after you stepped inside. That's when I figured we were both in for a nap, just wanted to find out why Powell wants you sleeping."

A tremor ran up Butch's spine. He didn't know what kind of swindle Musante was playing with his head. He didn't like it though, mostly because he'd had the same conversation with himself a few dozen times. He didn't belong in the company of men like Powell, men like Musante. Butch knew that. He'd taken the job because he was tired of the road; because the money was a hell of a lot better than the strong man act and wrestling exhibitions with Mack Mack McCauley's Traveling Wonder Show.

"Got you thinking about it now," Musante said. "If you'd'a asked yourself some questions thirty minutes ago, you might be on a train to Nebraska breathing easy. Now I'm thinking you best be happy with any breath you got left to take. See, I'm thinking there's a shotgun or a tommy outside that door and as soon as I give over the package and show you out we're both going to be introduced to sweet St. Pete, so I figure I'll talk a bit, clear my throat and my head. Get a few things offa my chest, because I'm ready to go, just not quite ready this very minute."

"You're crazy," Butch said, but the confidence in his voice was gone.

He looked away from Musante, fixed his gaze on one of the ugly green walls. It seemed to breathe, moving with the sudden pulse behind his eyes. Disturbed by the illusion, he dropped his gaze and caught sight of a deck of cards on the table beside him. It was a tarot deck, the kind the carnie mystics used. He didn't like the sight of those either; most of the folks in the medium rackets were okay, but he'd met a couple that had made his skin shrivel.

He looked back at Musante and said, "I haven't done a single thing that was out of line with Powell."

"Maybe yes. Maybe no. His lady like the shape of you? You're a big guy, lots of muscle, and your face ain't bad. She spend some time looking you over?"

"Haven't noticed," Butch replied. That was true enough. "Only met the lady once and she seemed happy with her situation."

Musante walked to the corner of the room where a rickety wooden table leaned against the wall. He snatched up a bottle, pulled its cork and threw back a long slug. Then he reached into the front pocket of his trousers and lifted out a package, no bigger than a pulp novel, wrapped in brown paper.

"I guess I'm ready as I'm ever gonna get," he said.

"You really think you're gonna get snuffed?"

"Been around a long time, Butchy," Musante said. "I know what I know."

"You're nuts," Butch said, stepping forward. He reached for the package and noticed the tremble in his fingers as he waited for Musante to hand it over. "If you really thought that, you'd have skipped."

"Where am I gonna go?" Musante asked. He pushed the parcel into Butch's hand and stepped away. "I got this shack and a place on Lake Wisconsin. Had a lady friend up that way. Saw the place and figured it wasn't bad at all, dropped the cash on it right then. Can't go there and can't stay here. Can't hide this face anywhere they won't find it. A candle's only useful while it's got wax. After that, nothing but a burnt bit of string, and that's me Butchy. They lit me when I was a kid and I'm all burned down, just waiting for one last hot puff of air."

Butch felt certain Musante was the one pushing hot air. No man just surrendered to death; it didn't matter how little chance he had. Butch had heard this kind of tough talk his entire life—from schoolyard friends and naval buddies—but it was talk, empty chatter. You see a gun coming for you and you run or you duck, or you try to talk your way around. You don't walk toward it.

The package in Butch's hand weighed so little; it could have been empty. And what if it was? What would that mean? After another uneasy glance at the tarot deck, he shook the package. The contents made no sound, nothing knocked against the sides of the box. What could be so important? It wasn't heavy enough to be a meaningful amount of cash or dope. He stared at the brown paper enveloping the thing as if a clue as to what was inside might appear there. What if Musante wasn't crazy?

Butch slid the parcel into the pocket of his overcoat.

Musante stepped around him. The ugly little man walked with his shoulders back, his chest pushed out, like a cocksure grappler strutting the ring. At the front door, he grasped the handle and gave it a twist.

"Hey," Butch said, unable to shake the shawl of dread from his shoulders, "wait a minute."

"Nice knowing you," Musante said as he pulled open the door.

Butch didn't even hear the gunshot. One moment Musante was speaking to him and the next the man stumbled back, following a mist of his own blood. Musante dropped hard to the carpet. The next shot Butch did hear. It popped like a snapping twig, and the second it sounded Musante's body twitched with the bullet's impact, and then fell motionless.

Butch stood in shock, disbelieving. Musante, the son of a bitch, had done just what he'd said he would. He'd known death waited outside and he hadn't done a thing to avoid it. How? It wasn't sane. Butch couldn't figure it.

And there was no time to put it together now, not unless he wanted to join Musante on the floorboards.

Butch spun on his heels and charged through the small dining room toward the kitchen. The bare fixture cast a glare of light over faded yellow wallpaper and wooden flooring so old every plank had cracked like the fingernails of a corpse. Ahead of him was the back door, a simple sheet of wood painted gray, and he made for it with every ounce of speed he could muster.

The door cracked open before him, but instead of rethinking his direction, Butch threw coal on the fire and put more speed in his step. The guy who'd shot Musante was still behind him somewhere, possibly over the front threshold and making his way across the living room. Butch knew his only chance was straight ahead.

Then he saw the second man just beyond the opening door, and then it was thrown wide. Butch caught the impression of a face beneath a cream-colored fedora: rounded cheeks, black mustache, eyes growing wide and white as Butch barreled down. The visitor held a .38, but when he tried to swing the gun for aim, the doorjamb got in the way.

Butch bent at the waist and collided with the shooter, burying his shoulder in the guy's gut, doubling him over with a blast of breath and a pained grunt. Once he felt the weight of the man against him, Butch uncoiled and launched the shooter off of the threshold. The guy soared, clearing the porch and coming down hard on a pile of bricks barely hidden by the first snow of winter.

Butch followed him off of the porch and landed at a run. He kept his footing in the slick accumulation and made for the fence at the back of Musante's yard, never slowing and never looking back. Gunfire sounded behind him and a chunk of snowy fence popped away like a kernel of hot corn. Another gunshot and Butch felt white heat rip the edge of his ear.

Then he threw himself over the fence, clearing it by a good four inches, and he flew and he thought he might never hit the ground, but then he did hit the ground, and he hit it hard enough to punch the wind out of his chest. A rock dug painfully into his hip, and for a moment he thought he'd taken a serious hit, but when he rolled away, he discovered his leg still worked and the pain was already receding. He scrabbled to get his footing on the icy ground and several more shots rang out, but they came nowhere near him. The shooter hadn't even reached the fence yet.

Butch climbed to his feet and dashed across a junk-strewn alley and through the back door of a tenement house. He ran the streets without pause in a zig-zag pattern into the center of downtown.

The wind cut and scraped. The snow kept falling.

• • •

THE killer stared at the fence, wondering how he'd missed a guy the size of Butch Cardinal. His heart pounded like pony hooves in his chest. He sucked in the icy air and pushed the hat back off his brow, scratched his neck just below his ear before replacing the Smith & Wesson in its holster. Done with the fence, he turned on his heels and caught sight of Lennon, still sprawled out on the pile of bricks, and it took him a moment to realize Lennon wasn't moving, The killer rolled his eyes with annoyance. Leaning over the body, he cracked his palm against Lennon's cheek and told him to snap out of it, but Lennon didn't move. *Peachy,* he thought with irritation. He shoved his fat fingers under Lennon's jaw and found a pulse ticking away.

After, he returned to Musante's kitchen, took another look at the man in the back yard and shook his head. *Pussy,* he thought. Then he lifted the phone from its cradle and dialed.

When a young female voice came on the line, he said, "This is Detective Conrad." He read off Musante's address and said, "Send backup, the coroner, and an ambulance. Officer down."

Then he hung up and walked into the living room and looked down at Lonnie Musante. As he'd done with his partner, Conrad jammed his fingers under the lowlife's jaw and felt around for a pulse. The skin was already going cold, and that was good enough for him. He pulled the weathered Mauser from his pocket. Since there was no way to plant the weapon on Cardinal, now, he wiped it down with his tie and dropped it on the floor. At first he didn't like the placement, so he kicked the ugly gun with the toe of his shoe, scooted it a little farther from the body.

Conrad returned to the back yard, where he stood on the porch, looking at his unconscious partner. He figured he should do something, but he wasn't a fucking doctor. The stupid son of a bitch wasn't even supposed to be there.

He shook his head, lit a cigar, and waited for the sirens and the hubbub. He ran his story back and forth until he had it solid.

• • •

Exhausted, Butch stopped on the busy street, to get his bearings and to catch his breath. His heart felt like an icy metal glove trying to punch its way up his throat. He flagged a cab on Michigan Avenue and climbed in the back, breathing heavily and sweating under the layers of his suit and overcoat. He held a handkerchief over his wounded ear. It burned and ached, and still bled, dripping warmth down his wrist as he tried to hide the injury from curious pedestrians. The kid behind the wheel twisted round and fixed Butch with a grin. "Big night?" he asked.

Feeling exposed as if every winter-wrapped shape on the street was gunning for him, Butch slunk down in the seat and turned his face away from the window. He gave the boy, who couldn't have been more than twenty years old, his address on the west side of town and said, "Keep the chatter down." He'd heard more than enough talk for one night.

With little success, he tried to think around his temper, but the anger screamed in his head; it demanded bones for breaking and blood. But who the hell had set him up? Musante hadn't been whistling in the wind. He'd known exactly what was going down, and Butch should have listened. He should have asked some questions of his own. Questions about Impelliteri, about Powell.

He considered Musante's suggestion that Powell's woman had made him a target; it didn't fly, and neither did the idea that one of the other guys in the crew—Terry or Hank or Joey—would have something against him. He did his job—did it right. He didn't get into their business. He barely even knew them. It wasn't like he socialized with the men he worked with, didn't take much joy in shooting pool or trying to talk through the noise and smoke of the speakeasies; he entertained himself with the ladies Powell paraded through his clubs like cuts of veal on a meat cart, but kept his involvement with them shallow, skin and banter; he had no opinions to share about Hoover or Roosevelt. He went to the pictures, went to the lake, went to the gym owned by his friend Rory to keep his muscles up; ate his dinners at the Emerald Cafe, breakfasts too. In the evenings he bounced the door at Elysium, Powell's upscale club off the lake. Every few days he'd get a call—Joey or Terry or Powell himself. Butch would be given an address; told an amount to collect or the description of a package to pick up. He wasn't close enough to any of those sons of bitches to step on their toes.

The cab hit a hole in the street, bouncing Butch against the window and driving his kerchief across his bleeding ear. He bit down on a groan and squeezed his eyes closed.

He'd find a doctor to stitch the wound, if he had the time. Ears always made good show wounds; they hurt like a fucker, and they bled enough to make a substantial mess—a fine display for the crowds—but they weren't much of a deal. Herb Tenor had lost his whole ear, grappling with Del West and it hadn't done him in. It could wait. He had BC Powder in his room and a few rolls of gauze and tape. He could patch himself up until he found a professional to do the job right.

At his apartment house, the driver pulled to the curb, and turned to face Butch, still grinning like he knew all the secrets of the world. "You have a good night, mister," the kid said after Butch paid him.

The lobby of his building was icebox cold, but it kept the wind off his face. Gloom filled the entryway and staircase like ink, one hue of gray atop another coalescing into fluid shadows. His landlord was a cheap bastard. All of the light fixtures on the stairwell and in the hallways had been left empty to save a few pennies on the power bill, and the heat came on for about three hours every night to polish the edges off the icy air, but the building was never warm. It was cheap, though. That had been the point. Butch wanted nothing these days but to save money, build a good bank. Chicago wasn't home, just another place on the road. Had he not just witnessed Musante's murder, he might have stayed for another year, maybe two, but that option no longer made sense. He was leaving this particular place in the road as soon as he cleaned up his ear and grabbed a few things, then to a hotel to ride out the night. In the morning, he'd visit the bank, and then the train station after that. From a distance he could make calls, find out who he should plan to visit once the dust settled. Or maybe he'd just stay gone.

This kind of life was for lower men, and he'd only signed on because the world had left him few options.

He used to dream about another time, used to dream about home: a sturdy house on good land in a valley beneath endless sky. He dreamt of a porch and a comfortable chair and a glass of beer. In the house someone put away dishes, or fiddled with the stove or poured another drink, making him wait. But that was okay, because in the dream they had all of the time in the world, and in the dream there was warmth and there was trust and there was familiarity—no transient acquaintance to be left when the train pulled out of the station, no face to escape when lust was sated and nothing remained in its place. He rarely mentioned the dream to anyone, and on those few occasions he had discussed it, he'd failed to make himself clear.

Those listening believed he had meant a return to childhood terrain when he spoke of home. They mistook a dream for a memory, and a memory was no more a dream than yesterday was tomorrow.

Childhood, his childhood, had been a cold, ugly place. Back then he'd been called "Billy," but he'd left that name in Burlington along with his parents, his church, and every other fucking thing he'd hated. In the Navy his shipmates had tagged him "Butch," and he'd liked it well enough. Like the tattoo of the swallow on his shoulder, the name had gotten in deep enough to stick.

His ear began to throb and ache in earnest as he made his way up the stairs. The numbing effect of adrenaline—minimal as it had been—was fading, leaving the sharp screaming pain. He grasped the railing tighter until a wave of nausea passed over him. In his room he sat down and waited for the place to stop spinning, and despite taking immense comfort in the soft cushions of his davenport, he forced himself to his feet only two minutes later. If Powell had set him up, it wouldn't be long before Terry or Joey came knocking on his door.

Butch stripped off his overcoat, and looked with unease at the smear of blood covering the right shoulder. He'd need to clean that up before he tried booking a room for the night. Most desk clerks knew to keep their mouths shut, but he wasn't going to take any chances. He removed the jacket of his suit and loosened his tie.

After removing his collar and tossing it on the floor, he made quick work of the wound. It was hardly a nick, but it felt like half his ear had been taken off. Butch cleaned it with a molar-grinding splash of alcohol, a square pad of gauze, and a few strips of tape. From the shelf above the sink he opened a pouch of BC Powder and dumped it on his tongue, hoping the pain medication would be sufficient to quell the sting and the ache. He washed it down with a pull from his tooth glass, and then he leaned on the sink and caught his breath.

In the mirror, he saw a haggard face, wet with sweat and wind blushed. He splashed his cheeks with tepid water from the tap and ran a comb through his hair, pasting it down tight to his skull, and then he dragged the comb through his mustache and let loose a noisy sigh.

From the wardrobe, he pulled a fresh shirt, and tossed the one he'd been wearing, its cuffs spattered with blood, on the floor. Butch affixed a collar and cinched a new tie. He lifted his topcoat to the sink. The parcel Musante had given him made a lump in the pocket that bumped against his stomach as he hoisted the coat. In his rush to get home, Butch hadn't even thought to open the thing. He removed the box and carried it to his bed. His muscles went loose the moment he dropped to the edge of the mattress, as if they believed the night was over. The feeling couldn't be entertained for long, he knew, but it would have been damn nice to just lie back and close his eyes for a minute and let his head catch up to all that had happened to him.

Instead he tore the paper away from the package, revealing a simple cardboard box. He lifted the lid and pushed air against the back of his throat like a growl. Just cotton padding. The fucking package was a dummy, a prop in a game. Butch threw the parcel against the wall and was surprised to hear the clink of metal hitting wood. He stood from the bed and walked over. In the gloom, he saw the snaking chain of a necklace, affixed to a smudge of reddish gray. He bent down and lifted the jewelry. Immediately, he questioned its value; it didn't have the color of a precious ore—not gold, not silver. The metal had a red cast, a genuine red, not the approximate red of copper. It seemed to weigh less than a strip of tin. Butch leaned to the side so the pendant could get some light.

"Shit," he muttered.

It was ugly and it was cheap, and as far as Butch was concerned the box might as well have been empty. He slid the thing into his pants pocket and then returned to the sink with his overcoat. He scrubbed at the shoulder and cuffs to get the worst of the blood off. Some salt would help scrub away the stains, but he wasn't going to take the time to grab any out of the kitchen. Instead he rubbed with a wet towel, grinding one fabric into the other.

When he returned to the living room he was feeling better, felt like his control had returned. He eyed the davenport, the rickety table in front of it, and the rug beneath them both. Under the furniture was a loose board below which he kept the bulk of his money; sure, he kept some cash in the bank so he could write checks, but he kept most of his capital close. Butch leaned forward and grabbed the edges of the table, but before he hoisted it off the floor, he heard a ticking sound at his front door. He let loose his grip and straightened up. The noise at his door became a rattle and then silence.

Someone was testing the lock.

Butch remained quiet, easing to the side of the room where he'd left his overcoat. Knuckles rapped on his door, and a thin voice—Terry McGavin's voice—slid into the room. "Hey, Butch, open up. Gotta talk."

Backing away, Butch pulled on his overcoat. What little trust he might have had for McGavin and the other boys in Powell's crew was gone. He hadn't recognized the shooters at Musante's, but McGavin had sent him to that house, and for what? An ugly chunk of metal at the end of an ugly thread of chain?

Butch hurried to the far side of the room and unlatched his window. He looked over his shoulder at the flimsy table and the rug beneath it. His money waited there, nearly enough for the good house on a fine parcel of land, but he'd have to return for it. McGavin was turning the knob again. Butch had no idea if the man was alone, but he knew damn well he was armed—McGavin liked his guns, called them his "ladies."

Though he tried to open the window quietly, it scraped in the frame, and Butch shoved it upward.

"I hear you in there, buddy," McGavin called. A moment later, a shoulder collided with the door.

Butch climbed out and sat on the windowsill. Another booming collision was followed by the creaking of distressed wood. One more solid hit and the door would go.

Unwilling to face another gunman, Butch dropped into the snow. He landed hard and a twinge of pain shot through his knee, but he ran nonetheless, slipping and sliding on ice and snow, and making his way far from the room he called home.

Chapter 2
Wake Me When It's Over

Hours later, Detective Roger Lennon opened his eyes and instantly regretted the decision. Beside the hospital bed was a small lamp with an exposed bulb. Needles of discomfort and a penny nail of serious misery drove into the back of his right eye. Then the other pains surfaced. His skull felt like a bag of shattered glass, every edge and point scraping raw nerves. He groaned and reached for his head and groaned again. Another mistake. His back felt like it had been used for punting practice. After lowering his hand, he remained as still as he could, trying to figure how he'd made his way from a State Street speakeasy to a hospital bed.

After a shift, far quieter than most, he'd gone to the Zenith Club and had been throwing back shots of Canadian whiskey. As Lennon drank, the piano player tapped out a dreary rag on the upright against the back wall, his shoulders and arms moving sinuously behind a cloud of blue-gray smoke, his head locked in a downward and cocked position. Lennon was eyeing one of the new girls, who worked the tables on that side of the room. She wore a snug dress in a shade of pale green that reminded Lennon of pond water. Her eyes were big and her legs were fine, and Lennon watched, smiling against his glass, as the waitress fumbled with a lighter, trying to produce a flame for the cigarette of another detective, who worked homicide on the Southside.

His name was Smith, and he was built like a football, wide in the middle, with a head that looked absurdly small on his shoulders. Because of his portly build, the suit he sported had to have been finely tailored so the buttons on his jacket didn't pull trenches across the lapels.

Lennon knew Smith was on a couple of payrolls: one was the city's; the other was the Northside gang's: "Bugs" Moran's Irish crew. The Italians and the Bug had split the entire city, and that included the city's employees. Lennon himself collected an envelope once a week, but his bonus came from the Italians on the Southside, once ruled, and some said *still* ruled, from a prison cell by Al Capone. Between that and his salary, Lennon could still barely stay in the black. The house his wife wanted, the clothes she wanted for their daughters and herself—damned if he could rub a couple of dimes together by the time payday came around again. He certainly couldn't afford a suit the quality of Smith's.

He ordered another drink from a waitress who wasn't nearly as fresh as the girl in green. Then his partner, Curt Conrad, appeared beside him, shuffling into view like a diseased rhino. The fat man pinched a cigar between two sausage-plump fingers and carried his hat in his fist. Conrad sat down, and they started gabbing.

But Lennon couldn't remember what they had talked about. It hurt to try like his thoughts were weighty bastards, and they tromped on the broken glass in his skull as he attempted to line them up.

He'd been in a bar.

Now he lay in a bed.

With as much care as he could muster, he rolled his head on the pillow so he no longer faced the scalding light, and Lennon opened his eyes again. In the chair by the door, his wife Edie sat slumped. She was sleeping. Her hands rested in her lap: one clutched a wadded kerchief, and the other draped over her handbag, which in the gloom resembled a napping black cat. Briefly he wondered where his daughters were. Normally, Edie never let Gwendolyn and Bette out of her sight—not that a night in the hospital had anything in common with normal.

Lennon sensed movement in the hallway, hisses and mutters and displacements of light that might have been shadows or just defects in his vision. Across the corridor, the silhouette of a woman appeared in a doorway a moment before it closed.

Lennon wondered if he was dreaming because nothing he saw was in focus. Nothing felt solid, except for the pain. The pain felt hard and hot, but aches could slip into dreaming minds, couldn't they? A tickle of panic went through him. He vaguely remembered a determined face bearing down, remembered the collision of muscle and bone and the sensation of swimming backwards, and then nothing. What if Lennon wasn't in the hospital at all, but only dreaming of it? What if he were still lying in that yard with his head split open and his brains leaking into the snow? His panic swelled. He struggled against it, called out for Edie, and at first she didn't move, and Lennon felt certain he was trapped in a terminal dream. He bolted up in the hospital bed and the pain coalesced unbearably; so much so that he answered it with a harsh, gravelly shout, which seemed to do the trick.

"Roger!" Edie cried. Fright broke her voice as she bolted from the chair.

A squad of men appeared in the doorway behind her, and they all rushed in, and suddenly he was surrounded by familiar faces, many of whom smiled to see him awake. And then there was talking—ridiculous questions about how he felt—and finally Curt Conrad, his partner, a man he'd never considered particularly compassionate or bright, told the crowd he was getting a doctor, and Lennon thought that was a fine idea.

Edie sobbed into his neck, and he wished he could get his mind off of the pain long enough to appreciate her concern, but her hair smelled pungently of floral perfume and the scent all but made him gag. He coughed and each spasm was like getting slugged by a heavyweight. A wave of gratitude ran through him when the doctor entered the room and cleared it of well-wishers before setting into his examination, which consisted of simple questions (*How many fingers am I holding up?*) and a bright beam of light drilling through Lennon's retina and into whatever part of his brain telegraphed anguish.

"Detective Lennon," the doctor said, "Do you remember the events leading up to your injury?"

There was a girl in a green dress that reminded him of pond water, and then a man with a determined jaw was closing in, only steps away, and then he thought about water again.

Swimming. Sinking.

"Not really," Lennon said. "Bits. Pieces."

"That's natural enough. You took a nasty blow to the back of the head. Your memory got rattled. You might have even lost some of it for good. It's hard to say in these cases. Just don't let it worry you. You seem to be functional. We'll want to keep you awake for at least a few hours to make sure you remain responsive. I'm afraid you'll have to suffer through without morphine at least for the time being. We don't want to addle your mind with drugs until we know the extent of the damage."

"How about aspirin?"

"Not until we're sure you're not hemorrhaging internally."

"When will you know that?"

"Another couple of hours should do it."

"And if I am bleeding into my skull?"

"Don't worry yourself, Detective Lennon," the doctor said. "In these cases, if you can open your eyes, you're probably just fine. This is all just precaution."

The doctor patted Lennon's forearm and left the room. Then Edie returned, handkerchief to her face, still crying. She quickly resumed her place against his neck, smothering him with the scent of lilacs.

"That's enough, now," he whispered into her ear. He didn't dare lift his arms to try to push her away, though. The more alert he became, the sharper the pain. "Come on, sweetheart. Ease off. I'm one big bruise."

Edie pulled away, and Lennon was struck by the panic in his wife's eyes. Edie was fragile and unworldly; she'd never really grown up, had never endured anything more than imagined discomforts. Swaddled in a soft environment, she couldn't imagine a life without her husband.

To his complete surprise, Roger realized he hated her in that moment. Her tears were accusations, prosecuting him for being wounded, for being weak. He could have died, and her wet eyes asked, "What about me? Did you ever think what would happen to me?" The grim emotion disturbed him with its suddenness and virility. And the grief in his wife's eyes only fueled his irritation, because he knew he was bound to fail her. In Edie's world, heroes were bronze statues, impervious and static. Her heroes never bled, they never fell down. But he couldn't live on a pedestal; he couldn't be a radio-drama husband who said and did all of the right things, and made promises that would last forever because the show needed to end on a high note and Frances Langford was singing them out.

Quit looking at me like I'm disappointing you, he thought.

"Gwendolyn and Bette are with my parents," Edie told him, expectantly as if waiting for congratulations for having made a sound decision on her own. "When Curtis called, I was beside myself, so I called mother and…" Edie rolled her eyes and sniffed gingerly and tried to smile. "And I haven't even asked how you feel? I'm so sorry. Darling, are you okay?"

"You know those headaches you get that keep you in bed?" Lennon asked.

"Of course."

"Like that, only scalp to sole."

"Won't they give you anything for the pain? They must have something."

"No," he replied. "Not just now."

"How can they just let you suffer?"

Please go away, he thought.

"Roger," Edie asked, sounding one part concerned and one part perturbed.

"They have to wait with head wounds. It won't be long. It's okay."

Curt Conrad appeared in the door behind Lennon's anxious wife, and for the first time in years, Lennon was glad to see his partner. He couldn't shake the way Edie was making him feel. His irritation with her grew with every tear she attacked with her handkerchief. He should have been grateful for her concern, thankful that she needed him so completely, but he was stuck with the rigid pain and it was staining his mood.

"Come on in, Curt," he said.

Startled, Edie twisted at the waist to watch Conrad waddle into the room.

"Honey," Lennon said, "I need to talk with Curt—about last night."

"Have you caught that animal, yet?" Edie asked.

"No, ma'am," Conrad said.

"Are you even looking?" Edie demanded.

Conrad stopped and fixed Edie with a hard glare. He pulled the stump of cigar from his lips and said, "Road blocks. Train station. Lakefront. Nobody's getting out of this city."

"As it should be," Edie said, apparently satisfied that his colleagues were taking her husband's treatment seriously. She turned back to Lennon and said, "Can I bring you anything?"

"Not just now," he said.

Edie dipped forward and kissed Lennon's cheek, filling his nose with her awful perfume one more time before telling him that she would be back soon and that she loved him. As she left she turned her head away from Conrad as if he were a hobo making lewd remarks and stormed out of the room.

"Lennon," Conrad said, grasping the back of a chair. He slid it toward the bed and asked, "How's your skull?"

"Still attached," Lennon replied. "You want to tell me how I got here?"

"What do you remember?" Conrad asked. In the chair, he stared at his hands, seeming more interested in the dirt under his nails than Lennon's response.

"We were at a house," Lennon said.

"Yeah," Conrad said, nodding. "You know whose house it was?"

"No. I don't even know why we were there."

Conrad hummed deep in his throat. "Guy's name was Musante," he said. "I got word that someone wanted him dead, and it wasn't the wops. Impelliteri sent us over to keep an eye on him and make sure nobody tried to take him out."

"I thought we stayed out of that shit," Lennon said.

"We do," Conrad told him, using his thumbnail to dig beneath the nail of his middle finger. He hadn't looked at Lennon since taking the chair. "I told Marco it was a one-time thing. A favor. I like it when he owes me favors. So we drive over and park outside and not much happens for about twenty minutes and I get to thinking that maybe Musante is already face down. So I take the front; you take the back. Next thing I know, *bang bang*. I go in, but the perp is already fast-assing it out the back, where he introduced himself to you. Hopped a fence, and…"

"And what?" Lennon asked.

"And nothing. He was gone. I got off a few shots, but there was no way I was going to catch him. Cardinal may be big, but it doesn't slow him down none."

"You already identified the guy?"

"Sure," Conrad said, flicking a bit of filth from his thumbnail to the floor. "Got his name on the radio fast. William Cardinal. 'The Butcher.' That wrestler who does muscle work for Powell and Moran. He's not going anywhere. Like I told the missus, roadblocks are in place. Train station is covered. If we don't get him, the wops will."

Son of a bitch, Lennon thought. He'd seen Cardinal in the ring. The match had gone on for nearly three hours, until the Butcher had managed to take down Dicky Reed once and for all. Lennon remembered it as one hell of a match. The corners of his mouth ticked up in a grin.

"Something funny?" Conrad asked, finally looking at him.

"Not much," Lennon said. "I just feel better knowing I got my ass tossed by a pro like Cardinal."

"You can pay your respects soon enough."

"He should have stayed on the mats."

"Yeah, well, a million shoulds aren't worth a speck of moth shit. He's gonna have his face plastered all over the papers—name all over the radio. He'll be in a cage or ice cold or both by this time tomorrow."

Chapter 3
A Lovely, Simple Frame

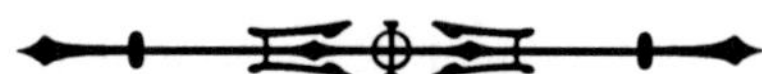

Butch Cardinal wasn't dreaming of home; he wasn't dreaming at all. He'd dozed off only an hour ago, and now a door creaked open and a flashlight cast glare over him. In the beam of light, he saw the snub nose of a revolver, and his muscles tensed.

Blinking and squinting against the torch's blaze, he lifted his hands, partly to keep the light from his eyes and partly in surrender. He'd thought the gym would make a safe place to flop. Only now was it occurring to him that safety was a thing of the past.

"Get up," a rough yet familiar voice said.

"Rory?" Butch asked.

"Are you expecting someone else?"

Relief flowed through him. Rory "Ripper" Sullivan was one of the few people Butch knew in Chicago outside of the rackets. They'd met on the legit wrestling circuit as Sullivan's career in the ring was ending and Butch's was just building steam. The man had acted as Butch's mentor for half a year, before calling it quits and buying this building in Chicago. Rory lived in the apartment above the gym with his daughter, Molly. Without enough cash in his pocket for a room at the Y, let alone a hotel, Butch had taken a cab north, putting a good amount of distance between himself and his room. With no place else to go, he'd made his way to Ripper's Gym.

He sat up and swung his feet off the side of the cot.

"And that's as far as you go," Rory said. The gun slid closer as if riding the beam from the lantern.

"What's this about?" Butch asked.

"I think you've got about two seconds to answer that question yourself," Rory said. "I've been hearing things. In fact, it's about all I can find on the radio. Now, I want to hear some *things* from *you* about a guy named Musante."

Butch stiffened. Had Musante's murder already made the news?

"I don't understand," Butch asked.

"You don't understand," Rory mocked. He ratcheted on the overhead fixture and turned off the flashlight. Rory was on the short side, but he looked like he'd been carved out of stone, with a wide chest, thick arms and a square face. The gym had been more than a business for Rory; it had been an obsession. Even in his advanced years, Rory had the musculature of a fighter in his prime. Cold blue eyes stared out beneath white brows. His chin was notched. Normally, when he spoke only a ghost of his Irish accent was apparent, but the angrier he got the more pronounced his brogue became. "The likes of Powell aren't nothing but poison and gristle, and you would have known that if you'd ever listened to me. Now start talking."

Butch explained what had happened at Musante's in as much detail as he could manage. Reciting it back to Rory, hearing it all out loud, Butch found every moment implausible. Unreal. Rory wasn't helping much. His face was like a mask, showing no more emotion than he would if he were listening to someone complaining about the fish at a restaurant he had no intention of visiting. Butch ended the story and leaned forward making a bridge of his hands and resting his upper lip against it.

"And you came here?" Rory said, dryly. He leaned against the doorjamb and shook his head. "I can't have you here."

"I'm not looking for a hideout, Rory," Butch said. "I just didn't know where else to go."

"Tell me about the cops."

"What cops? After the shooter killed Musante, I ran. I didn't stick around until the cops came."

"You dumb sack of horse meat," Rory said, "The shooters were the cops."

Butch looked up stunned. "That isn't right. Not right at all. How do you figure?"

"Because your name's all over the radio. The cops said they walked in on the murder, so if you didn't do it, then they did." The Irishman lowered the gun and stepped away from the door. "Get your kit together and come on out to the office. I'll put some coffee on."

"I should go," Butch muttered as if speaking to himself. Rory didn't need this kind of trouble.

"Oh, you'll go. But it sounds like you're up to your eyes, and the only thing panic is going to get you is more panic. So let's take a few minutes to think things through before you go tearing out of here."

"Sure," Butch said. "Thanks."

"Don't thank me," Rory said, "My opinion isn't going to change your luck. They're still going to fry your ass if they get their hands on you."

With that, Rory left the doorway and a stunned Butch, who covered his face with his palms and scrubbed viciously as if his troubles were a film of dirt he could remove with a bit of elbow grease. Except these troubles were in deep, a stain. If Musante was right, Butch should have been dead on the floor alongside the ugly old man. But why?

He pushed himself off of the cot and stretched out his back. A twinge of pain shot up his left knee from where he'd landed in the alley after escaping his apartment. Compared to his ear, which stung like hell, the minor twinge was hardly a concern. He shook it out and walked through the lighted gym. In the office, Rory had already set a percolator on the electric burner he kept on top of his filing cabinet. Photographs, yellowing newspaper clippings, and post bills with Ripper Sullivan's name printed in big black letters cluttered three of the walls. A half wall, open from waist level to ceiling, squared off the fourth side of the room. Rory kept his desk against the partition so he could collect dues from the men entering the gym and so he could keep an eye on his equipment. Unlike the walls, the desktop was clear—the wood dry and split like Lonnie Musante's kitchen floor.

"I didn't mean to bring this mess in here," Butch said. "I should get going."

"Sit your rump down," Rory said.

Butch hesitated. He wrung his hands and then smoothed the hair on the back of his head.

"Sit," Sullivan repeated. Butch did as he was told. "What did I always say about the first thing you do when you get into a ring?" Rory asked. "And I don't mean that exhibition nonsense; I mean a real match."

"Size up your opponent," Butch said.

"That's right. Glad you remembered something useful."

"But how am I supposed to size this up? None of it makes sense. The Irish? The Italians? The cops? I haven't stepped wrong since I got into town, haven't skimmed so much as a nickel. I play the game clean."

"Bodies stacking up in barber shops and on the sidewalks and you think it's a game?"

"You know what I mean." He wasn't in the mood for a semantics lecture. *Any* lecture.

"No, I don't," Rory snapped. "I don't know what you mean. Fill me in. How is this a game, Butch? I offered you work at the gym five minutes after you settled in town. Solid work. Real work. I told you to get away from Powell, but you laughed. What did you tell me? You told me you weren't really involved."

"I'm not," Butch said. "I bounce at his club, and sometimes I collect a few bucks."

"Every tooth in a shark's mouth is involved. You think you just go along for the ride and no blood gets on you?"

Butch lowered his head. He felt cornered, and a hot rage boiled up the back of his skull. "Rory, we should talk about something else."

"You telling me I'm wrong?"

"No," Butch said. He couldn't even comfort himself with denial. Like Rory said, he was in the shark's mouth and he was there of his own choosing, but Jesus if that explained what was happening to him. "The other way around. I know you're right and it makes me gut sick. But it's done. Now I've got to deal with it. That doesn't mean I have to go over it a hundred times."

"Well, you don't have the luxury of letting this one slide, Butch. You need to size up your opponent and find a hold that'll take him down."

"Between the cops and the gangs there are about two thousand opponents, Rory. And if you heard about this on the radio, then that number is just getting bigger while I sit here."

"So what's your plan?"

"I don't know."

Rory lunged forward and slapped the side of Butch's head. "You'd better know something, Butch. Now what's your plan?"

Grateful his friend hadn't hit his bad ear, but distracted by a ringing the attack had brought to his head, Butch sat back in the chair. How could he have a plan? He'd only just found out the extent of his problems. Rory crossed his arms and sat up straight and glared, wanting an answer. He had to say something.

"I'm going back to my room. I've got some money stashed there. When the bank opens, I'm going to get that money out, too, and then take a train east. I'll catch a boat, go back to Paris. I did a tour there…know some people. I can lay low."

"Except you can't," Rory countered. He stood and poured coffee into two tin cups. He handed one to Butch and said, "The police are involved. They're already at your place, and anything you think you want, *they've* already got it. You walk into that bank, and they'll walk out *with* you. You walk through the doors of that train station and—"

"Okay," Butch barked. "I get it." But the import of what his friend was saying had only just reached him, the cry inciting an avalanche. Everything he had, every *damn* thing, was gone, and if not gone, inaccessible, which was the same thing. Years of work and saving and living like a bum just to have enough money for a house, and peace, and quiet… Meaningless. Wasted.

"But why is this happening?" he asked. How had he crossed Powell or Impelliteri in the first place?

"What makes you think there is a why?" Rory asked. "Case you haven't been paying attention, your buddies don't make up the sanest group of folks this side of the Mississippi. They get ideas—foul, rotten ideas. They get these ideas and they can't get rid of them until they do something about them."

Butch nodded his head, but the explanation fell short. The Italians and the Irish gunned each other down the way most people did their laundry, but there was always a reason—even if it wasn't particularly rational.

"So what do I do?" he asked.

"Right now, this city is your opponent, and it's too big and too well-trained for you to do anything but forfeit."

"I told you I was leaving," Butch said.

"Okay." Sullivan shrugged. "Where are you thinking of going? With no money and little chance of finding enough work to feed yourself?"

"Does it matter? I can't stay here. Maybe I'll head south and see if I can pick up with one of the carny tours. I can't take the chance with a vaudeville troupe or serious promoter up this way. They're all tied into the syndicates."

"What about that sister you used to talk about?"

"First place they'd look, and I haven't spoken to her in a long time."

Not since the fight. Not since the night he'd rushed her to the doctor. A sudden flash of memory—split knuckles, his sister screaming, so much blood. After what he'd done, she wouldn't welcome him at the door, not unless she was holding a rifle to his chest when she did it.

"Any other family?"

"None that could help."

"Friends?"

"They're all on the circuits," Butch said. "No place to hide. Too many eyes."

"Okay," Rory said. "Okay. Okay. Let's circle this thing, eye its backside. What was in the package?"

"Huh?"

"The package," Rory repeated. "You said Musante handed you the package before he got himself shot, so what was in the package that's so god damn important?"

"Nothing," Butch said, "I mean, I don't know. Just some ugly piece of jewelry. No diamonds or rubies on it. Looks like lead—ugly rusted lead."

"You got it on you?"

"Yeah, I got it," he said and reached into his pocket.

Butch withdrew the pendant, and handed it across, laying the chain over Rory's thick palm. The man sneered and squinted and tested the ornament's weight in his palm before shrugging again and handing it back to Butch. "You're right. It doesn't look like much. Musante say where he got it?"

"I don't even think he looked inside the package," Butch said. "I think someone handed it off to him, and he handed it off to me."

"Sounds like a hell of a puzzle for a few fillings worth of metal."

"I'm thinking I should send it on to Powell. Might take the heat off."

"Don't be feeble," Sullivan scolded. He huffed out a breath and looked away in frustration like a disappointed parent. "Those two cops expected to walk away with that thing last night, and they didn't expect to leave anyone who'd touched it breathing. And don't count on this being Powell's racket. It could be Impelliteri and the Italians. Either way, the cops and the gangs are the same thing. I don't trust the cops in this town any further than I can piss, but they follow the money and do what they're told. You work a deal with whichever side wants that thing, and this Musante business will go away."

"If I live long enough to make the deal."

"Finish your coffee," Rory said. "I think I can get you out of the city, and I have a good idea about where you should go."

"Where's that?"

"New Orleans. I've got a friend down that way named Rossington. Owes me a favor or two."

"Name's familiar."

"He was a second-tier grappler. Had a lot of flash and style. Not much on the technical side, but he was good with the crowd."

"Why'd he throw it in?"

"Couldn't really get used to the life."

Butch didn't like the sound of this. Rory was the straightest arrow he'd ever met, but putting his life in the hands of a stranger at this point, after what he'd already endured, was just plain foolish. "You trust him?"

"Like I said, he owes me. I'll call ahead."

Butch would keep it in mind. It was a long shot, but maybe his only shot. He needed time to think it through. Another concern was at the top of his mind. "Rory, I hate to ask, but I need you to do something else. It's important, and if it doesn't help me, maybe it will help you."

He leaned over the edge of the desk and whispered to Rory, the way he would if they sat in a crowded room, surrounded by strangers. Butch told his friend about the loose board under the davenport in his apartment, told him about the money.

"Maybe the cops won't find it. Once things cool down, you could go by my place and pick it up."

"And you want me to send it along?"

"Unless things go south," Butch said. "Then you keep it. There isn't enough money in the world if things go south."

Chapter 4
Like Postcards from the Inferno

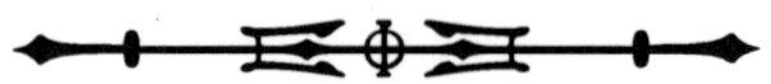

1.

Detective Roger Lennon sits in an armchair. He wears a cream-colored cotton robe. A white bandage wraps his head like a turban and blends seamlessly with the lace doily draped over the back of the chair. Smoke rises in a twisting column from the cigarette he's placed in the crystal ashtray on the table beside him. His daughters sit on the floor at his feet. Both wear crisp, golden-yellow dresses tied at the waist with white sashes. Their hair has been parted down the middle and pulled into pigtails. They look up at him, mouths open, bombarding him with questions. Edie leans over him from the back; her arms rest on his chest and her lips are pressed in a kiss against the strip of bandage above his ear. The corners of his mouth are lifted in a shallow smile. His gaze is distant, removed, as if staring at something miles away, like a convict imagining a field of grass, an open road, a room built of anything but concrete and steel bars.

2.

A man in a double-breasted, forest-green suit stands before the door of a crematorium. Flames jump behind the grate. A blanket of coal and coal-coke glows orange at the bottom of the incinerator. The name etched into the clay pad nestled beside the cheap wooden casket reads *Musante*. Fire climbs the coffin's sides. Smudges of char ring the box in black waves. The observer's name is Marco Impelliteri. His hair is thick and the salt and pepper strands lie neatly against his head. Agitation is clearer on his face than grief. He clutches a crucifix in his plump palm, which he holds firmly against his hip.

3.

Butch Cardinal stands on a desolate road. The highway lies beneath three inches of snow. Fields on either side of him are the icy blue-white of an arctic wasteland. No homes. No barns. The few trees that remain are skeletal, showing no more signs of life than the snow-blanketed fields or the steel gray sky above. Butch's ruined overcoat is fastened tightly at the neck. The collar is raised. His thumb is extended in anticipation of an approaching car.

4.

Sunlight cuts through a bedroom window like a golden ramp, ascending from a dull cotton carpet to the upper window frame. A white chair rail circles the walls. Above the rail, a dense linen-textured paper with a magnolia blossom pattern rises to the crown molding. Below it, the wall is painted violet. Across the room is a narrow bed. Two men are tangled on the mattress. One man is short and burly, his skin is pale and smooth and unblemished. The other man is darker, tall, hirsute, and bulky in the manner of an athlete who has let his muscles soften. He lies on his back and the younger, smaller man straddles his hips.

Chapter 5
Oh, When the Saints...

Hollis Rossington lived in the converted slave quarters of a French Quarter home owned by a young man named Brugier. The two-story bungalow stood across a courtyard dense with succulent foliage. A narrow balcony, painted the same bright white as the building's trim, ran the length of the sky-blue structure. The building had been updated with the latest comforts—a serviceable kitchen, indoor plumbing, a telephone of its own—and while it lacked the elegance of the main house, the residence more than met Rossington's needs. Besides, the rent was cheap, and these days, that was far more important than grandeur.

He slid from beside Lionel, his companion of the past two months, and climbed off the foot of the bed. Lifting his dressing gown from the floor, he noted the twinge in his lower back, a reminder of his age. He wrapped himself in the robe and passed into the hallway. The phone bell rang again. It seemed to have been ringing all morning. He'd never grown accustomed to the sound. It grated on his ears like the squeal of a pig being hauled hoof-high over a killing floor. To make matters worse, he rarely received welcomed calls. There were the occasional dinner invitations, but generally, the calls came from angry bookkeepers insisting they receive their checks before the week's end.

At the midpoint of the hall, he grasped the iron rail of the spiral staircase and began the task of cautiously descending the steps. Though he admired the architectural benefits of the case, he'd more than once slipped on its metal rungs and brought his knees to misery against one of the cold metal spindles.

Downstairs he gazed to his right toward his kitchen. The phone pealed yet again. He turned left.

The parlor was a small front room, barely large enough to entertain guests. Red velvet wallpaper, the kind Rossington had only seen in bordellos, covered the walls, and the sofa and chairs, with their intricately carved frames and plush, richly colored materials, added to the impression. The rooms had been furnished and decorated when he'd leased them, and though they did not reflect his taste, they struck him as generally cheerful.

He picked up the phone and an operator informed him he had a call holding from Chicago. The caller's name was Rory Sullivan.

"My god," Rossington chirped happily. He hadn't heard from his friend in ages, and the call reminded him that he owed the old man a letter. "Hello? Rory? You there?"

"Hollis?" a scratchy and distant voice asked, sounding like the moan of a ghost with bronchial complications.

"Rory, I don't believe this. How are you? It's been too long."

"This isn't exactly a social call, Hollis."

Typical of Rory to get right to the point. He didn't bother with subtlety and he didn't need to. Rossington generally found his friend's directness refreshing after all of the silk-over-horseshit conversations in which he found himself. "Is something wrong? Is Molly okay?"

The line between them was scratchy. Mysterious pops and crackles punctuated Rory's words. "Fine, Hollis. Fine. I'm calling you about something else."

Rossington listened through the static as Rory told him about a friend who was in trouble. Because of the poor connection he had a difficult time making out the exact nature of the problem: something to do with the *obs*?

"Hold on, Rory," he said. "What are obs?"

"Mobs. *Mobs,*" the Irishman shouted, "He's in trouble with the mobs, but he's a good guy, just a little naïve."

"A young kid?"

"No," Sullivan said, "not young. Just kind of ignorant to the depths of shit he's stepped in."

"Okay," Rossington said, also shouting. "What can I do?"

"I sent him your way, Hollis. I need you to put him up until he gets his balance back."

Rossington would have said yes to nearly any request the man made of him. Giving a beleaguered gentleman a bed and a roof was a paltry request—or should have been—but there were things Rory didn't know about Rossington's current situation, things (like Lionel) he didn't *need* to know. Still, could he say no? He didn't see how.

"It's a lot to ask," Sullivan said. "This guy is in deep with some nasty people. Sounds like he's got both sides of hell closing in on him. It could—"

"I didn't catch that last bit."

"Dangerous," Sullivan said. "It could be very dangerous to have him in your house."

"Who is this guy?"

It took three tries before Sullivan's voice came through clear enough for Rossington to catch the name: *Butch Cardinal.* Rossington smiled. Had he heard that correctly? He remembered Cardinal, had even seen one of his bouts in Kansas City. Good-looking kid, as he remembered it. Even for a wrestler he was big, and not the kind of big that came from padding his physique with fat: pure muscle, that one. On top of that, he was one hell of a wrestler. He'd pinned Joe Means in less than thirty minutes and had hardly broken a sweat.

Rossington had to admit he liked the idea of connecting with someone from the ring. He'd left the mats himself a decade ago, and except for taking in the occasional bout, and his ongoing friendship with his dear friend Rory Sullivan, he'd completely severed himself from the sport. It would be nice to have another wrestler in the house, if only to swap war stories over whiskey and cigars. But athletes, too many of them, had rather limited tolerances; the ones he'd met had proved to be less than accepting of uncommon emotional perspectives.

How would he explain Lionel's presence? The place wasn't nearly large enough to pull off some screwball cinematic subterfuge. He could always ask Lionel to find alternate lodgings for a time. Lionel had been a popular visitor, if not exactly a houseguest, for a number of Hollis's acquaintances. Certain transactions of skin and spit were invariably negotiated in those instances, which made Hollis all but immediately discount the idea. Still he didn't mind the idea of Lionel being gone for a time. Frankly, Hollis could use the break.

More and more, the kid's presence grated on his nerves. Some time apart might be just the thing they needed. But Lionel wouldn't be easy to relocate. Any way he looked at the situation it came out awkward.

"He may not be comfortable here," Rossington said, finally. "I can get him set up in one of the hotels in the Quarter and keep an eye on him if that helps."

"He's tapped out, Hollis. He needs to lay low and he needs to do it on the cheap."

"Okay," he said. "I'll handle it, Rory. When will he be here?"

"No idea," Sullivan said. "But I gave him your number."

"That's fine."

"I'm counting on you, pal."

"It's the least I can do," Rossington said.

They spent another few minutes on the telephone, trying to get caught up, but the connection continued to deteriorate. By the time they said their goodbyes, Rory's voice was little more than a thunderous buzz. Rossington hung up the phone and turned away from the desk only to discover the young man staring at him from the archway. His mouth was ticked down into a frown. His arms crossed over his bulky chest.

Chapter 6
Out on a Rail

Three days after witnessing Lonnie Musante's murder, Butch woke disoriented and freezing in a house on the outskirts of Cincinnati. He sneezed. He sniffed and wiped at his nose with the back of his hand; a cold had set up shop in his head and throat. The night before, unforgiving weather had about done him in, and he'd considered breaking down and renting a cheap room for the night to escape the winter chill. Then he'd seen the house with its *Foreclosure* sign nailed to the front door. He hadn't even had to break in. A hobo, a thief, or local children had already cracked the backdoor's lock, so Butch had simply stepped in out of the wind and made himself at home. The ousted family had taken most of the comforts with them, but a large sofa—perhaps too bulky to relocate—faced off on the fireplace from the center of the room, and Butch found a set of thick brown curtains in a second-floor bedroom. He carefully removed these from the rod to use as blankets. The possibility of diligent neighbors kept him from lighting a fire, and though the layers of fabric—his clothes and the curtains—didn't keep him warm, they had been enough to keep him from freezing to death.

He rolled his head on the arm of the sofa. On the wall next to the fireplace was a hole the size of a fist. A scrap of plaster hung from the ragged upper edge against ribs of lath. It was one of three such holes that marred the wall separating the hearth from the dining room.

The hole in the wall and the frost on his bones recalled fragments of his childhood. He hated that time in his life. It was ugly. Confusing. So many of the memories were alike, it was difficult to place them in a rational chronology, particularly since he'd spent so much time trying to erase them completely.

His mother wipes a tear from her eye, the lids and cheek already growing puffy and discolored. In the next room, his sister, his only sibling—Clara—screams. A crack, like gunfire—a father's hand across the soft cheek of his daughter's face ended the shrill cries, leaving only sobbing echoes to ooze through the walls. The scene is familiar, as common as fish on Friday and church on Sunday, and Butch doesn't know anything else; he only knows he's scared, and Clara is wonderful, and their father should know that. Robert Cardinal should know his daughter is wonderful. Butch—who wasn't yet Butch but rather Billy—tries to get off the bed. His sister's muffled sobs gather and coil in his stomach and turn hard and aching, and he doesn't ever want to hear the sound again. His mother holds his shoulders and shakes her head and more tears spill down her cheeks, and Butch tells her he has to talk to his father. She tells him he can't because his father isn't really there at all.

Sitting up on the sofa, squinting through the diffused light seeping in around the paper on the front windows, Butch knew it was time to head south. No matter what else happened, the weather would only be getting worse in the northern cities. He felt uncertain about taking Rory's advice, looking up Hollis Rossington. Butch didn't know the man. Rossington might have owed Rory a favor, but how strong was that obligation? Strong enough to house a fugitive? He'd thought about going to New York and losing himself in the swarms of unemployed while he tried to sort out what had happened to his life, but Butch only had the money in his pockets—another gift from Rory—and it would have to last until he managed to wrangle some work. In New York, he might find labor on the docks or in a warehouse—the kind of jobs he'd done fresh from the Navy—but no one was getting fast work. It could take some time, and what would he do until then? The idea of scrounging in a bread line was too shameful for him to consider, and he couldn't imagine enduring weeks of bitter cold in some confiscated shelter.

No, he had to go south, and there was no reason not to choose New Orleans. Even if Rory's friend Rossington didn't pan out, Butch could get by cheap in that city. Between the brothels and the burlesques there were a hundred places he could bounce, and the people there knew how to keep their secrets.

A sneeze took him off guard and the two that followed were each more powerful. He sniffed and rubbed his watery eyes. He preferred the sneezes to the coughing. He'd started coughing the night before, and each barking hack produced instant agony.

At the window, he pulled back an edge of butcher paper, which had been used to cover the glass. The weather kept the neighborhood quiet. No one occupied the sidewalks or streets. At a mirror in the upstairs bath,

Butch combed his hair down and did his best to straighten his jacket. For three nights he'd worn his clothes to bed. Creases lined his jacket and his slacks. The gauze on his wounded ear looked foul. Blood and sweat soiled the cotton padding. He tried to peel it off, but the cotton was glued to the wound, and he felt certain if he ripped it away, he'd ruin another collar and further stain his overcoat.

He coughed violently, producing a thick wad of phlegm that he spat into the sink, which he leaned on until the worst of the ache faded from his chest. He released a deep breath in slow, measured sighs, afraid that expelling the air all at once would produce another round of painful coughs.

In New Orleans, he could get his feet under him. He'd have time to think through his situation. He had enough money for a train ticket and maybe enough to get him through a few days in a cheap flop.

It wasn't much. It was all he had.

• • •

AT the train station, he bought a ticket for the Pan-American line. Then he sat on a bench and nearly fell asleep. He'd exhausted himself crossing town from the empty house. His chest felt heavy and his head felt light. The train wouldn't be leaving for hours. In the men's room Butch cleaned up a second time, grateful for the hot water that scalded the chill from his fingers and cheeks. His suit looked worse in full light. He might as well have been one of the bums curled on the benches of the station. Unshaved. A filthy bandage over his ear. He admitted that vanity was a peculiar thing to worry about, but he'd spent his life running from the little boy with ripped trousers and smears of mud on his knees, and now that same little boy peered from the mirror at him. Butch left his reflection, left the men's room, and bought a newspaper from the stand. He took a bench. His nose ran and his head throbbed. The chill he'd felt for days now radiated outward, rather than in. Opening the paper, he searched for his name, and more importantly a picture. He found both on page seven, and though initially the sight of himself staring from the page startled him unpleasantly, he realized the photo the papers had rounded up was more than seven years old. He hadn't even had a mustache then, and the young man with the pronounced muscles, striking a threatening pose, looked so little like the ragged man he'd left at the toilet mirror Butch felt relieved.

He folded the paper and then he relented and made his way to the bank of phones at the back of the station. He had a call to make, a call he had been putting off.

After telling the operator to connect him with a number in Chicago, he tapped a finger against the side of the booth as he waited for the call to go through.

"Yeah, this is Powell," a reedy voice answered.

"Angus, this is Butch."

"Is it?" Powell asked.

"Yeah, look—"

"Where the fuck are you, Cardinal?" Angus Powell's bellowing voice filled his ear.

"That's not important."

"Oh, so now you know what's important? You stupid piece of shit. Now *you* know what's *important*? You ice one of Impelliteri's cabinet without orders?"

Butch swiped his palm down his face. He checked over his shoulder to make sure no other travelers were within earshot before saying, "I didn't kill anyone."

"Save your bullshit, Cardinal. Just tuck that shit right in your cunt, because we got a war on our hands, and we got that war because you spent your day off popping some greasy, little fuck. You think the Italians are spraying bullets for grins? This is vendetta shit, and you brought it down on our heads."

"The police killed Musante," Butch said. He coughed violently into a fist as he pulled the phone away from his head. By the time he got the earpiece re-situated, Powell was in the middle of another rant.

"...work for the Italians. They don't wipe their asses without clearing it with Impelliteri. So try another one, Cardinal. Better yet, get your ass back here. Lie to my face. See what kind of pain that brings you. Think you're so fucking tough? Well, you ain't shit, Cardinal."

"Talk to Terry," Butch said. "He's the one that called me. He sent me to Musante's. He's the one that set this whole thing up."

"Terry?" Powell shouted. "I've known Terry since we were kids, pinching candy and tobacco. You telling me I should take your word, the word of a side of beef I bought secondhand, over a guy I've known my whole life? You really think that's gonna play, Cardinal?"

"Okay, Angus." Butch closed his eyes and ground his teeth. Powell's tirade was working on his headache like a pickaxe.

"Okay? Nothing is *okay*. You get your ass back here so I can feed you to Marco Impelliteri, and then things will be okay."

An announcement played loudly from a speaker above Butch's head. "The Continental leaving Cincinnati serving stops in Lousiville—"

"Cincinnati," Powell said.

"I gotta run."

"You do that," Powell said. "I got another call to make. You're dead, Cardinal. You know that, right? You're—"

Butch hung up the phone and hurried back into the station as if a paper screen rather than hundreds of miles of wire separated him from the furious thug. Once he had a moment to settle himself on a bench, his head cleared. He saw that the phone call had actually been useful. Powell wanted him dead, no question, but the man had had no idea what was going on. He hadn't said word one about the package, the necklace. Powell didn't seem to have a clue about the cop-shooters or the set-up. Terry might have called Butch, might have sent him to that miserable house, but he hadn't done it on Powell's order.

Butch didn't know exactly what that meant. Did Terry have a personal beef with him? With Musante? Was Terry working his own swindle, playing the sides against each other?

When they called boarding for the Pan-American, Butch walked with his head down all the way to the platform. He sat at a window with no one beside him and no one facing. He slumped down low in the seat, covered his face with the front page of the newspaper and drifted off to sleep as the whistle blew and the wheels began their chugging rotations, and…

Sleep.

Butch woke, and snatched the paper from his face. The musty chemical reek of the printers' ink remained in his nostrils; it felt alive, squirming down the back of his throat.

A woman had taken the seat across from him. She was a fine-looking woman, with a round face and button nose and thick brunette hair swept back and held in place with a number of pins. She wore the smart jacket and skirt set of a secretary.

A sneeze came over him so quickly he didn't have time to cover it.

The woman winced in disgust and covered her own mouth and nose with a gloved palm.

"I'm sorry," Butch said.

She offered him a tight smile. Her eyes flicked a gaze at his wounded ear, and then she hugged herself as if cold and turned her head to the window. He followed her example and stared through the glass, surprised to find the sun setting over a distant ridge of hills.

• • •

WHEN he woke the second time, the car was dark. His head ached and his chest felt as if it were stuffed with cotton. The disapproving secretary had apparently found another seat and a portly man with a scruff of graying beard snored lightly in her place. Full night had fallen. A thumbnail moon hung on the horizon.

Butch sneezed twice in quick succession and the man with the gray beard mumbled in his sleep. Folding the paper, Butch decided to stretch his legs. He felt miserable just sitting there, stewing in the cold. The train wobbled as he got to his feet and the motion nearly sent him crashing back into his seat, but he steadied himself and began walking down the aisle, occasionally glancing at the faces bathed in gloom. Briefly he wondered what took these other people from Cincinnati to New Orleans. Were they traveling toward something—the promise of work, loved ones—or were they running away like Butch?

The idea of skipping out sat wrong with him. He understood the repercussions of remaining in Chicago and taking on Powell or Impelliteri, but he'd never surrendered before, even when Jerry Simm had cheated him out of the title and sent Butch on the downward slide. Even then he'd held his own, though it hadn't done him any good.

After his return from an exhibition tour in Europe, Butch had begun training for the match of his career. He would be taking on the World Champion, Jerry Simm, in front of thousands of spectators in Madison Square Garden. He'd heard the rumors about Simm: how he'd oiled his body to defeat Krasner in Milwaukee, and how he'd hired a Russian to cripple Morey the morning of their title bout in Kansas City, but Butch had let the rumors roll off of him. Simm was a sportsman, and he was at the top of the game.

Simm didn't want the match, Butch had heard, but the promoters called the shots. This sort of manipulation was all part of the show. The championship belt had to switch hands every so often or the audience lost interest. Fixes were made. Fights were thrown. The promoters controlled the game top to bottom, and they understood the value of showmanship, likely more than they understood the value of athleticism.

Audiences needed a constant supply of heroes, as they grew tired of the ones they were given. So the word had come down that "Butcher" Cardinal would be taking his place at the top. Maybe for a week. Maybe for a month. It didn't matter. A championship win would solidify his future, and he wanted it. Not only for what it would mean to his career, but also because Butch knew he was a superior athlete to Simm, and he wanted the chance to take the man in a straight shoot.

Three days before the match, Butch had been sparring with a young Hungarian named Dobos, who had been recommended by the owner of the Hell's Kitchen gym where Butch had been training. Dobos was a bear with a thick shrub of beard and his hair sheared flat on top to make his face look absolutely square. The kid had twenty pounds on Butch, but he was graceless, and on the first day, Butch had found it easy enough to throw holds and bring the enormous Hungarian to the mat. The second day, the kid planted a knee in Butch's balls, and while he was incapacitated,

Dobos wrenched his arm behind his back. Without so much as a "fuck you," Dobos snapped Butch's wrist and dislocated his shoulder. And that was it.

Simm's manager refused a rematch, telling Joshua Liszt, Butch's representative, that most kids never got that close to the champ, and if you were given the opportunity, you didn't muck it up. Opportunity knocking once and all. Furthermore, the promoters, though not pleased with Simm's behavior, knew he was a cash cow, and they weren't about to put him to pasture. Liszt had told Butch to let it go. The promoters ran the circuits, and if you got on their bad side, you might as well get used to digging ditches.

Butch hadn't listened.

Once his wrist had mended, he'd tracked Dobos to a club in Alphabet City, and the second the square-headed cheat laid eyes on Butch he sprang to his feet and produced a spring-knife with a four-inch blade. Butch wasn't concerned. He wrestled the knife out of the kid's hand with remarkably little effort and then dropped him with a punch to the jaw. Then Butch had Dobos on his feet, locked in a full nelson with the kid's head shoved into a corner of the bar. From there it had been easy enough to get the story. Simm's manager had slipped the Hungarian five hundred bucks to make sure Butch didn't make the bout in the Garden.

Instead of confronting Simm, Butch had gone to the papers, but they had unanimously dismissed his account: not because they didn't believe him, but because they didn't care. Simm had greased wheels and palms, and the sports reporters could expect perks from a guy like him. They didn't know what, if anything, Butch Cardinal could do for them. Besides, they all knew that wrestling was a game, a show, no different from the fan dancers in a burlesque to them. Most of the matches were fixed to begin with, and Butch was just showing his naïveté—or flat-out ignorance—by thinking sportsmanship played any part in the goings on.

He couldn't let it go, though, no matter how hard Joshua Liszt insisted.

Bouts were canceled and new ones never materialized. Liszt dropped him as a client. Two months later, the manager signed Dobos and started selling him all over the Northeast.

Butch's career collapsed, but it didn't end there. His friends in the sport deserted him, refused his calls and turned away when they saw him on the street. Even those that sympathized with his plight and believed his account of the fix made it clear they couldn't be seen to take his side in the matter, not if they wanted to keep careers themselves.

He hadn't done anything wrong. He'd played by the rules, except he hadn't truly understood that the rules were different for people with real money.

Butch opened the door between cars and stepped into the night. The bitterness was out of the air, and he wondered how far south they'd traveled already. He sneezed twice, and a small voice from above said, "Bless you."

Butch craned his neck and saw the face of a little boy peering over the roof of the next train car. He smiled and waved at the boy and said, "Thank you."

But the boy was gone before the words were out of his mouth. Butch thought he heard voices from up there, but the train's grinding chug and the rushing wind made it impossible to say for certain. Not wishing to exacerbate his burgeoning cold, Butch returned to the car and his seat.

Instead of replacing the newspaper and going back to sleep, Butch stared out at the night and the crescent moon, remembering things he'd rather not remember.

Because of Simm, his career had been derailed, though Butch believed the setback a temporary one. Free time on his hands, he'd decided to visit his sister and her husband in New Hope, Pennsylvania, but that had ended in a night of blood and screaming and what Butch could only consider another betrayal.

With no other skills, Butch had joined Cal Lawrence's Vaudeville Extravaganza and performed exhibitions and feats of strength under the name "Ivan Borgia." He couldn't use his own name because the promoters had their fingers in the Vaudeville pie as well. Since he wasn't a headliner, no one saw his face until he came on the stage. He'd grown a thick beard and cut his hair to the scalp, and the disguise must have done the trick, because no one had blinked or said boo. Those days had been good, if not satisfying. He'd had money and security and he'd made friends among the entertainers, and had taken up with a singer named Mildred Olin. He could have made a decent future in the traveling shows, except he couldn't put aside his past. On more than one occasion, his sparring partners complained of rough treatment.

It was just a show after all.

It all went sour one afternoon, when during a matinee, Butch grew frustrated with a townie, hired for the weeklong booking. The man was not a wrestler by any definition. He threw illegal moves—kicks and punches—night after night, and Butch took it all in stride, because the man's bulk was showy, but there was little muscle beneath his layers of flab. His punches struck powerlessly, but on that afternoon, the townie landed knuckles to Butch's Adam's apple, causing him to choke. The townie ass pranced around the stage like he'd done something heroic, and Butch's temper boiled thick and dark, like molasses.

He grabbed the townie and hoisted him toward the lights. The man squealed and threatened and slapped the air as Butch held him like a trophy overhead. Then Butch carried the man to the edge of the mats and slammed him to the wooden stage, where he lay motionless on the boards. Ultimately the man recovered, but Butch was fired on the spot. He left that night while Mildred was on stage. Too angry to offer any kind of civil farewell he wrote her a letter after he settled in with Mack Mack McCauley, but he never heard back from her.

Then Powell. Then Musante. Now the train.

Butch closed his eyes, eager to reach New Orleans. He was due a break, and he had to believe one waited at the end of the line.

Chapter 7
Dancing in the Attic

"Do you visit often?" the girl in the crisp white uniform asked.

"What else would I be doing?" Paul Rabin replied warmly.

His wife lay on the bed before him. In the morning sun her skin more resembled an accumulation of dust than tissue, kin to the motes that swam in the buttery light bathing her face and neck. He'd insisted on a room that gave Irene morning sun; she loved it so. He touched the back of his hand to the dry skin of her brow and stroked gently. "She's all I know."

"How long have you two been married?" the girl asked.

"She was sixteen, and I was twenty," Rabin said, "and the century had just begun, and we felt certain it would be our century, so we had a wedding and a honeymoon, and we expected a hundred years of bliss." He chuckled without mirth. "We were children. Foolish romantic children. And here it is only a third of the way into the century, and we're hardly there at all anymore."

The nurse's face softened with sympathy or envy or the offspring of both. Tears pooled on the lower lids of her eyes. "Do you have children?"

"We weren't so blessed," Rabin said. He grasped Irene's hand lightly and bent to press his lips to her fingers and wished the nurse would leave him alone—leave *them* alone—because he found the timbre of the nurse's voice abrasive, and he preferred his mornings with Irene to be uninterrupted. Peaceful. He understood that the girl was new and eager to show interest in her patients and the families of her patients, and she'd probably learned this behavior in a college course that stressed the importance of such interactions. The nurse wouldn't realize her peskiness, so Rabin considered addressing it. Most mornings he arrived with his newspaper and a thermos of black coffee and he perused the *Tribune* and read certain passages aloud if he thought Irene would find them interesting, and sometimes she'd ask him to read the passage again because she liked the way his voice sounded pronouncing certain words. Of course, she wouldn't ask him to repeat anything this morning as she'd had a difficult evening. The hospital handled her difficult evenings with drugs, enough to keep Irene sleeping entire days.

Raving, the doctor had said. *Striking out.* One orderly had commented sourly that Irene had even managed to scratch a poor nurse's cheek.

That's my good girl, Rabin thought. *Don't you take any of their guff.*

Irene's official diagnosis was pre-senile dementia. It sounded ugly to Rabin. He preferred the name Dr. Kenfold used. Kenfold was one of the younger doctors who spoke in long, technical sentences as if constantly quoting from a psychiatry journal. He called the illness, Alzheimer's, named for a German who'd studied the condition extensively. Unfortunately, Alzheimer had done a wonderful job in identifying symptoms, but he'd done nothing in the way of curing the affliction. Mental capacities diminished. The brain dissolved. The patient died, lost in a stew of disjointed sensations, words, and images.

Rabin could imagine little worse in the way of fate. The idea of losing his faculties, losing control, made his neck perspire.

On the table, beside the window, Rabin noticed the vase of flowers he'd brought on his last visit. The carnations were looking wilted. Sad. Usually they lasted through the week. He stepped closer to the table and reached out a finger, drawing a line in the light film of dust that had gathered on the top.

"I'm sure tonight will be much better for her, Mr. Rabin."

"Oh, I have no doubt," he replied. "Her spells come and go. No harm."

"Yes, sir."

Rabin grasped the vase and lifted it. "It's a shame how they wither," he said. "The beautiful things never last long enough to overstay their welcome."

"I can take those..."

Before the nurse could finish her sentence, Rabin released the vase, fumbling after it as if the act were the result of clumsiness, rather than a premeditated act of destruction. The nurse gasped in harmony with the shattering glass. Rabin hopped back and regarded the mess with an expression of dismay.

"What have I done?" he asked.

The nurse rushed forward. "I'll get that. Please. Let me."

"No. No. No." Rabin said, kneeling down to begin retrieving pieces of the broken vase.

Then the nurse was next to him, insisting that he let her clean up the mess—such a helpful girl. Like Rabin she carefully pinched her fingers on the smooth shards, cautious of the jagged edges. She picked with one hand and stacked the glass in the other. Rabin waited until he had her rhythm in his head and then went for a particularly thin shard. He snatched it and pulled the sliver upward, drawing a cut along the back of the nurse's hand. It was shallow, hardly wider than a tack point. The nurse squealed and jerked her hand away.

"I'm so sorry," Rabin said, but every muscle in his body sighed with satisfaction.

Then the nurse was assuring him it was nothing and insisting he let her finish with the mess, and she hurried from the room, allowing Rabin the opportunity to smile, and when she returned with an orderly, who held a broom, Rabin apologized profusely and the nurse waved his concern away, and then the glass and dead carnations were swept into a pan, and the orderly sopped up the water with a rag and told Rabin to watch his step. The orderly made a hasty retreat with the debris, and yet the nurse remained.

"You should have that cut looked at," Rabin said. "I feel just terribly about this whole situation."

"It's barely a scratch, but I should at least daub it with iodine."

"You do that," Rabin said. "And thank you so very much. You've made my visit particularly pleasant."

The girl smiled and bent at the knees in an odd and completely unnecessary curtsy, as if he were a suitor at a cotillion, and after she left, he stood by the window and shook his head, wondering exactly what her performance was meant to mean. A curtsy? Really? What must be going through that child's mind?

Once Rabin felt certain the nurse had made her way to the next victim of her curiosity, he pulled a chair to Irene's bedside and unfolded his paper, and he read her the headline about a missing schoolgirl, and the story about the wrestler who had murdered a man named Musante and was successfully eluding capture, and he read her the article about the World's Fair which would be infesting the city, and he read her the latest developments in the Al Capone trial and he thought he saw his wife's lip twitch upward when he mentioned the gangster's name, and he smiled, because Irene had often said the man looked like a gorged toad. She felt certain some sly fox would gobble him up in due time.

Like so many people, she believed in justice. Radio dramas. Picture show fluffs. Biblical passages. These were the sources of Irene's comfort, just as they comforted the millions who wagged their fingers and shook their heads and said, "He'll get his," when learning about some new perpetrator of atrocity. So ingrained was the desperation the reverends called "hope" it castrated men and further mollified women to the point only a handful of truly depraved men ever saw justice. Those that did became not only infamous for their crimes, but also false icons that suggested justice existed, that it reigned, when in fact every villain in custody had a hundred counterparts left untouched, roaming the world and spreading their gospel. The convicted were the exceptions to the rule; and they proved nothing.

Rabin thought the belief in justice was the belief that someone else would handle the bad men. Yet another opiate of the masses. It was simple logic really—all very Darwin to Rabin's mind. The bad men were the fittest, inclined toward greed, deceit, and violence. The fit survived, and the fit were not concerned with hope beyond the proliferation of hope in others. Hope made sheep and sheep were for fleecing and for eating.

"And the president is certain we'll be seeing an upturn in the economy in no time at all," he said to his unconscious wife. "I'd say it's about time," he added.

He read through the sports page and amid the scores he found a notice for a wrestling exhibition, and he thought of the wrestler, William Cardinal known to fans as "The Butcher." He returned to page three of the paper and looked over the story a second time. He winced upon reading the name Curtis Conrad, one of the detectives investigating the crime. He knew the man. At least he knew enough about him to dislike him intensely. After gathering what information he could from the piece, he studied the accompanying photo. The picture was old and in it William Cardinal had struck a common pose for one in his line of performance: arms out, knees bent, face attentive as if expecting attack from any side. Well-muscled. Intimidating in a brutish way. Rabin looked closely at the dots that made up the lines and shadows of Cardinal's face, and he squinted at the image and leaned back. After lowering the paper to his lap, he offered his peaceful wife a soft smile.

"This one looks like he'd fight back."

Rabin returned to reading the paper, putting William Cardinal out of his mind for a time. When he finished the news he kissed Irene's brow and held her hand before excusing himself. Quietly, he slipped the paper into the pocket of his overcoat and retrieved his thermos of coffee, which had gone untouched because the curious nurse had disturbed his morning ritual. He gave Irene a last wave and exited into the hall, where he said, "Good day," to the various members of the staff charged with caring for his wife.

Outside, he pulled his muffler tight to his throat and shivered. The snow had ended the night before, leaving the world white and bitter. Glare hit his eyes like acid and he made a visor of his gloved hand as he walked to his car. He drove home slowly, not because the icy roads concerned him, but because the other drivers on the road were, generally speaking, idiots. He thought about Irene and the lies her doctors had told him: lies about her condition improving, about her being able to come home soon. Though he wanted to believe their prognoses he wasn't a fool. He'd never been a victim of hope. As he understood it, Alzheimer's was a progressive and devouring disease, and even if she were to accompany him home, she would be back in the sanitarium's care only days later, because that's what it had come to, because that's how the world worked, because life was a series of random inequities, made tolerable for some by their gods and for others by illusions of control.

He loved Irene. She was the only human being he'd ever been capable of loving—if he understood the term correctly—but the toys in her attic had gotten the rhythm in their feet, and they'd started to dance, and nothing was going to settle them down until the music stopped once and for all.

A car idled at the curb in front of his house. Upon recognizing the vehicle a tingle singed his chest, not for the visitor, or course, because he loathed the man, but because he understood that the man only visited his home with exciting news.

Rabin pulled into the drive and leaned to the glove box, from which he retrieved an ice pick. He slid it into his breast pocket. He left the thermos on the floor and stepped out of the car before crossing to the idling Police Flyer and climbing into the passenger seat. The driver was obese, unshaven and reeked of cabbage, bad gin, and old sweat. The disgusting man's only concession to vanity was a narrow, well-groomed mustache, like a neat and perfect line drawn across a mound of excrement.

"Detective Conrad," Rabin said.

"We have a job for you," Conrad said, and then sniffled loudly.

"And by *we* do you mean the fine men of the Chicago Police Department?"

"Don't crack wise," Conrad said. He sneezed and drew the sleeve of his overcoat across his nose, collecting a broad glistening trail on the already stained wool. "I'm here for Impelliteri."

A cog turned in Rabin's mind, and he said, "This is about that wrestling fellow."

"How'd you know that?"

"I read the paper."

Conrad grunted. Nodded. "Butch Cardinal. We lost him. Your guys and my guys. I don't know how he slipped but he did it. He might've gotten out of town. We don't know, so Impelliteri wants you to find him and do whatever the fuck it is you do."

Rabin sat in the car, enduring the stench of the detective, listening to the plan that had failed and the steps his employer was taking to correct that failure. Rabin thought it providence that he should have considered Cardinal such an interesting opponent, only to have the opportunity to find out firsthand dropped in his lap. Near the end of their conversation Detective Conrad mentioned an item of interest, a trinket Rabin was to recover for his employer, but the details were, at best, vague.

"How am I to know what the item is if I don't know what I'm looking for?"

"Well, it's not like I've got a picture of it. It's a necklace, and it doesn't sound like shit to me, but Impelliteri wants it. He said it looks like a squashed rose. Cardinal probably won't be carrying too much jewelry, so it shouldn't be all that tough to figure out."

"Indeed," Rabin said. "Is this item of sentimental value to Mr. Impelliteri?"

"Does Impelliteri strike you as sentimental?"

"Remarkably on point," Rabin noted.

"Just don't come back without it."

Conrad slapped his fat hand down on a wide envelope. "We got what we could about Cardinal in here. Didn't do us a shitload of good, but you seem to have your ways. Everything we know about him is in here. Plus your retaining fee, of course."

Rabin lifted the package and asked, "Officer Conrad, how much of a commission did you remove from this envelope before I arrived home?"

Conrad sneered and shook his head like the question was an inconvenience rather than an insult. "Delivery charge," he said.

Rabin considered the ice pick in his pocket. His heart beat against its handle. Killing the detective would only take a second. It would feel so very good. But it would complicate things with his primary employer. Maybe another day.

"Have a fine day, Officer," Rabin said. He let himself out of the car and frowned. Despite enjoying the notion of a new project to keep him busy, the detective's visit, like the earlier imposition of Irene's nurse, had soured his morning.

Rabin returned to his own car to retrieve the thermos of coffee before walking up the stairs to his home. He quickly unlocked the front door and entered. After securing the three bolts to lock himself in, he paused to enjoy the comfortable surroundings. He'd stoked the furnace before leaving to visit Irene, and the heat wrapped around him like a blanket. His breakfast of bacon and fried tomatoes still scented the air. If he closed his eyes and pretended, he could imagine hearing Irene in the parlor, could hear the clicking of her knitting needles as she made a sweater for one of the unfortunate children at St. Michael's. With her gone such dreams were all that remained, and sadly the illusion couldn't last.

Rabin had to clean up some old business before he began his new assignment.

"Sooner than later," he whispered, and then he opened the basement door to descend the stairs.

Much cooler than the rest of the house, the basement nonetheless brought pleasures of its own. To his right was a broad alcove he'd made into an office. Here he had a small rolltop desk and a comfortable wingback chair for contemplation and reading. Rabin placed the pick on the desk and began unbuttoning his vest. He removed his coat and vest; his money clip, cufflinks, and studs went into a fine china saucer on the desktop.

After rolling up his sleeves, Rabin closed his eyes and breathed deeply, letting his mind drift, waiting for serenity to welcome him. He'd learned the meditative technique from a palm reader on Clark Street, and though her talent to see the future was decidedly in question, Rabin had found her relaxation regimen thoroughly effective.

Now peaceful, Rabin opened his eyes and retrieved the ice pick from the bench. He turned to face the center of the room, where muffled sounds called to him.

"I'm sorry," he said, "but I've been called away on business."

The man sat tied to a sturdy wooden chair. He was short and round and fat with a thick pelt of hair covering his belly and his chest. The shrub at his crotch was so thick that the man's meager sexual apparatus was all but obscured. He tried to keep his eyes on Rabin, but the lids drooped from exhaustion and pain. His head lolled. Disappointing, really. Rabin had hoped to spend a few more days in his company. The only benefit to his wife's affliction was a level of privacy with which he could explore his craft more fully. But like the carnations in Irene's room, the man wilted. Bruises stained his neck and shoulders. Tiny cuts ran like ruler marks along his hairy upper arms. Blood had seeped from one to the next like a marble water installation Rabin had seen in New York many years before.

His name was Barney. Hardly of any importance. He was a numbers man whose numbers didn't add up. Normally, such a meaningless specimen would get a bullet to the brain and cease being a problem once they hoisted his bulk from the sidewalk, but Barney had connections that went higher than Impelliteri, which was why he'd assumed his theft would be overlooked. Marco Impelliteri overlooked nothing. Not a ledger page, not a slight. The man wanted his ducks in a row. It made them easier to shoot. Impelliteri did know how to cover his tracks, though. Instead of a public execution, a common enough warning to the other Southside scavengers, Barney would disappear along with a sum of cash sufficient to imply an early retirement. The questions would be few. The rumors unsustainable.

Rabin crossed to the chair and placed his hand on the man's forehead as he'd done with his wife only two hours before. Beneath his palm, dry red eyes pleaded with him. Barney mumbled something into his gag, and then Rabin stepped behind him. He stroked the man's bald pate a single time and then grasped his forehead firmly. Applying all of his strength, he yanked the head back as he drove the ice pick through the base of Barney's skull, and then he waited for the convulsions to cease before smoothing the hairs over the seeping wound.

Once the fine texture of the hair became thoroughly damp and matted with blood, Rabin stopped petting and stepped away. He crossed to a faucet, which jutted from the wall, suspended over one of two large drains he'd found intriguing when first viewing the house. He rinsed his hands in the icy water, and then dried them on a towel. As he did so, he checked his shirt and suit trousers for spots of blood but found the fabrics unblemished. Satisfied, he returned to the alcove and his comfortable chair. Rabin drew the envelope from his desk. He opened it. Then he began to read everything the Chicago police knew about Butch Cardinal.

Chapter 8
Mumbo Jumbo

Roger Lennon had arrived at the station with a sense of relief, having an excuse to be out of the house and away from rooms full of exaggerated concern, but when he'd received his orders, his good mood rapidly eroded. Because of his doctor's report, Lennon would be on desk duty for a week, and possibly longer, pending a follow-up examination. So instead of sitting at home with Edie eyeing him and asking him how he felt every goddamn minute, he had to sit in the smoke-filled office, reading reports that had already been compiled, congratulating his colleagues on cases that had been solved without him, and hearing about the action on the streets.

These days there was plenty of it.

Musante's murder had sparked a street war between the Northside and the Southside gangs. So far, there had only been two fatalities. Unfortunately both victims were bystanders, but last night two gunmen had sprayed the front of Elysium with their tommys and the doorman had only managed to save his ass by diving behind a concrete planter. Cardinal had worked the door at Elysium, so the message wasn't exactly subtle.

Lennon leaned back in his chair. He still couldn't remember much about the night at Musante's. Something about Conrad's story didn't click with Lennon but he couldn't pinpoint it. Add to that the fact that Cardinal made an unlikely shooter, based on what Lennon had read in the wrestler's file, and the day's frustration just grew thicker.

He had no doubt that a man with Cardinal's background could kill. That wasn't the issue for Lennon. He'd seen fairy lounge singers go blood crazy because their dope supply was running low, and he'd seen fine and proper housewives busted in warehouse brothels with their asses in the air because they wanted bigger iceboxes or a string of pearls. Nothing a person did surprised him, but the syndicates weren't people. They behaved with a far more predictable logic, and using a high-profile guy like Cardinal to hit a smalltimer like Musante—a geezer any kid with a .38 could pop—made no sense. Of course Cardinal could have been flying solo, but what was his beef?

Which led Lennon to his next question: who the hell was Lonnie Musante anyway? Why wasn't that file on his desk? Anyone who'd spent real time on Impelliteri's crew had a record. Even if the geezer had managed to avoid a rap sheet, there should have been a background file accompanying Cardinal's. A coroner's report. Something. Conrad was out, probably stuffing his face, so Lennon checked the man's desk, pushing aside piles of papers that should have been filed weeks ago. When this turned up nothing, he walked across the station to his sergeant's desk.

"I'm looking for a file on Lonnie Musante."

"Conrad may have it," Palmer said, gruffly as if his time were too valuable to be wasted on his job.

"It's not on his desk."

"Maybe he took it home."

"Conrad doesn't take work home."

"Then it's a mystery. Don't detectives solve those?"

"Fuck off, Palmer."

"Kiss me first."

On his way back to his desk, he waved a rookie uniform over and told the kid to run down to records to see what he could bring back on Musante. He also wanted whatever they had on file for Cardinal. Then Lennon went into his office and made a phone call.

All the paperwork in the world wasn't likely to get him close to an answer, but every now and then useful information showed through the dreary veneers. More times than not, the real information, the raw skinny, came from the streets, and Lennon was more than happy to dredge the gutters for bits of shiny fact, even if he had to wade through filth to get it. Which was the only reason he was making an appointment with a man he so thoroughly loathed.

"Hey, Valentino," Lennon said. "I need a word."

"Is this Lennon?"

"Yeah."

"Heard you took a good knock. Went out like a kitten."

"I'd be glad to discuss that face to face."

"Can't do it, Lennon."

"And then I say, *you will,* and then you say, *there's no way,* and then I remind you of all the prison time you could do and you whimper and grumble and we dance for five minutes on the phone, and I don't have the patience for that shit, so meet me at Cucina Napoli in thirty minutes or all of the bad things I always have to threaten will happen."

"I hate you, Lennon."

"Why wouldn't you?" he said and hung up the phone.

• • •

CUCINA Napoli was an upscale Italian eatery with the best pasta in Chicago, and an extensive wine list available to patrons who could afford to eat in one of four private dining rooms. The restaurant catered to a clientele certain to be discreet about the serving of spirited beverages, as the customers were the men who profited from their distribution. Lennon was led to a booth at the back of the restaurant, near the kitchen. He always got lousy tables when he came in, but he always got seated, even if the lobby was swarmed. The place had red velvet wallpaper and white tablecloths and tiny lanterns—wicks burning in oil—in lieu of candles.

Henri Fiori arrived ten minutes after Lennon. Fiori was a Corsican who passed for Italian. He was uncommonly handsome, if on the feminine side, which was how he'd earned the nickname Valentino. Despite having a soft and pretty face and mannerisms not altogether masculine, Valentino was no fairy. He had been considered a prize by the socialite ladies of whom he'd made a career. These days his addictions to opium and cocaine were drawing deep and dark lines across his face, but in dim light, like the restaurant's, he still carried a movie star patina.

For the most part, Lennon despised the man and his vices. The gigolo was a dope fiend and a gambler, and he tossed other people's cash around like rose petals in a ritual of constant seduction like a charming virus that had stricken Chicago years ago and continued to infect. But he was useful.

"I really do have some place to be," Valentino said, sliding into the booth across from Lennon.

"Then let's not waste our time together. Tell me about Lonnie Musante."

Valentino laughed and shook his head. "Are you off your nut? Why would you care about a freak like Lon?"

"Well someone must care. Your boss declared war on the Bug's crew because Lonnie was killed."

"A baby cries if you take away a toy, even if he doesn't like playing with it anymore."

"What did Musante do for Impelliteri? Or was he lined up with Ricca and Nitti?"

"He was all Marco's," Valentino said. He peered around the restaurant. "He gave everybody the jimjams. For that matter, he gave Marco the jimjams, but they had a history. I need a drink." When this statement didn't make a server magically appear, Valentino slid from the booth and walked to a plump waiter with a fringe of gray over his ears. He spoke, laughed, pointed at Lennon, clapped the waiter on the back, and then returned to the table. "You'd think a place that charged so much for a plate of spaghetti would be on the ball."

"You said Musante made people nervous."

"Not nervous exactly." Valentino slid his palm across the hair above his ears to smooth it, even though it was already as smooth and shiny as a slab of wax. Then he started looking around the restaurant. "Where's that goddamn drink?"

"It'll be here. Tell me about Musante."

"You know us Italians, a lot of superstitions."

"You're not Italian," Lennon countered.

Valentino continued speaking as if he hadn't heard. "Well, superstition doesn't go away when you join the outfits. There's still a lot of old country hokum in our heads."

"What's that got to do with Musante?"

The drinks arrived. Scotch. Valentino downed half of his with a gulp. He kept hold of his glass and turned in the booth, again searching the restaurant. Lennon couldn't tell if the man was anxious, afraid, or just hopped up on a nose full of cocaine. His irises were like crickets on griddles, bouncing around and looking for a place to land.

"Look, Lennon, there's just not that much to tell. Musante came from an old family, and they had some sway in their day, but Lon fell from the tree and rolled way on down the hill, if you get my meaning. Marco and Lon grew up in the same Brooklyn neighborhood; that ties men together, you know? What's the confusion? Musante's dead. Let him rest."

"You haven't answered my question. What did Musante do for Impelliteri?" *Why had his death ignited a street war?*

Valentino rolled his eyes and shook his head. He lifted his glass and sipped this time, and then leaned back in the booth. "Eight months back, Lon was in a club, shooting his mouth off about a delivery: Scotch coming in over the Canadian line." He hoisted his glass and swirled the whisky. "The delivery never made it. Some Fed overheard him and the whole shipment was stopped at the border. Six men collared. Two men toe tagged. These were members of Capone's crew, part of Nitti's pipeline, and everybody knew Musante had done the damage. So why was he still walking around? Still breathing? Anyone else would have been target practice in less than a day, but not Lonnie."

Lennon chewed over the information, sipped his own drink. "He must have had some serious leverage against the syndicate."

This made Valentino laugh. "We all have serious leverage, Lennon. But most of us are smart enough to never even consider using it. Lon had something else."

"I don't follow."

"No, you really don't. And I'm not the one to guide you, because I've always thought it was all a load of horseshit anyway."

"All of what?"

"That mystic mumbo jumbo," Valentino said, as if he'd already said it a hundred times.

Lennon could see the lucidity leaving Valentino's eyes. No longer crickets on a griddle, his irises bobbed slowly, eyeing his glass and then the table and then his glass again. Apparently his system was coming down from the dope.

"One sentence, Valentino," Lennon said, leaning on the table. "In one sentence, tell me what Musante did for Impelliteri."

Valentino stared into the oil lamp on the tabletop, eyes now glazed. "He read his future."

The statement hung between them. Lennon shook his head and lit a cigarette and leaned back in the booth. "Is that code for something?"

"It is what it is," Valentino said. His chin dipped toward his chest. "Marco kept Lon around as a spiritual guide or some shit. Hell, I wish someone would pay me for looking into a drained tea cup or at their palm for a few seconds."

"But Marco believed Lon was legit?"

"Medieval witch shit in the bright and shiny city," Valentino muttered. Then he barked a sharp laugh and lit a cigarette of his own. "Lon couldn't have been all that good or Marco would have made his mint at the track instead of running booze. Hell, if Lon had been any good he wouldn't have been home the other night, you know?"

"And that's it? Lonnie didn't work the rackets?"

Valentino shrugged. A thick film had fallen over his eyes and his chin lazily bobbed as if he were trying to stay awake.

"I'm asking you a question."

"Nah," Valentino said. "He ran some numbers, but even that was more than Lon could handle. The guy was pretty much useless. They should have just done it and saved everyone the headache."

"Done what?"

"After the Canadian import went south—or *didn't*—Marco sent Lonnie an invitation." He drew on his cigarette and released the smoke slowly so that it oozed over his upper lip. "It's one of those invitations that you don't refuse—to an event you usually don't leave."

"So Impelliteri *did* order a hit on Musante?"

"Yeah," Valentino said. "Then he called it off the next day. Never heard of that happening before. Nobody talks their way out of an invitation to the dance, but Lon did. No dancing for Ol' Lon. So maybe he had a different kind of leverage. Hard to say."

"Then what?"

"Then the Bug sends the Wrestler to kill the Fortuneteller, and my good friend Lennon asks me to lunch."

Valentino barked another laugh, drew on his smoke, ground it in the crystal ashtray and began looking around the restaurant again, presumably to have his drink refilled. After a quick wave to the gray-haired waiter, he turned his muddled eyes back to Lennon.

"You look like you're about to fall over," Lennon said.

"Perhaps a visit to the gents," Valentino muttered.

"You do that," Lennon said. He stood and withdrew his money clip and counted bills onto the table. "Tell me something before you go."

"Hmm? Sure?"

"Where do pretty boys go when they aren't pretty anymore?"

"Straight to hell, detective."

Chapter 9
A War on Crime

Hours later and miles away, Marco Impelliteri, a man whose cunning business sense and quiet brutality had earned him a position near the apex of the Chicago syndicates, strolled across his office to his expansive mahogany desk and lifted the ringing telephone. He'd been in a lousy mood for days, ever since watching flames consume Lonnie Musante's coffin and its contents: a man he'd known since childhood. The street war wasn't helping his disposition. He'd called it, wanted it, but the fucking Irish were doing too good a job of dodging his boys' bullets. He was sending messages, but nobody was listening.

He picked up the phone, cleared his throat, and said, "Yeah?"

"Marco, this is Lou."

"Yeah."

"Powell's goons took out two of my boys this afternoon. Frank isn't happy. Your vendetta is drawing too much attention, and nobody but you is missing that fuck Musante. Frank says to shut it down."

The line went dead and Marco Impelliteri looked at the conical earpiece as if it were the statue of a sainted martyr that had just whispered obscenities into his ear. He slammed the thing into the cradle and broke the metal arms loose. Marco lifted the telephone off his desk and threw it on the floor. It was the sixth phone to be scrapped in as many months.

Marco went to the window and put his brow against the cold glass. He didn't like what he saw outside. The electric lights in his back yard illuminated a field of melting snow with great patches of brown grass appearing like lesions all across the ground. It looked horrible. It looked like rot.

Frank said. Frank said. Bullshit.

Nitti was nothing but a front, a face for the outfit that wasn't as contentious as Paul Ricca's. The only reason Al had anointed Frank in the first place was because the guy's record made him look like a choirboy alongside the other lieutenants. Ricca gave the orders these days, probably had since the day Al went into the slam. Marco wasn't impressed. That Old Country fuck, Ricca, could suck his cock. Yeah he had the skills, certainly had the brutality, to lead the outfits, but he was a thug. Immigrant filth. He ordered hits with his Sicilian "Make 'im go away," bullshit, an accent so thick Marco could barely make out what the shit-heel was saying. But Ricca was in charge. He had the muscle, and nobody, not even Nitti, said boo when Ricca opened his mouth. Nitti was weak, as weak as a damp rag puppet, but he knew how the game was played.

Regardless of his feelings for the man, Marco had learned a thing or two from Nitti, learned to pass on the wet work, learned to keep his hands clean and his face out of the papers. That's why he retained a small crew of hitters, kids who were young enough to move fast and were looking to make names for themselves. It was also why he'd retained a psychopath like Paul Rabin for the more complicated, delicate assignments. Rabin had been a hand-me-down from "Big Cheeks" Collasanto, a Capone lieutenant who'd taken a bullet to the throat in '27. Impelliteri had gone to Collasanto, needing help with a matter outside the rackets, something that required secrecy and expediency, and Collasanto had been accommodating, if vague.

"You put the assignment and the money in an envelope and you have one of your chumps drop that envelope off. You don't want to meet this man, don't want Paul Rabin to know your face if you can help it."

Impelliteri had been about to laugh in Collasanto's face. Considering the level of bat-shit crazy exhibited by the gang boys he'd bummed around with on the streets of Brooklyn and later Chicago, it struck him as pretty damn funny that he should be warned away from a contract man, but before he let this train of thought lead him to laughter, he considered Big Cheeks' history, knew the currents of violence that had lifted and carried him to Al's side. The life he'd lived. The shit he'd done. If this man was concerned enough to keep a distance from Rabin, then Impelliteri would do the same.

When he needed Rabin's services, he sent the fat cop. Let that slob say the wrong thing or do the wrong thing and take Rabin's heat. The life of a cop meant less than a turkey neck to Marco. He had a hundred cops in his pocket.

Cermak and his war on crime, now there was a laugh.

And Marco had to admit Rabin knew his business. Men that were supposed to disappear, like that piece of shit Barney Orso, disappeared and never surfaced. If a more public display was necessary to throw a scare into Moran's crew, Rabin could manage that, too. The killer did his job and that was all that mattered. Soon enough, Rabin would introduce himself to that meathead Cardinal, and he'd open the wrestler up—slowly if Rabin followed Marco's instructions. He wanted that son of a bitch to pay.

Every time he thought about that fucking wrestler his stomach turned sour. He pictured Lonnie lying dead, a guy he'd known since they were both pissing diapers, and he thought about the package Lonnie was supposed to deliver, and Marco's vision went red. He wanted Cardinal to suffer all the way to his soul, and he wanted every Paddy on Powell's crew to follow him into the ground, and then he wanted the rest of the cunts in Moran's outfit to follow *them*.

Nitti wanted him to shut it down, told him it was done. Nothing was fucking done, not until the Irish were under dirt or under water, and Marco was shown the respect he deserved.

He left the window and crossed his office. In the hallway he looked up the stairs and then over his shoulder as if someone were following him. Impelliteri climbed the stairs, turned left on the landing and walked to the first door: his daughter Sylvia's room. Carefully he turned the knob and pushed the door open, allowing the light from the hall to cut a line from the threshold to his daughter's bed. Upon seeing her, the red rage all but vanished. Sylvia faced the wall, her beautiful black hair sprayed over the pillow like bands of satin. Her silk duvet, the color of lavender, clutched tightly to her legs and rose in gentle swells at her hips and shoulders. The sight stirred Marco, made him forget Lou's phone call and the muddy thoughts it had stirred up. His beautiful girl. His light.

Marco took a step into the room, but a noise from the front of the house startled him, brought him to a stop. It might have been nothing more than the house settling, or a tenacious icicle finally releasing its grasp on the eaves, falling, and cracking against the walk, but a distinct change in the air followed the noise, as if it had thinned and fled. Escaped. Maybe his guard, Tony, had decided to do a sweep, or he'd noticed the office light on and decided to see if his boss needed anything. It was possible, but Impelliteri doubted it.

Backing out of the room, Marco listened carefully. He closed the door to his daughter's room and reached for the gun he kept in the pocket of his robe. Once he had a firm grip on the weapon, he returned to the top of the stairs and looked down. The entryway was empty, and the floor was clean, no muddy footprints to indicate intruders. He eased down the stairs, alert for both sound and motion. At the bottom of the stairs he stopped again, and he listened, and though he didn't hear anything, his belief that someone was moving around remained. It was the air. The air felt wrong. It shifted and rolled like a phantom draught. Marco retraced his steps to his office and outside he pressed his ear to the door. More silence.

Marco entered the room, holding the gun low and close to his hip. Tony stood behind his desk. Hands at his sides. The man's narrow face was tight with fear.

Before Marco could take in the totality of the scene, or completely understand the expression on his bodyguard's face, a hand slammed down on his wrist with so much force he dropped the gun and flinched. When he opened his eyes, he saw a hard, broad face and the point of a knife, hovering less than an inch from his eye.

"Mr. Brand," a voice said from the corner, "bring Mr. Impelliteri in and show him a seat."

A strong hand gripped Marco's arm and yanked him into the office. The door closed behind him.

On his left stood a tall, thick man, holding a metal bar about two feet long. For Marco, he called to mind a baseball manager, holding a new narrow bat. His partner, the guy with the knife, was a short, stocky piece of shit, and a freak on top of it. *What kind of a guy walks around a Chicago winter in an A-shirt and a butcher's apron? And what was with his arms?* The arm he'd used to drag Impelliteri into the room was thick with muscle, the other arm was like a stalk of broccoli—thin and flaccid. And he had something on his wing: a metal band, copper maybe, coiled around the scrawny arm from wrist to shoulder.

The shorter man tugged and shoved and forced Marco into the club chair beneath a wall of books. After gripping the armrests, Marco glared at Tony and a string of obscenities paraded through his head. Marco knew he should be afraid, should be pissing-himself terrified, but what he felt was rage. His guard, Tony, had let these men—men who didn't even have guns—into Marco's home. There was no excuse. If these guys were here, Tony should have been face-down dead in the yard. He should have done everything in his power to kill these motherfuckers or at least gotten a warning to Marco. Fire off a round. Scream his head off. Even if it meant getting his throat cut, Tony should have given his boss a chance.

"You piece of shit," Impelliteri said, glaring at the man.

Tony lowered his head in response.

"Mr. Impelliteri," the tall, thick man said, "we are here for information." He strolled up to the chair and placed the metal bar on Impelliteri's shoulder. "This should only take a few minutes, and if all goes well, no one will be hurt."

"You're already dead," Impelliteri said. "You think you can just walk in here and start shoving me around, you fucking lowlife shit-heel?"

The stocky man with the knife looked amused and startled. His eyes widened in surprise and his cheeks turned red as if he were some sheltered schoolgirl who'd never heard real men talk before. Only then did Marco wonder who these men were. He'd assumed they were sent by the Irish, just street thug hitters carrying out a contract for Powell or Moran, but the short man's reaction, not to mention the way the two dressed—like Halstead Street kitchen help—and the fact they hadn't plugged Tony right off and opened up on Marco at first sight threw that likelihood out the window. Were they members of Nitti's crew—a couple of out-of-towners brought in to lean on him? That didn't fly either, especially since they were asking for information. Who the hell asked for information? The law? These guys didn't look or act like cops. They sure as shit weren't feds.

"You're fucking feeble if you think I'm going to tell you guys anything." As he spoke he noticed Tony stepping to the end of the desk. One of his hands twitched as it eased behind his back.

Good, Marco thought. Maybe his guard wasn't completely useless. Tony probably kept a spare piece in a holster at the small of his back. All Marco had to do was keep the circus entertained for a couple of seconds.

"Who are you anyway?" he asked. He stared at the stocky man with the mismatched arms. "What's with your wing, kid? You do all your jerking off with the right and the left got jealous and died."

Again the guy's face went red, but this time Marco saw the anger building there. He figured that was good, kept the fucker's attention on him. The tall man at his side tapped his shoulder with the metal bar.

"That's enough, Mr. Impelliteri."

"Did I hurt your boyfriend's feelings?" he asked. "Or did I hurt yours? Is tugging his meat your job?"

Marco laughed, not only because of the comment, which he found extremely clever, but also because Tony was in the process of drawing down on these cunts. Another second and *bang bang* he could get back to his evening.

The tall guy raised the metal bar from Marco's shoulder. Across the room, Tony pulled the gun from behind his back, but he never got the chance to fire. With a motion so smooth and fast Marco could barely track it, the man at his side whipped the metal bar in a side-handed toss. The rod soared past the stocky man with the knife, and then it broke apart. Separated. Where there had been a single iron rod was now a swarm of dozens, maybe hundreds, of elongated needles that spread out like scattergun shot. Tony only managed to get the gun to his side before the needles hit him, giving off the sound of a hundred sighs. They simultaneously pierced his face, his neck, his shoulders, and torso and slid through him as easily as bullets through butter. Then the narrow spears reconnected, joined together, and a single metal bar hit the far wall with a *thunk*. It pierced the paneling, going deep into the plaster, and jutted out over the floor like an accusing finger.

Marco looked on, more amazed than afraid. His mind sprang open and stories, all of the stories Lonnie Musante had ever told him about steel and magic, flooded in. Despite a lifetime of friendship, he'd written off the bulk of Lonnie's tales, and with good reason. Not only were the man's stories loopy, going far beyond the logic of common mysticism, but also because it had taken Lonnie nearly fifty years to say a damn thing about his uncle and the sect of believers he called the Alchemi. A part of Marco, and it was a considerable part, hadn't believed in the mystery men or their metal magic. In fact, he'd considered such realms of magic absolute horseshit, but the men were real; here they were, and if they existed, then everything else Lonnie had told him must also be true. Marco's head spun with it. Weapons. Baubles. Bits of steel that looked useless to everyone but the men who knew how to use them.

Tony, his face and suit now covered in deep red freckles, fell to the floor. The tall man walked away from the chair, and the stocky man, the one named Brand, moved in and pressed the point of his knife to Marco's chin.

"My name is Mr. Hayes," the tall man said. He stood next to the bar sticking out of the wall. Leaning down he said, "And as I noted, my colleague's name is Mr. Brand."

The stocky man before him smiled, and then he tapped Marco's chin with the blade of his knife. "Nice to meet ya," Brand said.

Hayes grasped the metal bar and gave it a gentle twist before pulling it smoothly from the wall. He tapped the rod against his palm and sneered. "Mr. Brand, would you please attach the pin to Mr. Impelliteri."

"Of course," Brand said, reaching into the pocket of the leather apron.

"The what?" Impelliteri asked. The amazement he'd felt only moments before was gone as he understood the focus of the two men was now wholly on him. "You're not sticking anything in me."

Brand pressed the blade hard against Impelliteri's cheek. From his pocket he drew a shining silver item approximately the length of his little finger. Ridges ran over the arched top of the object, and a long, needle jutted from below. Brand lifted the thing for Impelliteri to get a good look, waving it with his puny hand like a child teasing a classmate with a toy. Then the stocky man reached down and in two quick motions pushed aside the lapel of Impelliteri's dressing gown and jabbed the needle into his chest.

Though the pain was minimal, hardly more than a light pinch, Impelliteri shouted and tried to launch himself from the chair, but Brand caught him with a shoulder and knocked him back into the seat. Marco reached for the pendant, eager to have it out of his flesh, but Brand knocked his hand away and returned the blade of the knife to his cheek. The point again hovered a quarter of an inch from the soft tissue of Impelliteri's eye.

Hayes tapped his hand with the rod as he returned to his place by Impelliteri's side. "That pin, Mr. Impelliteri, is a means of gathering the truth. If you lie to us, you will feel it. More importantly we will know it. I suggest you stick with the truth. Despite the unfortunate incident with your associate, we have no taste for violence, though we understand its efficacy and are more than willing to use it as we deem necessary."

"You're the Alchemi," Impelliteri said. "I've heard about you."

"From Mr. Musante?" Hayes asked.

"Yeah, Lonnie told me about you freaks."

Brand frowned and pressed the flat side of the knife hard against Marco's cheekbone.

"That was a severe indiscretion on Mr. Musante's part," Hayes said. "But he was never a particularly reliable individual. If he were still alive, I imagine we'd be forced to deal with him." Hayes paused and leaned close to Impelliteri's ear. "He's not alive, is he?"

"Who, Lonnie? He's as dead as shit," Impelliteri said. "Don't you freaks get the newspaper?"

"I think we can dispense with terms like 'freak,' Mr. Impelliteri. They are hateful and Mr. Brand is particularly sensitive to such derision."

"Indeed I am," Brand said.

"Like I give a fuck." Impelliteri fixed his eyes on Brand's. "I'm not the one walking around like a rag doll with a thread hanging off the shoulder. You got questions? Let's hear 'em."

"You gave Mr. Musante a large sum of money for an item that was stolen from us."

"Bullshit," Marco said. "I didn't…"

The lie had barely begun when a wash of pain, scalding and acidic, spread out along his pectoral. It climbed his shoulder and cascaded down his belly. The agony appeared so quickly it caught the scream in Marco's throat. He grit his teeth and managed to squeeze out a high-pitched whine. Then the pain receded, leaving a patina of misery in its wake.

"What the fuck?" he bellowed.

"You were given ample warning about the value of the truth," Hayes said. "So you've lied to us and in fact did give Mr. Musante the funds he needed to buy our item. We know the transaction occurred. We know Mr. Musante returned to Chicago soon after the acquisition with the intent of passing the item on to you. Did he do so?"

"What?"

"Did you take possession of our property?"

"No," Impelliteri said. "He was supposed to bring it to me the night that fuck of a wrestler gunned him down."

"Do you know where our item is?"

"The wrestler's got it," he said. "I mean, I think he's got it. I don't know. I had a man on the scene and it wasn't in the house, wasn't on Lonnie."

"And you're certain Mr. Musante is deceased?"

"He'd better be," Impelliteri said. "They put him in a coffin and burned the whole thing to char."

"But he could have tricked you," Hayes said.

"Would have been a really good trick," Impelliteri said. "I saw him in the box, and twenty minutes later I saw them put the box in the fire, and that's *after* he spent two days in the county morgue. You telling me you guys are immortal or something?"

Mr. Hayes' face pinched at the question. He walked around to the front of the chair his shoulder hovering over that of his buddy, Brand. "Do you know the name of the item Mr. Musante stole?"

"The Rose," Impelliteri said. "He called it 'The Rose.'"

"Do you know what it is capable of?"

"No," he said. Again the pain. He fought it. Struggled to keep from screaming.

"You certainly wouldn't spend so much on an item if you didn't know its purpose. What did Mr. Musante tell you about the Rose, Mr. Impelliteri?"

"He told me it could help me."

"Help you how?"

"He said it could help me keep faggots like you from trying to ass fuck me." The pain blinded him this time. He lost consciousness for a moment, and he wished it had been more thorough in knocking him out, because even in the second of oblivion the pain was as sharp and loud as shattering glass.

"How was the Rose supposed to help you, Mr. Impelliteri? It didn't help, Mr. Musante, did it?"

"He never said it would make me bulletproof. He said it would help me. Help me fix my head."

Lonnie swore it would take care of the fucking disease in my brain, so I can stop… I don't want to do it… My poor baby… I don't. Some kind of curse. Some kind of devil possessing me, making me… Fuck, I have to find it. It's real. The things I could do…

"So you believe the Rose is an instrument of healing?"

"Yeah, why? You saying it's something else?"

"We're done here," Hayes said. He backed away and held the iron rod out at his side, a pose that showed Marco he was more than ready to throw the uncommon weapon if he did so much as flinch.

Brand tapped Marco's cheek with the knife one last time and then yanked the pin out of his chest. He dropped it into the pocket of his apron and skipped back several steps, looking pleased as fucking punch, looking like he had a mouthful of canary. Marco hated the stubby little prick, hated his withered arm and his smug expression.

Hayes and Brand, he thought. *Hayes and Brand.* If he was still breathing when those shit stains walked out of his house, he was going to make a hobby of causing them pain.

Brand continued to the door of the office, but Hayes remained in the center of the room.

"I understand you won't take my advice, but I'll offer it nonetheless," Hayes said. "You're likely searching for the Rose. Perhaps you've sent some of your men after Mr. Cardinal or you've put out a bounty on his head. I would suggest you cease those efforts immediately. We have resources, Mr. Impelliteri. The Rose belongs to us; it belongs *with* us. If you gain its possession, I can assure you it will be for a brief and sorrowful time."

With the words still hanging in the air, the men of the Alchemi walked out of the study, leaving Marco with the remains of his bodyguard.

Thoughts ran through his head in a jumble of words and images. Each idea was critical. They raced like ponies on a track as Marco leaned back in his chair and let the pounding of his heart ease. The thought that led the pack was: *Lonnie hadn't been full of shit; the Rose was real and its power was real.*

This important realization lost ground to Marco's temper, which insisted he get on the phone so he could have his men begin the process of hunting down Brand and Hayes. He needed to show those fucks how much he enjoyed someone breaking into his house and killing his guard. This thought came on fast and hot, but it faded just as quickly when he remembered how little he'd done to track down the Rose.

He'd only sent Rabin, and Rabin was good, but he could only cover so much ground. Cardinal could be anywhere by now. The outfits had a long reach, and Marco decided that getting the word out was crucial; he would put an ample price on Cardinal's head, one so high no one would be stupid enough to let the wrestler slide.

Marco crossed to his desk, ignoring Tony's corpse, which continued to leak fluids through the innumerable holes in its skin. For a moment, he was confused because the space where he kept his phone was empty. Then he remembered and looked at the floor where the busted machine lay like another victim. He growled a stream of obscenities and walked through the house to the kitchen where he kept a second phone. The longest night he'd experienced in months was just beginning.

Part Two

New Orleans December 1932

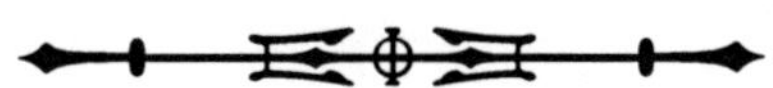

Chapter 10
Under the Weather

Butch woke to the sensation of someone rapping gently on his shoulder. He opened his eyes to a stern, round face with bulging eyes and plump, wet lips beneath the bill of a conductor's cap. With his amphibian eyes and fat cheeks, the man's face looked like it was about to explode. "New Orleans," he said, but Butch's plugged ears and addled mind turned the words into "Nawluns."

Threads of dream clung to him as he shook off sleep. Details from his dreams melted like paraffin but he knew with complete certainty that the dreams had been horrible. He felt so bad, they couldn't have been otherwise.

He nodded, which sent the conductor on his way, but Butch remained in the seat, looking through the window at the wooly, gray air, as he tried to compose himself. A chill ran through him as if his blood had been replaced with ice water. He trembled. Sweat coated his neck and brow. Fluid streamed from his scratchy eyes and his head felt as if it were full of rancid pudding. His throat hurt. His head ached. When he tried to breathe, he could barely get air to his lungs. His chest felt as if it were being used as a bumper between two trucks. Then the pain from his wounded ear surfaced, arriving after the other miserable sensations like the star of a show. It burned and throbbed. Butch coughed painfully and set about hoisting himself from the seat. At first, his muscles were like rubber, all but useless, and only with a tremendous act of will did Butch manage to get to his feet. He wobbled for a moment as he checked for his billfold and the scrap of paper with the name and phone exchange of Rory's friend on it. The necklace nearly slipped his mind. He reached into his shirt and felt the bauble against his chest and nodded. Then, with great effort, he made his way off the train.

The depot teamed with people, dressed against the weather. Every face appeared beleaguered and anxious. Butch shambled through them, struggling to keep his balance, feeling as though someone had filled his body with water that sloshed and sent him in directions he didn't wish to go. The sight of a man in uniform startled him, and Butch lowered his head, conscious of little except the illness and an overriding sense of suspicion, but what he'd taken as the neat blue suit of a police officer was just another conductor's uniform, and he approached the man to ask directions to the phone.

"You look like you lost a few fights," the conductor said.

"Won more than I lost," Butch said, though the defense of his fighting record seemed, even to him, like an odd thing to discuss. "I'm sorry. I'm a bit under the weather. Can you…" For a moment he'd forgotten why he was speaking to this man. He cleared his scratchy throat and searched over the conductor's shoulder for a clue as to what he needed, but his thoughts became a tangle of hemp, sinking below a swamp's surface.

The conductor, a young and healthy looking man, put his hand on Butch's shoulder. "There's a Salvation Army shelter in the Central Business District," he said earnestly. "They won't stand for no dope or drink, but they could get you squared for the night."

"No," Butch said, suddenly remembering what he needed. "I need to call a friend. I need a telephone."

"Telephones are in the back," the conductor said, though the pinch of his mouth and eyes showed he considered Butch's decision a bad one. He kept his hand on Butch's shoulder and squeezed in a gesture of comfort. "God will protect you and provide."

"Well, that would be nice for a change," Butch said. He thanked the man, who looked at him like he'd just spit on the floor and trundled away through the crowd.

Though the station wasn't large, it took Butch more than ten minutes to find the bank of telephones. He wandered in a daze, getting turned around. At one point, he stood outside of the depot, his body quaking with chills as a light mist settled on his face, and then he realized he needed the phone, and the phones were in the back.

Once seated on the hard wooden bench and facing the telephone apparatus, Butch dozed off, waking a second later when his head rapped against the wooden wall. He shook off the worst of his fatigue and reached in his breast pocket for the scrap of paper Rory had given him.

The letters and numbers of the phone exchange slid and smeared on the sheet like living creatures that didn't wish to be caught. Butch dug change out of his pocket and lifted the earpiece. He tapped the arm it had hung from until the reedy voice of an operator swam into his muddled mind.

Rossington, he thought, fixing the name in his head. *Hollis. Hollis. Hollis Rossington.*

"How can I connect you?" the operator asked.

He said the name and then squinted to discern the specifics of the exchange. These he read aloud.

"One moment, sir."

Then there was silence, and Butch thought the call might have been lost. A twinge of panic made its way through his tight and aching chest. What if he had the wrong name? The wrong exchange? Not even considering the fact he could always call Rory for clarification, Butch gathered the fabric of his trousers in a fist and squeezed tight in frustration.

Then a deep voice came over the line. The man told him that he had reached the Rossington residence.

Butch couldn't speak. What if he gave his name, and the man recognized it and decided to turn him in? He didn't have the strength or the money to last long on his own in this town. He didn't know the rules of the place.

"I can hear you there," the voice said. "You got something to say or not?"

Too exhausted to entertain any further paranoia, Butch said, "Hollis."

"This is Hollis. What can I do for you?"

"Hollis. Hello, uh, I'm a friend of Rory Sullivan's and—"

"Butch?" Rossington asked quickly. "Butch Cardinal?"

"Yeah, hi. Rory must have called ahead."

"He did." The voice had lost its bright timbre. Now the man sounded concerned, his tone somber. "Are you in New Orleans?"

"Just got in…off the train."

"You don't sound well," Rossington noted.

"A bit of a bug. Look, I don't know what Rory said—" A flurry of wrenching coughs fled Butch's throat, leaving him breathless and aching.

"Okay, Butch," Rossington said. "The thing is I don't know if my house is the best place for you."

He hadn't imagined this response. Rory had called ahead. He'd sealed the deal. Except he hadn't.

Butch hadn't imagined it possible that he could feel worse. All he wanted was to lie down in a warm bed and sleep. He was a thousand miles from threat, but he felt so haggard and miserable, he might as well have been facing the barrel of a gun.

"You take care," he said.

"Hold on," Rossington said. "Are you at the train station?"

"Yeah."

"The streetcar runs out front. Take it east and ask the conductor to let you out at the French Market. There's a little place called the Café du Monde. I'll meet you there in thirty minutes."

"You really shouldn't bother."

"So where are you going to go?" Rossington asked. "You sound like you're about to keel over. At least let me get some coffee into you and help you find a room. That way I'll know how to find you."

"Why would you need to find me?" Butch asked.

"Because I promised Rory I'd help you out," Rossington replied. "And I intend to do it."

• • •

HOLLIS Rossington walked down Dumaine Street carrying an umbrella. A light mist, not unpleasant in the slightest, continued to cover the French Quarter, muting the colors painted over the façades of shotgun and camelback homes. The downpour had cleaned the air, leaving behind a wet purity that would eventually, and sooner than later, succumb to the usual mixture of savory and foul odors emanating from the homes, shops, and restaurants. Rossington lit a cigarette when he reached Royal Street and crushed it out on the damp pavement a block later, suddenly concerned with the quality of his breath.

He was keen to meet Butch Cardinal, even excited at the prospect. Not only did he want to do right by the man out of respect for the promise he'd made to Rory, but also it had been years since he'd sat down with another athlete and shared stories. He had forty bucks in his pocket, which should get the man through the first few days of his stay without worry. After that, Hollis would do what he could.

If he felt he could explain Lionel Lowery to Butch without an uproar he'd have welcomed the wrestler into his home. He couldn't, though. Hollis had to believe that Butch was as conservative and traditional as any other man off the street, and his reaction to the exclusively masculine domestic situation would be a harsh one. A lie wouldn't work. Lionel was aggressive and vulgar, and he would never agree to playing a part in this kind of deceit, simply because it would strike him as more entertaining to offend and taunt their guest. Realizing this brought a pang to Hollis's chest. He disliked the near-constant frustration and suspicion he felt toward Lionel. They were supposed to be coupled, but the emotions Hollis felt for the kid had soured—faded like a daydream of supper, conjured in a starving man's mind. He didn't even like the young man, not really. Occasionally Lionel exhibited a good humor that was quite charming, but such moments were brief. More often he acted arrogant, needling those around him, daring someone to challenge him.

What did they always say? Any port in a storm? It would have been nice if they had noted what to do when the port was burning and the waves were throwing your vessel against the rocks. At least having Butch in town would give him an excuse to be out of the house more.

Though his memory wasn't quite sufficient to the task, he attempted to conjure Cardinal's appearance in his mind. The only time he'd seen the man had been on the mats, and Hollis had been near the back of the arena, so the image in his mind was of an enormous man, with a wall of chest and shoulders and tree-trunk legs that vanished into the snug red fabric of his shorts. This was all easy enough to imagine, but the face eluded him. He'd seen a photograph of Butch on a poster, and Hollis remembered thinking Cardinal was a handsome man, striking even. The exact details of the face, however, were lost to him. Still he wasn't worried about recognizing Cardinal at the café.

Hollis walked through the arched doorway of the Café du Monde and scanned the room, but found the patrons a disappointment. Four tables near the door had been taken by couples who chatted quietly. A working girl in a torn cotton dress sat against the back window, staring into her coffee. A male counterpart to this sad lady, a lone bum, sat in the far corner of the restaurant, head down, likely sleeping off a two-day drunk. His filthy jacket sagged and he seemed to have something pale attached to the side of his head, or maybe it was his ear. Hollis didn't let his gaze linger on the man, but moved it on to a group of four young people chatting excitedly, hands waving to animate the stories they were telling.

Hollis took one of the small round tables in the middle of the room. He sat in a wire-backed chair and again regarded the couples by the front door. It occurred to him that maybe Butch wasn't alone; he could have struck up a conversation with a lady friend at the café. No doubt the man did quite well with women when he wanted them, but none of the men matched up with Rossington's memory of Butch. They were all too short. Too fat. Too old. Too scrawny. And with no sign of the wrestler, he began to worry. If Butch had followed Hollis's instructions, he should have been halfway through his first cup of coffee by now. Even if he'd crawled on hands and knees from the train station, he would have beat Rossington to the place. It wasn't as if he could get lost. All he had to do was ask any random pedestrian on the street. Everyone in the city knew the café.

When the waiter, a squat black man named Williams, came for his order, Hollis said, "I was supposed to meet a friend here. Perhaps he's come and gone?"

"Yes, Mr. Rossington," Williams said. The corners of his mouth ticked down as he nodded his head toward the back of the restaurant. "I was just coming over to direct you to his table."

"He's here?" Hollis asked.

"Yes, Mr. Rossington." Again, Williams nodded to the back of the café.

This time Hollis looked over his shoulder in the direction the waiter had indicated, but he saw no one in the corner, except for the dozing bum. Hollis smiled, certain there had been some kind of mistake. "No," he said, "the man I'm looking for..." But he let the sentence trail away.

The man he was looking for had been on the run for at least three days and had traveled more than a thousand miles, likely without a change of clothes or a toiletry kit. He'd expected to be overwhelmed by Cardinal's size, yet on his first glance he hadn't noticed how completely the man was slumped in his chair. His unshaven chin pressed deeply into the lapels of his filthy shirt. And hadn't he said something about having caught a bug? Why had Hollis imagined Cardinal would be scrubbed and photograph ready after such an ordeal?

"Thank you, Williams. I'll have a café au lait, and bring us a couple orders of beignets, if you don't mind."

"Yes, Mr. Rossington."

Hollis stood and wove his way through the tables. As he approached Butch Cardinal he caught the sound of a wet, wheezing snore. The sleeping man looked too old. Beaten. An overwhelming sadness fell over Hollis as if he'd stumbled across a saint lying in a gutter, covered in his own vomit. Only common people were allowed such blatant weakness. In fact, they excelled at exhibitions of it, but a man like this, a *wrestler* like Butch Cardinal, deserved respect. He deserved some goddamn dignity.

Hollis gently shook Butch until a grinding hiccup replaced the rough snoring. A moment later, Butch reared back and fixed wild eyes on him, looking like a rabbit with the scent of a coyote in his nose.

The wildness in his eyes remained until Hollis said, "Hey, Butch," as if they were dear old friends. "Settle on down. I'm Hollis."

It seemed the name didn't immediately mean anything to the dazed man, but it sank in slowly and Butch's expression shifted and melted into fatigue. He managed a fraction of a smile; it pushed at the edges of his mustache. "Yeah. Hi. Sorry."

The voice was incredibly weak. Now that the surprise had passed, Butch looked as if he could barely keep his eyes open. Hollis extended his hand in greeting. They shook, and Rossington noted the sweaty, grimy texture of Butch's palm.

"Hell of a week," he said, taking a chair.

"Mmmm," Butch replied with a shallow nod. "A few more days like this and they'll have to bury me."

"Well, let's not have it come to that." Hollis couldn't even force a comforting smile. Butch's eyes were filmy and his skin was pale and sapped, like a fired clay mask. Spit had dried in the corners of his mouth. The bandage on the tip of his ear was a rainbow of foulness—yellow and brown and rusty red. The ear beneath was inflamed with infection. "I know a doctor. He's discreet."

"Mmm," Butch said. "I just need a good night's sleep."

"You need more than that," Hollis said. "Exactly how much trouble are you in?"

"How much is there?"

"You feel like sharing the details?"

"Rory didn't tell you?" Butch asked.

The man inhaled shallowly, and Rossington caught the ratcheting wheeze ticking away in his chest. The sound disturbed him. He knew bad lungs when he heard them. His father had died of tuberculosis. Hollis remembered sitting by the old man's bed, hearing the persistent grinding and bubbling that accompanied his father's every breath as he drowned in his own blood.

Clearly this wasn't the time for conversation. Butch could tell his story some other day. When Williams arrived with his order, he pointed at Butch's empty cup and nodded before dropping a bill on Williams' tray.

"Look, Butch," he said, "We've got something of a problem here."

"Good," he mumbled. "Can't get enough of those."

"No, listen to me. You need a doctor, and you need someone to keep an eye on you. The hospital is too risky. They find out who you are, and we got fat ladies singing."

"No hospital," Butch said. He barked out a flurry of damp coughs and snatched the napkin from the tabletop to press against his mouth. "I'll get by."

"The thing is, I have something of a rare domestic situation," Hollis said.

Butch hummed again and performed the shallow head bob, which Hollis took as agreement but the distance and murk in the wrestler's eyes suggested he might well have missed every word Hollis had spoken. His head lolled, and he drew in another ratcheting breath. "I'll get by," he repeated.

"No doubt," Hollis said with false merriment.

He'll be dead by morning, Rossington thought. *If he doesn't get someplace warm and get some medicine in him, he's going to die.*

When Williams came back with a second cup of coffee for Butch, Hollis waved him away. He had to get the man back to his house. He'd manage the inevitable conflict over Lionel when it arose.

Hollis stood and walked around the table, where he put his hand on Butch's back. "Come on, pal," he said. "We'll get a taxicab out front."

"Where are we going?"

"To my house," Hollis said as if it had been the plan all along.

Butch tried getting to his feet and dropped back into the chair. On his second attempt, Hollis slid close and helped the man up and wrapped an arm around his back. He was glad Butch's legs held him this time. Even in top shape, Hollis would have had trouble holding up a guy Butch's size. But between the two of them, they managed to make it through the restaurant, past the interested and humored gazes of the other patrons, and onto the walk in front of the café, where Rossington waved his hand at a man sitting in a mule-drawn carriage.

Chapter 11
Speak When Spoken To

Lennon sat on a stool at a counter in the evidence cage three floors below his office. Once a block of narrow holding cells, the cage was grim and cold. The stone floor, fenced in by rusting bars and chipped brick walls, was covered by any number of unwholesome stains. The place had been little more than a dungeon and it felt as if it still held many of the emotions loosed by the caged men who'd spent time there. Anger, fear, and hate were as palpable as mist. Squinting through the dim light added to his persistent headache, as did a frequent clicking behind the damaged bricks, which might have been a leaking pipe or the teeth of persistent vermin. Lennon imagined a prisoner lost over the decades, trapped behind the stone and attempting to dig his way free. The notion brought tingles to his neck, but he couldn't shake it whenever he heard the *click, clickety, click*.

He picked through the contents of two cardboard boxes—items removed from Lonnie Musante's home. Thumbing through the carton, he found the victim's belongings: cigarettes, matches, anything that wasn't nailed down and might belong to the killer. A banged-up Mauser 1914 lay in a small box, nestled among a handkerchief and a pair of gloves. The gun's handgrip was cracked and the barrel was scratched to hell. This was the murder weapon Butch Cardinal had dropped after shooting Musante. Nothing special. The German firearm was common enough. He and Conrad had pulled one off a vagrant just last month, after the guy had used it to hold up a grocery.

Lennon held the weapon, turned it in his palm. Satisfied that he had the all of it in his head, he replaced the gun in the evidence box, and reached in for a stack of cards. They were large with a white frame surrounding a field of black. He flipped one over and saw an intricate painting of a midnight sky with crimson dogs lifting their muzzles to howl at a silver moon. Over the years he'd heard about cards like these—the tarot, they were called. Carnie fortunetellers hauled them around. He considered what Valentino had told him, and Lennon couldn't help but wonder if a thug like Marco Impelliteri actually cut his path through life based on what Musante had seen—or at least, claimed to have seen—in a tarot deck? He found it hard to believe that anyone so firmly entrenched in the guns and blood of Chicago's outfits would hold close to such nonsense.

Medieval witch shit in the big and shiny city.

He flipped another card, showing a man in sapphire and emerald harlequin garb performing an exaggerated bow. The word *Fool* was written at the bottom. Lennon smiled, figuring that was the only card a deck like this one needed, then he replaced the cards in the box. Next he withdrew a brown leaflet with a number of holes punched through: a train ticket from Milwaukee. He turned it over and saw the date matched the day Lonnie Musante was murdered.

Lousy thing to come home to, Lennon thought.

The contents of the second box seemed to be the things the coroner's office had removed from Musante's pockets: a wallet with assorted bits of paper, mostly receipts; a money clip with three bucks pinched between tin fingers; a set of cheap false teeth as yellow as the front of a bum's drawers; three cigar stubs; a tin flask—empty.

Lousy life to come home to, Lennon added.

The scraping behind the wall returned, startling Lennon. He shook off the silly fear and rubbed his eyes, imagining it might remove a fraction of his headache. It didn't.

After feeling certain he'd committed the items to memory, he closed the boxes and returned them to the shelves, then he left the cage and wished Sergeant Jones, the cage's keeper, a good afternoon. Upstairs he sat behind his desk and looked at the collection of meaningless files, wondering all the while where Conrad had gotten to, but the afternoon passed with no sign of his partner, and then it was time to call it a day, but that meant going home to Edie and playing husband and father, even though he didn't feel he was through playing cop for the day. Lennon lit a cigarette and stared through the smoke and the windowpane at the coming darkness. He considered heading to the Palermo Club or the Grand for a few drinks and the company of a woman that would speak to him without making him feel regret. Before he could commit to the plan, however, another idea surfaced.

Lennon picked up the phone and called home to tell his wife that he would be working late.

• • •

LENNON reached Lonnie Musante's house after sunset. Pulling up before the darkened dwelling, a strange thought—perhaps a memory or some mental flotsam—played behind his eyes. He pictured Curt Conrad's fat face dripping sweat in the freezing cold car; his partner shook his head furiously, mouthing protests. Lennon couldn't remember the words, couldn't say for sure that he remembered the incident at all, but Conrad seemed to be arguing with him. He struggled to recall the moment, but instead Butch Cardinal filled his mind's eye—barreling down like a coal train draped in an overcoat.

Why did he drop his gun? Lennon wondered. *He pops a couple in Lonnie, and Conrad busts in and Cardinal tosses his piece? Why? Had he suffered the panic of the inexperienced?*

Leaving his car, Lennon strolled up the walk to Musante's front door. The place had been secured with a two-by-four nailed to the jamb. It came free with a good tug and Lennon tossed it on the icy lawn before trying the door. He'd expected some kind of lock to slow him down, but the knob turned easily in his palm, and the door opened with a squeak of rusted hinges. Lennon reached in and felt along the wall for the switch. He gave it a twist but the house remained dark. A second later his flashlight beam cut a trough through the center of the living room, and Lennon stepped inside.

He played the light over the space. The chalk frame of Musante's last pose remained on the floor, very white against the gray planks. Lennon noted the few pieces of shabby furniture and the bare walls. Thin clouds of breath rose from his nose and feathered the edges of the lantern's beam. The place smelled of stale cigars, old milk, cheap whiskey, and mold. At the center of the room, Lennon stopped. He'd driven to Musante's on a hunch, but now he couldn't figure out what he had hoped to gain by the trip. This wasn't his case. There was nothing for him to solve. So why was he here?

It was the near-empty house of a dead man: a box holding the trinkets of a life, likely misspent and certainly unenviable. Musante had been the pet mystic of a powerful man, with no ambitions of his own beyond scraping by at Marco Impelliteri's heels, making himself useful by weaving superstition and fantasy for his boss's…*what*? Amusement? Peace of mind?

But Musante had been free, Lennon thought: no mooring lines of guilt or obligation. Standing in the center of Musante's home with its tattered furniture and sad wallpaper, Lennon had rarely found the exercise of independence so repulsive.

He wandered to the kitchen and peered out the back window. There he saw the dark heap of bricks beyond the porch. Patches of persistent ice and snow clutched the blocks like lichens. And again he pictured Butch Cardinal charging him, and he remembered swimming backwards, and the darkness rushing up to meet him. Lennon shook the oddly substantial memory away and left the kitchen. In the hallway, he kicked a door open with the toe of his shoe and darted the light around an empty room with a badly cracked wooden floor. Dust covered the planks like a carpet, only marred by a series of footprints, likely belonging to Lennon's colleagues who had combed the place after Musante's death.

At the end of the hall he found Musante's pitiful bedroom. A short, narrow cot had been shoved into a corner and an old whiskey barrel stood beside it, a candle melted to the nub at the center of the drum. Lennon walked farther into the room, playing his light over the dirty window. The beam reflected back, and for a moment the sight of his own pale face on the glass startled him. His head began to feel light, and Lennon knew he shouldn't be spending so much time on his feet, but he had no intention of taking his rest in Lonnie Musante's bedroom.

A rap sounded in the front of the house, quickly followed by another and another: footsteps. Lennon turned away from the window and snapped off his flashlight. He drew his service revolver and moved quietly to the doorway where he listened to the sounds at the end of the hall. Whispers cut the frigid air like crackling static. He made out two voices, but he couldn't understand the conversation. The syllables were curt and delivered in breathy monotone, dying when they hit his ear rather than forming coherent phrases.

Lennon urged his eyes to adjust to the gloom flooding the hall as the voices and the echoes of footsteps worked their way down the corridor. His heart tripped rapidly. His palms sweated. When he felt certain the men were only a few steps away, Lennon lunged forward, thumbing on the flashlight.

But his light's beam fell on empty air. Confused, Lennon stepped back.

"Come out now, Mr. Police-man," a deep, dry voice called. "We're in the living room."

"Identify yourself," Lennon called.

"Our names would mean nothing to you."

"This is a crime scene," he shouted. "You're trespassing."

"Yes, we are," the man agreed. Distance and the drumbeat pulse filling Lennon's ears deadened the voice.

"What do you want?" he called. At the end of the hall just inside the archway opening onto the living room, Lennon paused and adjusted his grip on the gun. "Were you friends of Musante's?"

"Not in the least. But we are in some ways family. We came to pay our respects."

"They have funerals for that."

Lennon peered around the corner and saw a man sitting on the sofa. His body was a smudge of darkness atop the shadowed furniture and his face stained the gloom like a pale thumbprint. Lennon couldn't tell whether the man was armed, nor did he see anyone else in the room, though he'd heard two separate voices and two sets of footsteps.

"Where's your buddy?" Lennon asked.

"He's seeing to—" An ugly lamp, like a dead sapling in the corner, burst on, momentarily shocking Lennon's eyes. "He's seeing to *that*, Mr. Policeman," said the man on the sofa, pointing over his shoulder at the lamp.

"Stand up," Lennon said, "and keep your hands in sight."

The man shrugged. With his salt-and-pepper hair and thick neck, he reminded Lennon of his father-in-law, but Edie's dad had never worn such intensity in his eyes.

"I'm unarmed," the man said.

"Heard that one before," Lennon said. "Come on, stand up."

The man worked himself forward on the sofa cushion. Once standing he held himself tall and straight. His presence seemed to suck the air from the room, leaving Lennon in a frigid vacuum.

"My name is Hayes," the man said.

"Pleased," Lennon said, sarcastically. He threw glances around the room, checking the dining room on his right and the bit of kitchen he could see beyond. "Is your friend in the basement?"

"No," Hayes said.

An arm wrapped around Lennon's neck, throwing off his aim. He fired the gun, but the shot went wide. Then a glimmer of metal passed near his chin, and the warm blade of a long knife came to rest against his throat. Simultaneously, a sharp pain flared at his shoulder; it drove in deep and his hand spasmed. He dropped the gun. It landed with a *thud* on the carpet. His mind scrambled even as his legs began to turn soft and unstable beneath him. He grasped at his wounded arm and felt a long, oval piece of metal attached to his jacket.

"Leave it," the man behind him said. His breath stank of meat and onions.

"No one has to die here, Detective Lennon." Hayes said, his voice rich and commanding. "We have questions. You'll give us answers."

A strong palm planted itself in the middle of his back, guiding him toward the sofa. The knife pulled away from his throat and Brand shoved him hard. Lennon stumbled. He nearly righted himself but his shins crashed against the front of the sofa and he toppled onto the cushions. Quickly, he rolled onto his back.

Brand moved fast, climbing onto the sofa, keeping his knife close to Lennon's face. The burly little man straddled Lennon's waist and sneered down at him. He wore a sleeveless undershirt beneath a leather butcher's apron. Muscles bulged along his right arm and shoulder, but his left arm was shriveled in comparison. The knobs of his wrist and elbow rose like welts on the scrawny appendage. A copper coil wrapped the arm. In his hand Brand held a fat-bladed knife. Lennon had never seen anything like the weapon, curved and ornate, with what appeared to be gears in and among three arced blades and polished like a brand new dime.

"Mr. Brand," the man who'd called himself Hayes said, "is the pin secure?"

The man reached out and grasped Lennon's arm tightly, pressing the piece of metal deeper into the meat of his shoulder. Lennon winced and ground his teeth against the pain.

"It is, Mr. Hayes." Brand leaned back, but kept the point of his knife near Lennon's chin.

"You'll tell us the truth, now, Detective Lennon," said Hayes. He leaned in, his chin hovering above his colleague's shoulder. "If you don't, your experience will be thoroughly unpleasant."

"What do you want?"

"You aren't our enemy, Detective Lennon," Mr. Hayes said.

"I guess the knife at my throat confused me."

"We've encountered a number of aggressive men recently, and it seems violence is the only logic that resonates with them, except perhaps greed."

"Human nature," Lennon muttered.

"Yes, Detective Lennon, the nature of some. Why are you here tonight?"

"To remember," Lennon said before he could even consider his answer.

"The night of Mr. Musante's murder?"

"Yes."

"And have you remembered?"

"No."

Pain erupted in his arm as if the metal piece there injected pure agony into his veins. Lennon squeezed his eyes closed and bellowed. The suffering spread across his chest and back as if he were being submerged in acid. His body went rigid. He couldn't breathe, and the searing misery blossomed across the back of his head before it vanished completely.

"You remember nothing at all?" Hayes asked, appearing to have been saddened by Lennon's torture. His buddy, Brand, just looked amused.

"Nothing I can be certain of," Lennon said, speaking slowly, ready to stop himself should the pain reappear.

"What do you *think* you remember?"

"I tried to stop him," Lennon said. "My partner. I argued with Curt, because I thought he was doing something stupid, but I don't know what."

"What about the wrestler?" Hayes asked. "Do you know where Mr. Cardinal is currently?"

"No."

"As we understand it, he took something valuable from Mr. Musante."

"I don't know anything about that," Lennon said, wincing. Even though he was telling the truth, he felt certain the agony would return if he didn't tell them what they wanted to hear.

"Or perhaps you took the item yourself?"

"What item?" Lennon asked. "I was knocked cold about two seconds after I opened the door that night. Then I woke up in the hospital. What was taken?"

"It's not your concern, Detective Lennon. Do you have any notions about where Mr. Cardinal might be now?"

"South."

"Why south?" Hayes asked, cocking his head to the side.

"It's where I'd go," Lennon replied. "He couldn't get his money out of the bank, and if he has any friends, we couldn't find them. He won't freeze to death in the south, and the states down there keep things close to the vest. They don't trust northerners, so he could set himself up with a new name and live out the rest of his life and nobody would blink. Alabama might as well be Timbuktu."

"Why did you mention Alabama?"

"I have family there. It was just an example. What did you do to me?"

"As long as you tell the truth, it shouldn't concern you."

"It hurts."

"Did you know Mr. Musante before coming to this house, Mr. Lennon?"

"*Detective* Lennon."

"My apologies, Detective. Did you know him?"

"No."

"Do you work for the Italians or the Irish?" Brand asked.

"I work for the City of Chicago. I don't—"

Again the agony spread across his body like a pool of acid. Lennon screamed into the faces of his captors, neither of whom did so much as blink.

"Detective Lennon," Hayes said.

"The Italians." After he'd said the words, the pain receded. What had they attached to him? How could it know fact from fraud?

"Do they pay you well?" Hayes wanted to know.

"Yes."

"Do they pay you well enough to die for them?"

"No."

"And your family? Do the Italians pay you enough to put the necks of your family under Mr. Brand's knife?"

A gray fog of panic settled over him. He pictured Bette and Gwen playing on the stoop of their house, marching dolls across the living room floor, kneeling besides their beds and saying their prayers wearing matching sleeping gowns and slippers. He saw their laughing faces over the dinner table, remembered them chasing gulls on the lake shore. Then he pictured Edie's face, and she looked at him with disappointment—such a familiar expression.

"You haven't answered me," Hayes said. "Do the Italians pay you enough—"

"No," he barked.

"Very well," Mr. Hayes said, "we're going to take your identification, Detective Lennon. It will have your home address on it. You know what that means, yes?"

"I'll kill you if you go near my family."

"Well, we'll hope it doesn't come to that," Hayes said.

Brand shook his head as if in wonder of an idiot.

"We're done, Mr. Brand," Hayes said. He placed a hand on the muscular shoulder of his accomplice. "He knows nothing about what happened here or why it happened." Hayes turned his eyes back to Lennon. "Thank you, Detective. Perhaps one day we'll meet under kinder circumstances."

Brand reached out and yanked the metal pin from Lennon's shoulder. He flipped it in the air like a coin and slid it smoothly into the pocket of his leather apron. Then Brand hopped off the sofa and followed Hayes from the house, leaving Lennon stunned, ashamed, and intensely frightened. He rolled off the couch and struggled to his feet. He was in such a hurry to reach his car, he didn't bother closing Lonnie Musante's front door behind him.

Chapter 12
Monster in the Closet

Rabin sat in his car, staring at Ripper's Gym from half a block away. The neighborhood was typical. Drab. Low brick apartment buildings hovering over dismal retail spaces, a full third of which were empty, their windows soaped with instructions for prospective renters. Rusted ladders and steel grate platforms clutched the filthy exteriors like metallic insects. On the corner a boy with oddly sized features—ears and nose too large, barely enough chin to support his lower lip—hawked newspapers and occasionally blew warm breath into his palms. Rabin sipped from his thermos cup, having replenished his coffee at a diner down the street. Though he hadn't slept in thirty-two hours, he didn't feel fatigued. He was somewhat disappointed because he had not been able to visit his wife, but Irene had always understood about his job, even if she didn't know exactly what it was her husband did for a living. She'd taken him at his word when he'd told her that he worked for the city as a hog inspector, and since she rarely asked about the details of his day, the lie had been easy to maintain.

The police's failure to capture Butch Cardinal came as little surprise to Rabin. The authorities in this city had gotten lazy, so used to having their jobs done for them by the men they'd been hired to pursue. A few roadblocks and some dim-witted ox at the train station wouldn't be enough to catch a gaggle of nuns in full habit. Cardinal's file had revealed no personal connections, save for a sister named Clara who lived in Pennsylvania. Rabin already had that address, if he needed to use it. Otherwise the dossier had been useless, with one exception: the gym. He wasn't surprised a detective like Conrad would dismiss such a thing. A typical Chicago cop, though certainly not Conrad, might lift weights or skip rope in the gloomy basement of the police station, but few of them had any genuine commitment to physical fitness. To them, a gym was a place of annoyance and chore, but to an athlete like Butch Cardinal it would be as warm and comforting as a mother's lap. Likely the police had spoken with Rory Sullivan, the gym's owner, questioning him as they would any other acquaintance of Cardinal's, never understanding the deeper connection.

Of course Rabin had fashioned this logic retroactively.

He'd been watching Cardinal's apartment building. For three days, the place had been conspicuously observed by a number of police officers. A blind and slow child would have spotted them. Rabin first saw the white-haired Paddy on Monday. The burly Irishman, made all the thicker with a black overcoat and cable knit sweater, had sauntered onto the street and walked to the end of the block, pretending not to notice the officers on either side of the road. He'd reached the far corner, turned, and didn't come back that day. Rabin saw him again Tuesday afternoon, when the white-haired Irishman repeated the performance. Yesterday, however, the police had cut back their surveillance of Cardinal's building to the dogleg shift, and the Paddy had returned. This time he lingered on the block, pretending to look for an address. Then he'd walked to Cardinal's apartment building, unlocked the front door with a key and slipped inside. Less than ten minutes later, the man emerged, and Rabin followed Sullivan to Ripper's Gym.

From that point on, he'd foregone even the most cursory reconnaissance of Cardinal's apartment building. The Paddy was the key. Rabin knew it. The wrestler had skipped town, and by Rabin's thinking it was the smartest move the man could have made, but Cardinal needed something here, or at least needed to know where he stood, and the Irishman was acting as his connection to the city. Not a bad move, Rabin thought. The cops wouldn't give the old geezer a second look, as was demonstrated on more than one occasion. Rabin knew better. He'd figured it out and had taken to parking outside the gym, keeping his eye on the stout little Paddy and following him on any number of pointless excursions. Eventually, the old man would lead him to the wrestler.

Or you could just go in there and cut the information out of him, a small voice whispered to the back of his mind. Rabin shook the voice away, though he liked its tone and message. That side of his personality, the savage side, needed to be kept in check. He'd spent his entire adulthood managing the monster, keeping it in the closet, keeping it quiet, and only releasing it in the course of performing his duties. He didn't dare let it run loose.

Ahead on the street, a young woman stepped out of the entrance to the building. Her thick red hair fell over her shoulders in lush waves. The black pea coat she wore hung to her knees, so Rabin had no impression of her figure, but that was of little concern to him. She held a snow shovel in gloved hands and her breath appeared in soft clouds, like bits of soul floating skyward.

Then Rory Sullivan exited the gym and walked up to the girl. He spoke to her, and she didn't like what she heard. The cold-burn of her cheeks went crimson and her hands slapped the air in consternation. The white-haired man's demeanor did not change, and the redhead discarded the shovel before punching her fists to her hips in a stance of defiance. The man said something else, and she shook her head. Then Sullivan walked to the south, leaving the young woman fuming in front of the gym.

Sullivan turned left at the corner, and Rabin pulled away from the curb to follow the man. After a dozen blocks it became clear the Irishman was headed for the L station and a flare of rage ignited in Rabin's chest. By car he'd have to meet the train at every station to see if the Paddy disembarked, but he stood a greater chance of being seen on foot. Neither choice was satisfactory, but one had to be made. Frustrated he found the first available space at the curb and parked the car.

As he made his way up the stairs to the train platform, he questioned the move. If nothing else, he should have driven to the next stop and waited there. Either Sullivan would get off and Rabin could stay on his heels or Rabin would be overlooked, considered a random passenger commuting like all the rest.

At the top of the stairs, Rabin continued to the back of the platform and leaned forward, peering down the tracks. Then he backed away, checked Sullivan, and then dropped his gaze to the muddy smears on the tips of his toes. The Paddy was on guard. Checking his periphery, and doing a respectable job of it. Rabin would keep his direct observations of the man to a minimum.

The train arrived and Rabin walked into the car behind the one Sullivan entered. Rabin positioned himself by the door, standing, holding a strap. At the next stop, he turned and checked the platform to see if the man exited, and when he saw that he hadn't, Rabin resumed his casual stance. He repeated this ritual several times, until the train pulled into the Clinton Street Station and Sullivan disembarked. The Irishman walked south, and Rabin felt another tickle of annoyance, guessing at the man's next destination.

Men and women, bundled in layers and hunched against the cold, scurried along the slick walks. One unfortunate soul—a bum clad in tattered, gray rags—clumsily approached and stretched out his hand to Rabin in a silent act of begging. Rabin smiled in response. A flicker of anger showed in the transient's eyes, all but daring Rabin to voice what he found so amusing. The bum ground a damp toothpick between his teeth and pulled up his chin as if in defiance, perhaps to say, *You wait until I'm back on my feet.*

Rabin could all but hear the echoes of similar sentiments bouncing off the brick buildings around him.

It seemed every other man on the street was a down-and-outer, a guy who'd been somebody just a few years ago, only to be hollowed out and left a panhandling shell. They wandered, dazed, as if disbelieving life could have betrayed them so wholly: discarded by the society they'd helped build; forgotten or ignored by those who feared sharing their fate.

These were glorious days for Rabin and the men who employed him. Notions of community and compassion eroded under the constant abrasion of personal uncertainty and loss. Rabin knew humankind *could* join together, *could* build wonderful things, *could* help one another, so long as it meant the individuals involved didn't lose too much in the process. When the individual had so little, they shared nothing, and their brains went primitive, clicking into a survival mode that created a splendid tunnel vision. Immediate needs had to be met. A desperate man robs and murders for a bottle of gin, and a woman will eagerly trade her body at the prospect of feeding her children. The hungry man spends the remainder of his life in prison, and the woman doesn't understand that a stranger might use her body in any number of ways, many of which would not result in the nourishment of her children. Granted, such trades were willingly made at any point in human history, but this depression had created winds that carried the pollen of brutish self-service across the entire nation. A leader with vision, one who understood the power of hope among the desperate, could conquer the world, and stand like a sun for all of the miserable weeds to feed from. What else did they have? They borrowed nickels and dimes at exorbitant interest rates; they hocked family heirlooms; they bet their final pennies on horses as floundering as themselves, and each ridiculous step was a gamble that they sincerely believed would pay out the beginning of an easier life. For mere heartbeats they forgot that their futures couldn't help but rise from the foundations of mud they'd built them upon, and instead chose to believe their destinies lay in sweet fields made bright and fertile with the rays of hope.

Every human being was a victim of something, whether it was desire, addiction, ignorance, or faith. Simple...weak...victims.

Rabin wouldn't have it any other way.

He checked on the direction of his target. His annoyance grew when Sullivan entered Union Station. He'd considered this possibility. Apparently, the trip was not coming to an end; it was just beginning.

• • •

RABIN considered himself an intelligent man, exceptionally so. He knew that if the Paddy had noticed him on the L platform, then being seen again in the train station would take away his advantage. Instead of following Sullivan to the ticket window to eavesdrop on his destination, Rabin paid a boy a quarter to do it for him, and when the boy returned and told him, "Indianapolis," the boy received his coin and a smile.

After that, it was a matter of staying out of Sullivan's sight, an easy enough prospect. Twenty minutes later, when the train boarded, Rabin again took the car behind the Paddy's, settled into his seat and lit a cigarette. The train pulled out of the station and Rabin noted his fellow travelers.

Ahead and across the aisle, a young couple snuggled under an ugly woolen blanket. The boy's cheeks were unshaven and the girl's hair, despite having been bundled and fastened atop her head, frayed with untidy wisps. The man sneezed twice and blinked, and the woman quickly drew her hand from under the blanket. She held a white handkerchief, which she used to wipe the man's nose like a mother tending a baby.

Rabin warmed to the display, but not because of its tenderness. The sight merely confirmed a notion he had long held to be true.

The entire country had been infantilized. An adult could weigh his options and think a problem through, but children only knew want; they demanded immediate satisfaction of that want and were more than willing to sacrifice any number of needs to have it. The young threatened and wailed and gnashed, but if they were supplicated—with kisses or candy—they would forget for a time that their diapers hadn't been changed, and that they remained swathed in their own shit. Anyone who had enough cheap candy—a criminal, a factory owner, a reverend, a government—could keep the soiled babes distracted indefinitely, and the children would know nothing but the pleasure that momentary sweetness brought to their mouths and the want—the *Hope*—for another piece.

Beautiful, Rabin thought.

Thirty minutes later, Rabin sat at a table in the club car and looked out on the magnificent world. Despite his lack of sleep he felt exhilarated, wanting nothing more than for the Irishman to lead him to Butch Cardinal. They would both die. That was indisputable. Rabin had received no demands for discretion. Impelliteri wanted a necklace and the knowledge that Cardinal had taken his last breath. All else was up to Rabin, and though he felt elated, he did not feel charitable. In fact, he couldn't imagine synonymy between the two emotions.

He turned his head from the window to greet the white-jacketed Negro who'd come to take his order, and the face of a boy, standing at the bar caught his eye. The kid couldn't have been more than sixteen years old. Black hair. The toned, etched face of a marathoner or a child enduring starvation. Ears and nose too large. Nothing of a chin. He wore a sleek gray suit with a narrow black tie. A cigarette jutted from his full lips.

Rabin didn't know the young man's name, but he knew his face; he'd seen it outside of Butch Cardinal's apartment building more than once. He'd been hustling newspapers on a corner, standing there for hours until his supply was gone. The boy's performance had been convincing. Rabin hadn't thought twice about the youth, but he didn't believe in coincidence. A paperboy didn't belong on a train headed to Indianapolis. Not this train.

He ordered a soda water with lime from the waiter and immediately turned his attention back to the window to consider the boy's affiliations. Marco Impelliteri hadn't sent him; that was a given. Rabin had made it clear that if he accepted an assignment, he did so with the understanding that no one else was offered the contract. The police might use a boy that age for his eyes and ears, but they wouldn't send him traveling. That only left the Moran syndicate, possibly trying to recover the necklace that seemed so important to Impelliteri, or perhaps to kill Cardinal themselves and present his corpse as a peace offering to the Italians. Maybe the outbreak of violence had gotten to Moran, or more likely the lesser man, Powell, but again, the boy's age made this supposition less than promising. You didn't send a novice on this kind of hunt unless you intended to lose him. A friend of the Irishman? Someone to watch his back?

A twitch of agitation skipped through Rabin's thoughts. He didn't like uncertainty.

Chapter 13
Life Expectancy

Lennon carried the last of his wife's luggage down the stairs, and she stood at the bottom waiting for him. Her arms were crossed and her mouth was fixed in a pout.

"Are the girls in the taxi?" Lennon asked.

Edie dipped her chin, nodding.

"Good. This is the last of them. Be sure to call me at the station when you get to Raymond's."

"I still don't understand why we have to leave."

"Yes, you do. You just want to know more about the *why*, and I'm not telling you that." Lennon wasn't even sure what he'd tell her. It had to do with two men, one of whom carried a knife that looked as intricate as a watch mechanism. They had his identification. His address.

"But Roger…"

"Look Edie, I told you when we were married there might come a time when I packed you off for a vacation, and you promised you wouldn't ask me why, so now I'm holding you to that promise."

"How am I supposed to not worry about my husband?"

"I'm fine, and I'll be fine, but right now the city is a bad place to be. I want you and the girls as far away from here as possible for a couple of weeks. You're always complaining about not spending enough time with your brother's family anyhow. Well we've got two birds and one stone."

"You know I didn't mean this," she said, exaggerating her petulant frown.

"Yes, I do. I also know you'll be late for your train if you don't get a move on. Everything should be fine in a week or two, and then you can bring the girls back and we'll think about taking a trip of our own. How does Florida sound?"

"You can't bribe me, Roger."

"I don't have to bribe you, Edie. You're going, like it or not. You can spend your time being angry at me, or you can spend your time looking forward to sand and swimming and sunshine. Your choice."

"I love you, Roger, but I don't like you very much right now."

"Duly noted."

He ushered his wife out the door ahead of him and placed the final bag in the trunk with its companion pieces. He kissed his daughters goodbye, pecked Edie on the cheek, gave the driver money and then stood in the slush in front of their home, waving at the taxicab as it rolled down the block. When it disappeared around the corner, Roger raced up the stoop and into the house. From the jar in the pantry, he took money—to replace the cash that had been in the wallet Brand and Hayes had stolen—and then he gathered up his keys, strapped on his holster, and wrapped himself in an overcoat before leaving the house.

At the station he poured coffee into a mug and carried it to his desk. He sent a formal request to the evidence room for the items retrieved from Musante's home and then looked at the low pile of files sitting on his desk. The coroner's report, along with two disturbing photos of Musante's naked corpse; medical reports; memos from Brooklyn, NY; bank statements; everything he could think to dredge up on Lonnie Musante sat before him.

He started with the photos, which showed Musante on a metal table. The first picture was a close up of Musante's face. His eyes were closed and his upper lip had retreated in death, revealing the stub of a single tooth. The second photograph showed Musante from the waist up. His ribs were visible through the tight skin of a spooned chest. The two bullet holes appeared neat, small, and black in the center of his sternum. A misshapen lump, about the size of a lime had risen to the left of Musante's navel; it looked like a mouse had curled up beneath the lowlife's skin. Lennon leaned closer to the picture, wondering what the hell had taken up residence in Musante's gut. But he could draw no obvious conclusions from the picture.

Next he read through the memos from New York. He knew that Musante, like a lot of Capone's crew, had come from back east. Last night, after his encounter with Hayes and Brand, he'd gone home to make sure his family was safe, and then he'd called precincts all over New York City to find out anything he could about Lonnie Musante. When he mentioned the name to a detective in Brooklyn, the man had laughed heartily.

"I never thought I'd hear that piss weasel's name again."

Lennon informed the sergeant that a dispatcher would be contacting him for details, and if he could assign someone to read Musante's files to the woman, he would be most grateful. The sergeant was more than happy to help.

What he found in the folder were two typed sheets with the details of Musante's criminal past.

(Detective Lennon, Sergeant Lipman was very helpful, though his language was highly objectionable. I have taken down his statements as spoken. I apologize for the harsh verbiage. That noted, he worked in the victim's neighborhood during the years in question, so he was quite familiar with him.)

Sergeant Lipman comments: Musante was in trouble most of his life. Petty theft. Numbers. Attempted assault. He was a typical Brooklyn rat, except he wasn't, because the little prick just wasn't any good at the crime business. In fact, he was lousy at it. I'm surprised he lived long enough to have any kind of record at all. Let me see what I've got here on him.

1885: Perpetrator, age 13, arrested with four other youths for setting fire to a fruit cart.

1885: Perpetrator, age 13, escapes from Ronson Juvenile Facility with Marco Impelliteri and Jupiter Leone. Apprehended two days later.

1887: Perpetrator, age 15, implicated in the murder of Jupiter Leone. Never charged.

1888: Perpetrator, age 16, apprehended during the burglary of the home of Anthony Scaramellino (perpetrator's uncle). No charges filed.

Sergeant Lipman comments: The family protected their own, even the rotten little piss weasel. Don't know how he fell so far from that tree. The Musantes were good folks generally speaking. You know, for immigrants. One interesting thing, Musante was with his uncle in the fall of 1890, when the old man got gunned down by persons unknown. The family insisted on treating old Anthony themselves. They must have one hell of a doctor in that family or I saw things wrong, because I could have sworn old Anthony took one to the lung and a week later, I see him strolling down Coffey Street as fit as you please. The old guy just passed away a couple weeks back, according to the papers. He lived a good long life. Must have been near ninety years old.

1889: Perpetrator, age 17, admitted to hospital with severe contusions.

Sergeant Lipman comments: Had his ass beat good and proper by the owner of a candy store for trying to extort money. The candy store owner broke Musante's jaw and freed a good number of the fucker's teeth. Hope the weasel didn't like beefsteak. Lipman laughs.

No charges filed.

1893: Perpetrator, age 20, throws in with Giovanni "John" Torrio.

Sergeant Lipman comments: And ain't that something? The dumbest, worst-lucked little shit Brooklyn had ever produced, manages to work his way in tight with the shrewdest gangster in the Five Boroughs. Guess his luck changed. He brought Impelliteri into the gang and while Impelliteri continued to put notches on his record—including time for an assault rap—Musante was never again implicated in criminal activity. But you know the piss weasel didn't go straight. No way. Maybe some of Torrio's smarts rubbed off on him. He was seen frequently at Torrio's billiards parlor in Coney Island. He grew old in the place as the real players, Capone, DeStefano, and Glaister, grew up in it. In 1920, Musante followed Impelliteri and Capone to Chicago with a good chunk of Torrio's crew. So thanks for taking those shit stains off my hands. Lipman laughs.

(The rest of Sergeant Lipman's comments were general and were focused on the qualities of my voice and how they might relate to the physical attributes he admired rather than relevant to the victim's history.)

Lennon read over the statement twice more, underlining passages that interested him. Then he put the pages aside and opened the report from Musante's doctor. He'd meant to read through it methodically, but his eyes were drawn down to the center of the page where words in all capital stood out:

CANCER OF THE STOMACH. TERMINAL. PATIENT'S LIFE EXPECTANCY: 3-4 MONTHS.

Resistant to X-radiation treatments.

Surgery not recommended due to proliferation of the disease.

Son of a bitch, Lennon thought. *Musante was dying.* Lennon returned to the photograph of Musante's torso and focused on the lime-sized lump growing beside his navel—a tumor, a death sentence.

He read the rest of the report, none of which was surprising or even interesting—occasional dyspepsia, sore joints, bad back—typical complaints for a man of advancing years. But the all-capital letters drew Lennon's eyes time and again. He didn't know whether he should consider Musante's murder a blessing or not.

Lennon's mother had died of lung cancer, or might as well have done. Her last months had been spent wheezing shrieks of pain into a pillow. The morphine the doctors had prescribed hadn't alleviated the old woman's suffering much, except when it had knocked her out cold. In the end, she'd shot herself up with half a bottle of the dope and brought her heart to a stop.

It was an ugly and humiliating way to go, Lennon thought. A couple of bullets might have been a blessing.

Conrad appeared at the station an hour after his shift had begun. Before saying a word to Lennon, Conrad took a seat and started devouring a ham and egg sandwich that dripped butter like sweat onto the desktop.

"I got the information on Musante," Lennon said.

"So-oo whah?" Conrad said around a mouthful of half-masticated bread and meat. "Fuh-ers stih de-ahd."

"Yeah, he is and it's our job to figure out why."

"It's not our job. It's not our case. And if it was, our only job would be to find Cardinal and make him fry for it."

"If Cardinal was the shooter."

Conrad eyed Lennon angrily. He snatched a dirty handkerchief from his breast pocket and scrubbed the butter and egg from his lips. "We saw the fucker do it. What the hell else do you need?"

"I didn't see anything," Lennon said.

"Right. You were napping."

The insult stirred his belly, but he didn't respond to it. Conrad wasn't worth additional aggravation. The man was the epitome of self-serving and he'd have no part of logic unless it happened to corroborate what he already believed. Lennon figured he should have sent the two freaks with their knives and their pain device in Conrad's direction. He'd like to see the fat son of a bitch squirm inside his lies.

"It's not our case," Conrad concluded. He lifted the sandwich and ripped off another mouthful. "Sow-sies pro'lem."

Yes, it was the Southside's problem, their case. Even if Musante had been gunned down in a northern precinct, the Captain would never have let Lennon investigate a case in which he was considered a secondary victim. That didn't mean he was just going to drop it. Desk duty bored him to tears, and something about the Musante case just didn't add up. The more he knew about the man, the more chance he'd find the answer to why Musante was murdered.

"Musante was dying," Lennon said, not that he expected his partner to give a shake.

"Looks to me like he did a good job of it," Conrad replied. He again scrubbed his lips with the foul handkerchief. "Now how about you drop this shit? It's fucking up my digestion."

Lennon pushed the photographs and papers back into his file and closed his eyes so he didn't have to see Conrad sloppily eating his breakfast. He refused to believe this was just a run-of-the-mill mob murder. Hayes and Brand, the strange men who had asked so many questions, weren't connected to the outfits, at least no outfits Lennon had encountered in Chicago's streets. A dying man was murdered and his killer stole something of considerable value from him. That's what Hayes and Brand had wanted. They'd made their disinterest in Musante clear, even though they'd referred to the man as family. It was what he'd been holding that interested them. Maybe it was this same item that interested Marco Impelliteri, Angus Powell, and every other thug now chasing Butch Cardinal.

But what was it? he wondered. What the hell could be so important?

Chapter 14
Delusions in a Strange Bed

. . . And for a moment he was home: a sturdy house on good land in a valley beneath endless sky. He had his porch and his comfortable chair and a glass of cold beer. In the house someone fiddled with the stove, making him wait. He was impatient to see his companion, whoever it might be. He needed an explanation for the weight in his chest and the pain in his head. But like all of the other dreams sweltering in his mind, home was a transient place, nothing more than a wispy mist, easily burned away to reveal a fresh, hidden place and a new, fleeting sentiment.

He found himself crouched on the floor of his sister's house in Burlington, holding her head in his lap as blood ran a line from her lip to her chin. Clara cried. Two minutes later, she was on her feet, shrieking at him, pointing her finger. So much hate.

Butch woke and gasped for air because he felt as if he'd been held under water, at turns ice cold and scalding hot, too long, but the gasp agitated his chest and throat and did nothing to alleviate the suffocating sensation. He sat up in bed. He coughed violently, so violently that it felt like his sternum and spine were meeting in the center of his chest, displacing his heart and sodden lungs. The cough continued, bringing a cramp to his sides and spikes of misery to his temples. He crashed back on the pillows and took in the details of a room made filmy by the scrim of moisture covering his eyes.

Sunlight cut through a crack in scarlet drapes to his left. Columns of a similar red alternated with gold creating the design of expensive wallpaper. The paper ran from crown molding to a deeply etched chair rail. To his right, an armoire with an intricately carved cornice stood against the wall.

Ahead, the varnish on a matching secretary's table glimmered in the rod of sunlight running over its surface. Butch craned his neck to find a small lamp and a ceramic bowl occupying another table only a few inches from his head.

Where the hell is this? What am I doing here?

His chest convulsed and another flurry of coughs dislodged the questions; they fell into darkness. And his thoughts turned hazy again, and his vision lost focus and the bar of light cutting the far wall expanded and blossomed before turning black.

He woke some time later, brought from the hot swamp of dreams to find a figure standing at the end of his bed. Though not wholly certain, Butch told himself this person, a young man with a sour face, was real and not another scrap of delusion.

The kid was short and stocky with pale skin, accentuated by a sheer white shirt that hugged his shoulders and chest.

"Who are you?" Butch asked.

"This is my house," the kid said.

"I don't understand."

"Hollis brought you home. You've been stinking up our guest room for two days and making Hollis act like a complete ass."

"I'm sorry," Butch replied. A whisper of self-consciousness blew through the miserable aches and pains. But at least he knew where he was and who he was with.

"Yeah, well, sorry and a nickel…" The kid crossed his arms over his chest and sneered. "At least you're easy on the eyes."

Butch tried to make sense of the comment, but his feverish and fatigued thoughts melted together like candle wax. He shut his eyes for a moment, just a second to rest them, and then he was asleep, drifting through fragmented images.

Chapter 15
Interrogating Humphrey

The young man's name was Humphrey Bell. Rabin knew a lot about him now. For instance, he knew Humphrey was twenty-two years old, and not the teenage boy Rabin had thought when observing him on the train. Humphrey's oddly proportioned features and slight build had given Rabin the mistaken impression that he was still in his growing years. Further, Rabin knew that Humphrey was only visiting Chicago. A long time resident of Red Hook, New York, Humphrey had been sent—by whom he would not say—to the windy city, where he had rented a room in a building across the street from the former residence of Butch Cardinal with the intent of keeping an eye on the property. Another thing Rabin knew was that the kid was bleeding all over the floor of the room; he was sobbing quietly into his gag, a filthy piece of shirt already sodden with tears and spit and snot.

"This is my job," Rabin said, leaning against the counter of the kitchenette. "Which is to say, I have nowhere else to be right now. I can stay here for a few more seconds or a few more weeks."

From his chair in the center of the room, Humphrey sniffed loudly and closed his eyes.

Indianapolis had proved frustrating for Rabin. He'd endured the train ride surrounded by pitiful humanity only to watch the Paddy, Rory Sullivan, leave the station and climb into a car. The old Irishman hadn't so much as paused to adjust the vehicle's mirrors before speeding away. Rabin had flagged a cab and they'd followed Sullivan for thirty minutes, but it became clear that Butch Cardinal's friend was doing nothing more than retrieving his vehicle and returning to Chicago. The gym owner had not come south to help the wrestler; he'd already helped Cardinal by loaning the man a means to escape. For all Rabin knew, that act had ended Sullivan's complicity. He wasn't ready to write Sullivan off, but the man was not the shortcut Rabin had hoped.

In the cab, returning to the train station, Rabin had grown more incensed with the situation, and he nearly asked the cabbie to pull to the side of the road, where Rabin had intended to release a bit of his annoyance on the driver, but he'd thought better of it, and the decision turned out to be a good one. Had he indulged himself with the cabbie, he would have missed the train back to Chicago. In and of itself not a significant event, but on the return trip, he'd again seen Humphrey in the club car, appearing as frustrated as Rabin himself.

Back in Chicago, he'd followed Humphrey to his room, which overlooked the same street as Butch Cardinal's, and there he'd secured the young man to a chair. Going through the man's pockets he'd found identification, which had given him Humphrey's name and an address in Brooklyn. But why he was in Chicago and following the same man as Rabin was the question. He wasn't a hitter. No chance of that. Humphrey's eyes were too clear, filled too full with hope and dreams. So what *was* he, and why had his path crossed Rabin's twice in a single evening?

Still leaning against the counter, Rabin removed the ice pick from his jacket and tapped the tapered spike against his palm. He looked away from Humphrey who seemed to have drifted into unconsciousness again, and sneered at his surroundings. Wallpaper peeled away from seams, had been torn out in great swatches, exposing dirty plaster like wounds. Once the color of wheat and grass, the paper had fouled from age and dirt and nicotine stain and now resembled the colors of infection. The floor was buckled and warped. Long deep scratches bit deeply into the planks. The furniture and linens and window shades were of the lowest quality. Only the radio beside the window was as yet untarnished by time and indifference. How could a man call himself human and install himself in such a sty?

Leaving the kitchenette, Rabin walked past the dozing man. At the window, he pulled the shade aside and peered into the street. Pedestrians bundled against the bitter, gray air scurried like vermin—rats seeking their sustenance. He'd missed another morning with his wife, and it was because of the kid in the chair. Of course, Rabin was here voluntarily. It was his choice, but it was Humphrey's *fault*. He released the shade and turned to the radio.

A moment later, the raucous and tinny music of a big band clamored into the room. Humphrey shot upright in his chair. He knew what the music meant; it meant questions, and it meant pain.

At the chair, Rabin leaned close to Humphrey's ear so that he could be heard through the music. "I'd like to say that I admire your courage, but the truth is I don't understand it. I cannot fathom the notion of enduring personal discomfort for another man, even less for an ideal. Apparently, you've convinced yourself that silence is bravery's equivalent. But you're not a friend of Butch Cardinal's. You don't even know the man, do you?"

Humphrey shook his head. This fact had been established early on.

"You were sent to find Cardinal, as I was. But you don't work for the police or the Irish or the Italians. You don't work for anyone in Chicago." This had also been established. "So, we know what you're not. I want to assure you, we will be together until I find out what you are." He lifted the ice pick and placed the point against the skin beneath Humphrey's lower eyelid. A moment later, the man was trembling violently as if he were riding a carriage over rough roads. Tears spilled from his eyes like rain from a gutter spout. The reaction interested Rabin greatly.

"You have sincere eyes," he said. "I'd like to keep them in a jar as a reminder of our time together."

With that, the tremors shaking Humphrey's body became a series of convulsions. Wet, clear snot bubbled from his broken nose; it drained over his lip and was quickly absorbed into the filthy gag. He swung his head from side to side and panted frantically, releasing a high-pitched whine through his nose.

Every man had a particular weakness, a fear that overpowered all pretensions to bravery. Rabin was glad he'd stumbled onto Humphrey's.

He pulled the ice pick away and slapped the back of Humphrey's head with a palm. "You'll want to pay attention, Humphrey," he said. "I'm going to count to five. At the count of five, I will either learn what I came here for, or I will puncture your eye." Rabin stepped around and knelt down so that he could meet Humphrey's gaze before he said, "And I'll do it slow, Humphrey. So…very…fucking…slow."

The young man's eyes grew comically wide and white. His convulsions returned in spasms that rocked the chair, making its legs click against the floor like the feet of a brain damaged tap dancer.

"One," Rabin said.

Humphrey shook his head violently from side to side.

"Three," Rabin said. The fact he'd skipped the number two had not been missed by Humphrey, whose face had turned as red as a beet beneath the film of greasy sweat covering it. The stink of ammonia rose as Humphrey's bladder released a stream of piss into his trousers.

"Just nod your head, Humphrey. Tell me something fascinating. No one else ever needs to know."

Then as if what remained of his strength had drained away with the urine, Humphrey's body relaxed and slumped.

"Four," Rabin whispered, just loud enough to be heard over the music.

Humphrey nodded his head. Rabin nodded, too. He stood and walked around behind the chair. With the ice pick back in his pocket, he set his fingers to work on the knot of the gag. "You know what will happen if you call out. You know what will happen if you lie to me." The young man nodded again. Rabin pulled the filthy scrap of shirt free and threw it on the floor.

Humphrey gasped for breath. He coughed and wretched dryly. Finally, he managed to say, "The Alchemi."

"Pardon me?" Rabin asked, returning to his place in front of the chair.

"The Alchemi," Humphrey whispered.

"What is that?"

"We gather the metals and protect them."

Rabin felt a tide of rage rising behind his face. The punk kid was playing him for a fool. In a swift motion, he yanked the ice pick free and lunged forward, pressing the point against the soft flesh beneath Humphrey's eye. "What did I say about lying?"

"Cardinal stole the Rose," the young man babbled. "It was stolen from the Alchemi and sold to Lonnie Musante and then Cardinal murdered Musante and stole the Rose. I was sent to find him, sent to find the Rose."

Rabin pressed the ice pick deeper until the dimpled skin nearly broke. Through the crimson haze of his anger, he remembered something that swine Conrad had said about a necklace that was incredibly important to Marco Impelliteri. Was this "Rose" the item in question?

No, he thought. *The little fucker is testing me. Take his eye. Take it right fucking now!*

Disturbed by the screeching voice that suddenly filled his head, Rabin pulled away and took a deep breath. He needed a moment to clear his thoughts, to silence the shrill demands for violence. Blood would come soon enough, but he had visited Humphrey with a purpose. Once he'd gotten what he needed, then he could entertain the needs of that scraping voice. Until then, his thoughts had to be lucid. He wasn't an animal.

"Tell me again," Rabin said.

"I belong to the Alchemi. We gather the thinking steel and harbor it, protect it."

"What is thinking steel?"

Humphrey seemed confused as if Rabin had asked him to define air or water. "Long ago, the sky rained ore. It fell like God's wrath all over Europe and the Orient."

Rabin considered the possibility that he'd already done too much damage to the young man. Perhaps Humphrey's mind had snapped from fear and trauma. Whatever the case, Rabin wasn't accustomed to forgiving regardless of the excuse. "I'm losing my patience, Humphrey," he said.

"It's the truth. Or I think it is. It's what we're taught. The ore rained down on the earth, and it was discovered by the tribes of men. They used the raw ore to create alloys and from these they fashioned weapons and icons. Over time, the items were lost, or they were hoarded by immoral men who exploited the powers of the metal. The Alchemi was formed to protect the thinking steel."

"Your eyes must mean very little to you."

"I can prove it," Humphrey said. "I can. Just wait."

"What kind of proof?" Rabin asked.

"I was just sent to watch, so they didn't give me a weapon, but I have something else. You took it out of my pocket when…it's there, on the counter."

Rabin looked about the room and saw the low pile of items he'd removed from Humphrey's pockets: a wallet, some loose change, a handkerchief, a cheap spring blade knife, a ring that held two simple house keys, and yes, there was something else. Something strange. It was an arced metal band, no longer than Rabin's pinkie finger. Attached to this simple arm was a sheer plate of metal that ran diagonally from the bend. He crossed to the thing and lifted it. He remembered taking this from the inside pocket of the young man's overcoat but he couldn't remember having asked Humphrey about the item, though it certainly was odd enough to warrant such an inquiry. More than likely he hadn't thought to ask because the device had not appeared to be a weapon, at least not a useful one. He lifted the thing from the counter and rubbed it between his fingers. The metallic surface was cold and presented an uncommon velvety texture.

"What is it?" Rabin asked.

"It's for listening," Humphrey said quickly. "You see that depression near the bottom of the angled arm? That goes in your ear. You can hear everything."

"That's your proof? That's your magic? A hearing assistant?"

"Put it on," Humphrey said. "The band goes over your ear like a spectacle stem. You'll understand."

Rabin gave the device a thorough examination, searching for some hidden lever or spring mechanism that might identify the thing as a trap, but it had no moving parts, just two lengths of metal no wider than a cigar band attached by a thick and clumsy weld. Seeing no apparent danger,

Rabin slid the arced band over his ear and positioned the flat metal over his left ear.

At first, he heard only crackling like sturdy paper crumpled in a strong fist, and then a blast of noise punched the side of his head. He squeezed his eyes against the roar and quickly realized it was the tinny music from the radio amplified to ear splitting volume. Furious, he snatched the device from his head, but the screaming music echoed in his head like tortured souls, only far less pleasant. A groan escaped his throat, and he drove a fist into Humphrey's cheek for not having warned him about the radio. Shock came and went quickly over the young man's face.

Then Rabin's prisoner smiled. The pathetic little shit actually smiled, revealing a grin of bloody teeth. As the din of shrill horns and thundering drums faded, the voice of Rabin's monster picked up the song, screaming wretched orders, demanding punishment for the trick that had been played on them both. Rabin lifted the ice pick and struggled against his every instinct, fought to keep from driving the metal rod into the punk's eye socket and through to his brain. The monster wanted the asshole dead, wanted his eye juice and blood to warm his fingers to slick everything up good and proper for the other socket, but Rabin battled the urge. He took deep breaths and pushed them through his teeth, sending flecks of spit showering over Humphrey's face.

"It needs time to adjust," Humphrey said. "After it adjusts everything is okay. I swear it is."

Rabin punched Humphrey a second time, which seemed to placate and silence the monster for a time. After all, the young man hadn't lied. The device, a simple strip of metal, had indeed acted as an amplifier, and were it not for the radio, which was already playing at an excessive volume, Rabin might well have found the device effective. This did not mean that he accepted Humphrey's fairy tales, but a kernel of belief had been planted.

He returned to the radio and switched it off, and then he crossed to the chair. Again he slid the device over his ear. In his other hand, he held the ice pick to his lips: *shhh.*

Another moment of static was followed by two distinct pulsing rhythms, and soon enough Rabin identified those stuttering thuds as his heart and that of his prisoner. Then he heard more scratching, only instead of random static, Rabin understood the sound came from the walls, or rather the insects moving behind them. And then he heard voices, a choir of them crept into his ear. In a room at the end of the hall, a couple fucked on the floor, and he could hear the sound of flesh slapping flesh and he could hear the woman's moans and the man whispering, "Fucking bitch. Fucking bitch," in a soft rhythmic chant that almost sounded tender. And in a room above and to the north someone urinated and the sound filled his ear like the crashing of a waterfall, and more conversations—arguments over bills, children spouting irrelevancies—and more private moments poured into his head. Rabin considered the value of such a toy, understood the secrets he could gather like gold if he were in the vicinity when such valuable information was shared.

He removed the device and slid it into the pocket of his suit jacket, and Paul Rabin smiled, which was an expression generally reserved for his wife. With a nod of his head he patted Humphrey's shoulder.

"Now you're going to tell me about the necklace Cardinal stole," he said. "Tell me everything."

• • •

At least Humphrey hadn't begged for his life like so many of the men Rabin had encountered over the years. That was admirable on the young man's part, and completely rational by Rabin's estimation. He grabbed the back of the chair and dragged it into the corner, next to the radio, and once he was out from behind it, he shoved the chair to the wall with his foot. Humphrey's body rocked forward, spilling more of the viscous red tears from the holes in his eyes. Once satisfied with the position of the body, Rabin went to the window and opened it wide. A gust of icy wind blew over him. It felt soothing. Pleasant. With the window open and the room's temperature already dropping, Rabin turned the knob on the radiator off and then yanked the window shade down and closed the curtains. The eager wind tossed the window coverings about, but would sufficiently obstruct a prolonged and direct view into the room. This finished, he pulled the blanket off of the bed and tacked two corners above the door jamb, and then he tacked the lower edge of the blanket to the door itself, making sure to leave enough play in the fabric for him to exit. Between the cold and the bedding, it could be weeks before anyone noticed a suspicious odor emanating from the room. Of course, a landlord or caretaker would be in sooner than that if the rent wasn't paid through the month, but Rabin wasn't interested in secreting the body forever, just long enough for anyone who might have seen him entering or exiting the building to forget his face.

Satisfied with his preparations, he turned to Humphrey, who appeared to be gazing into his own lap, and Rabin stared at the top of the young man's head.

Why didn't you beg for your life? he wondered. *Do you believe glory awaits you wherever you've been sent?*

Such a strange thing, begging for one's life. For a good man, a religious man, death should have been considered welcome, an early jump on blissful eternity. For most of the men Rabin encountered—falsely religious and in no way good—their begging was ludicrous, because they had to know their ends had come. What was more rational, begging to live through days and days of agony or having two slugs behind the ear, having fear and pain turned off like a light? Rabin understood even if he found it puzzling. It was Hope. It was that ridiculous light at the end of the tunnel that men and women reached for, and they'd crawl over glass and through lakes of shit in the service of Hope. People were willing to endure battering and burns and cuts to the bone for hours and days, and they begged to be allowed to live to continue enduring their torment because Hope tricked them into believing some different, and wholly irrational, outcome might be seconds away.

But this young man, this Humphrey, he hadn't begged for his life. *Why?* Rabin wondered.

The thought followed him out of the room and down the stairs of the apartment and it lingered like smoke around his head as he walked to his car. And then the wonder was gone. Rabin thought about Irene and decided to pay his wife a late visit, after stopping by the florist for a spray of brightly colored blossoms. He would have to go home first and change his clothes and wash his hands a little more thoroughly, and he would need something to eat. His stomach was growling and kicking for sustenance, so, yes, he'd stop at the deli before going to the florist, and then he'd spend a leisurely afternoon with his wife.

And though he thought about what Humphrey had told him, even grew excited at the possibilities of what he'd been told the Rose could do, he never again thought of Humphrey or why he hadn't begged for his life. To Rabin, the young man had been a conduit of information, no more important than a phone line stretching across the plains of Kansas.

Chapter 16
The Hot and the Cold of It

After another day of vague reality and vivid delusion, Butch woke to find his breath came easier and the ache in his head had receded, more a memory of pain than a true ache. Sweat cooled on his brow and neck, and it felt good after so much heat. With some effort, he managed to sit up in the bed. The room was murky, shadows on shadows. The space between the drapes was dark. He listened for sounds in the house, but he only heard the distant clopping of hooves on stone.

Sliding his legs around to dangle off the side of the bed, Butch took a cautious breath, filled his lungs. The air rattled in his chest, and the fluid there bubbled. He coughed painfully and brought up a thick wad of muck. On the table beside his bed he found a ceramic bowl and he spit into it and managed another deep breath, which along with the cool sweat were the only pleasant sensations he could feel. His body hurt all over. He couldn't remember a single wrestling bout or bar fight that had left him so thoroughly miserable. Even when the Hungarian, Dobos, had snapped Butch's wrist, the pain and incapacitation had been isolated, and he'd felt healthy despite the injury. Now he simply felt weak and beaten, but he was on the mending side of the sickness, whatever it had been. He was certain of that.

Butch eased off the bed and stood. The floor wobbled beneath his feet, but he managed to stay upright. He took a step and then another until his stride had competence if not confidence.

Uncomfortably aware of his nudity, Butch felt his way around the room, searching for his suit. He didn't want to put it on; simply wanted to know it was there if he needed to dress in a hurry. When he reached the armoire he leaned against it and took several shallow breaths, orienting himself before opening the wardrobe. Though his eyes had not fully adjusted to the gloom, Butch could see that his suit was not inside. He felt around, regardless, and his fingers slid across a panel of silk. Butch removed the dressing gown from the hook and wrapped himself in it. Though a bit tight in the shoulders, the robe fit, and once it was secured he closed the doors and leaned back against them.

It then struck him that if his suit was gone, then so was his wallet, and worse still, so was the necklace: his only leverage against the men who wanted him dead.

Uneasy, he made his way across the room and turned the light switch. Three weak bulbs from an overhead fixture bathed the room in grim, yellow light. Not a pleasant glow, but useful. He returned to the armoire and opened the doors, but it was, as he'd known, empty. He searched the desktop and even lowered himself to his knees to check under the bed, but there was no sign of his belongings. A flare of panic lit in his chest and Butch walked on unstable legs to the archway. He left the room and entered a parlor with walls so red they looked as if they'd been hosed down in blood. Again he listened.

A noise from above caught his attention but he couldn't identify it. A gasp? A hiss?

The house struck him as oddly constructed. It seemed to be comprised of two broad hallways stacked atop one another with partial walls to separate living spaces. In the kitchen, the gasping, hissing sound came again and he cocked his head toward the spiral staircase. Though he questioned the courtesy of wandering through a stranger's house, the need to find his belongings compelled him. He crossed to the spiral stairs and hunched over to begin the climb. The metal rungs were like ice beneath his feet, sending a chill up to the base of his neck. Halfway up the twisting case he paused to catch his breath.

On the second floor the gasping announced an occupant in the room ahead, and he walked toward it. He thought to say something, to declare his presence, but a wave of dizziness crashed behind his eyes, forcing him to turn to the railing. He grasped it tightly and peered down into the kitchen, which swirled and blurred. The vertigo passed a moment later, but it left Butch breathless, clutching the railing with white knuckles. A fresh icy layer of sweat covered his face and neck. He breathed deeply until he regained his composure and then he turned toward the room ahead. The door (it seemed to be the only door in the house) had been left open.

At the threshold to the room, he stopped. He blinked. He tried to comprehend the sight before him.

A man with a gnarled gray beard, dressed like a tramp in tattered layers of clothes and a hat with a brim that looked as if it had been gnawed by rats, stood at the end of the bed. The gasping noise emerged from his parted lips. A younger, thickly built man, knelt before the grizzled hobo. His head moved back and forth in smooth motions, his lips sliding along the hard shaft of the older man's cock.

Butch's head grew light again, only this time it was not the whirling sense of vertigo, but rather the heart-racing sensation of plummeting from a great height. Butch's face burned hot and the uneasy fire spread through his whole body. He told himself he was disgusted, but he couldn't look away.

The old man, whose eyes had been fixed downward on the scalp of the boy servicing him, groaned and gasped and then lifted his head. He noticed Butch and a flicker of concern skipped across his face before vanishing. He raised his grimy hand and waved Butch forward.

The foul invitation startled him out of his dazed state. Butch flinched and backed away and made for the spiral staircase as quickly as his feet would carry him.

Back in his room, Butch stomped from one wall to the other. His fists clenched tightly. His heart pounded in his chest. The perverse act he'd witnessed above was wholly unspeakable. He couldn't get the weathered hobo's face, mouth, and filthy beckoning hand from behind his eyes.

Had Rory known what kind of a place he was sending Butch to? Had he known that Rossington was lodging a fairy? Was Rossington a fairy himself? Butch remembered so little about his meeting with the man he couldn't even conjure a face to go with the name. Still he refused to believe Rory would knowingly have sent him here. Maybe it was just the kid. Rossington might not know a thing about what the punk got up to when he wasn't home. If he didn't then someone needed to tell him, needed to wake him up and set him straight. If he did know…

All of the pacing burned away his minimal energies, and Butch forced himself back into the bed. He pulled the blankets up high on his chest, just under his chin. He closed his eyes but the wrinkled face with the rat's nest beard surfaced against the dark screen of his eyelids. Then he was seeing the man's cock, thick with pronounced veins, and the punk's lips sliding over it. More memories emerged, older memories. A summer's night on the edge of the lake near his father's house, lying on the still-hot rocks and looking at the sky, talking to his older cousin Michael as the two of them masturbated. Gazing at the stars, lost in the miracle of speckled lights, Butch grew nervous when he felt his cousin's hand moving over his belly and taking over the task of stroking… A freezing night in a rundown boarding house in Indianapolis. Touring with Mack Mack McCauley's Traveling Wonder Show, he shared a room with a comic named Hatteras. On stage, Hatteras was all energy, dancing and sliding from wing to wing as he delivered off-color jokes and sang songs that would have been inappropriate in legitimate theaters. Off stage, Hatteras presented a different personality. Quiet. Sullen. Behind his back the other performers had taken to calling the comic "The Weeping Clown." He drank excessively and snorted cocaine when he could get it. One night, when the weather was so brutal it hadn't allowed excursions outside, Butch had joined Hatteras in a binge. In the early morning hours, Hatteras began to undress Butch, whose moral cloth was saturated with bad whiskey. Then Hatteras undressed himself, revealing a surprisingly toned body. He sat Butch on the edge of the bed and proceeded to perform the same act Butch had just witnessed upstairs. In the morning it had been easy to write the incident off as drunken tomfoolery. He'd been out of his mind, soused. It was all the excuse he needed, until it happened again and a third time.

The sound of footsteps on the metal staircase and whispered voices startled Butch out of his dazed reflection. He rolled in the bed, turning his back to the archway. The front door opened and closed. A moment later the air in the room shifted, and Butch felt certain the punk had entered his room. He kept his eyes closed and pretended to ignore the existence of such a man.

Chapter 17
Nostalgia and the Blank Page

The soles of Rabin's shoes rapped loudly on the cold tile floor as he entered the lobby of Crane Hospital. He waved a good morning to the aging bald man behind the welcome desk. The man smiled, waved back, and then returned to reading his newspaper. In the corridor, Rabin turned right onto the staircase and climbed to the second floor where he made another right and continued down the cold corridor, which smelled of ammonia and lemon. He paused at the nurses' station, but only for a moment to say "Good morning" to the women there. Three nurses of varying age, all wearing wool cardigans over their white uniforms, returned his greeting. He did not notice the overly inquisitive nurse among them, and he hoped he wouldn't find her in Irene's room.

When he entered he was surprised to see his wife awake, and more surprising than that, she actually smiled when she saw him in the doorway. He couldn't remember the last time she'd regarded him as a welcome visitor rather than just another stranger.

"How's my girl?" Rabin said.

"You came," Irene replied.

"I did."

Rabin walked around the bed to the window and set his newspaper and thermos on the table there before going to Irene's side and leaning over to kiss her brow. When he looked at her, he saw her eyes were not clouded by drugs or by disease, and he felt a surge of happiness. It was a similar emotion to the one he'd felt earlier, holding the ice pick in his hand, standing over the young man who bled out on the rug of a filthy apartment. They were not the same emotion, but they were unquestionably related.

"And how are you feeling this morning?" he asked brightly. He scooped up her hand in his.

"A bit chilly," Irene said. "We could use some more logs on the fire."

"I'll speak to the nurses."

"You say the funniest things," Irene told him, amused and shaking her head.

She doesn't know where she is, he thought. The joy he'd felt skipped like the needle on a 78, but it came back to the groove when she said his name.

"Paul," she said.

"Yes, darling."

"I've been here a very long time."

"Too long."

"Seems like I've always been here, Paul. Even when I wasn't lying in this bed, it seems like I was, and the other times—the days, the years with you in our house—seem like a dream and I'm waking up and can hardly remember them anymore."

"You aren't well." He stroked her hair and squeezed her hand. The warmth of her palm soothed him, coaxed a bit of the joy back.

"Paul, I've been here a very long time," she repeated. "And I'm scared."

"I know," he said, "but I may have found something to help. I'll be leaving in a couple of days to retrieve it, and then you'll be home with me and your knitting, and everything will be like it was. You'll see."

The corners of her mouth twitched as if she were trying to smile.

"Do you remember our wedding day?" she asked.

"Of course."

"And Christmas and the Fourth of July?"

"We've shared many of those. Which do you mean?"

"Any of them," she said. "I know I should remember them, know they mean something, but there's nothing there except the words."

"It'll come back," he told her. If he'd extracted accurate information from Humphrey Bell, he could use the oddly named "Rose" to repair Irene's damaged mind. It would fill the holes, bridge the gaps. "All of it will come back."

"Do you remember the night of the street fair?" Irene asked. "The first one? Right after we were married?"

They'd eaten frankfurters and sauerkraut and paraded up and down the streets near the apartment he'd rented. They'd held hands and said very little to one another, pleased enough with one another's companionship, strolling from one makeshift booth to the next, eyeing the food and trinkets offered at each. Surrounded by hundreds of their neighbors, Rabin had felt that he and Irene were completely alone in the sense that they were different, somehow blessed. The other men and women and the children they had bred were nothing more than animated puppets trudging about like a display created for the happy couple's amusement. They were all so gray and dull. They didn't share the light that had ignited and warmed Mr. and Mrs. Rabin, and therefore they were not the equals of this couple, more like a bland, mimicking species that had not yet evolved to this place. It was a youthful conceit—the notion that only he and his bride could know such happiness, such love, such life.

It had been a wonderful night up until Irene had taken sick with a stomach malady, most likely from a poorly cooked sausage.

"Of course I remember," he said.

"And after the fair? Do you remember that?"

"You were very sick."

"After the fair, you had to go out."

"Did I?" Rabin asked.

"You had to meet a friend."

"I can't imagine leaving you that night. You were very sick."

"That was later. I was fine when we got home. But you had to meet a friend, and you told me you'd be back before ten."

Rabin considered what he remembered about that day. Amid the images of the fair and standing outside the bathroom listening to the grating sounds of Irene's sickness, he recalled a face, now smeared by decades of distance. It belonged to a slovenly, obese man, whose name he no longer remembered. But names rarely mattered. What mattered was getting the rope around the disgusting neck and placing his knee in the center of the flabby back and pulling and twisting until the man—whom he now remembered was dying because he'd welched on a bet—stopped struggling.

"Who can remember?" he asked, patting Irene's hand.

"I've been here so long," she whispered. "Paul, I've been here forever."

"I'm going to make you well."

"You can't. This isn't about you or about the doctors. It's me. I did this to myself. I know I did."

"Don't be ridiculous."

"Some things you want to forget, you wish you didn't know. You wish them away. You wish to forget. *I* wished to forget, and now my wish is coming true."

"Why would you want to forget?" he asked. "We have had a lovely life together, haven't we?"

"Together," she said and closed her eyes.

"That's my good girl," Rabin said. "You rest and quit exciting yourself over such nonsense. You'll be right as rain in no time."

"This is my punishment." Her eyes flashed open. She looked around wildly and yanked her hand out of his. "The one thing I want to forget is the only thing I can remember. This must be Hell. This must be just like Hell. Wishing to forget and losing everything but the thing you most want gone."

He tried to calm her, reaching for her hand, which flapped madly in the air, and shushing her to no avail.

"The street fair," she cried. "The damnable street fair and those awful sausages and the stench—all of those people smelling of dead flowers and the slaughterhouse and coal. And you. And that man. And the rope. And his eyes, bulging. And you, smiling. *Smiling.*"

A nurse appeared in the doorway and Rabin whipped his head toward her. "Get out," he said through gritted teeth. The woman flinched, mouth dropping into a ludicrous *O*. Then paralyzed like a man facing a gun barrel. "Get out!" he roared, and the nurse fidgeted as if experiencing a minor seizure before fleeing the threshold.

"I can't" Irene cried. "I can't get out. I'm lost."

Rabin backed away from the bed and his wife. Sobs racked her now and her hands slapped at her sides.

She knew. She always knew. All these years, pretending…lying! How could she? How could she know and still live with me, live with herself?

A doctor ran into the room, followed by a nurse and an enormous orderly. They pounced on Irene: the nurse and orderly holding her arms down as the doctor yanked a hypodermic from the pocket of his white coat and targeted the crook of Irene's elbow.

"I've been here so long," Irene wailed.

Rabin slipped into the hallway. He hurried toward the stairs, and his wife's voice echoed, accompanying the rapping of his shoes on the cold tile floor.

Chapter 18
The Way It Is in Rossington's House

Four A.M. and the club was winding down. The second dancer had left the stage more than two hours ago, and Bones had climbed onto his piano bench to send mellow jazz into the smoke-thick air. His tunes prowled and sank beneath the skin, rubbing against bone and organ like affectionate predators, soothing flesh but eyeing the soul. Only a few patrons remained in the main room of Lady Victoria's. Hollis Rossington made a lap through the club, checking on the paying customers.

A good house tonight, he thought. *People feel bad and we make them feel good.* He'd feel better himself if more of the deadbeats left their flasks at home and bought their hooch at the bar. Maybe then he'd get ahead of the accountants.

Most of the customers paid their thirty cents to enter the club, and their wallets promptly snapped shut, unless they were buying something sweet and cheap in which to pour their rum. He'd tried enforcing a drink minimum, but the results had been disastrous—all but empty chairs for two weeks running. The fact no customers were purchasing liquor didn't change the fact that Hollis still had to pay the cops and the city officials for the privilege of having booze on the premises. As a result, Lady Victoria's was a place of pleasant distraction, not the gold mine outsiders assumed, much to Hollis's frustration. More evenings than not, they barely managed to scrape enough together to keep the dancers paid and the lights on. Before Black Friday, Lady Victoria's had featured six dancers a night: half of them women, and the other three boys in gowns. The boys were the real draw. Dancing ladies were a dime a dozen in New Orleans, but a feminine veneer with something different between the legs brought out the wallets, or at least it had.

Now he could only afford two dancers per night, one of each, and keeping them satisfied with spotty payment was getting harder every day, though Hollis couldn't imagine anywhere else they might make a profit.

He crossed the club, nodding to the dregs, waving, forcing a hard smile to remain on his lips. At the bar he nodded to Mickey, a sign that he was ready for his coffee. This was a nightly event, so the percolator was already gurgling on the plate behind the bar. The barkeep filled a glass mug with the rich liquid and then poured in the cream, which swirled and spread like a storm cloud. Mickey stirred the beverage with the handle of a spoon, clinked the silver against the glass rim, and then handed the drink across the bar. Carrying the steaming mug, Hollis left the main room and entered a gloomy L-shaped hall. In his office, a small, windowless, paneled room; he locked the door behind him, shutting out the prowling piano music. An aged phonograph with a dented bell sat on the table to his left, and he cranked the handle with a smooth, precise motion, in time with music not yet playing. He placed the needle on the disk and a static hiss filled the office before the first whining strains of a guitar echoed through the bell. A mournful voice followed, singing of hope and loss. Hollis proceeded to his desk, where he dropped into his chair. He sipped his coffee and the rich beverage coated his tongue with the dueling flavors of smooth cream and bitter roasted bean.

He cleared his mind. The guitar twanged in sorrow and he hummed the melody in a smooth baritone register.

Hollis pictured the record's musician on a dusty track of road in front of a ramshackle home in which the woman he loved ignored his impassioned melody and pretended he didn't exist. Hollis opened his eyes and looked at the ledger on his desk. After another sip of coffee he considered the hours ahead, the tedious job of totaling the evening's receipts and going through a stack of bills. He thought about Butch, terribly ill and confined to his bed. Thoughts of Lionel quickly followed, and he hoped the kid wasn't making things difficult for their houseguest. He'd instructed Lionel to steer clear of the guest room, which on reflection was a mistake. Hollis knew that if he placed boundaries around Lionel the kid's primary goal would be to kick them down.

As with most evenings, he put off the calculations and administrative annoyances so he could enjoy his privacy. This was the only time he could listen to music and breathe his own air and be with his thoughts. It never happened at home. Lionel was so demanding of his time and attention. At the club, he was in constant demand—meeting and greeting his customers, shaking hands, chatting and telling jokes. He lived a life that often startled him. The good of it, the bad of it: the whole of it was beyond the imaginings of a kid from Oregon.

Hollis slid his chair back. He crossed to a narrow closet door and pulled it open. Carefully he slid a box away from the back of the space and reached behind it, awkwardly balancing on the balls of his feet to get the greatest reach. His fingers grazed a cardboard edge, and he leaned a shoulder against the jamb for support. Once he had a firm grasp on the card, he lifted it free. He carried the mounted poster to his desk, opened the long top drawer and propped the poster inside, where it sat like a piece of art on an easel.

Holding his coffee, Hollis leaned back in his chair and stared at the image of himself, a dozen years younger, clad in snug black shorts and matching boots. Where had that kid gone?

Having Butch in the house had rekindled an intense nostalgia in Hollis, a longing for his days on the mats. The training. The packed arenas and theaters. Cheering admirers. The company of athletes. The crowds had loved his flamboyant boasts and strutting gait, and they'd paid good money to sit in his shadow as he stalked the mats, teasing an opponent before dropping the lug on his tail. His coach had always told him to focus on the science of the sport, and maybe the old man had been right, but even if he'd perfected his holds and his breaks, his career would have ended just as quickly.

Some scandals passed like dust at your heels; others buried you deep.

Hollis's dishonor had come as fast and low as a leg reap, and he'd hit the mat and fallen through, dropping good and fast into the sewer flowing beneath his career, and it was all because he'd misinterpreted a situation, had made a stupid mistake.

He'd just won a bout against a bulky Norwegian kid and had finished his shower in the dressing room. He stepped out to find the place nearly empty. Most nights his coach corralled the members of the press and let them babble and jot notes while Hollis dressed, but upon emerging from the shower, Hollis encountered a single man, sitting on the leather sofa and holding a highball of whiskey. The man had a look about him, a look Hollis liked. When it came to men, nothing did him in quite so quickly as a rugged face. Unfettered masculinity. And the man on his sofa, despite a neatly tailored suit and hard-starched shirt, fit that bill nicely, looking like a dockworker or an aging boxer who'd lost more than his share of fights. Hollis introduced himself and learned that the man's name was Croger.

"I cleared the place out," Croger said.

Looking back, Hollis imagined post-bout exhilaration and more than a little arrogance had put his mind in a place it shouldn't have been. He'd had his share of willing fans—men and women—who'd found their way to dressing rooms and hotel rooms with his body on their minds. Though he should have known better, he'd assumed the strong-jawed stranger was another of that familiar species.

Hollis had kept things superficial and friendly. Usually, he knew better than to move too quickly in these situations, so he waited until he'd gathered what he considered sufficient evidence: the way Croger's eyes moved over him when they spoke; certain phrases Croger used that were so common and meaningless, Hollis had had no business reading so much into them. Then Croger had suggested they get together for a drink at the hotel later, and Hollis had suggested they just take a bottle to bed with them.

In less than a second, a hot sheet of outrage replaced momentary confusion on Croger's face. The insulted man threw a punch and Hollis dodged it easily. The scuffle was ridiculous and Hollis won it.

But Croger was the brother-in-law of the local promoter, and all the while Hollis believed he was being seduced, it turned out to be nothing more than Croger greasing the wheels for a business proposition he'd intended to pitch him over drinks. It could have been funny. It wasn't. Thanks to the promoter Hollis became an overnight pariah, and he sank fast after that. Newspapers throughout Florida carried accounts of the misunderstanding, using brutal code words like "unnatural" and "sinner." He didn't even attempt to maintain a career.

His coach summed things up with icy precision: "This ain't a sport for punks. You're good and done now." With no purpose and no prospects, he slid headlong into a truly ugly place. Night and day, he drank until he was a soft and useless knot, curled on a rickety bed in an Atlanta hotel.

Then Rory Sullivan found him. The Irishman had heard all about the ruckus and wanted to know why Hollis was taking the flack lying down, as if he'd done nothing more than got himself into hot water over some man's wife. Rory stayed with him for three weeks, getting him off the booze and helping Hollis see a different kind of life for himself. Taking in Butch was supposed to pay back that debt, but to Hollis's mind no favor would be great enough to balance the account.

Further, he'd wanted to meet Butch, "The Butcher": the ring's golden boy. The man had entered wrestling fully formed, his skills and physique already perfected for the sport. Rory had told Hollis the story—different from Rossington's but with similar results. The grappler from Vermont should have been a legend, but he'd crossed the wrong men. Made the wrong moves. Hollis understood completely. Where the hell did you go once your dream ran you down?

Apparently you go to New Orleans, he thought.

He stood and lifted the poster from the desk drawer, returned to the closet and leaned the card against the back wall. After sliding the box into place, he closed the door and felt a tug as if the poster were attached to him, a piece of him that had been partially, but not wholly, severed.

Hollis wanted to hear stories about the sport he loved and get caught up on what had happened to the grapplers he had once faced in the ring. He missed those conversations as much as he missed the sport itself. If Butch had gotten wind of Hollis's dark days, it hadn't showed in their first meeting, not that Butch had been in his right mind. In fact at the café he'd seemed about as close to death as anyone Hollis had ever met.

An hour passed before he set to the frustrating task of totaling and notating the receipts. When this was accomplished and the wholly inadequate figures laughed at him from the page, he turned his attention to the bills, many of which were past due. He let the phonograph go silent as he wrote checks and addressed envelopes. The sound of his pen on the dry paper was the soft-shoe slide of a drunk. Halting and uncertain. He set the bill for the building mortgage aside; there wasn't enough money in the bank to pay it yet. Maybe by the end of the week.

He'd gotten used to overdue account notices, had rarely even blinked at the warnings and threats his postman delivered, but Lady Victoria's had been treading water for a long time. Things weren't getting better and showed no signs of turning around.

After filing away his ledger and locking the receipts in the safe, Hollis lifted the stack of envelopes from the edge of his desk and left the office.

• • •

At home, Hollis checked on Lionel and found him sleeping soundly in their bed. Not quite ready to sleep himself, Hollis returned to the first floor and poured himself a brandy, which he enjoyed on the sofa. Through the wall at his back, Butch slept. Hollis pictured the serene features beneath the unkempt beard, imagined the round, full muscle of Butch's shoulders and chest.

Warmed by the drink, but not calmed by it, he stood and crossed to Butch's room. He stood at the threshold, peering through the gloom. The rustle of blankets surprised him.

"Good morning," Butch said.

Hollis turned the light switch. The fixture lit, and Butch slid up in the bed to rest his back against the headboard. A ridge of sheet and duvet ran low over his belly. Hollis was pleased to see his energy, if not his appearance, had vastly improved. The whisper of longing he'd felt for Butch became a chant. He didn't want to feel this way, not about this man. It complicated things, but the song persisted even when he shouted for silence.

"Hollis?" Butch asked. His face had wrung into an expression of concern.

The uncomfortable memory of Croger flickered and died, and Hollis began to realize how foolish he must seem. Still unable to bring himself into the room, he turned his attention to the curtains where morning light filtered soft and pink between the crimson drapes until Butch said his name a second time.

"I'm sorry," Hollis said. "It's been a long night. And besides, it wouldn't be polite to enter unless you invite me in."

"Sure is a fancy carnival you're running here," Butch said. Maybe he'd meant the comment to ring light, but his rough voice only made it sound aggressive. Hollis felt a mask of disapproval tighten over his face, and Butch must have noticed, because he quickly said, "Sorry, Hollis. Please, come in. We need to talk about something."

Hollis walked into the room, hesitantly, but he wouldn't let himself approach the bed. Instead he turned to the drapes and pulled them back to allow warm light to flood his face. He stood before the panes, head cocked back, eyes closed as if beneath a shower's spray.

"Not nearly enough sunlight in my line of work," he said. Butch said nothing, but Hollis hadn't really expected a response. "You had something you wanted to say?"

"Yeah, it's about that kid you've got living here," Butch said.

He attempted a frown to show Butch he would be surprised by whatever news he was about to receive, but in truth, any mischief Lionel performed was unlikely to surprise Hollis.

"Lionel?" he asked. "What about him?"

"Did you know he was a fairy?"

"Oh, that," Rossington said as if Butch were reminding him of an irrelevant errand. "Has he approached you in some way?"

"You're taking this awfully cool."

"Well, it's not news, Butch, and as far as I'm concerned it's not an issue."

"How can it not be an issue? He brings men into your house and... Well, I'm not going to say it. What exactly is this kid to you?"

And here, Hollis found himself at a loss. He *was* surprised. He'd expected to hear many things from Butch: Lionel flirting; Lionel dropping hints about his relationship with Hollis; Lionel stirring up the pot to enjoy a bit of excitement. Hollis had not expected to learn that his companion was bringing men into the house—the house Hollis paid for—when he was at the club. More surprising was the sudden realization that he'd known this was not a first or second indiscretion. He'd suspected for weeks, but he'd denied the possibility. And why? He couldn't say.

"I think you better—" Butch said.

Hollis interrupted the wrestler by lifting his hand, though he continued to look through the glass. "I don't expect you to remember our first conversation. You were pretty gone with exhaustion, but at the time I told you we had an unorthodox household, and I stressed the fact that you'd have a difficult time adjusting."

"Yeah, but—"

"And you're talking again," Hollis said, shaking his head. He turned from the window and finally allowed himself to approach the bed. Though Lionel's betrayal stung, and he would certainly deal with the son of a bitch, he needed to make some things clear to Butch first. "I have something to say, and I'm as tired as a whore three days into leave, so let's be clear and quick. Having you here presents a threat to the people under this roof. Now, I knew that when I brought you here. Rory made it very clear when he called, but I figure there are enough people getting ground up by the way things are, so if I could keep someone…you…from becoming more gear grease, I'd consider it worth the risk. But there are realities in this house that I don't think you'll ever be able to live with."

"For fuck's sake, Hollis," Butch said, throwing back the blankets and sliding off the bed. Either oblivious to his nakedness or indifferent to it, Butch stood and faced off on Hollis, who backed up a step. "You got some sick punk running around your house."

"And who does that hurt?"

"You're kidding?" Butch looked about the room, as if searching for someone to support his position. Absently, he scratched his chest and shook his head.

Hollis was taken off guard by his unabashed guest, though he knew he shouldn't have been. He'd shared showers and locker rooms with dozens of men. It had been a common practice for years, but Hollis had been removed from that world for a long time, ever since Croger. In recent years, the only unclothed men he encountered were on their way to or from his bed. He became self-conscious about his manner, feeling certain there was a way he should have been behaving that he wasn't. His shoulders and neck felt like concrete as he made a conscious effort to keep his eyes on Butch's angry face.

"What do you mean, who does it hurt? It isn't normal." Butch walked to the wardrobe and opened the door. He pulled a robe off of a hook and slid it on.

With the body covered, Hollis felt his poise return. "Butch, this is what I'm talking about. No one here, in this house, is particularly concerned with *normal.* And quite frankly, Lionel is one of my less complicated acquaintances."

"You can't be serious?"

"Dead serious," Hollis said.

Butch walked toward him, shaking his head. "It's your house, pal. I'm just visiting, but I'll damn well be sleeping with one eye open."

Apparently, the fever hadn't boiled any of the ignorance out of the man. Further, he was holding on to a heap of arrogance for a guy who'd pretty much hit bottom, but Hollis understood that. On a downhill slide, you reached for anything you could hold on to, anything that felt stable and secure. Butch's ego had suffered one blow after another—his career and future toppling away like gravel no matter where he'd tried to find purchase. Every root and stone he'd clutched had torn out in his hands. On this one point, Butch felt certain he had a firm grasp because the illusion of its truth had been reinforced on playgrounds and locker rooms and churches throughout his life, but if things were going to work out, Hollis would have to kick Butch's grip loose and let him slide a little farther.

"Butch, let's look at your normal world. Men are standing in soup lines, stripped of every ounce of dignity. They are killing each other over bits of bread crust. Then you've got the moguls and politicians who designed this fucking nightmare and are living above it, riding it out, wholly amused by the festival of shit they've staged. And let's look at your good friends in Chicago, the *real men* who toss bullets like wedding rice, not giving a fuck where those grains land. Those are the *men* who decided what was natural, and what was normal, and what good has it done you? Did following their rules do you any good when Simm was bum-rushing you out of the sport? Did it keep you from being the patsy of a couple of booze thugs? You ask me, you're stuck to the bottom of normal's shoes and you're about to get scraped off, so why the hell are you defending it? What's it ever done for you?"

"Right and wrong don't change," Butch said, though his confidence had paled.

Hollis leaned in close. "You think throwing fists for Bugs Moran was *right*?"

"I didn't work for… never mind," Butch said. "I needed the work."

"But you didn't. You had a job with Mack Mack McCauley, playing strong man and doing exhibitions. And if not with Mack then with any of a dozen other outfits on the circuit. You didn't need work. You wanted easier work and more money for it. And to get it, you made a conscious decision to break the law. In that regard you're no different from Capone or Moran or any petty thief on the street."

Butch pulled his shoulders back, his brow furrowed and his jaw went tight, but even so his eyes held questions, confusion. He looked trapped and maybe a little scared. Then the defiance vanished in a blink, and Butch's face collapsed into sad perplexity. Hollis pulled away and walked to the end of the bed. He grabbed one of the posters and leaned against it.

"There are millions of ways to live a good life," he said. "You need to understand that."

"But it can't be chaos. There have to be rules." Butch mumbled the words. Fumbled them. He struggled as if each word had to be voiced in an exact way to make the statement true.

"Maybe so," Hollis said, "but your short life is going to be nothing but misery if you think the people making those rules are following them. They aren't. Not even a little. Politicians and churches tell us to shut up and take it; toe the line and one day—one glorious day—we'll get ours, as long as we don't cause any trouble along the way. Ideologies are just the armies they use to clear and quell crowds so the assholes who promote them can get where they're going with minimal trouble."

"You sound ridiculous."

"I accept that as very likely," Hollis said. "But I don't think a man has to live within the tight little grooves he's been trained to follow. I didn't, and for the most part I live better than the majority of guys who trudge their trenches from cradle to casket. Rory understood this. Hell, he taught me to think this way."

"Rory wouldn't have let that punk stand."

"You're wrong, Butch. Completely wrong." Hollis waited for a response, but Butch gazed at the wall, his features leaden, his mouth locked in a frown, his eyes lost. Hollis had broken Butch's handhold, and the man was sliding again with yet another of his beliefs having failed to support him, and that was a good thing. Hollis figured Butch would find firmer ground farther down the slope. "Rory understood and enjoyed the company of people who were uncommon. He's the most regular guy on the planet but he doesn't attack or degrade those who don't share his beliefs."

"Whatever," Butch muttered distractedly. He lifted his hands to the back of his head, and with his fingers clawed, he scratched his scalp in a clear demonstration of frustration. "I'm sorry, Hollis. None of this makes sense to me. Not Chicago and not here. Maybe no place will make sense. It's like I woke up one morning and everyone was yelling at me in a foreign language, you know? And every word out of my mouth just makes them yell louder. But it's not words. It's everything. Ever since Simm every damn step I take breaks through the floor. Do you have any idea what that's like? Being afraid of every move but knowing you can't stand still?"

"Yeah, I know that feeling," Rossington said, thinking about Florida and Croger and the months following one poorly chosen question. That had been his slope, and he'd muddied it with booze and frequent indiscretions, but he'd slid low and found a solid place to put his feet. If he had anything to do with it, Butch would too. "That's why I let Rory tell me where to step, and that's why I listened. Rory's not here, but maybe I can get you on the right track."

"There may not be time," Butch said.

"Should be plenty of time. You're safe here. But we can't have any more trouble. Do you understand that? You're the one who has to adapt."

"I don't know," Butch said.

"So you'd rather run and fight for every damn thing under the sun? You don't have to live that way. In this house, we make our own rules for how we live. Be courteous and kind, and you can be anything you want to be here."

Silence moved between them like a draft. Hollis waited to see some sign of understanding on Butch's face, but the man was looking at the floor. He shuffled from foot to foot nervously and then shoved his hands in the pockets of the dressing gown.

"Jesus," Butch said. "I don't... Look, this is your house and even though I haven't done a damn thing to prove it, I am grateful for what you've done for me. The rest of it...? I guess it's none of my business, and I need to keep my mouth shut."

The words were encouraging. They implied progress. Still, Hollis didn't understand why all of this meant so much to him; it had to be more than his promise to Rory, more than saving a soul as lost as his own had been. It would have been foolish to deny his attraction to Butch, just as it would be foolish—perhaps devastating—to ever act on this attraction. Fortunately, Hollis wasn't a schoolboy, made feeble by romance and lust. If anything, acknowledging the way he felt allowed him objectivity. Control. So why? he wondered. Was it one thing or all of the things in his head and heart that made him determined to protect this man?

Butch walked to the window. As if mimicking Hollis's earlier performance, he turned his face into the bath of morning sun.

"We'd better try and get you figured out, then," Hollis said.

"What do you mean?"

"What do you want? Are you here just to hide? I suppose that's fine if that's what you want to do."

"No, I don't just want to hide," he said. "There's this necklace, and someone thinks it's important. Or I think they do. Either way, I have to figure out what it is."

Hollis reached deep into his slack's pocket and grasped the chain and charm. He pulled it free. "Do you mean this?"

"Yeah," Butch said, lunging forward to take it from Hollis's hand. "I thought that punk had pinched it while I was out cold."

"Okay, I can help you with that." Hollis knew a number of people that dealt in jewelry and antiquities. "I can put a list together of the people you need to see. What else? You said you were tapped?"

"Flat broke," Butch admitted. "I'll need to find work, need to scrape up money in case I have to disappear for good, and I'll have to lay pretty low while I'm here."

"That isn't going to work," Hollis said. "Not in this city."

"Why? What do you mean?"

He really is naïve, Hollis thought. The guy was thinking like a rube right off the carrot cart.

"Butch, you ran from Chicago, a mob-woven spider's web. And where did you go? New Orleans, which is just another web. We have as many runners and gunners as Chicago, and they're all connected, so if you try to get work in one of the clubs here, you're shaking hands with close cousins to the folks who want you dead. You could try humping crates at the docks, but that's not much different."

"Shit," Butch hissed. He lowered his head.

"Don't worry about the job," Hollis said. "You've got a roof and food."

"Yeah," Butch said. He didn't sound convinced.

"And on that note, I'd better go talk to Lionel. I have a feeling it will be a rather unpleasant conversation." *Cheating bastard.* "When you're feeling up to it, get dressed and fix yourself something for breakfast. We should have plenty in the cabinets and icebox. We keep the devil's hours around here, so you probably won't see me until two or three this afternoon."

"Okay," Butch said. He moved away from the window and held out his hand for Hollis to shake.

The man looked miserable, frustrated, beaten, but Hollis felt certain he was on the right track. He shook the hand and offered a tight smile. As an afterthought, he clapped Butch on the shoulder before saying, "Take care."

Chapter 19
Simpler Times

Curt Conrad unlocked the door to his apartment and stepped inside. After removing his gloves, he shoved them in the pocket of his overcoat, and then he removed his hat. He dumped his winter clothes over the coat rack by the door. The hat fell off. It hit the floor. Conrad thought about stooping to pick it up, but it was a flicker of a thought, quickly replaced by a decision to grab it later on his way out. For now, he wanted a drink and then some shuteye. Last night had been a late one; one of many. So he took his sleep where he could get it, even if it meant skipping out of the office a couple hours shy of his posted schedule.

Not that leaving the station early amounted to a tower of air. He hadn't worked a full eight hours in three years; it was one of the perks of being a detective. The simple phrase, "Tracking something down," was all it took to shut up his superiors and his partner, Lennon, who was becoming a serious pain in his ass.

The guy wouldn't shut up about Musante. Conrad didn't know why his partner was so hard for information on the shit-heel. A guy like Musante wasn't worth the gray juice it took to think him over, and if Curt hadn't pulled the trigger himself, he wouldn't have given the dirty little wop a second thought.

A yawn erupted over his round face. Conrad removed his holster and swung it across the back of a chair and continued through the living room. In the kitchen he poured himself a shot and threw it back.

When he returned to the living room, he found Paul Rabin facing him. The man had removed Conrad's service piece from its holster, and he aimed it at the detective's chest.

"Greetings," Rabin said merrily. Conrad flinched and stepped back. Rabin was dressed, as always, like a politician in a fine three-piece suit. Pressed. Slick. "Take a seat," Rabin said. The three dry syllables rolled over a desert before leaving his mouth.

"What the fuck are you doing here?" Conrad asked.

"Take a seat, detective."

Tremors of fear began in his knees and worked their way to his throat, causing his voice to rattle when he said, "Impelliteri is going to tear your ass apart when he hears about this."

"Then it'll be our little secret. Now sit down. I won't tell you again."

He sat on the wooden chair, his father's chair, by the window. Conrad didn't know much about Rabin, but what he knew was enough to keep him from testing the man. A dozen times he'd delivered packets to Rabin; each envelope had contained a significant amount of money and the name of a guy who was never seen again. In remembering those envelopes, he couldn't help but recall the cash he'd removed from them. He'd helped himself to a share of Rabin's commissions, and the man knew it. But it was just money. Conrad could get his hands on plenty if he had to. He could fix this.

"Is this about money? I can get you money."

"No," Rabin said. He walked forward and stopped three feet in front of Conrad.

Conrad looked past the barrel of the gun at Rabin. His face was hard and flat like a death mask. His eyes glittered but it was the shimmer of candlelight on a polished coffin lid. Cold. Lifeless. These were the eyes his victims looked into for mercy.

"What do you want?"

"I'm confused," Rabin said. "Why would Marco Impelliteri, our kind employer, hire you to murder his closest confidant?"

"You got some bad information. Cardinal killed Musante."

A twitch tugged at the corner of Rabin's lip. It was a subtle reaction—two rapid tics that came and went so quickly Conrad might have imagined them. But when Rabin stepped forward his movement was distinct and unmistakably odd. To Conrad it appeared as if Rabin were struggling, pushing forward, like the madman was walking while someone was trying to hold him back. "No. Cardinal was a pawn. Did you arrange his setup?"

"Come on, Rabin, I just go where I'm told. Same as you."

"No." Rabin lifted his foot and kicked it down between Conrad's legs, where it rested on the edge of the chair. "Times have changed. So much of what I have believed has turned out to be false. I can't afford to be wrong anymore. Who told you to go to Musante's house?"

Sweat rolled down the back of Conrad's neck and pooled at his collar before soaking into the starched fabric. Conrad had never had a bit of trouble throwing lies, but by comparison those had been small, all but meaningless fibs with little on the line. The lies he told now were important; they could keep the red under his skin where it belonged. "Marco told me, same as always."

"That's a lie, and it's the last one I'll allow. Tell me another and I'll start taking pieces off of you."

Conrad needed a name to feed the madman, but his calm was shattered. He couldn't think of anyone to point a finger at except for the man who had actually given him the order. "It was Terry McGavin."

"I don't know that name." Rabin kept his foot on the chair, but leaned forward, slowly pushing the gun toward Conrad's shining fat face.

"He's with Moran. On Powell's crew."

"You work both sides." Rabin nodded his head. "Powell wants the Galenus Rose for himself."

"The what?"

Conrad saw the fucker was as crazy as he'd always believed, and that was a bad thing, considering which one of them held the gun.

"But how did Powell even know of its existence?" Rabin wondered aloud. "No. This is wrong. You're lying."

"I'm not lying, you crazy son of a bitch. I picked up a few easy hits from Terry here and there. Simple low-profile shit. I didn't want word getting back to Impelliteri, and I didn't want Powell thinking he had me on a leash."

"And what did Terry tell you about the necklace?"

"Nothing," Conrad said.

"But you knew about it," Rabin said. "You made quite a to do about it when we met last week."

"That was Impelliteri. All Terry told me was to wait outside of Musante's and pop him when he came out and then do the wrestler the same way. He gave me the time and the place. That's it. I didn't hear about the fucking necklace until after I called Marco to let him know about Lonnie."

"Terry didn't ask you to retrieve anything from the scene?"

"Not a fucking thing."

"Curious."

"I don't know about that, but it's true." Conrad squirmed in the chair. "What about Impelliteri? Are you going to tell him all of this?"

Rabin removed his foot from the chair and stepped away. "I'll be severing my connections with Mr. Impelliteri. What is said here, remains here. I see no reason to involve him in this matter."

"No reason at all," Conrad agreed.

"And your partner, Detective Lennon? He was working with you?"

An idea presented itself and Conrad grabbed hold of it. Roger Lennon had been an annoyance since day one. If Conrad could get Rabin off of his back and put him onto Lennon's, his life would not only be a lot easier, but it would last a whole lot longer.

"He was the go-between," Conrad said. He made it sound as if the information was obvious. "Between Terry and me. If Terry said anything about a necklace it was probably to Roger. I can ask him at the station tomorrow."

"That won't be necessary."

Once Conrad had told the lie, it hung before him like a rope ladder and he reached for it, swatted at it, knowing it was the only thing that would get him out of this pit. "I'll call him. Give me a minute, and I'll get him on the phone."

"Don't trouble yourself."

"You can ask him anything you want." Conrad knew he sounded too eager, too desperate. The ladder was pulling away, but he had to let it go. The panic in his voice wasn't doing him any good.

"I don't see the need to trouble Detective Lennon at this time," Rabin said. "I admit to some curiosity, what with you being so eager to throw your partner to the lions. There must be quite a history between the two of you, and I've recently grown interested in the ease with which those closest to us can deceive and betray. But, thank you, no."

"He's the one you want. I can get him for you."

"I assure you, if necessary, I can get him for myself," Rabin said. "What about the wrestler?"

"Cardinal? What about him?"

"Have your people turned up any information on the man? His whereabouts? I'm curious."

"Nobody's told me anything. I figured you'd get to him long before we did."

Rabin nodded. "Yes, I imagine I will. There's an old Paddy I've been far too coy about questioning. I imagine it's time to get serious about that one."

"If you need a hand, just say the word."

"Very kind," Rabin said. He stepped away and lowered the gun before retreating to the entrance of the living room. Rabin threw a glance over his shoulder at the door. "If you don't mind, I'll just let myself out."

"Sure."

Conrad was confused. Relieved but confused. In fact, everything he knew about Rabin suggested Conrad should be face down on the floor, bleeding. But there Rabin was, turning the knob, pulling the door open, leaving the apartment. It wasn't the smartest move, because Conrad was going to find the old prick and put a bullet in his head, but there was no reason to bring that up just now.

He exhaled and closed his eyes. He only allowed himself a momentary respite, though. The detective wanted a locked door between himself and the killer. Taking a second deep breath, he opened his eyes, pushed himself from the wooden chair, and headed across the room. Conrad stumbled when he noticed the door opening again.

Rabin poked his head in. "I still have your gun."

"Keep it," Conrad told him. Guns were cheap. Easy to find. He didn't care about it, at least not enough to invite Rabin back into his home.

"Don't be silly." Rabin opened the door the rest of the way and stepped over the threshold. He held the gun in his palm. His finger wasn't even looped through the trigger. Once inside the apartment he closed the door behind him. "Professional courtesy and all."

"Yeah," Conrad said. "Thanks."

Rabin met him in the middle of the room and held out the gun. Uncertain, Conrad stared at the weapon like it was a dead bird.

"Should I just return it to your holster?" Rabin asked.

"Nah, that's fine. I'll take it."

And Conrad reached for the gun. He grasped the handle and in a smooth motion, lifted it level with Rabin's eyes. He pulled the trigger.

The hammer hit an empty chamber with a hard *clap*.

Rabin's polished-coffin eyes didn't blink.

"You…" Conrad began to say.

Rabin delivered a quick, vicious punch to Conrad's nose. The detective's vision blurred from pain and from a wash of tears that instantly covered his eyes. Conrad stumbled back, disoriented. From reflex, he threw his hands to cover his injured face. He still held the gun and it smashed into his aching nose. Blood gushed over the grip before Conrad dropped the weapon on the carpet. Rabin strolled forward and buried his right fist in Conrad's belly, doubling the man over.

"I spoke with my wife this morning," Rabin said.

Though he still couldn't see, Conrad uncoiled and whipped his fist toward the voice. It passed through the air, sending him off balance. Tottering and blind, he waved his arms with steadying flaps until he was certain he wouldn't topple.

Then he felt the rope slip around his neck.

"It wasn't a pleasant conversation," Rabin said, "but it reminded me of a simpler time."

Chapter 20
Things to Feel

Lennon worked late. The station remained bustling with the third shifters. Tobacco smoke rose thick, casting haze over the wooden desks and the men in their suits. In a shadowed corner, a man pecked at the keys of a typewriter. Two men sat on the edge of a desk, smoking cigars and laughing heartily. Al Jolson sang "Sonny Boy" through the radio static. For Lennon, this setting offered greater comfort and familiarity than his house on Whitmore Street. The sense of camaraderie came easily. He and his colleagues shared this space and they shared ideas and they shared a language. To his mind, the station was more akin to a gentleman's club than a place of work, and with Edie and the girls out of town, Lennon didn't have to worry about checking in every thirty minutes, or being interrupted by calls from home. Edie questioning. Needling. Wanting his attention when it was needed elsewhere.

For the twentieth time, he looked over the information he'd gathered about Lonnie Musante, a man who struck Lennon as an ever-growing mystery. The creep was completely useless to the syndicate, and yet he was dear to Marco Impelliteri. Why? In a business that thrived on substance and exploit, Musante seemed irrelevant—a criminal failure with a terminal disease. He dealt in speculation, in superstition; he was impotent when it came to what the outfits truly valued: the cash, the blood.

On his desk sat two small evidence boxes he'd had sent up from the cage. Lennon went through the items collected at Musante's house piece by piece, a ritual he'd performed more than a dozen times in the last few days. When he came to the Mauser 1914 a familiar thought, the same thought he always had when he looked at the gun, ran through his mind. He'd seen the gun before. On the one hand, Lennon knew the familiarity of the weapon was easily explained; thousands of the things had been manufactured and sent to the streets. But it wasn't just the model that he found familiar; it was this particular weapon. The nicks. The scratches.

Lennon ran his finger down the wooden wrap-around grip and paused at a chip near the base, likely where a ring had gouged the wood while some lowlife was ramming the magazine home. His thumb traced the shape of the divot and then Lennon put the gun down on his desk as the realization of where he'd seen it before flooded him.

"Son of a bitch," he muttered. He shook his head.

Lennon sprang from his desk and ran from the office. When he found a rookie in blue, standing over a filing cabinet, he clapped a hand on the kid's shoulder and said, "Drop what you're doing. I need a file. A grocery store robbery. Went down a couple months back. Gladson's Mercantile. Perpetrator's name was Myer or Mayer."

"Who was the lead officer?"

"Curt Conrad," Lennon said.

The case all of his colleagues considered solved, all but closed save for the apprehension of their suspect, unraveled in his head. Musante. Cardinal. Conrad had set the whole damn thing up. His partner had involved him in a mob hit, crossing a line Lennon had sworn to keep at a distance. Premeditated and foolish, Conrad murdered one man and framed another, and dragged Lennon along for the goddamn ride. Once Lennon had the proof in his hands, he would be paying his partner a visit. The man owed him answers.

• • •

LENNON stood in the doorway of Curt Conrad's apartment, staring at his partner's corpse. The detective lay face down. A blood-stained rope snaked away from his throat. His arms were curled under him, like a baby sleeping on its stomach. The room reeked of sweat, grease, old cigar smoke, whiskey, and the combined death scents of blood, urine, and excrement. Lennon put a hand over his mouth. A door opened in the hallway to his left, and Lennon stepped into the apartment, closing the door behind him. He felt little in that moment. Nothing, in fact. A perplexing numbness had overtaken him the moment he'd pushed open the door, replacing the anger he'd carried with him from the station. He'd come for a confrontation and had found his partner was beyond accusation or explanation.

The room was a mess. Cluttered. Dirty. Typical for the corpulent son of a bitch. Conrad's service piece lay on the floor next to his body. A pile of bullets had been left beside it.

Lennon knelt and grasped Conrad's wrist. He checked for a pulse, but Conrad was already cold.

"Stupid," Lennon whispered. Playing both sides only doubled the number of people gunning for you.

Before calling the station, Lennon made a thorough search of his partner's home. In a beat-up nightstand he found a bankbook with a surprising total jotted in black ink on the last page. Conrad kept a rigorous accounting of his spending—from cigars and egg sandwiches to the car he'd bought last spring. It was, perhaps, the only evidence of organization in an otherwise cluttered life. Beneath the bankbook he found a small journal, bound in cracked black leather. Lennon flipped through the notes inside. The journal contained names and phone numbers, jotted down in no particular order. With no time to read every entry, and wondering if his own name was among those listed, Lennon put the ledger and the journal in his coat pocket.

Lennon finished his search, went to his car, and deposited the few items he'd taken from Curt Conrad's apartment in the glove box. Then, back in the apartment, he called the station. After the call, he returned to the living room and sat in a wooden chair by the window, waiting for the homicide squad to arrive, waiting to feel something about the man lying dead on the floor before him.

• • •

THE next hour played slow and murky for Lennon. He rose from the chair when his colleagues arrived, but it was like trying to swim to the surface of a mud pit. Everyone offered outrage and condolence in equal measure. Men clapped him on the back, expressing heartfelt sorrow that Lennon had lost his partner in such a violent manner. They assured him they would find Conrad's murderer: they would find the pig, the fucker, the son of a bitch, the rat. Lennon nodded through it all, unable to summon the same level of fury as his colleagues.

Lennon remained at the scene for over an hour, though he added little to the investigation. He listened in on conversations, speculations. He answered a few pointless questions. Just before leaving, a detective named Glaser, a smooth creep in an expensive hat, burst into the room to announce that one of the other residents had seen the killer exiting the building.

"She figured he was about my build," Glaser said. "Fifty years old. Dressed to the nines. She said he was a very pleasant and polite gentleman. He held the door for her and fed her some chit-chat before leaving the scene."

"How's that make him our killer?" Lennon asked.

"Like I said, he was holding the door while he was chatting the old lady up. She said she saw blood on his glove, said she knew what blood looked like."

Lennon catalogued the information, building a mental picture of the killer in his head. He noted Glaser's squared-off shoulders and short stature. He figured the detective's weight to be just around a hundred and ninety pounds, and then wondered how a middle-aged man of that weight could have kept hold of a rope with a guy of Conrad's considerable girth, trying to buck and shake him loose. The thought came and went quickly, though. It was apparent that Conrad's nose had been broken. Who knew what additional damage the killer had managed before getting the rope around the fat neck?

Back at the station, he mulled over his history with Conrad, which amounted to a combative six years. For Lennon, death had not polished away the tarnish of Conrad's life, the way it apparently had for the other men in the department, who made it a point to stop by his office and express their condolences. Lennon thanked the men, but he deflected all conversation meant to extol Conrad's virtues, all of which were nothing but the fantastical creations of his colleagues. Curt Conrad hadn't died in the line of service, at least not in the service of his city. He'd died a crooked death, but Lennon would be the one shamed if he exposed that fact. You didn't speak ill of the dead, especially under his brothers' roof.

Lennon packed all of the evidence he'd gathered on Musante, all except the Mauser 14, and sent the box back to the basement. He was flipping through Conrad's address book when he received a summons—the Captain wanted to see him.

In Captain Wenders' office he took a seat, once again accepted condolences that raked across his ears like sandpaper, and waved off the offer of a whiskey.

Wenders, a blubbery man with a shiny handlebar mustache, knocked back a shot and leaned forward on his desk. On the wall behind him were a dozen framed certificates of commendation. From the superintendent of police. From the chief. From the mayor.

"This changes things," Wenders said. "Those dirty fucks can kill each other until the cows come home, and that's not a thing I'll lose a wink of sleep over, but coming after one of ours? No, sir."

"You seem pretty sure this is connected to the syndicates."

One of Wenders' eyebrows ticked upward as if waiting for the punch line to a joke. "Everything in this town is connected to the syndicates."

Including you and me, Lennon thought. He'd seen Wenders picking up his monthly bonus from the same restaurant where Lennon collected his envelope. Once he'd considered it harmless. Irrelevant. Standard operating procedure. Now, it sickened him. The entire system ran on the syndicates' fuel. He'd always known it, had been a part of it since his first promotion, but he felt as if he had just turned this particular rock over to see the repulsive creatures writhing beneath. Suddenly the day-to-day corruption—predictable and bland—had taken on importance. It had touched too close to home.

"Now, I know you boys draw envelopes," said Wenders. "Most of the station does. I never put my nose into your business when it comes to that. Folks have to feed their families, but we have a dead detective, and that's not the kind of thing that money is going to make go away."

"No, sir," Lennon agreed.

"So which side were you two drawing from?"

"Sir?" Lennon shifted in his seat and leaned on the arm of the chair. He didn't trust the captain. For that matter Lennon wasn't sure he could trust anyone living in the city limits.

Wenders rolled his eyes impatiently. "You playing the coy whore with me? Your partner is dead, about had his head sawed off with a rope, and you want to pretend you never spread for the thug fuckers who done it?"

"Sir, it's not that simple." He looked away. His gaze landed on a framed commendation from the mayor, hung only a few inches above the trashcan Wenders kept in the corner.

"Look, Lennon, I'm not gunning for you. Like I said, I don't give a shit about your take. But I got a call a little over thirty minutes ago and I need some confirmation before I throw this department headlong into a gang war."

"A call?"

Wenders worked his lips silently as if testing the shape of the words before speaking them. "A tip-off."

"About Conrad?" Lennon sat up straight in the chair and turned to the captain.

"Yeah, about Conrad."

"What did they say?"

"You running things now?" Wenders asked. He sneered at Lennon, and then appeared to deflate as if too tired to sustain a performance of authority. "Just tell me who was slinging his envelopes."

"Curt was drawing from both sides," Lennon said.

Wenders' face went rigid. "Are you sure?"

"Yes. We both drew from the Italians, but Curt was also drawing from Moran's crew, likely somebody under Powell. I think I should leave it at that."

He wasn't ready to discuss Curt's involvement in Musante's murder, might never be ready. What good would it do? The guy was scum but hardly more crooked than anyone else in the department. Musante was one of the bad guys, even if he wasn't particularly good at it. When all was said and done, the world would keep on turning as it had. The only thing talking would accomplish was to earn Lennon the label of rat.

"You're not leaving it at that," Wenders said.

"Sir, there are extenuating—"

"Fuck your extenuating and fuck this bullshit. We have the Feds and the press spitting on their dicks, looking for a place to park them. Let's have it."

Lennon felt like a chicken on a spit, roasting under Wenders' angry impatience. He cleared his throat and swallowed twice. He could lie, but none came to mind. "I think, no, I'm pretty certain, that Curt murdered Lonnie Musante."

"Come again?" The captain's voice had turned to flint. Beneath his impressive handlebars, his mouth pinched tightly, as if daring Lennon to continue.

"The gun used in the Musante murder, the Mauser, was the same weapon Curt and I pulled off of Dickie Mayr for the Gladson's hold up. I checked the serial number on the weapon we found at the scene. It matches the Mayr piece. No way a guy like Cardinal could have gotten his hands on it."

"But you were there when Musante was shot."

"Yeah, I was there," Lennon said, again looking toward the certificate of commendation hung on the wall. "But I didn't see any of the action. I didn't see anything, except Cardinal fleeing the scene."

Even though the details of that night eluded him, Lennon knew what he was willing to do, and pulling a hit for the Irish wasn't on the list. Curt had taken the job. Considering how careless the fat slob had been, he'd probably bragged to Lennon about it. Whatever the case, Lennon knew he wouldn't have chewed the news and sat back while his partner made such a profoundly stupid move.

He pulled his attention away from the framed document and looked across the desk. Wenders wasn't enjoying the report. His fat jowls burned crimson and his eyes, already curtained by heavy bags of skin, were all but slits.

"Considering Musante's relationship with Impelliteri," Lennon said, "it only stands that the Irish made the call. They brought Curt in to make it clean and set up Cardinal to take the fall. He was a petty player. Expendable. They didn't want to risk any of their real talent, and they probably thought they could pass it off as a personal gripe between the two."

"I don't see it," Wenders said, shaking his head. "Musante was a penny among dimes. Hell, he was trouser lint. The Irish wouldn't start a war over a guy that small."

"But they did," Lennon said. "Don't ask me why. What I know is that Curt was supposed to be working for Impelliteri. If he moved *against* Impelliteri, then it was coming from the Irish."

"Fuck," Wenders said. He pushed himself away from the desk and knit his fingers behind his head.

"Sir?"

"The call I got. The tip off. The guy identified a lowball named Terry McGavin for Conrad's hit. McGavin is Powell's second-in-command."

"Does he match the description Glaser took off the old lady at the scene? Fifty years old? Five-foot-nine or ten? A hundred and eighty, maybe ninety pounds?"

With a weary expression, Wenders shook his head and said, "Not even a little."

"Then it's a set-up. Impelliteri's crew called it in to give Powell grief."

But again, Lennon had to wonder why. What had the gangster lost with Musante's death? Was Impelliteri really fighting a war over such a loser? A con man fortuneteller? Or was it something else entirely? Lennon considered the two men who had put a knife to his neck in Musante's home. They hadn't been worried about Musante at all; their concern was for some bauble Musante was supposed to have had. They'd threatened Lennon's life and the lives of his family in order to extract everything Lennon knew about the trinket, which was nothing. Maybe Musante had muled the thing, run it from a seller to Impelliteri.

"Yeah, it's probably a set-up," Wenders said. The loose skin on his plump face sagged further as if someone had poured water into reservoirs behind the flesh.

"McGavin is already here," Lennon said, realizing what the frustration weighing Wenders' face meant. "Christ, he's a dead man."

"They just brought him in," the Captain said, placing both palms on the top of his desk as if trying to soothe the piece of furniture. He pushed air from his mouth, a silent whistle achieving little but the flutter of his lips. "These fuckers keep playing us like bums."

"Only because we let them." Lennon stood. He needed to get to McGavin while the man was still alive.

"Hold on. We've got a story to get straight." Suddenly the strength was back in Wenders' voice. He'd made up his mind about something, and he was ready to deliver an order.

"What story?"

"The incident at Musante's. You need to forget about Conrad," Wenders said. "You didn't say it. I didn't hear it. As far as this department is concerned, Butch Cardinal killed Lonnie Musante. He acted alone. That part of the story doesn't change."

Lennon leaned forward on the desk. He couldn't believe Wenders wouldn't even consider the evidence. "You're going to let an innocent man take the fall?"

"I don't give a good god damn about Cardinal," Wenders said. His eyes glared from the soft face like two marbles nestled in a wad of dough. "The dumb fuck was in the wrong place at a very bad time. He's not my problem. On the other hand, I *do* care about this department. I am not going to let *it* take the fall. We already have citizen groups hanging from the walls, and the Feds have taken just about every decision out of our hands."

"Maybe that's not such a bad thing."

"Really? And how's that?"

"Most of them aren't playing the angles. You may not have noticed, Captain, but you just signed contracts on the lives of two men tonight: Butch Cardinal and Terry McGavin. And for what? From what I can see, the Feds are trying to uphold the law. What the hell are we trying to do?"

Wenders' expression didn't change. He glared at Lennon with his hard marble eyes, and the indifference captured there swallowed light. The face disturbed Lennon; it disgusted him. And the well of emotions that had eluded him for hours suddenly gurgled into life. And it gushed. And it plumed.

He stormed out of Captain Wenders' office and headed for the stairs.

• • •

By the time Lennon reached the interrogation room, Terry McGavin had already been questioned within an inch of his life. It didn't take long for Chicago's finest to telegraph their displeasure to a suspect, and when the life of a cop had been taken, they sent a lot of messages. Subtlety went out the window. With the real movers of felony, even if they happened to be innocent of the charges they'd been hauled in on, nobody trod softly.

When Lennon entered the room, McGavin was face down on the table amid a stippling of blood. The wall to his left was made of brick. It had a narrow, barred window. The other walls were plastered and painted the dull brown of dead grass, not that the color was easily identifiable this evening. A single, glaring bulb hung low. Its conical shade directed all of the light onto the table and the suspect, leaving much of the walls and the corners in gloom. The skin on the nape of McGavin's neck looked bloodless under the harsh light. The man groaned and wheezed.

The two detectives who had been interrogating the suspect stood off to the side, smiling, wiping their knuckles with their handkerchiefs. When they saw Lennon, their eyes lit up and their smiles broadened.

"Give me ten," Lennon said. He knew they wouldn't argue the request. His partner had been murdered and the man suspected of doing it was bleeding all over the table in the middle of the room. Cops had a code. Partners had rights.

"Take as long as you need," Detective Glaser said.

Lennon dipped his chin toward the detective. Considering his mood, he'd rather have Glaser in the chair. The piece of shit had taken the old lady's statement, and he knew damn well McGavin didn't match her description. But that hadn't stopped Glaser from beating the prisoner senseless. He wouldn't let something as insignificant as the truth keep him from throwing pain. He enjoyed making men scream, liked to see their blood paint the table. For guys like Glaser, every interrogation was a wedding night.

"Make Curt proud," the other detective added.

"Thanks," Lennon replied. "Go get yourselves some coffee. I'll let you know when I'm through in here."

After the men left, Lennon took the chair across the table from McGavin. He sat but said nothing for a time. Instead he listened to the struggling breaths of the suspect, and considered the position he was in. He didn't know McGavin, but he knew he didn't like the man, and he didn't like the fact that things had gotten so cockeyed he had to consider an Irish mobster a closer ally than the men in his squad. The whole mess was like a knot of wires behind a fuse box, and he didn't know which ones were live and which were safe to touch.

Finally he said, "How long was Curt working for you?"

McGavin made a sound, wet and deep. A cough? A laugh? He groaned and lifted his head. With his pale skin and numerous contusions, the suspect looked like a circus clown made up in the colors of violence. His right eye was purple and swollen. A deep gash over the left brow dripped blood into the socket, and McGavin blinked furiously to clear it away. A knot the size of a walnut had already swelled on his jaw. His lips were split and pulled back in a grimace. Blood ran into his mouth and framed his teeth like mud being pushed through fence boards.

"You were his partner," McGavin said. Lennon nodded. "You have my sympathies. Before and after."

Lennon took a deep breath and released it loudly. The last thing he needed was lip from a creep he was trying to help. "That mouth is going to cause you trouble, Terry. Why don't we start again?"

"Because I didn't kill the fat fuck. He was strangled. What kind of street trash uses a rope? If I wanted someone dead, I'd use my ladies."

"Your ladies?"

"Guns," McGavin said. He turned his head and spat a wad of red phlegm on the floor. "I let my ladies do the sweet talkin'. Or I *would* let them if I were to ever hurt a living soul, which I wouldn't."

"Of course not. You're a good Catholic boy."

"Indeed true. Saints preserve." McGavin's lips twitched up in an oily grimace.

"Here's the thing, Terry," Lennon said, leaning on the table. "Detective Conrad kept a bank ledger and he kept an address book. Any guesses whose name I found in them?"

McGavin's expression didn't change with the news. He continued to squint and blink.

"Your name, Terry. Your name was in Curt's ledgers. Now from what I can put together, Detective Conrad did quite a lot for you and Mr. Powell, including a hit on Lonnie Musante."

At the mention of Musante's name, McGavin winced. He sniffed blood back into his nose and looked away.

"I was there that night," Lennon said. "He did the job, framed another man. But you must have known that using Curt was dangerous. After all, he worked for the Italians. If Powell or Moran sniffed that out, they might figure you were playing both sides."

"You tell good stories," McGavin said. "You know the one about the cop who went and fucked himself?"

Lennon leaned across the table and slapped the side of McGavin's head, causing the man to groan. "Pay attention, Terry. I'm telling that story now, and the cop's name was Curt Conrad, but you've got some luck on your side. Neither you nor my late partner will be implicated in the Musante affair. It wouldn't look good for the department, so you'll walk free and clear on that one. That should be a big relief."

"Maybe. If I believed it."

"Regardless," Lennon said. He stood and began to pace the room, hoping to stomp his agitation through the soles of his feet. "More good news for you. Since you're a known associate of Angus Powell and Bugs Moran, the Feds will be coming to whisk you off, and they will have more concern for your well-being than my colleagues do. My guess is, no one here is planning to make that call until morning, and the way things are going, you won't live through the night—cop killer and all. You give me something I want, and I'll go make that call right now."

McGavin's swollen brows knit. His lips finally closed over the blood-smeared teeth. Lennon had offered the man something important, something crucial. He didn't expect the offer to put McGavin on his side, but it might clear the way for a conversation.

"You don't seem too torn up about your partner's death," McGavin noted.

"I'm getting around to it," Lennon said. "I didn't like the man. He was a slob and he was rude and he was a dog's hind leg, but we were on the force together a long time. That does something. It takes men beyond issues of *like* or *hate*."

"I didn't kill him," McGavin said evenly. "I was with my family all day, and they'll swear to it in court, even though it won't change the way things are. I know that. I know how the game is played. You fucks need someone to blame."

McGavin was right, of course. As with Butch Cardinal, guilt was no longer an issue. The department needed a name for the papers, an ass for the chair. "Maybe you can give us someone else to blame."

"Not my style."

Lennon walked around the table and leaned over the prisoner. McGavin peered up at him, harsh light bathing his face. "I can help you, Terry, but you have to give me something."

"How much?"

"I don't want money. I need a name."

"Like I said. Not my style." McGavin turned away, looked into the corner.

"And like I said, you can't go up on this one," Lennon kicked the chair hard to get McGavin's attention. "I'm not asking about Curt. This is about Musante. Cardinal is going to fry for that one no matter what happens. I'm not happy about that, but there's not much I can do to change it. So you've got a free pass here, Terry. You give me a name, a name I can't do a damn thing with. I call the Feds. You live to see sunrise."

"If you can't do anything with the name, why do you want it?"

"I just want to know."

"What?"

"Who ordered the Musante hit? Who on your crew is so fucking stupid they'd start a street war over a glorified fortuneteller?"

"Oh, you wouldn't like that answer," McGavin said. The bloody grin opened across his face again.

Lennon was finding it harder to keep control of his temper. The guy understood his situation: he was maybe thirty minutes away from getting his brains bashed in. McGavin had to know that. Was he so stupid he'd rather play his tough-guy games than add some years to his life?

"And why wouldn't I like the answer, Terry?"

"Your partner wasn't the only one playing both sides, detective."

"Both sides? Are you saying Impelliteri ordered Musante's murder?"

"No. But someone from his crew did." McGavin attempted a shrewd expression that pinched his face, making him look anguished rather than clever. "The guy approached me a few years back. He needed cash, and he had some information. It helped clear certain paths for us. So I've kept him on the line ever since. I paid him out of my pocket, knowing Powell would pay off double for the information the guy gave me. A couple of weeks back the guy calls me up and tells me he needs a big favor. Musante was the favor."

"Did Powell know about this?"

"Hell, no," McGavin said. He hawked another wad of red phlegm and spat it on the floor. "Powell is like Moran. They think the Italians are a different species—just greasy apes who know how to pull triggers. They won't make deals with them. But the thing is it's not about Italians or Irish, and it's not about Northside or Southside. It's about money and power. When you've been around as long as I have, you figure you've got all the power you're going to get—no way you're going to be top of the heap. So you settle for the money and whether the money passes through Rome or Dublin it spends the same in Chicago." Pain brought creases to McGavin's face. He tried to smile through them. "He used to say that."

"He?"

"The two-face in Impelliteri's operation," McGavin explained. "He was a talker. Fucker could go on for hours when he got an idea in his head. Most of the time he was just ass talking. On this point, though, I happened to agree with him."

"And he knew you had Conrad on the line?"

"Sure. He liked the idea of having a cop pull the trigger. When he came to me with his plan, I made the arrangements."

Lennon gave up pacing and returned to his chair. "So Cardinal was his idea?"

McGavin cocked his head to the side. Shrugged.

"Time is running out, Terry. Once my buddies get back from their coffee break, you're out of my hands."

"Cardinal was my idea," McGavin said bitterly. "He was a smug fuck. Came in all cocky, kept his distance like we weren't good enough for him. Powell just ate it up, acted like he'd gotten himself a big-shot pet. I figured we could do without him."

Lennon could hear the jealousy in McGavin's voice. It wasn't a surprise that a man who'd done nothing of value with his life should get his hair up over a man who'd tried to make a name for himself. The fact the wrestler had hit hard times made it all the easier to dismiss him. So Butch Cardinal had been given a death sentence because he'd rubbed a lowlife thug the wrong way. No genuine slight. Certainly no threat. McGavin simply had no tolerance for anyone he considered better than himself, which to Lennon's mind must have been a good, long list.

"And Detective Conrad?" Lennon asked.

"It should have been an easy night for him. I already had the wrestler lined up for the fall. He comes in, pops Musante, pops Cardinal in *self-defense*, plants a gun, neat and tidy."

"Except Cardinal got away."

"I did not see that one coming," McGavin said. He fell silent, shifted his weight in the seat, trying to find a comfortable position in a chair that hadn't been designed for comfort. Finally, he said, "You ever think that maybe Cardinal is the one who killed your partner? I'd think he's got more than enough piss in him by now to want payback."

Lennon shook his head. Cardinal was on the run—might be in Mexico by now. Besides, he looked no more like the man the old lady at Conrad's building had described than Terry McGavin did.

"I'll keep him in mind," Lennon said. "Right now, I want to know the name of your contact on Impelliteri's crew. I'd like to speak with him."

"No chance of that."

"Why not?"

The prisoner's face was lowered, staring at the table. Even so, Lennon could see his smirk. "He's dead," McGavin said.

"That's convenient for you."

"In more ways than you know."

"How so?"

"My contact was Lonnie Musante." McGavin paused, waiting for a response. His battered lips pulled wide when he caught the look of confusion on Lennon's face. "He ordered a hit on himself, detective. Said he had the cancer real bad and was on his way out. Said he couldn't kill himself because of being Catholic and all. Suicide being a mortal sin."

Lennon needed a moment to comprehend what he'd just been told. He knew Musante was a terminal case with cancer building tumors in his gut. When he'd read the medical report, Lennon had considered bullets a blessing in comparison to the misery the disease promised, but the news stunned him anyway. Lennon leaned back in his chair and searched

McGavin's battered face for signs of deceit but saw only self-satisfaction and amusement.

"Why did he make it so complicated?" Lennon finally asked. "You said it was all his plan, so why did he need someone like Cardinal there?"

"Who knows what a dead man is thinking?"

"Yeah," Lennon said. He stood from the chair and leaned forward on the table.

"You going to make that call for me?" McGavin asked.

"I am." Lennon stepped around the table and stood over the man. McGavin craned his neck and looked into the detective's face. "But I have to knock you around a little."

"I know," McGavin said. "Gotta look right for your friends."

"Something like that."

"Well, do what you gotta do."

Lennon landed a fist to McGavin's jaw, but the punch was weak. Halfhearted. That wasn't going to work. The wounds needed to be convincing. So he pulled his fist back and gave it another go.

Chapter 21
Human Sacrifice

Hayes and Brand walked up the block and paused outside of the building where their associate, Humphrey Bell, had taken a room. Wind blew angrily over them, racing in great gusts down the street. The apartment house was tall and narrow; its bricks and the veins of mortar between them were nearly black with grime. Two days had passed since the young man had checked in, and while such silences often occurred in the course of an investigation, Humphrey was still being trained in the field, and he was held to stricter guidelines than a seasoned associate. During that time, Hayes and Brand had covered the city, speaking with its degenerates and its criminals, searching for information about the outfit to which Lonnie Musante had been affiliated, but while every gun-toting insect in this city knew Mr. Musante by his unfortunate and comical reputation—his service as Marco Impelliteri's mystic—no valuable information had surfaced.

"The phone lines have been down," Mr. Brand said. "The last storm took a good number of them out. He probably didn't want to leave his post."

This was the third time his partner had mentioned the downed lines, but both men knew that if Humphrey had wanted to contact them, was *able* to contact them, he could have left a note at their hotel. Hayes had already pointed this out to Mr. Brand on several occasions, but now he remained silent out of respect for his associate. Mr. Brand had a special affinity for young Humphrey. He had mentored the boy for years, teaching him the history and the application of every weapon in the chambers beneath 213 House. To add to their fraternity, Mr. Brand had begun courting Humphrey's older sister only the year before, and he was on the verge of proposing marriage to the girl.

Though his life had been troubled since youth, fighting his way through the cruel gutters of Brooklyn with his handicapped arm, Mr. Brand had managed to grow into something of a romantic, and he felt things deeply and carried them silently. Although he rarely allowed his sentiments to escape through word or voice, emotions lived in Brand's eyes.

"The phone lines," Hayes said. "I'm sure you're right."

"I should have visited him. He's still in training."

"And part of that training requires independence. I'm sure Mr. Bell is fine, Mr. Brand. He was instructed to watch for Mr. Cardinal's return and follow the man if necessary. You have given him excellent instruction over the years. He would never take action on his own. If he's not in his room, we'll wait and clarify the proper procedures with him when he returns."

"Yes," Brand agreed.

To his sadness, Hayes believed little of what he'd just told his associate. Looking up at the sky, which again wore a blanket of furious gray clouds, Hayes struggled with pessimistic thoughts. Their work rarely brought them into contact with good men, and the days they'd spent in Chicago had done nothing but reinforce Hayes' disdain for a corroded humanity. He vilified the entire city, though he knew it was no worse than his neighborhood in New York, nor was it worse than the neighborhoods surrounding his. Maybe it was no worse, at least no different, than any bloated city. What bothered Hayes so greatly here was the celebrity afforded to the gangster faction. Chicago's killers and thieves were heralded, celebrated like movie stars and royalty. Hayes could understand weak men cutting a crooked path through a society, but he could not understand a society that not only accepted such deviation, but also aspired to it with shameless zeal. In this place, this Chicago, all that mattered was power. Commerce was God, and He had a taste for human sacrifice.

"I intend to set that kid straight," Mr. Brand said, again speaking of Humphrey Bell. "I'll give him a couple of good knocks in the head if that's what it takes."

Hayes tried to chuckle, knowing Mr. Brand would do no such thing, but the fabricated laughter fell on his tongue like ash. He turned to look across the street at the building in which Butch Cardinal had rented a room. It could have been a twin to the building at his back, except it was squatter by two floors.

Unable to put it off any longer, Hayes pivoted on his heel and walked up the stoop. When he opened the door a blast of warm air that smelled of cabbage, garlic, and cat urine washed over his face.

"I'll bet he met a girl," Mr. Brand said.

"Then you will have my permission to knock him in the head."

"I'll do more than that."

Hayes fixed a tight smile on his face, listening to Brand's speculations and threats, which followed him to the third floor of the building. Outside of Humphrey's room, Hayes knocked on the door and listened, but the only sound was an undulating moan of wind. The noise made him uneasy. It was too cold to leave a window open. He knocked a second time. Mr. Brand nudged him aside and rapped more forcefully. "Mr. Bell," he barked. Hayes gently tapped his associate on the shoulder and waved him back. Then he removed a four-inch steel pin from his pocket and slid it into the lock. The metal melted and bent, all but disappearing into the mechanism's hole. What remained was a knob, approximately the size of a dime. Hayes turned this and the lock disengaged. Once the newly fashioned key was removed from the hole, it shifted its shape, lengthened and narrowed, until it was again a narrow pin, which went back into Hayes' pocket.

He threw open the door and was startled by a length of cloth, a blanket, that dropped over the top edge of the door. Freezing air blasted into the room from the open window. Gusts of it animated the simple shade and the white curtains which danced like ghosts. To the left of the window, beside a large console radio was a chair bathed in gloom, and in the chair was Mr. Bell.

Beside him, Mr. Brand emitted a groan so filled with pain it momentarily bested the howls of the wind. Both men stepped cautiously into the room. Mr. Hayes went directly to the bound and tortured body of his associate, while Mr. Brand stomped heavily across the floor to close the window. Observing the door remained open, Mr. Hayes hurried back and closed it before returning to Mr. Bell's remains.

He noted a number of cuts and bruises on the young man. Crusts of rust-colored scab marred his arms and throat. A gag had been tied so tightly that the skin of Mr. Bell's cheeks rose in ridges around it. But it was in seeing the eyes, or rather where the eyes should have been, that made sickness blossom in his gut; the sight punched Mr. Hayes and he covered his mouth and he stepped away. Behind him, Mr. Brand paced between the window and the door, his footsteps heavy and brutal on the stained boards. To the window. To the door. He resembled a wild cat that had taken all of the captivity he could endure.

He turned back to the poor young man's body and winced. All morning, he'd expected to find a sad tableau inside this room, but his imagination had taken him no further than the likelihood of finding Mr. Bell lying on the floor with a gunshot to the head. The level of savagery exhibited in the young man's treatment would never have occurred to him, and if he were being honest with himself, the fact that someone could perpetrate this kind of violence on the young man terrified Hayes. This wasn't the clean kill of mob muscle; this was the work of a madman.

"Humphrey. Humphrey. Humphrey." Mr. Brand spat the name in time with his tromping steps.

They would have to clean the room and remove the body and Mr. Bell's belongings, which would need to be searched. The corpse would need to be thoroughly bathed to afford the sad young man his dignity. A report would have to be made. The remains would need to be secured and transported back to Red Hook for a proper burial. Mr. Bell's family would have to be notified—his dear sister would be devastated. But Mr. Hayes refused to focus on this particular issue. His mind was incapable of managing the sight of the bloodied, eyeless body, and he couldn't endure thinking about the young man's last moments of life. Instead, he wanted distraction. Tasks.

First, Mr. Bell had to be unbound and properly, carefully, wrapped so he could be taken from the room and… And what? They couldn't carry him back to their hotel. They couldn't prop him on the seat of a train like an old, rolled rug.

"We need a car," he said.

"I'll rip his head off," Mr. Brand said. "When I catch Cardinal, I will cut his throat and tear his fucking head from his carcass."

Hayes hadn't considered the identity of Mr. Bell's assassin, except in the broadest of terms. His mind had been filled with gangsters, the highbrow cousins to the street scum they'd interviewed over the past two days. Oddly, he hadn't thought of Butch Cardinal once, but now the name was lodged in his mind, and his anger began to form around it like a pearl hardening over a speck of grit. Except he could not let his emotions loose. Not now. There were tasks. Details. They needed to focus and manage this place and care for Mr. Bell's earthly remains. Then they could pursue justice.

"We need a car," Hayes repeated. Brand continued his vicious pacing from one side of the room to the other, oblivious to the statement. "Mr. Brand," Hayes said tersely. The tone of his voice did the trick and Brand came to a stop. "We need a car to transport Mr. Bell's body. You will go and buy a vehicle. It should be used, but not so old that we are likely to need it repaired. I will remain here and put the room in order and prepare Mr. Bell."

The muscles on Brand's face twitched and shifted as if parasites scrambled beneath the skin, but then the spasms calmed and he appeared earnest. Only his eyes remained disturbed. Anger and loss came through them as if the emotions were cast by a projector at the back of his skull. Brand faced off on Hayes and threw back his shoulders. He brought his arms to his sides like a soldier awaiting command, though he'd already received his orders.

"You know where the money is kept in our room. At the hotel, send a wire to 213 House so that an apprentice can be sent by train. He will drive Mr. Bell home."

"I have to go with him," Brand said. "I have to tell Marie. She'll need me."

"You're needed here, Mr. Brand. I'm sorry."

The burly man's expression didn't change. "This is unacceptable."

"We need a car," Mr. Hayes said again. "You will go and buy one."

His chest ached with regret as he gave the orders. He knew Brand should return with the young man's corpse, but they couldn't afford that kind of delay. They were facing something Hayes had never imagined. He quickly looked at the dead boy bound in the chair and then yanked his gaze away. No longer did he believe they were in the land of men; this place was far darker and inhabited by vile things. A soulless beast was leading them away from civilization and would one day turn on them; Hayes could feel it. What waited ahead was not simply criminal. It was sinister. It was evil.

Chapter 22
...A Man When He's Down

Hollis never did answer Butch's question: What is Lionel to you?

Butch didn't really need an answer. It was clear enough. For two days, ever since he'd confronted Hollis and been summarily knocked down a few pegs, Hollis and his housemate had done nothing but argue, sounding like a married couple, reminiscent of Butch's parents, only without the inevitable bloodshed. They were at it again, and the angry tones drove Butch outside.

Vines and succulent plants filled the courtyard. Even so late in the year, flowers blossomed white and violet amid low shrubs of green. The scent was a sugary perfume of rose, sweet olive, and jasmine, and Butch filled his lungs with the cool fragrant air. It felt good to be outside after so many days cooped up in his room. He'd experienced a similar cabin fever in Chicago, where the brutal winds had forced him inside and kept him there for entire days unless work called him away. But the weather here was agreeable. Cool but not cold. A soothing climate, particularly after so much snow. And it was a pretty place. At the center of the flagstone patio stood a granite fountain like a stone wedding cake. Ivy blanketed the brick wall, and the house rose like a sheer mountain precipice, above which a square of sky revealed dove-gray clouds.

Behind him, the door opened and Lionel emerged, slapping a cap on his head. The kid fixed Butch with a hateful glare. Then he smirked and stormed away, slamming the gate behind him with a clanging crash.

Butch had managed to avoid the punk for the past couple of days. He heard Lionel Lowery stomping about the house, climbing the spiral staircase, playing records in the upstairs bedroom, but they'd seen little of one another, and that was just fine with Butch. It was bad enough he couldn't clear his mind of the act he'd witnessed Lowery performing. The scene frequently interrupted his thoughts, leaving him baffled and agitated. He didn't need to interact with the kid who'd put those thoughts in his head.

Hollis appeared a few minutes later, looking worn out. The man crossed to Butch and handed him a folded sheet of paper and then clapped Butch on the shoulder and turned back for the door.

"Hey," Butch said.

Hollis paused and asked, "Yeah?" over his shoulder.

"I'm sorry about the ruckus," he said.

"Well, I think things will be a lot quieter now."

"How's that?"

"I've asked Lionel to leave." Hollis turned. His lips curved down in a frown. His eyes appeared dull with exhaustion. "He's never been a good fit for my life. Best to just accept that and get on with things."

Butch wanted to say something comforting like "It's probably for the best," but he had no right to make such a claim. In fact anything he said, outside of praise for Hollis's decision, would have been forced, inappropriate, or fraudulent. He thought he might like Hollis, figured they'd be friends under different circumstances. Maybe they were anyway. He felt comfortable in Hollis's presence. The man's strong yet kind face and powerful physicality reassured him. Hollis had been good to him, and he felt pretty low about hurting the man. But he did believe it was for the best. Fairy or not, that Lionel kid was trouble. It showed on his face and sounded in his voice like a snake's rattle.

He unfolded the paper Hollis had given him and found a list of names and addresses. "What's this?"

"A few jewelers and antique dealers I know. It should get you a good start on finding information about that necklace."

"Thank you."

"You're welcome," Hollis replied. "Now, if you'll excuse me, I think I'll lie down for a bit before I head into work."

"Sure," Butch said.

"Oh, one other thing," Hollis said. "I'll be packing Lionel's belongings in the morning. He'll be by to pick them up tomorrow noon. I don't want him in this house while I'm out."

"Sure," he said again. "Okay."

Then Hollis left him alone in the courtyard. Butch walked across the flagstones, approaching the big house. It was a grand place. He wondered who owned it. He hadn't seen so much as a drape move in the breeze since his arrival.

Not long ago, only a handful of years, Butch might have pictured himself owning such a house. During his rise through the athletic ranks, he'd often imagined an opulent lifestyle, but after the Hungarian and the ensuing battles with the wrestling establishment, he'd toned down his fantasies, had come to terms with simpler wants and wishes. He wanted nothing more than a small, comfortable home on a good piece of land. A place of his own, where he made the rules. Even that humble dream seemed unlikely now.

The gravity of his situation returned with startling focus. His life was eroding, slipping away, and he didn't have a clue how to manage the slide. The path of his life had taken him through crooked territory and his only companion had been bad fucking luck. The journey had eaten away at his competence and his strength, leading him from the ring into the underworld and leaving him powerless against the forces he'd found there. Now he was forced to live in a stranger's house, trapped with his rules, not knowing how to behave.

He returned to the bungalow and tried to call Rory, but there was no answer. In his room, he lay on the bed to stare at the ceiling fan. Its blades revolved slowly, casting shadows on the ceiling.

His only real hope was the money he'd kept under the boards in his apartment. If he could get his hands on that—*if, if, if*—his prospects would open up. It wasn't enough to get him through the rest of his years, but it could get him started in a town far from Chicago where nobody knew his face, and he could live his life without worrying about lies and humiliation and bullets and knives. But with each day, the hope dwindled. No word from Rory. The police had probably found Butch's bank, and it was rotting away in an evidence box, or worse it was currently lining the pockets of one of the shady bastards who'd set him up in the first place.

When this is over...

But he couldn't finish the thought. It would never be over, not while he was drawing breath. This was life, his life, and it was going to be a series of holds and blows and wounds and takedowns. A fight to the death. He couldn't imagine the fine house on good land, and he couldn't imagine a companion at his side. In the end, he would be another casualty of the era. A zero. Quickly forgotten. Once certain he would enter the pantheon of legendary athletes, Butch now believed his legacy would be nothing more than a slick of sweat, rapidly drying on the earth's skin.

• • •

EARLY the next morning, Butch was woken by Hollis's return from his club. The man moved quietly but Butch heard every step. The clink of a glass stopper told him that Hollis was pouring himself a drink, and the sudden change in the tone of footsteps—from light rapping on tile to a hushed whisper—informed Butch that Hollis was having his drink in the parlor just outside of his room.

He gazed into the shadowed ceiling and willed himself to stay put, but the urge to leave the bed and join Hollis in the next room gnawed at him. He remembered Hollis's words: *No one here, in this house, is particularly concerned with* normal. *There are millions of ways to live a good life. In this house, we make our own rules for how we live.* He imagined Hollis standing in the doorway, gazing at him, and then stepping forward, without a word, to join Butch in the bed. His mind grew raucous with images and imagined sensations, and through all of the turmoil a sliver of anger pushed itself.

You're still sick, he told himself. *You're exhausted and your mind isn't wholly recovered.*

When this excuse failed to quell his agitation another surfaced to replace it: you've been alone too long, months since you've shared skin with anyone. It's natural your body would seek some kind of release. It's no different from your cousin on the rocks by the lake or the Weeping Clown in a shabby rooming house. Except it was different, because those encounters had been spontaneous. He'd anticipated neither of them, nor had he brought himself to turmoil over them.

Don't do anything stupid, he warned. *Just go to sleep. Tomorrow you'll find out what the necklace is worth, and then you can leave. You can work the deal with Impelliteri or change the plan according to what you find. Either way you'll never have to travel this muddling landscape again.*

He didn't sleep, though. Not for a long time. The circuit of thoughts he'd just completed started over, running through his mind time and again. He heard Hollis leave the parlor and walk across the kitchen to deposit his glass in the sink. He heard the man's footsteps on the spiral staircase, and despite the warring messages filling his head he wanted to follow.

Chapter 23
Failure

Only an hour after returning to sleep, Butch woke, dressed quickly, and left Hollis's house. With little knowledge of the city, he wandered for some time in the morning sun, zigzagging through the streets until he came upon a restaurant that didn't look pricey. He ordered his breakfast and gobbled it, guzzling three cups of coffee in between bites of egg and toast and bacon. After, he made his way toward the river until he came upon a newsstand. There he bought a map and a nub of pencil and five minutes later, he was in another café, very near the Mississippi, perhaps even the same café where he'd first met Hollis, though he couldn't be certain. He spent the next hour searching the map for the general locations of the addresses Hollis had given him. He circled areas and put an X on the intersection near Hollis's home so he could find his way back.

Away from the confusing atmosphere of Hollis's bungalow, he felt better. His mind was clear now. He had a purpose. If the necklace had any value at all, a clerk at one of the shops would be able to tell him. All he needed was information and once he had it, he could be on his way.

Unfortunately, the first shop he visited, Francine & François on Royal Street, set the tone for his morning. It was a large store, despite having a narrow and misleading shop front. Butch entered to the tinkling sound of a bell and made his way through the ornaments of prosperity, all tucked neatly behind glass, to the counter at the back. No one emerged to greet him, and it occurred to Butch that the owners weren't particularly concerned with their merchandise as he could have cleaned out the cases by the door and fled into the street in the time it was taking the proprietor to investigate the bell.

Butch peered through the glass case before him. Diamonds and sapphires glimmered from gold settings. Finely crafted pieces of silver shone against the black velvet. He considered the necklace in his pocket and felt ridiculous.

A woman in an obviously expensive dress, the color of coral, pushed aside a navy blue curtain draping the doorway. She moved with elegance, the light catching her own jewelry, pearls at the throat and diamond teardrops on her ears. She smiled a hard porcelain smile, and regarded Butch with suspicion.

"Can I help you?" she asked. Her eyes roamed over his cheap suit and wrinkled shirt. Her expression was pure disdain.

"I'm trying to identify a piece of jewelry," he said. "A friend said you might be able to help me out."

"Really?" she asked, touching the string of pearls at her throat. "I'm not in the consignment market, you know?"

Butch wondered how many men and women had come into the shop trying to hawk their family heirlooms. How many bums had trudged in to pawn off their St. Christopher medals and crucifixes and military honors for the opportunity to put bread on the table?

"I'm not looking to sell the thing," he said. "I don't think there's anything precious about it, but maybe you've seen something like it before."

"Well, let's see what you have." The shopkeeper's disinterest came through as clearly as if she had wearily sighed.

He removed the necklace from his pocket and set it on the counter. The woman leaned to the side, fingers still resting against the pearls at her neck. A soft clicking noise rose in her throat and she shook her head.

"I don't believe I can be of any assistance," she said.

"So you've never seen anything like this before?"

"If I have, I've quickly forgotten it." The smile fixed to her face took on a cruel property. "Have a pleasant day."

Having been dismissed, Butch retrieved the necklace and returned it to his pocket. He fumed and turned for the front of the store.

In his heyday women like this had cooed over him, petted his muscles, embarrassed themselves in front of their husbands at cocktail parties. Oh, they always started out with the cold, holier-than-thou crap, but as evenings progressed and drinks were consumed, they'd warmed to him. He couldn't count the number of propositions he'd entertained for late-night rendezvous, slurred into his ear by some socialite. Now, he couldn't even get a shopkeeper to show him civility.

And the next shop proved no different. Nor did the one after that. By the time his morning came to an end, Butch's humiliation was complete.

No matter how many times he explained that he simply wanted information, shop owners sneered and sent him on his way with the assurance that he wouldn't get a nickel for the necklace, and beneath such statements was the implied scorn that he—a bum—should have been ashamed for wasting their precious time.

Maybe they were right. For all he knew, Musante had been given a dime-store ornament, a prop in a drama meant to end with his and Butch's death. Butch couldn't figure the why of it, but if the necklace meant nothing then what other answer could there be?

• • •

He pushed open the gate and walked along the narrow alley running between the converted slave quarters and the high brick wall on his left. As he stepped into the courtyard he paused to take in the foliage and the fountain. Lionel Lowery barreled into him a moment later, sending him momentarily off balance.

"Watch where you're going," Lowery said.

"Hey," Butch protested after regaining his footing.

"Fuck off," the kid said.

He stomped into the alley, swinging a brown cardboard suitcase. In his other hand he carried a hobo's pack made from an old gray towel. Midway down the corridor, Lowery stopped and released his luggage, letting it drop to the flagstone path. He whipped around, glaring at Butch.

Butch tensed, prepared for a fight. After a morning of frustration and shame, he wanted a fight, wanted the chance to prove, if only to himself, that he wasn't completely useless. It wouldn't be much of a fight, though. He had six inches of height on the kid and a good thirty pounds, not to mention years of training on his side.

"Something on your mind?" he asked.

"Got plenty on my mind," Lowery said. "Most of it ends with you face down and bleeding."

"I've got the time if you do."

Lowery's cheek twitched with the invitation, but he remained where he stood and scowled. "You couldn't keep your mouth shut. Couldn't mind your own fucking business."

"Maybe you shouldn't have been playing Hollis for a chump."

"We got along just fine before you showed up."

"I imagine Hollis will still get along fine."

"You shouldn't have crossed me."

Butch grinned at the threat. "You gonna talk me to the ground?"

"You'll see," Lowery said. "Hollis took your side because he wants to ride your tail, and from the looks of you, you'll let him, but don't get too comfortable. I know your name, Butch Cardinal. I know your name."

Anger like matching swarms of hornets teemed in his gut and behind his eyes. The kid's grubby claim brought heat to his face. Butch tightened his hands into fists and took a lumbering step forward. He liked the look of fear the movement put into Lowery's eyes. A part of his mind screamed through the buzzing fury. It demanded he cut his losses. The kid might be easy to drop in a fight, but that didn't mean he was harmless. If Lowery talked to the right people he could bring a lot of trouble down on Butch and Hollis.

"You better leave now," Butch said through a clenched jaw.

The fear cleared from Lowery's expression. Satisfaction replaced it. The kid sneered at Butch and dipped low to retrieve his baggage. "You'll see," Lowery taunted.

"Get your ass out of here."

Butch watched the kid walk to the gate. Once Lowery was gone, he relaxed a bit. He breathed deeply.

He'd made a mistake. God damn it. It was bad enough he had all of Chicago chasing him down, now he would have that snake Lowery slithering through New Orleans, spitting venom at anyone who got close. Hollis had said the southern syndicate was closely tied to the northern. Butch's name could have gone out over a wire, might be printed large on a sheet of paper with a dollar amount beneath it. Every thug in the city might have it. Did Lowery know those people? Would they be hard to find if the punk went looking?

Inside the bungalow he found Hollis in the kitchen, standing beside the sink and holding a glass of water. Hollis's eyes were half closed and his expression showed extreme sadness or advanced exhaustion. Butch didn't want to add to the man's burden, but he couldn't stay quiet about Lowery's threat.

"He said something similar to me," Hollis said. He put the glass on the counter and turned to Butch. "This was one of the reasons I was worried about having you stay here. Under ideal circumstances, Lionel is barely stable, and our circumstances have moved a good ways from ideal. Still, it may be hogwash. My guess is his first move will be to find a new place to lay his head. He never had trouble with that before. If he settles into a comfortable situation he might forget all about us."

"You don't believe that."

"No," Hollis said. "No, I don't believe that at all. But he doesn't really know anything, Butch. More than anything else, he was needling you. I didn't spill your life story to him. I said you were in some trouble up north and needed a place to get back on your feet. That's it. I didn't mention the police or the syndicates. He might put it together, but I don't see how. You didn't make the papers down here. I haven't heard a thing on the radio. And Lionel's not from the city. He doesn't exactly have friends. He'll need to get settled, as I said, and then he'll have to start asking questions. If he's determined, he'll figure it out, but it won't happen fast."

"What'll happen to you if the gangs find out I'm staying here?"

"Hard to say. I'm not particularly useful to them. I'd imagine the only threat I have to worry about is if I'm around when they come after you."

"Then I shouldn't be around."

Hollis stepped away from the counter and placed a hand on Butch's shoulder. "Don't be silly." He forced a weak smile that made him appear even sadder.

The sensation of Hollis's fingers pressing on the fabric of his jacket and the muscle beneath ran through him, warm and reassuring. Butch felt a strange and sudden urge to step forward and wrap his arms around the man, but he fought it back. He didn't understand the connection he felt to Hollis Rossington, but he knew better than to encourage it. He needed to know the necklace's secret, if it had one, and then he needed to go.

"Truth is," Butch said, "I'm having no luck with that list you gave me. I'm pretty certain the necklace is a dead end. I'm heading back out after I grab some lunch, but if I don't come up with something, it'd be best if I got out of here."

"Give it some thought," Hollis said. "I'm heading up for a couple hours of sleep before I have to go in to the club." He lifted his hand from Butch's shoulder and clapped him on the back. "Don't let that prick get under your skin. He's a manipulative and utterly miserable kid, but he isn't the genius he thinks he is."

"Yeah," Butch said. "Okay."

Except the uncertainty and fear persisted. He knew he should have handled things differently with Lowery. He didn't need any more enemies.

• • •

THE man's name was Seward. He was a short and slender man with a neat thatch of white hair that gently receded from his brow. A crimson velvet bow tie clashed with his blue seersucker suit, but the effect wasn't wholly awful. If anything, it added to the man's impish appearance. Seward's shop, a retail nook hardly larger than the room in which Butch stayed, stood between a tobacconist's and a haberdasher's on Decatur Street near Canal. In his small hand, Seward held the necklace. He lifted it close to his eyes and then pulled it away as if a change in focus might reveal something astounding.

"What do you think?" Butch asked.

"I think you're on the wrong track," Seward said. His pinched, nasal voice was so pronounced, it sounded like a put on, like a radio comic impersonating a child. "You're speaking with jewelers and the like, but not everything has an obvious value."

"I don't understand. Do you know what it is?"

"No sir," Seward said. "But that doesn't mean much. Like I said, you could be on the wrong track." The diminutive shopkeeper eyed Butch through his lashes and frowned. "You don't look like the sort that puts much stock in the otherworldly."

"Come again?"

"The supernatural. The occult. Alchemy. Mysticism."

"If you're asking me about the spook rackets, no I don't think much of them."

"Can you accept the notion that other folks think very much of them?"

"Sure," Butch said. "People waste their time with all kinds of horseshit."

Seward's lips curled, and Butch realized he'd made another mistake. The shopkeeper, the first one to do more than rush him out of the shop, was offended, and Butch had done the offending.

"Regardless," Seward said, "there are a number of organizations the world over who are devoted to the investigation of and are in service to the *horseshit* you referenced."

"I'm sorry about that. I—"

Seward clucked his tongue and held up a hand. "No need. No need. The ignorance of the masses is what gives these organizations their power. I know of only a handful, and by 'know,' that is to say I have heard of their existence, though their specific practices are unfamiliar to me. It's clear that you feel this object is incredibly important, though it appears to have less than no value. As such, it could be assumed that you—or one who has influenced you—believes the object is precious, perhaps even immensely powerful in the right hands. So I would suggest you discard your current list. There are really only three people you need to speak with. If what you've got there is a talisman or a spiritual icon, one of these three will know it."

Seward retrieved a sheet of lime-green notepaper, and he removed the pen from the holder on his countertop. After dipping the pen tip in ink he began to write.

"Thank you," Butch said.

"Eh, now, don't get too excited. You may find you're holding onto nothing more than a bit of scrap. And I'd suggest you refrain from comments about horseshit and the like. The people on this list are believers. They won't feel particularly generous to some bull who starts crashing around their respective china shops. Show them a bit of respect."

"I will. Thank you."

"You're welcome," Seward said. "And give my regards to Hollis. He's a fine gentleman. I'm glad to learn he's done away with that Lowery fellow. Nothing but darkness around that boy."

Butch readied himself to respond, then realized he had not mentioned Hollis at all to the man. He certainly had said nothing about Lionel Lowery or his recent eviction from Hollis's home. Had Hollis called ahead to grease wheels with the shopkeeper?

"It's not all horseshit," Seward said. He smiled warmly and his eyes twinkled. "Good luck, Mr. Cardinal, and I promise your secrets are safe with me."

"Yeah," Butch said uneasily. He backed away from the counter. "Sure."

"One more thing," Seward said.

"Yeah?"

"Despite what you've been through and what you will go through, there is still joy in the world. Don't argue yourself out of it, and don't let others take it away. For most men, joy is the only magic they will ever know."

"Okay, sure," Butch said, feeling the cryptic message worm its way into his mind.

He turned and lifted his hand in a wave. Then he fled the shop.

Chapter 24
Top of the Morning

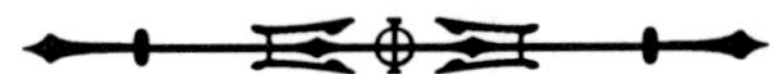

Rory Sullivan's wife, Maureen, had been dead for the better part of a decade, but still her face greeted him every morning when he woke. Smiling uncomfortably, she peered at him from a silver frame. Maureen had been a beauty, but cameras brought her panic. She hated the idea of having her image captured, frozen, unchangeable. Once she'd told Rory that she imagined being trapped in a picture, paralyzed and forced to see the world from a single angle for all of eternity.

Maureen had a lot of strange thoughts, and he remembered these as fondly as he remembered the curve of her hips and the shape of her ear-lobes.

It was five A.M., and as was his custom, Rory left his bed and went to the bathroom. He splashed his face with water and using his palm sluiced it over the crown of his head so that he could tame the tangles of white hair with a comb. He avoided the oils and pomades that were all the fashion, because he thought they made men look too polished and because they invariably made his scalp itch.

He dressed in gray trousers and his favorite green shirt, a gift from his daughter Molly.

At his chest of drawers he paused and looked over the box of cash he'd spent the previous evening wrapping in butcher paper. Once the police had given up watching Butch Cardinal's apartment, Rory had let himself in and made his way to the loose board in Butch's floor. To his surprise, the money Butch had stashed there remained untouched. Even more surprising was the amount: far more than he would have expected a shlub like Butch to sock away.

Rory ran his hand over the smooth paper. He hadn't addressed the package yet. Something told him it wasn't a good idea. Until he was in the post office and certain he hadn't been followed, he would refrain from writing Hollis Rossington's address on the box.

His concerns weren't imagined. Rory knew he was being followed by at least two parties, neither of whom struck him as representatives of the law. Granted, one of the guys, a young kid who'd pretended to push papers outside of Butch's apartment house and had sniffed around the exterior of the gym a few times, hadn't shown his face in a couple of days, but the other one, the older guy, was still on Rory's tail. He'd seen the old guy at the Indianapolis train station on the evening he'd traveled south to retrieve his car, and he'd seen the same man a day later, sitting in a Packard at the end of the block. The guy played it casual, pretended to read his newspaper as Rory passed on his way to the bank, but he'd recognized the cruel face under the fedora.

Likely enough the men were hoping Rory would lead them to Butch, but that wasn't going to happen. He might never see his friend again. Mailing the package to New Orleans might well be the last contact he ever had with Butch. He couldn't say the thought didn't sadden him a good deal, but he knew it was for the best. Likely his friend would be on the run for the rest of his life, and that life would prove very short if he didn't lay low. Besides, Rory had Molly to think about.

In the kitchen, he smeared strawberry jam on a thick slice of bread and carried his breakfast downstairs to the gym, which he opened promptly at six every morning, except, of course, for Sundays.

He opened the back door and took a moment to let the scent of the place waft over him. The average Joe might only detect pungent sweat and leather and liniment and rubbing alcohol, but the odors transcended simple sensory stimuli for Rory. Those mingled scents comforted and summoned nostalgia; they spoke of the past and of the future. These were the scents that had perfumed his youth when wrestling was a respected sport. Back when athletes, not ridiculous show-biz hulks, entered the ring to pit strategy and muscle against one another. Back before the fixes and the flashy exhibitions. Those were the days when a man like Butch Cardinal would have shined, but he'd missed the era by a good number of years. He'd begun when the *sport* of wrestling had given way to the *pageants* of wrestling. Sad. No life for an athlete. As for the future, which Rory also detected in the mixed odors, he considered a Spanish boy named Manero, who trained daily with Marfus Cole. That Manero kid had the bulk, the dexterity, and the strategic mind that would raise him above the typical grappler. He had himself a fine future if he learned to ease off the gin.

Rory crossed through the unlit changing room and walked over the mats, headed for his office. With everyone pinching pennies and asking Rory to run them tabs on their workouts, he had had to trim corners. The lights stayed off until he was ready to open, and even then the gym remained in gloom. Half of the fixtures hanging from the ceiling were without bulbs.

He fixed coffee and sat in his chair and bit into the jam-frosted bread. Ten minutes later, he had finished the meal and poured himself a cup of coffee. He placed the sign-in ledger on the counter outside of his office, and he had his cash box—empty as it was—unlocked and ready to receive the day's receipts.

The back door opened and closed with a *thack* that startled him, and he considered the possibility that the overly-curious strangers had decided that following Rory wasn't enough. But more than likely, Rory's daughter had come downstairs with a question.

"Molly?" Rory called.

Lately, his daughter had taken to waking nearly as early as he did. It wasn't uncommon for her to check on him mornings when he was alone in the gym. She was worried about him, what with all of the interest bad folks were taking in his friendship with Butch Cardinal. He'd even caught her standing in the alley behind the building one morning, holding the Colt pistol he'd kept in his nightstand, because she thought she'd seen a suspicious man.

Rory didn't approve of guns, generally speaking, but the weapon had been given to him by a beat-up old boxer who couldn't afford to pay Rory's daily gym rate. Rory would have let the unfortunate pugilist use the facility for free out of professional courtesy, but he knew it was an issue of pride for the man, so he'd accepted the weapon and then promptly put it away. After the incident with Butch, he'd told his daughter to hold on to the weapon, and he'd given her two dollars to buy bullets and to have the weapon inspected and cleaned. He didn't want the thing blowing up in her face.

"Molly," he called a second time. He left his desk and walked into the darkened room. Facing the back wall, the heavy bag and the ring were to his left. On his right were medicine balls, dumbbells and barbells. The tumbling mats were at the back, near the entrance to the changing room.

He looked over the familiar shadows and then focused his attention on the archway across the room. A shadow too large to be Molly's entered the opening and then passed through.

"We're not open yet," Rory said. His voice echoed like the whispers of ghosts against the high ceiling.

A soft padding of footsteps in the right corner sent chills over his shoulders. He knew every inch of the gym. The intruder was walking past the low rack of dumbbells. The footsteps stopped, and the silence was worse. Rory couldn't tell if the man had ceased moving, or if he'd managed to mute the sound of his shoes on the floor. The possibility that the prowler was creeping closer through the gloom sent a drum roll through Rory's chest. He backed up, making his way to the light switches on the wall beside the front door. When his shoulders bumped the plaster, he reached out and turned the switch.

Paul Rabin barreled across the center of the gym. Of course, Rory did not know the man's name. He only knew him as the cruel-eyed stranger from the train station, the guy who sat in a Packard at the end of the block. A small black gun led Rabin's way like an accusatory finger. His face was hard-carved with determination, and he cut the distance between them in a matter of seconds before pressing the muzzle of his gun to Rory's temple.

With his wide mouth and pronounced brow, the intruder reminded Rory of a jowly, aged Frederick March. But the man was no silver-screen star putting on a show. Everything about the man, from his earnest, cruel eyes to his obvious strength, told Rory that Rabin was built for violence.

"Greetings," Rabin said. "No games now, Paddy. I left all my patience in a hospital room."

"Is that a joke?" Rory asked.

"You're a quick one," Rabin said. "Where is Butch Cardinal?"

"I don't know," Rory replied.

Rabin's eyes flashed with a furious light. His lips pulled in tight across his teeth. "That's a lie. You only get one."

"Why don't you put down that gun and fight like a man?"

Rabin's face flickered with amusement and he exhaled hot breath over Rory's cheek with a growling hiss. He hissed a second time before saying, "That's one idea. Would you like to hear mine?" Rabin ground the gun barrel into Rory's temple. "My idea would be to put a hole in your head and then go upstairs to fuck your daughter with my knife. How's that sound?"

The statement, brutal and vulgar, shocked Rory so badly his skin went cold and shriveled tight to his muscles. He closed his eyes so he wouldn't have to look at the madman, so he would have a moment to think clearly. A level of savagery was to be expected from a man like this, but the glee behind Rabin's words and the raw animal hate that suffused that glee like venom were unnatural. Rory felt as if he were facing a cobra, a rabid dog, or a shark. Reason was beyond this creature, and knowing this hollowed Rory out.

"You strike me as a close family," Rabin said. "I'll bet she knows exactly what you know, but I might have a better time getting the information from her. Can you imagine me slipping a hunting knife into her—"

"Stop it," Rory whispered. He still had Molly's first pair of shoes, the first ribbon Maureen had ever tied in their child's hair. This monster had no right to share the same world with Molly, let alone the same room. He would do anything to keep Rabin away from her. "She doesn't know anything."

"Then tell me what I want to know. Point me to Cardinal and I'll save the good stuff for him."

Rory opened his eyes. The face in front of his had lost its crazy contortion. Instead, it rested in a serene, even bland, expression. But the eyes were cold and dark and threatened to pull Rory into their depths like twin wells, hard-edged and bottomless. "He's in New Orleans," Rory said.

His thoughts jumbled and frayed. They blurred. Guilt stabbed through the haze, but he'd had no choice. The man was threatening to force horrible things on Molly, and there wasn't a doubt in Rory's mind that the killer would follow through on them. He thought about his daughter—he had to protect her—and about Butch, for whom there could never be enough apology now, and he recalled memories of his wife and his great battles in the ring, and through it all, he heard a child's voice, his voice, reciting the Lord's Prayer as he'd once done every night before bed.

Our Father in heaven,
hallowed be your name.
Your kingdom come…

"New Orleans is vague," Rabin said. He twisted the gun barrel painfully into the soft skin at the side of Rory's head. "Give me the name of a hotel. Give me an address."

"I don't know," Rory said. "I don't know."

"How much of your daughter's blood would it take for you to remember? Maybe a flood pouring from between her legs? Hmm, Paddy? You think a flood would do it? It'd feel good on my hands." Rabin licked his upper lip with a flicking tongue. "It'd feel great on my cock."

Rory silently begged Butch to forgive him, and then he prayed his Lord would show similar pardon. "He's not in a hotel. He's staying with a friend. Hollis Rossington. He lives at—"

A gunshot filled the room with deafening noise. The blast silenced Rory's frantic babbling, and he squeezed his eyes closed, certain that Rabin had decided to end his interrogation. But Rory felt no pain, no sudden lurch from a bullet's trespass. When he opened his eyes, he didn't see Rabin. He saw Molly. Standing on the far side of the gym, aiming down the barrel of the Colt he'd given her.

"Son of a bitch," Rabin rasped at his side. The shot had sent the killer spinning into the wall.

Molly fired a second time. A spray of plaster rose up from where the bullet hit the wall, equidistant between the heads of Rory Sullivan and Paul Rabin.

Then Rory was being shoved forward. Rabin's arm wrapped around his neck and a sharp point, like the tip of a spike, pressed under his chin. He didn't know what had become of the killer's gun, and though he felt a moment of gratitude to know Molly was safely distanced from the animal, the point at his chin meant the threat to Rory was still very present.

The hard muscle of Rabin's chest pushed against his shoulder blades. The killer's blood, hot and wet, seeped through the back of Rory's shirt.

"Holy mother of fuck," Rabin said into his ear. "I forgot how much this hurts."

"Let him go," Molly called, positioning the gun so that it seemed to be aimed at Rory's forehead.

"Unlock the door," said Rabin. He squeezed his forearm against Rory's windpipe. "Do it or I'll kill you both before I drop."

Molly cried, even though the face beneath the tears showed ferocity and resolve. Her hands shook violently, making the gun barrel bob and nod. Rory couldn't count on her saving his life again…or her own.

He reached out and turned the bolt lock on the front door.

"Don't," Molly called. "Don't you let him out."

"Think of her blood pooling on the floor, Paddy. Think of the things I'll do to her," Rabin said. His breath wheezed hotly on Rory's neck. "Open the fucking door."

He did as he was told and turned the door handle, throwing it wide to let in a gust of freezing air. Rabin walked him forward, and then the arm left his neck and the point was gone from beneath his chin. Ahead, Rory saw Molly's face contort with dread. She screamed. Rory spun, ready to confront the man who had invaded his business, his home.

But Rabin was already halfway through the door, and he was driving an ice pick downward. The spike buried deep in Rory's shoulder. It punctured his muscle and clicked against bone, sending a white-hot bolt across his chest and turning his legs to rubber. Rory fell forward, slamming the door with his weight before his legs failed completely, and he collapsed to the floor.

Pain shot across his torso, and he knew it had nothing to do with the steel shaft sticking out of his shoulder. It felt like someone was laying into his ribs with brass knuckles, only from the inside of his chest. He imagined his heart made of glass. Shattered by the driving fist. Its edges cut and tore the nearby organs, and all of the pain he had ever known radiated from its jagged edges. He gasped for air. Tried to stand. Failed. He dropped onto his back and watched the ceiling swim and blur.

Molly is safe, he thought. *The beast is gone and Molly is safe.*

Please let her be safe.

Chapter 25
Shit on a String

The day after meeting with Seward, the shopkeeper, Butch got an early start on the man's list. The first place he visited was a house just outside of the French Quarter on Esplanade Avenue. It belonged to a woman named Mrs. Dauphine Marcoux. Bright blue paint slathered the siding of her home in an eye-aching hue. After ringing the doorbell, he fidgeted on the stoop, rocking back on his heels and making fists in his pockets. He drew his gaze upwards and noted the ceiling of the porch had been painted in a softer sky blue.

Footsteps approached the door. Butch stopped rocking and removed his hands from his pockets. When the door opened, he found himself facing a beautiful, plump Asian woman. Her hair was tied back into a loose ponytail, and she wore a red silk robe. A poorly rolled cigarette dangled from her lips. She looked as though she'd just climbed out of bed.

"Yeah?" she asked.

"Dauphine?"

The woman smirked and shook her head, releasing a thick cloud of smoke as she did so. "Do I look like a Dauphine?"

"I don't know."

"Well I don't, and I'm not." She drew on her cigarette, the end burning hot orange and fast, consuming nearly a quarter of the smoke in a single drag. Her exhalation cast a blue-white cloud around her face. "What do you want?"

Her voice surprised Butch. She spoke with a pronounced accent, but it had nothing to do with the Orient. She sounded more like a Brooklyn housewife than a China Doll, and Butch found this so intriguing he didn't immediately reply.

"Are you feeble?" she asked, annoyed.

"No," Butch said, taken aback. "I'm here to see Dauphine."

"Don't you mean Mrs. Marcoux?"

"Yes. I'm sorry."

"And what is your business with Mrs. Marcoux?"

"A man named Seward suggested she might be able to help me identify a piece of jewelry."

The woman licked her upper lip, and then plucked a bit of tobacco from her tongue with two talon-long fingernails, coated in ruby red polish. "She doesn't take visitors before lunch. And you'll need to make an appointment."

"Can I see her this afternoon?"

"If you make an appointment."

"How do I—"

"What time to do you want to see her?" the woman asked testily. She drew on her cigarette again, and blew smoke in Butch's face, waiting for his reply.

"Two o'clock?"

"No. She's busy at two o'clock. Come back at three-thirty, and maybe she'll see you. She's preparing for a trip, so you'll just have to take your chances."

And then the door closed in his face.

• • •

OVER the years Butch had visited New Orleans a number of times, but he only remembered it in darkness. Nighttime. After an exhibition bout or a meet-and-greet with local snobs who happened to be sports enthusiasts, he'd gone out to Bourbon Street, seeking the sweet drinks, lively jazz, and sociable women the city provided in abundance. Those were wonderful days.

At three in the morning he might share a plate of oysters with a young lady or a particularly entertaining drunk. He might walk the lamp lit streets from Canal to Esplanade, admiring the façades of homes and shops, none of which looked quite real to his eye—all seeming to be part of a child's toy village. One evening he stood on the corner of Chartres and Ursuline, holding a bottle of Scotch, head cocked back, counting stars. On the bank of the Mississippi River, he finished that bottle as he gazed in amazement at the motionless moon, hanging steadfastly above the rushing current. The air was scented with cayenne and cumin and cinnamon. Other nights, he joked and laughed in rundown clubs. He stomped his foot in tempo with the trombone player and the drummer who hit his skins with stripped tree branches. In a room made gray by cigar smoke, he played poker with four lawyers and a toothless old hag named Penny, who the lawyers treated with absolute reverence. He made love to a woman whose Creole accent was so thick he couldn't understand a word she said.

He had many fine memories of the city, but sunlight touched none of them.

He remembered the people being friendly and boisterous, but he had seen little of that throughout his recent visit, and he wondered if it was the night itself that brought joy to the city.

The second address on his list denoted a location on the southwest corner of the Quarter, only a few blocks from Seward's tiny shop, near the train station. Butch walked the streets in a zigzagging pattern, passing clubs that reeked of sickness and sour booze, and restaurants that pumped pure ambrosia into the air. Trash cluttered the gutters and as he approached the river he caught the dense stench of mule shit. When he reached his destination, a small antique shop with the name Mercer painted in gold across the window, he again found himself fidgeting before reaching for the handle and letting himself into the shop.

A fog of dust roiled in the door's wake. Butch coughed heartily.

On first glance, everything in the shop appeared to be common for such an establishment. Armoires, desks, leather chairs, Chinese screens, bronze and marble statuary, but as Butch looked closer at the items, he noticed oddities: a hat stand that seemed to have been constructed of bone; a chest of drawers with intricate carvings covering its surface, but no pulls for any of the drawers; an armoire that wore a wig of Spanish moss; a marble bust of a grinning man whose teeth were sharp and angled like those of an alligator; a severed arm in a glass case with a black tattoo running from wrist to elbow. The thick symbols etched in the skin meant nothing to Butch but they made his skin pucker nonetheless.

"Good morning, sir!"

Butch turned away from the painted arm. The voice had come from a counter on the far side of the shop. Behind it, a wiry little man in a white suit with oil-polished hair stood straight-backed with his hands folded behind him.

"Good morning," Butch said.

He made his way down the aisle. Though he tried to keep his attention on the man ahead, he occasionally noticed the details of the displays around him: a hand mirror ringed in what appeared to be human teeth; a piece of furniture that might have been a desk or dining table, but which more than anything looked like a funeral slab; the skull of a goat with some kind of star carved into its brow.

"Lovely morning," the proprietor said. "Might get us some rain later this afternoon, but that's a future we cannot know."

Butch smiled. Despite the questionable, even repugnant, items that filled the shop, at least he was faced with a courteous soul.

"It is a fine day," Butch agreed.

"And what can I do for you?" the man asked, pushing on the bridge of his wire framed glasses.

"Are you Edmund Mercer?"

"Indeed I am."

"I was told you might be able to help me with something."

"Something to sell? Something to buy?"

"No," Butch said. "Mostly just telling me what something is."

"I see." Mercer made it sound like the most interesting proposition he'd ever heard. "And what is the nature of this item?"

"It's a necklace," Butch said, and then added, "Well, here, I have it right here."

He freed the necklace from his collar and presented the pendant on the flat of his palm.

Mercer leaned over the counter. He pulled a hand from behind his back and asked, "May I touch it?"

"Yeah, sure."

Mercer wrapped his palm around the pendant and closed his eyes. Butch stood perplexed, wondering why the shopkeeper was holding the thing rather than looking at it. Finally, Mercer opened his eyes and released the pendant and stepped away.

"Is this a joke?" Mercer asked good-naturedly.

"No," Butch replied.

"I'm afraid it must be if you think you can pawn such a thing off on me."

"You didn't even look at it. Besides, I'm not trying to pawn anything. I just want to know what it is."

"Well, as far as I'm concerned it's a piece of junk," Mercer said. His good nature had apparently been tested. The smile vanished. Indignation rose on the man's face, a pink sheen that grew deeper as his voice grew louder. "And I have no idea why you'd think it had any value at all. It's clearly worthless, just a chunk of bronze or pewter stained red. I am a respectable merchant. I buy and sell precious items. I'm not a rubbish man. I am not a joke. I am *respectable*. Who sent you to me?"

"Okay, that's fine," Butch said.

"Did Elspeth put you up to this? This has her stench all over it. Sending you in here with shit on a string and trying to pass it off as arcane. She has always been jealous of my collection. Always! Well you can tell her I am not to be toyed with. I am not."

Butch thanked the man, though Mercer was too busy shouting to notice. He walked out of the store as the lunatic shopkeeper's voice reached a shrill, nearly incoherent screech. On the sidewalk, he smiled at Mercer's preposterous behavior. And then he chuckled, which became a laugh—a great booming laugh, like warm bubbles of amusement coursing up his throat.

• • •

ANGRY gray clouds began to creep across the sky as Butch waited for the streetcar on St. Charles Avenue. Initially, he'd been amused by Edmund Mercer's outburst. Obviously the twerp had a serious self-image problem and it took little to tease it from him. But now, on a small thatch of overgrown grass, waiting for the streetcar, he felt what little optimism he'd regained slipping away. If the necklace was garbage, as Mercer suggested—as all of the clerks at the traditional shops had suggested—then Butch was wasting his time. Marco Impelliteri had simply wanted him dead, along with Lonnie Musante. Butch didn't know why and he had no one to ask.

The streetcar's brakes squealed, and Butch climbed inside.

Arcane. Strange word. It began to gnaw at him. Mercer had used the word casually, but Butch had heard it before, plenty of times. The old broads in the spook rackets whispered it to the chumps on the far side of their crystal balls, making it sound dangerous and mystical.

As a boy he'd believed in magic. He had needed to believe in something grander than the dirty walls surrounding him, the misery on his mother's face, and the pain that came from his father's tongue and knuckles. Evenings, when it wasn't too cold outside, his sister would walk with him to the creek and she'd tell him stories. Often enough Clara recited old fairy tales—fanciful myths she'd heard in school or from their mother before their father had put an end to such things. Butch had wanted to steal Jack's golden goose, had wanted to awaken Sleeping Beauty with his kiss, had dreamed of saving Hansel and Gretel from the witch before he devoured her sweet, sticky house.

More thrilling than the stories were the times that Uncle Spencer had come to visit. Spencer worked the tracks, a conductor with the Seaboard Air Line Railroad, and while he had dozens of funny and shocking stories to tell about his travels, he also knew magic. He could pull coins from behind Butch's ears and produce fire from his fingertips, and he could always guess what card Butch had taken from the center of the deck. One evening Uncle Spencer gave Butch a rusted key and told Butch it could unlock invisible doors—doors that were hidden throughout the world; doors that entered into impossible landscapes of beauty and danger. And holding that key in his chubby palm, Butch had seen those doors. Really *seen* them. It felt like the rusted metal had been made of pure electricity and grasping it had sent signals to his brain, showing him portals made of wood and glass and gold—some over the water, others in the middle of busy streets. He had not wanted to return that key to Uncle Spencer, because it had many more secrets to reveal, Butch knew, but Spencer had demanded its return.

In ominous and reverential tones, Spencer told the story of Punjab, an ancient man from Bombay, who had revealed, before his death by enchanted poison, his otherworldly secrets to Spencer and had presented Butch's uncle with the mystical key.

Butch had worshipped his uncle Spencer, but that all changed one freezing January night. Robert Cardinal, Butch's father, drunk as he'd ever been and bleeding from a split lip, likely earned in a fight at Dingle's Tavern, had burst into the house shouting, catching Spencer in the middle of showing Butch a card trick. Robert Cardinal had ranted, knocked the table over and sent a confetti of cards to the floor.

"The deck is marked, you idiot," his father bellowed. "There are symbols on the backs and they tell him what each card is. He's not a magician. He's a fucking cheat. These are just tricks he learned to entertain the ladies. Did he tell you about that? Did he tell you about getting fired from the railroad because of that girl in Baltimore? Another man's wife, she was. A mother, no less."

His father snorted a laugh and stormed through the house, into the kitchen, leaving Butch to look for an explanation from his uncle. But Spencer just righted the table and picked up the cards. He wouldn't look at his nephew, simply muttered, "He doesn't know what he's talking about."

A long time passed before his Uncle Spencer visited again. By then Butch had put away his faith in magic, too old to believe in witches or gold-laying geese or sleeping princesses. Uncle Spencer's tricks were the last enchantments in Butch's life. Once they were gone, so was any illusion about the world waiting for him. It was his father's world. Hard as granite. Ugly as shit. And the only things of value were the things you could touch with your fingers.

He left the streetcar and in less than five minutes discovered he was lost. He checked the map several times but could not seem to orient himself in the street. The sky above had turned the color of bronze, with jaundiced lines running like infected cuts through the bulbous accumulation.

After more than an hour of searching, Butch finally found the home of Delbert Keane. It stood tucked in the back of the Uptown District like a shameful secret. The Victorian structure was tall, narrow and grim, seeming to have been painted with the same colors that currently stained the sky. A waist-high wrought-iron fence ran around the periphery of the yard, each spindle capped with a pointed spike. The yard was neat. The porch was kept tidy. But the house looked malicious, as if it had been summoned in a dark ritual, rather than built of wood and nails.

Butch let himself through the gate. As he began down the walk a man appeared at the side of the house. The man kept his head down, apparently distracted with thoughts, as he stomped to the front yard. He stopped before the porch stairs, looked up at the angry façade and put his hands on his hips.

"Mr. Keane?" Butch called.

The man lifted a hand to wave but did not turn around. He wore a white cotton shirt with the sleeves rolled past the elbows and black trousers that had accumulated bits of brown grass and dirt on his backside.

When Butch reached a point just behind him on the walk, he said the man's name again.

"Yeah, that's me," Keane said, still staring up at the house.

"My name's Butch Cardinal, and I was hoping you could help me out."

"You need something to eat? I don't got any work for vagrants if that's what you're fishing for."

"No, sir," Butch said.

"Good," Keane said. He lifted his hand and used his palm as a visor. His forearm was heavily muscled as if he'd spent a lifetime doing hard labor.

Butch found it odd the man was shielding his eyes, since there was little light in the air and certainly no glare. He looked up at the house, but could find no explanation for the action.

"I was told you might be able to help me identify something."

"Yeah, maybe so," Keane said distractedly. "How much paint you think I'll need to cover this place? Can't afford to buy a surplus but would like to get some of the dingy off the place."

"Couldn't say," Butch told him.

"Don't have much of a calculating mind myself," Keane said.

"Can't you buy it as you go?"

"Nah, can't do that, unless I use raw white. It's mixing in the color that causes the trouble. They can never get it exactly the same each time. I'd like a light walnut color, but if they mix it wrong, who knows what kind of mess I'd end up with. Don't think I'd like to live in a mottled house. But I might. Can't really say."

"I wish I could help you out."

"Not a problem," Keane said, lowering his hand. "About to get a big wet coming down. Won't be able to do much about this anyways." He extended his hand to Butch and they made a proper introduction. Then Keane asked, "What can I do for you?"

"I have this necklace."

"And you want it appraised? I don't really do that kind of thing."

"Maybe you could just tell me what it is."

Keane's eyes lit up and his brows arched. "A mystery, huh? I like mysteries. Let's go on to the back and have a sit down. I've been working in the garden all morning, and then I got the idea to paint the house, so I been walking in a circle for about thirty minutes, trying to figure how many gallons the old gal will need."

Butch followed the man around the side of the house. Behind the Victorian a wide vacant parcel of land ran to a line of low trees. Keane stopped at a small picketed gate and opened it onto a space not unlike the courtyard at Hollis's place. The backyard had been squared off with a tall fence and numerous panels of latticework. Vines covered the barriers in lush green skin. Two wrought-iron chairs with thick floral cushions sat in the middle of a flagstone court. Between them stood an iron table with tiles inlaid on its top.

"Nice place," Butch said.

"Working on it," Keane replied. He took a seat and waved for Butch to follow suit. "So what have you got? You said a necklace?"

Butch pulled the pendant out of his collar. Instead of holding it on the flat of his hand, he removed the chain and passed the whole thing over to Keane. The man gave the piece a smile. Turned it over in his hand. Bounced it against his palm testing its weight.

"And you think this is valuable?" Keane asked.

"I think someone does."

"Hmm," Keane muttered. He rolled the pendant on his palm and nodded his head. "Let's start with what it's not. There are a number of trinkets that look like very little but might actually have value. An ancient coin, for instance. If this here were currency, say Greek or Roman, you might have something. But it isn't. There are no inscriptions, no marks at all really. That tells me two things: it isn't a coin, and it isn't likely the product of a known artist. Even if it were the latter, the fact it has no signatory mark means it could never be authenticated. So that leaves a few options."

"Like?" Butch asked.

"It might be of personal value to someone. An heirloom passed down through a family with an interesting history. Or it could be an icon."

"Come again?"

"An object a coven or mystical sect would use in rituals. There are hundreds of such icons. Nearly every early culture had its charms and runes.

The Gaul. The Germanic with their Thull mythology. Pagans certainly. Even our own local brand of magic, Voodoo, comes with a set of talismans."

"So it's just symbolic?" Butch asked. Seward had said something similar to him. Talk of the occult and mysticism. "It doesn't really do anything?"

"More than likely," Keane said. He opened a metal box on the tabletop and withdrew a cigarette. Keane handed the necklace across the table. "Can I ask where you came across this piece?"

"A friend."

"And what makes you think it has any value at all?"

"Certain people seem very eager to have it."

"Really?" Keane asked. His eyebrows rose with interest. "Maybe you should leave it here. I can test the metal and see if there's something I'm missing. Check my books."

"I can't do that."

"Of course," Keane said. He quietly smoked his cigarette and looked at the sky.

With no useful information to be had, Butch grew frustrated. Keane was pleasant enough, didn't seem to be as crazy as Mercer, but if Butch had hit a dead end, he needed to turn around and get moving. "Long story short, you don't know what this thing is?"

Keane lazily shook his head. He put his cigarette in the ashtray at the center of the table and then stood. With a look of startled humor he said, "But I'm being a terrible host. Can I get you a coffee or a beer?"

"I don't want to waste any more of your time," Butch said.

"No trouble at all. I insist." Keane stood. He walked across the court, climbed the steps and entered the gloomy interior of the house.

So that's it, Butch thought. His life hadn't come undone over a charm of incomparable value; it had been bartered for a bit of junk. The only other name on his list belonged to some broad in the spook rackets, and she was going to be about as helpful as tits on a boar. Aggravation welled in him, and he considered abandoning the courtyard, leaving Keane's home, and then perhaps leaving the city of New Orleans altogether. Nothing good was going to come from remaining here.

• • •

Delbert Keane held the earpiece of the phone and looked out the window, keeping an eye on Butch Cardinal who had leaned his head back to look up at the sky. The operator told him to hold while she attempted to patch through his call to Jackson, Mississippi. His nerves jangled like a prisoner's chains and his foot tapped an arrhythmic beat on the tiles of his kitchen floor. The percolator sat on the stove's fire, but there was no coffee in the filter, because he had no interest in hospitality; he'd just needed an excuse, time to make the call.

He could never have imagined finding the Rose under these circumstances. Holding the sacred piece proved all but overwhelming, and he'd struggled to maintain his composure and the steadiness of his hand so he didn't give too much away to Cardinal. Had his lies been detected? He didn't think so.

The telephone connection snapped and crackled in his ear. Impatient, he set the earpiece on the counter and raced across the first floor of the house. In his study, he opened the top drawer of his desk and removed the knife he kept there. This he carefully slid into his belt at the small of his back, and then he returned to the phone, returned to watching his guest.

Cardinal struck him as an oddity—a man somehow incongruous with himself. Obviously, he had stolen the Galenus Rose, though he claimed to have no understanding of its power, and this claim seemed to be validated by his appearance at Keane's home (though he wondered who had sent Mr. Cardinal to him in the first place). Keane held no doubt that violence, perhaps murder, was involved in the theft of the invaluable charm, yet Cardinal didn't carry himself like a killer, certainly not a calculating, experienced murderer of men. If anything, he seemed cowed, frightened, which were emotions discordant with his obvious strength and vitality. Further, if he had stolen the Rose with some inkling of its gifts and had only come to Keane for verification or elucidation, then why was he behaving so civilly? Wouldn't he be waving a gun and demanding answers? Wouldn't he be threatening violence? Veins of peculiarity wove throughout the entire encounter. Not that it mattered. Not really. The Galenus belonged with the Alchemi. This was not even an issue for argument. Keane simply found Cardinal's behavior interesting, considering the circumstances.

Finally his call was put through, and the distant phone rang, and he checked on Cardinal again—*He looks like he's dozed off*—before a stern male voice said, "437 House. Mr. Evanston, speaking."

Delbert said hello to Ramsey Evanston, but he did not instigate the niceties of banter. As quickly as he could he explained the situation and demanded that Evanston tell him whatever he could about the theft of the Galenus and the man who had stolen it.

"That would be inappropriate," Evanston said. "That is business kept within the Alchemi and as you are—"

"He's here," Keane said, interrupting the man's overly pompous explanation. "A man calling himself Butch Cardinal has come to my home, and he has the Rose. I need information before I proceed."

The silence on the other end of the phone line left Keane listening to the crackle and hiss of the connection. His foot tapped frantically as he waited for some response from his former colleague, and his hand slid around to the small of his back to touch the hilt of his knife.

"Mr. Keane," Evanston said, finally, "Cardinal is suspected of murdering two of our associates—Lonnie Musante and Humphrey Bell—in addition to his theft of the Galenus Rose. At this time, your priority is to take possession of the Rose, regardless of the means necessary to do so. I will forward your message to 213 House. Please contact us immediately once you have the Rose in your possession."

"Thank you, Mr. Evanston." Keane hung up the phone.

His hand wrapped around the handle of the knife and he squeezed it tightly. The grip had always fitted his palm well. Keane walked to the stove and turned off the flame, and then he breathed deeply to settle his frantic nerves before taking his first step out of the house.

Chapter 26
One Single Thing

The decision to help Butch Cardinal came to Roger Lennon as he watched the sheet drop over the body of Terry McGavin, though Lennon didn't know that was the decision he was making at the time. Lennon had done as he'd promised and called the Feds, but in the hour it had taken them to get their paperwork together, McGavin had been murdered and then returned to a cell.

Like the government agents, Lennon listened to the story Detective Glaser wove with furious incredulity. After his interrogation, McGavin had returned to his cell and committed suicide by beating his head against the edge of his cot. It was ludicrous. Impossible in every regard. The Feds didn't buy it, but the sworn statements of four officers who corroborated Glaser's fairy tale meant they wouldn't bother with a costly and ultimately futile investigation. He should have stayed with McGavin until the agents arrived, but he'd been called back to Wenders' office to once again be warned against spreading his story about Curt Conrad's involvement in Lonnie Musante's murder. By the time he'd made it to McGavin's cell the M.E. was already on the scene, draping the Irishman's body in a rough white cloth.

And Lennon knew it was his fault, not for any single reason or act, but because of a pattern of behavior he had practiced for as long as he could remember. He had taken money from the Italians. He was complicit in their crimes. He was as guilty as Conrad and Glaser and every thug on the street.

He couldn't make it right, not all of it. There was no way in hell he could dismantle the Chicago machine, but if he could do something—any *one* thing—to fight the twisted system he had helped construct, then he might be able to consider himself human again.

His opportunity came after a rough, sleepless night; it came in the form of an elderly gymnasium owner by the name of Rory Sullivan.

At the station, holding a cup of coffee that tasted like one part battery acid and three parts spit and leaning against a counter dazed from exhaustion, he heard a uniformed officer mention "Ripper's Gym" in regard to a crime scene. Though he'd not been an official investigator on the Lonnie Musante case, he'd pored over the file they'd compiled on Butch Cardinal a dozen times, and the name of the gym had stuck. After questioning the officer, who seemed confused by Lennon's babbling interrogation, Lennon had deposited the mug of foul coffee on a filing cabinet and left the station.

• • •

He drove through a light snowfall to the hospital. Inside, he found the hallways poorly lit, and the stink of ammonia burned his nostrils. Lennon hurried past the information desk, waving away a question thrown his way by the bald old man behind the desk. He didn't need directions. All crime-related victims ended up on the second floor in the west wing of the hospital, unless they went directly from the emergency lobby to the morgue. The officer had said that Sullivan took a shiv to the shoulder and had then proceeded to have a heart attack, but he was alive or had been two hours ago.

Lennon jogged up the stairs and turned left on the landing. Immediately a shadow fell over him as he passed into a short unlit corridor of stone walls. After twenty feet the hall opened into a ward with only slightly better illumination. He stopped at the nurse's station and asked for directions to Sullivan's room.

When he stepped into the room, a beautiful young woman with blue eyes, red hair and a murderous look accosted him. She lifted her hand and held it firmly to Lennon's chest.

"You can just keep yourself in the hall," she said. "My father needs his rest."

Over her shoulder Lennon saw Rory Sullivan lying motionlessly on the bed, bathed in a cone of sickly, yellow light. A gray blanket covered the lower half of his body. He wore a sleeveless hospital gown, revealing thickly muscled arms, lined with pronounced veins, and were it not for his current location and prognosis, Lennon would have thought the man an exceptionally healthy specimen, but with his lips parted, and his eyes closed, he could have been nothing more than an impressively formed corpse.

Lennon returned his attention to the young woman. He introduced himself and learned that her name was Molly. "I'm with the Chicago Police Department."

"All the more reason for you to leave him alone." She crossed her arms over her chest and glared, daring him to try getting past her. "I've told your friends everything there is to tell. My father needs his breath for living."

"Then you'll have to tell me."

"I don't *have* to tell you anything."

"I see it differently," Lennon said. The sleepless night had frayed his nerves and he found himself overly aggravated with the woman's attitude. Normally, he knew how to manage a beautiful woman, but rarely had the type he'd met exhibited such strength, and while he might admire the trait, it was seriously grating behind his eyes. He tried to think his way out of the anger, but his temper scratched the inside of his skull like a rat trying to escape.

"See it anyway you please," Molly said, fixing him with a scowl. "Now, get out of my father's room."

Lennon shot out his hand to grab Molly's arm. He'd shake the information loose if he had to. But he didn't get that chance.

Molly snapped her arm across her body in a smooth, powerful swipe that knocked Lennon's hand away before he could fix his grip. Then she slid to the side and with a motion that looked like an underhand toss, she planted her hand in Lennon's crotch and squeezed until he doubled over. Nausea rolled around his gut and began climbing his throat.

Anger and embarrassment joined the sick feeling that roiled in his belly.

"Enough," a weak voice said from the room in front of him.

"Dad?" Molly said, turning her attention away from Lennon, whose nuts she still held in her hand. "You're awake."

"Mmm," the old man agreed. "I wish those were flowers you were holding."

Molly turned back to Lennon, who was about to drop to his knees. Mortification blossomed across her face. Quickly, she snatched her hand away, and Lennon could breathe again.

He leaned back on the doorjamb and gasped in the stink of ammonia. A steady pulse, like drum beats, filled his ears. Over the years he'd grown uncomfortable, even contemptuous, of his wife's compliance. Looking at Molly Sullivan, he knew a woman like this would never ask his permission for...well anything, and despite the ache in his groin, or rather because of it, he found himself admiring the young woman for more than her milk-white skin, fine bones, and a body of movie star proportions.

She crossed to her father's bed and asked, "Why won't you leave him alone?"

"Best listen to her, son," Sullivan whispered, his voice quiet but harsh as gravel. "She'll change your tune—baritone to soprano in under a second."

"I noticed," Lennon said. He tried to smile to make light of having been bested by a woman, but the expression felt false and he let it fade. "But I'm trying to help Butch Cardinal, and I think you have information I need."

"He's with the police," Molly said—a warning to her father.

"Then we have nothing to say."

He's a smart one, Lennon thought. If he were in the old Irishman's position, he'd keep his mouth shut, too.

"Will you at least tell me what the man who stabbed you looked like?"

"I gave a description—"

"I know. But I don't want anyone at my department to know I'm looking into this. I don't much trust them myself."

Molly cast a look at her father, who was rolling his head all but imperceptibly on the pillow: *No.*

"You set him up," Sullivan croaked. "Butch was a good guy, a gentleman, and you've thrown him to wolves."

Lennon knew that Sullivan was speaking in general terms. By "you" he meant the whole crooked brotherhood of the Chicago Police Department, but Lennon took it personally.

"I need to get a doctor. They'll want to know Dad is awake," Molly said. "And you need to leave. Come on."

She grabbed his arm, much in the way he'd attempted to grab hers before she'd shown him how little she liked the idea. Yanking at him, she tugged until he quit the bedside and followed her into the hall. Once there, she led him away from the room. Near the end of the corridor at the top of the stairs, she whipped around and fixed him with an ugly glare.

"He's in New Orleans," she said.

"Cardinal?"

"Yes," she told him. "He's staying with a man named Hollis Rossington. I don't know the address. I don't know anything else about it."

"So you believe me?" Lennon asked.

"No," Molly said. "The fact is, I don't care. I don't give two goddamns about Butch Cardinal, but I want you to lay off of my father. He nearly died this morning—twice. So if telling you how to find that muscle head will keep him safe, then I'm happy to tell. But if another one of you thugs tries to strong-arm my dad, and I don't care if you're wearing gray flannel or blue wool, I will get my gun and lay you flat."

"Duly noted," Lennon said. "And the man who shot your father?"

"Old," Molly said. "Not as old as dad, but getting there. Around fifty. Average height, maybe on the short side, but stocky, and as crazy as a snake on a stick."

Lennon thanked her. She scowled at him and set off to find a doctor, leaving him alone to consider what she'd told him. She'd provided a familiar description for her father's attacker. But if the man worked for Impelliteri, Lennon didn't know him, which meant he wasn't one of the usual hitters on the Italian's crew; he was something different. Outside talent? A lunatic Marco Impelliteri kept crated until a special case presented itself?

"Crazy as a snake on stick," he muttered. The term made him smile.

Lennon started down the stairs. He slapped his hat back on his head and began thinking about New Orleans.

Chapter 27
Killing Grounds

In the far south of the city, Paul Rabin lay on a hard, cold table. The man hovering over him, Dr. Louis Somerville, poked and prodded the hole in Rabin's side with a cold shining instrument and hummed a popular tune that Rabin couldn't identify. Rabin swam in and out of lucidity, riding waves of morphine up toward the shockingly bright light, and then back down to a gray murk of random thoughts and images. When he was lucid, his mind absolutely clear, he considered his actions of the past two days—the boy, the cop, the Paddy. Those attacks worried him in that they suggested a loss of control, something he found unacceptable. He'd always been rational when performing his services for Impelliteri and others. Calm and precise. But his conversation with Irene had sent him tumbling; her words had stripped away his carefully maintained character, sending him back to the feral, reckless days of his youth. Before her revelation, he would never have allowed someone to sneak up on him while he was working. For that matter, he never would have casually stood and conversed with the neighbor of a victim, giving her time to analyze his face. As a boy, making a reputation, he'd exhibited such ridiculous arrogance, but he'd thought those days were long gone. Buried. To see them return so virulently was unsettling. He needed to cage the monster again. Needed to rebuild his mask.

"Went clean through," Dr. Somerville said. "I'll get you stitched, and after a couple of weeks you'll probably be fine as frog's hair. My only concern is that the bullet may have nicked the liver. Nothing I can do about that. I just do quick patches."

Somerville began humming again. He indelicately slapped a wad of gauze against Rabin's side and fixed it in place with a broad ribbon of tape. Then he helped Rabin roll onto his stomach, where the hard tabletop pressed against his jaw. Instead of watching the doctor, Rabin closed his eyes. He felt a tugging at his skin as the doctor sutured the exit wound but no real pain.

He slipped deeper into the morphine. It was warm and fluid, like a bath in mud, and memories swam there, sliding up to Rabin and revealing themselves before being pushed away, covered, and replaced by some other long-ago moment. Men died, kneeling before the muzzle of his gun. Men died, tearing their necks apart with fingernails as they tried to loosen Rabin's rope. Men died, surprised by the cold and efficient shaft of his ice pick. A dozen lives on the end of his knives. A dozen more keeping his bullets warm.

And Rabin wandered the street fair, holding Irene's hand. Smiling. All around them, nondescript people paraded up and down the blocks. Children ran through the shifting forest of legs, and they shrieked their pleasure to the brisk evening air. Irene looked at them with joy in her eyes, perhaps imagining a mother's future. Rabin squeezed her hand, as if to assure her he shared her hope for parenthood. His façade, carefully constructed and wholly convincing, covered him like armor. They stopped for glasses of beer and Irene cooed at a cheap brooch made from tin and glass. It lay on a black cloth, which fell over the merchant's table like velvet in a jeweler's display. On the far end of the table, Rabin saw a hunting knife. Its thick blade twinkled though it was late evening and there seemed to be too little light for such an effect. Rabin grasped its ivory handle and held the weapon in the air.

Then his bones and organs and muscles came apart. Every molecule separated, leaving him as a dense cloud, though still able to hold and to control the knife. Irene looked at him and clapped her tiny hands together. Smiling. Rabin felt his cloud-body expand and contract and begin to wring itself. He moved like a tornado into the crowd. Happy children. Young lovers. The aged and the frail. They passed before him and they fell behind him. Up and down the block he flew, rising and falling like a child's balloon on heavy currents. Ahead of him, Butch Cardinal crouched, arms out in a typical grappling pose, and Rabin wondered how he might recognize a man he'd never met, and then he remembered a photograph in a newspaper. And then he didn't remember it at all. He knew Cardinal because he'd always known him, was fated to know this opponent. Beside the wrestler, Marco Impelliteri held out an envelope. The gangster's head was lowered and the brim of his hat concealed the man's face, but it didn't matter what expression rode his flesh. It would all be paste soon enough. Rabin shot toward the two men and in moments they disappeared into a frothing cascade of blood and meat. Then he continued through the fair, leaving holes and bloody lines on everyone he passed, and in seconds, no time at all, he again stood before Irene. The knife in his hand had transformed into something red and pulsing and alive. Irene swept her head from side to side, observing her husband's handiwork.

No longer suitable for carriages or pedestrians, the streets had become an abattoir. Blood, made black by moonlight, painted the heaps of meat and clothing littering the pavement. Across from the trinket table, a woman sat propped against the wheel of a mule cart. Her eyes were gone, leaving pits that spilled tar black blood down her cheeks. In her arms she held the headless body of a child.

Smiling, Irene pressed her palms together under her chin as if in giddy prayer. She turned to Rabin and said, "I love you."

Chapter 28
Into Fire

The clouds rolled overhead, great black foam shot through with steel-gray veins. Though he had dozed for a minute or two, to daydream about beaches and sunlight, a sudden, piercing dread brought on by a momentary recollection of Lonnie Musante's murder—the twig-snap sound of the gunshots, the blood—flooded Butch's system with adrenaline. He sat up in the chair in Delbert Keane's courtyard and rolled his neck to loosen the muscles there. As he did so, his host emerged from the house, scratching his back with his left hand. His right hand was empty.

"No coffee?" Butch asked.

"It'll need another minute to perk," Keane said. "I didn't want you to think I'd forgotten about you."

"You really shouldn't have gone to the trouble. I should be on my way."

"Don't be ridiculous," Keane said. He had reached the bottom of the stoop and was walking toward Butch, still scratching at his back with his hand. "Stay."

"You've done enough. Thank you, Mr. Keane." Butch stood and held out his hand to shake that of his host.

"You misunderstand," Keane said. He pulled his hand away from his back. Gripped in his fist was a knife, unlike any Butch had ever seen. Layers of sharp planes wove and jutted like flickering silver flames from the handle. "I can't let you leave."

"Son of a bitch," Butch said. He had been ready to leave the property believing the charm in his pocket really was nothing but shit on a string as the shopkeeper, Mercer, had told him.

He slid to the side so that the heavy iron table with its tiled surface separated him from Keane.

The man gripped the edge of the table and knocked it away. The metal frame clattered. Tiles soared free and shattered on the rock.

"We're not done, yet, Mr. Cardinal," Keane said. "And I'm not letting you leave with the Rose."

In the middle of his patio garden, beside the upturned table and chair, Keane crouched in a fighting position. His knife moved with subtle fluidity as he stirred the air with the flame-like blades.

Butch backed up a step and planted his feet. Already the gears in his head were clicking into place. He understood fighting. Though he felt uneasy about his opponent's weapon, he was on familiar ground for the first time in days.

"So you *do* know what this thing is?" Butch asked.

"I know it doesn't belong to you, and I know you've killed men, my associates, so that you could steal it. I also know that you are going to give it to me and face a tribunal for your crimes or you're going to die where you stand."

"I didn't kill anyone, and I didn't steal it."

"The tribunal will decide what you did or didn't do." Keane stepped forward. He slashed the blade through the air, waving it like a conductor's wand.

Butch examined the situation. He checked his immediate surrounding for resources and settled on the heavy chair he'd just vacated. With a smooth pivoting motion, Butch scooped up the chair and launched it at Keane's legs. The wrought-iron frame cracked against the man's shins, sending him tumbling to the stone patio. This gave Butch the opportunity to move in, but Keane recovered quickly, rolling backward and getting his feet under him. He again took a fighting stance, facing off on Butch.

He needed to keep Keane off balance. He stepped wide with his left foot. Keane did as expected and moved his right foot back, which also drew his fighting arm away. Now Keane would have to reach across his own body to slash. It wasn't a dramatic advantage, but it meant Butch would have more reaction time when Keane attempted to cut him.

"What is this Rose supposed to do?" Butch asked.

"That knowledge stays with the Alchemi."

"The what?"

Keane shook his head. "You don't know anything, do you?"

The man lunged forward, sidestepping the chair. He drew the knife low across his waist and when he neared Butch, he whipped it upward. Butch saw the trajectory of the attack and bent backwards and to the side. The tip of the knife cut through his shirt and nicked his chest. Head filling with the familiar rush of adrenaline, Butch spun out of the way, and Keane's second attempt missed him completely.

As he backed away from Keane a scorched scent reached Butch's nose, and he discovered it came from his own body. The edges of the tear in his shirt were black. They smoked. He felt the sting of blisters rising at the sides of his minor wound. He didn't know what to make of it. Had Keane heated the blade on the stove fire?

Keane, his mouth set in a determined frown, came for him again. He held the knife low as he charged. Butch hurried backward until his back pressed against the wall of ivy on the far side of the patio. When Keane was within four steps, Butch faded left and then danced to the right. The bluff worked. Keane turned toward where he thought Butch would be and yanked the knife upward with a vicious slash, drawing a black line along the green blanket of ivy. Bits of vine, smoking and with embers burning at their cut edges, dropped to the patio and smoldered.

From the side, Butch threw a left jab and connected solidly with Keane's jaw. He followed with a battering right to the man's eye, and though Keane wavered, he propped himself against the wall and remained on his feet. Butch moved in and reached for the man's wrist to get the uncommon blade under control, but Keane touched his blade point to Butch's forearm. It scalded like hot grease and Butch relinquished his grip and backed away as Keane came slashing at him. Distracted by the man and his knife, Butch nearly tripped over the wrought-iron chair he'd thrown at Keane, but managed to keep his balance.

At this point, Butch knew something about his opponent. The man was armed, but he was not an expert with his weapon. If he had been, Butch's wounds would have been far more severe, or he'd be lying dead on the patio. The fact the man was a lefty threw him. Even though the attacks were easy to predict, they came at uncommon angles and Butch had to recalibrate his thoughts to them. Still, he knew he could win this fight but he needed to keep that blade off his skin.

He lifted the chair and held it in front of him like a trainer taming a lion. It occurred to him to once again throw the chair and use Keane's distraction to make his escape, but the man recognized the necklace; he might have the information Butch needed to stay alive, so he couldn't just run. Not yet.

"How about you give me the Rose?" Keane said. "Then you can walk. We *will* find you, but you could consider this a reprieve."

"I don't think so," Butch said. "Not until I know what it does."

Keane leaned to the right then dodged to the left, but Butch anticipated this fake and he kept the chair between them. Sweat covered the older man's brow. His eyes ticked wildly from side to side looking for a hole in Butch's defense.

"You don't even know what you have," Keane said. "Why die for it?"

"That's the question I keep asking, but no one's answering it."

Butch stepped forward with the intent of backing Keane to the wall. Up to this point he'd let the man lead the fight, but it was time to get this situation under control. Keane went where Butch herded him; he kept the knife up and checked his periphery to make sure he didn't trip as he backed to the wall. Finally, realizing the corner he was facing, Keane dodged to the left and Butch lifted the chair high and threw it, putting all of his strength behind the toss.

The iron chair crashed into Keane's head and the back of his neck. The concussion sent the man sprawling to the flagstones, and the knife skidded away from his hand, coming to rest against a bit of shattered tile from the tabletop. Butch ran to the weapon and lifted it. Once his palm secured around the handle, needles of electric charge shot up his arms, and he experienced a moment of dread, briefly believing the knife had been booby-trapped. Except he knew this feeling; it was the same buzzing current he'd felt holding a key given to him by his uncle Spencer, only instead of seeing an array of doors, Butch saw a series of people who came and went in rapid succession. He didn't know these people, yet he did. He knew that they'd all fallen victim to the blade, knew it as surely as he knew his own name. Men and women. The guilty and the innocent.

Butch shook off the intense reaction, and the faces behind his eyes vanished. He checked on Keane, who lay face down, moaning, and then Butch looked at the knife still thrumming in his hand. The arcing blades shifted and rippled. More than ever he had the impression of metallic flames flickering from the broad handle. He couldn't make sense of this anomalous weapon but, just as he'd known the faces in his head had belonged to victims of this knife, he knew the dagger was his. It was an extension of his arm, no different from fingers or thumb.

He righted the chair and then hoisted Keane by the collar of his shirt, all but dragging him to the seat. Keane slumped forward, nearly collapsed. Butch placed the sole of his shoe on the man's chest and pushed him back so that he sat upright in the chair, and then he waited for the man to come fully around.

Keane did so slowly. After several minutes, he reached up and cupped the back of his head. He moaned. His chin dipped as if he were again succumbing to grogginess. Finally, he pulled his head up and his eyes focused.

"What am I in the middle of?" Butch asked.

"I…I don't…"

"Tell me about the necklace. You called it the Rose? What is it supposed to be?"

"Not…for you…" Keane said. His speech was slow. Muddled. "Only the Alchemi…"

"Who are the Alchemi?"

Keane frowned. He closed his eyes.

Butch removed his foot from the man's chest and leaned in, grabbing his shirt with one hand and placing the knife in front of Keane's face with the other. "I am not fucking around," Butch said. "And I'm sick of this mysterious mumbo-jumbo. Now tell me something I can use."

Keane opened his eyes and peered at the knife. His frown deepened until he wore an expression of immense sadness. "It dances for you," he said. "It never danced for me."

Butch glanced at the blades, and saw that Keane was right. The metal seemed to have turned soft, all but liquid, and the blades undulated and rippled like flames on a hearth. "Tell me about the necklace."

He yanked on Keane's shirt to get his attention, but the man was fascinated with the ripple of the blades. Butch repositioned the knife, taking it away from the man's face and pointing it at his chest. He needed his attention, but already he saw tremendous distance in Keane's eyes.

"So many years and it never danced for me," Keane said. "Never for me."

A tear appeared and slid down the weathered cheek, and the older man began to cry. He clutched the arms of the wrought-iron chair, and his face collapsed into misery. Shallow sobs sent tremors through his body as he stared at the ground, unable to stop the morose outpouring.

"What the hell is this?" Butch asked.

The sight of a man crying unnerved him. A man wasn't supposed to behave like a disappointed child. He shook Keane, thought about slapping him or maybe using the tip of the knife to scald him back to his senses.

Instead he shook the man again and said, "Hey."

"I spent my life studying the metals, learning their secrets, but they never lived for me. And you—an accident, a blind and ignorant accident—for *you* they dance."

"Put away the bullshit," Butch said, "and tell me about the Rose."

"You'll find out," Keane said. His knuckles were white on the arms of the chair. "Soon enough, you'll know more than I was ever allowed to know."

With that, Keane pushed himself forward onto the knife. It passed into his chest as easily as a pin entering wet clay. Convulsions shook him. The scent of burning skin and hair poured thickly from his pierced chest. He threw his head back in agony, mouth gaping open. Butch stumbled away, leaving the knife wedged between the man's ribs. In an instant Keane's clothes ignited in flame; they burned like paper, revealing skin already bubbling with blister. Blast-furnace hot, the gusting air pushed Butch farther across the patio. Amid the consuming fire, Keane's skin blackened and cracked and fat reduced to clear bubbling streams sizzled through the fissures. Fire erupted from his open mouth and burned through his eyes, creating puddles of flame in the sockets, and the stench of roasting meat grew thicker, cloying. Disgusting in its savory aroma.

For a time, Butch could do nothing but look on in stunned silence as the flames consumed Keane. They rose like a pillar around the chair and the man seated in it. The knife handle remained visible like a sturdy branch protruding from a rushing orange river; the body that held it was shriveled, sunken, and charred. Butch turned from the pyre and ran.

Chapter 29
The Cold City

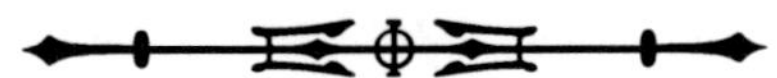

Mr. Hayes stood on the balcony of his hotel room. Bitter afternoon wind sliced his cheeks and neck. He peered over the city—a filthy place. Soot and the fat of rendered meat covered the buildings in grim paste. His spirits had been low for days. The death of Mr. Bell and all that had followed—preparing the body, waiting for an intern to arrive from 213 House by train to collect the car and the macabre bundle stored in its trunk, writing the report to his associates—were exercises in draining morbidity. He didn't sleep well, unable to push away thoughts of Mr. Bell's last living moments (*How horrible they must have been*) and he'd begun to feel a persistent haze clouding his mind as he moved through the days. Mr. Brand was similarly distracted, and this too added to the problem. Guilt as thick as the filth covering the downtown buildings had settled on Hayes for having ordered his colleague to remain in this city, away from the woman he loved, who was about to find out her brother had been murdered. It was an ugly business and one that didn't leave sufficient room for compassion.

At his back, the door opened and Mr. Brand stepped onto the balcony. He held one of his daggers in his withered hand and a polishing cloth in the other.

"213 House just rang," Brand said. "They reported a call from 437 House in the South. Delbert Keane, a former associate, told them that he'd found Butch Cardinal, said he'd seen the Galenus Rose."

"Keane?" Hayes asked.

"He's an associate who left the Southern Home a number of years ago. Outside of research, he showed only a sliver of talent. When it became clear he could not attune himself to the metals, he retired to New Orleans. That's where the call came from."

"So he has the Rose?"

"They don't know," Brand said. He rubbed the edge of his knife with the cloth. "Keane said he was going to take it from the wrestler. No word since. 213 House received the call a little over thirty minutes ago."

"Did Keane leave the Alchemi in good standing?"

"He was not dismissed, if that's what you mean. Not like Musante."

"Thank you, Mr. Brand. You should begin packing your things. I'll go to the lobby and retrieve the train schedules from the concierge."

"I'm going to kill him," Brand said, speaking about Butch Cardinal. He eyed Hayes, as if challenging his associate to protest.

But Hayes had no intention of protesting. "I know you will," he said. "Now, please get your things together. We may have to leave when I return."

Brand stopped polishing the blade of his dagger. He appeared uncertain, eyeing Hayes with suspicion, something that should never rise between them. But Brand knew Hayes was a stickler for procedure, and killing the wrestler might or might not prove warranted, depending on the circumstances. Hayes knew his partner had expected a lecture, a recitation of rules and regulations, but he didn't have the strength to even feign commitment to Alchemi policies on the matter. Anyone who could subject a boy like Humphrey Bell to such agonies was beyond the protection of procedures. More than likely Cardinal would need to be killed in order to retrieve the Galenus Rose, but whether need entered the equation or not, Hayes felt the same as Brand. He wanted the man dead.

Chapter 30
Violent Sport

Rain poured in hissing sheets. The storm had begun after Butch stepped onto the streetcar and it had intensified steadily during the brief ride. Butch trembled but not from chill. The wounds on his forearm and chest stung something fierce, but these didn't preoccupy him either. His thoughts were filled with flame and confusion. The scent of cooked meat remained in his nostrils, and he thought it might never fade. Keane had brought about his own death. Butch had been no more responsible than a desk drawer in which the blade could have been wedged for Keane's suicide, but he felt guilty and, standing in the streetcar, gripping a strap so tightly his hand ached, he believed everyone sharing the trolley had been a witness to the crime—*his* crime—and they simply waited for the right moment to accuse.

He should have kept the knife. That was the thought that continued to circle in and around his paranoia. The weapon held power, or he'd given the weapon power, Butch didn't know. He just knew he should have had the thing tucked into a pocket, close to him.

Holding that knife had woken something. Seeing what the blade had made of Keane, cinder and char, had recalled his childhood and a brief encounter with magic, but it was more than that. He'd felt the knife unite with his palm, felt it become part of his body. Unless he had completely lost his senses, Butch was not only a witness to magic, but also an instrument of it. He'd felt no such union with the necklace, the bauble Keane had called the Rose, but it must carry a power of its own—a secret like the inferno harbored in the knife's blade. Butch reached into his pocket and wrapped his palm around the charm and squeezed, hoping to feel a communion with the cool metal, but no bolts of charge worked into his palm. Not so much as a tingle of static.

Battering rain met him as he stepped off of the streetcar. He jogged across the road and continued running, sidestepping gray pedestrians and their black umbrellas and splashing through low puddles as he hurried back into the Quarter. Taking shelter in the lobby of a hotel, Butch saw by the large clock behind the front desk, that he still had two hours before his appointment with Dauphine Marcoux, an appointment he could no longer imagine keeping. His nerves hummed miserably. He felt sick. He needed time to think. Time to recover from the sight of a man burning alive.

If only he'd gotten more information from the man. There was no doubt in his mind now the Rose meant something, perhaps had a power equal or greater to that of the blade, but the nature of the thing remained a mystery. And what of the Alchemi? Keane had spoken of the outfit like they were famous and important. Another gang? Another pack of predators on his heels?

If that proved true, then the progress he'd made with Keane amounted to a step forward and down. He knew something more about the ugly piece of jewelry, but he had also discovered this new threat: the Alchemi. As if the cops and both sides of a Chicago street war weren't enough.

The men behind the hotel's front desk leaned close to one another to confer. Butch assumed he was the topic of conversation. Figuring he had enough trouble at this point, he pushed on the door and returned to the rain.

• • •

HOLLIS's home was unnervingly quiet when he entered. In his room he stripped off his suit jacket and his shirt, and then realized he had no change of clothing. The wound at his chest, two inches long, had cauterized instantly, but blisters had formed at its edges. He touched these. Winced. A single red welt, hardly a burn at all, marred his forearm where Keane had pressed his blade. The injuries were a minor annoyance, likely to heal in no time at all. But he couldn't leave the house in his ruined shirt. He was still a wanted man, and the last thing he needed were eyes lingering on him, putting together violence and his face.

Hollis must have spare shirts upstairs, Butch reasoned. He climbed the spiral staircase and crossed to Hollis's bedroom, where he found the man standing before a wardrobe. He wore only a pair of hunter-green trousers and smiled as he saw Butch in the doorway.

"Got a deluge, huh?" he asked.

"Sure," Butch said. Hollis's powerful musculature, despite having softened over the years, remained impressive, and Butch found himself distracted. Having always been as smooth as a child above the waist, he found himself fascinated by the density and richness of the hair covering Hollis's torso. When he realized he was staring, he forced himself to look away. "Yeah."

"Happens a lot this time of year," Rossington said. "I imagine you didn't find the umbrellas in the stand downstairs?"

"No, I left early. Wasn't thinking about the weather."

"What happened there?" Hollis asked, indicating the wound on Butch's chest with a nod of his chin.

"An accident," Butch said. A momentary flash of image startled him. He saw Keane on the end of a knife, flames guttering up around his chin, shooting like fountains from his eyes.

"As long as you're not badly injured. You've spent enough time using this place as a hospital room. It's about time you started enjoying your visit."

Though he saw no chance of that, Butch thanked him.

Hollis crossed the room and eyed the wound closely. "Are you sure you're okay? This looks nasty."

"No, I'm good," Butch said. The scent of Hollis's shaving soap put him off guard. It was a familiar brand. Butch used it himself. His father had used it. He took a step back. "I was just wondering if you might have a spare shirt? Mine's about done in."

"Of course," Hollis said. "I should have realized you couldn't wear the same clothes day after day."

Hollis displayed good spirits for the first time since Lowery's departure. His smile was friendly and his eyes were lit with the anticipation of having an enjoyable project ahead of him. He crossed the room and clapped Butch on the shoulder. His chest brushed lightly against Butch's arm as he did so. "I have some suits from a few years back that might just about fit you."

Butch's face went red. His heartbeat stampeded up his throat and into his ears.

"I really just need a shirt," Butch said. "The suit will dry okay."

"Don't be silly. Any luck with that list I gave you?"

"A bit."

"So you've found something?"

"Nothing concrete," Butch said. "But I think I'm on the right track."

"Well, fine," Hollis said. "I keep my older clothes, the ones I wore before my gut took over, in the room at the end of the hall."

Butch followed his host into the hallway. Hollis gave him a crisp white shirt and a fresh collar, and the man chatted amiably as Butch changed into the garment. As Butch examined a rust-colored tie, Hollis said, "I was thinking of taking a night off from the club."

"Yeah?"

"I thought we could use a night out. A *gent's* night. We can forget about this Chicago business for a few hours and gab about the ring."

"Sure," Butch said. "Sounds good."

Hollis slapped him on the back again. "Excellent. We'll have supper at Galatoire's and see where that takes us." Hollis retrieved a forest-green fedora with a brown band from the shelf of the armoire and handed it to Butch. He then reached into the back of the wardrobe and removed a matching trench coat. "And be sure to take one of the umbrellas from the stand if you're going back out. These rains can go on for days."

"Thank you," said Butch, fitting the hat on his head. It sat well on his brow, but he'd gone without wearing one for so long it felt awkward, restrictive. "But I think I'm in for the day. Haven't quite shaken the bug. I'll see you at dinner."

"I'm looking forward to it," Hollis told him. "Good luck."

After Hollis left the bungalow, Butch rested on the guest-room bed and stared at the ceiling. The sight of Delbert Keane's last moments played behind his eyes, but it wasn't alone there. In addition to the despondent man's suicide, Butch thought about Hollis, about the way the brush of his chest had brought a flush to his face. Keane's shirt erupted in flame. Hollis Rossington grasped him by the arms and pulled him close. Fire plumed from a dead man's eyes and firm lips pressed against his as a strong hand slid down his belly and…

Seward had told him that he could still find joy in the world; that for some men it was the only knowable magic. For *some* men that might be true, but Butch knew that additional magics littered the world. He'd seen them. He'd felt them. But in that moment on a bed in Hollis Rossington's home, he believed that joy might be the one magic that would undo him completely.

Chapter 31
Bleach

Death makes angels of us all.

Lennon thought this as he slammed the highball glass down on the polished counter of the bar in the banquet room of McMaster's Chophouse. The room was full. Beneath the chandeliers and between the finely paneled walls, the place brimmed with police officers and low-level city officials, all of whom had turned out to celebrate the life and commiserate the death of Curtis Michael Conrad. All evening, whispers had been running through the room that the chief of police and the mayor would be attending Conrad's funeral and making speeches. If that were true, the planting ceremony tomorrow would be a circus. Neither of the officials had known the detective; both were likely memorizing his name or jotting it down on note cards so they didn't embarrass themselves. Conrad had little in the way of blood relations, at least as far as Lennon knew. He had mentioned a brother in Milwaukee, a furniture salesman if Lennon remembered correctly. No wife or kids. That made the politicians' jobs all the easier because they wouldn't have to share the microphone with civilians, men and women who weren't part of the big machine, normal people who might not be able to lie with such abandon.

The bartender dropped ice in Lennon's glass and then covered the cubes with a hefty pour of Canadian whiskey. Nodding to the bartender, he took the glass and turned back to the throng. So many black suits. So many polished shoes on the expensive crimson carpet. So much bullshit. They were supposed to be the city's protectors, upholders of the law, and yet they stood around guzzling illegal booze, using it to toast the passing of a murderer.

A bland looking young man whom Lennon found vaguely familiar walked up and shook his hand and offered his apologies for Lennon's loss. "Those fucking Paddies are going to wish they'd never been born," the young man said. "Curt was one of the best. A fine detective."

Lennon agreed and then excused himself. Obligation had brought him to the wake, but he wished he could find a place to hide, wished he could grab one of the whiskey bottles and vanish into a corner, so he could observe the ridiculous scene rather than be a part of it. He wanted to be on a train. He should have been on his way to New Orleans to find Butch Cardinal, to warn him. The urge to do something to strike back against the mockery this entire night represented, to throw the smallest wrench into the big machine's gears, burned in his chest. But he couldn't leave before the funeral. No way. There was no excuse good enough to get him out of that, not as the partner of the murdered man.

A round man with a bad toupee waddled up and stuck out a palm. Lennon heard more wonderful things about Curt Conrad. The porker in the cheap wig called Conrad "Upstanding," and "Dedicated," and "An example we should all aspire, too." Lennon wanted to laugh in the man's face, or maybe punch him in the throat, anything to shut down the torrent of unadulterated shit spilling over his plump, wet lips.

All evening, he'd thought that there had been some mistake. The stories and condolences and the wishes for a peaceful rest couldn't have anything to do with the crooked son of a bitch who'd skulked through the station unshaven, more times than not with a drop of crusted egg yolk on his tie. A man who bragged about leaving bruised whores in alleyways once they'd finished him off. A man who hadn't done an honest day's work in years. A sloth. A slob. A murderer.

In death, Conrad had become a symbol of courage and honor. Hell, he'd become a fucking martyr. It was ludicrous, and it was disgusting. The entire façade confounded Lennon. Everyone in the room, or nearly so, knew that Conrad had been dirty. Many of them knew the darker streaks that ran beneath the grimy film of his personality, and yet they played this game. Why? Was it true generosity of spirit that compelled them to speak so highly of one so low, or were they simply wishing that others would say equally kind things of them when they went to the grave? With the mayor in attendance tomorrow, it was a certainty the press would be on hand, and they would spread the lie of Conrad's valor across the state, possibly throughout the country, and a murderer would be mourned and heralded and those who remembered him would remember the name of a saint. Death was bleach and it burned away the stains, leaving nothing but white.

It makes us all angels, he thought again. *What a crock.*

Across the room, Captain Wenders spoke with Detective Glaser. The two men were already drunk, smiling, leaning on one another as they shared stories. Wenders looked up and noticed Lennon and his smile faded. He nodded solemnly and lifted his glass, a silent toast. Reflex caused Lennon to return the gesture, and then he veered left and lost himself in the crowd. But this was a mistake. Men gathered around him, patted his back, filled his ears with more manure. It occurred to Lennon that he was the closest thing to a widow Curt had left behind, and as such he was being given the full treatment.

Late in the morning, he'd received a wire from Edie, saying that she and the girls were settled in nicely but she wanted to come home. Lennon had crumpled the telegram and dropped it in the trash. He missed Bette and Gwen, missed them terribly, but he didn't want them in the house either. With everything hanging over his head, he couldn't imagine being a kind father.

Lennon guzzled the remainder of his drink, hoping to excuse himself from the group to get another. Someone at his side insisted Lennon stay. "I'll get that for you," a man said with so much sorrow in his voice it made Lennon grind his teeth.

There was no escape. His life—work, home—had become a rash. It covered him from head to toe, and Chicago offered no quarter from the prickly discomfort.

Tomorrow he'd be on a train to New Orleans. He'd leave the charade and the machine behind. He didn't know if he could help Butch Cardinal, but it was enough for Lennon, at least in that moment, to know he was going to try.

Chapter 32
Where Have All the Good Times Gone?

Hollis Rossington and Butch Cardinal wore evening attire—dinner jackets and white waistcoats. Each had parted his hair impeccably, smoothing it against his scalp in sleek, oiled sheets. The large men cut impressive figures sitting at the table against the wall. Neither of them smiled. If anything, they seemed awkward in each other's company, though they did their best to hide it.

Similarly well-dressed patrons occupied the other tables in Galatoire's front dining room. Chair legs scraped over the small, white, hexagonal tiles. Hushed voices, like distant surf, murmured. The *click* and *clink* of silver on china and glasses meeting in toast, created a soft, syncopated rhythm. Enchanting scents from the kitchen and from fine cigars wafted through the room, and though the restaurant was lovely and the appetizers exceptional, Hollis found himself disappointed.

He'd expected something different from the evening. Galatoire's was Hollis's favorite restaurant, but all of the fond memories he attributed to the setting couldn't breach the crust of disenchantment. Though he could hardly afford the extravagant restaurant, he'd thought a night out would loosen up his friend, get his mind off his troubles, but Butch had carried his distracting concerns across the Quarter, and they'd dropped down in the chair with him. Though the clothes Hollis had given him looked quite fine, Butch fidgeted with discomfort, running his fingers under his collar and rolling his shoulders as if trying to dislodge something captured beneath his jacket. They'd already consumed salads and bowls of a delicious turtle soup, but Hollis had yet to engage Butch in easy banter. All of the talk of the "good old days" had never emerged, despite his numerous prompts.

"What do you think of the place?" Hollis asked, hoping to rekindle the conversation.

"The food is good. Thank you," Butch replied.

"I'm glad to see those clothes fit."

"Yeah," Butch said. He leaned back in his chair and folded his hands in his lap. Then he swept his gaze around the room. He seemed to have a difficult time looking at Hollis.

"Is something wrong?" Hollis asked. "I mean, I know a hell of a lot is wrong, Chicago and all, but is something else going on?"

Butch's eyes lost focus. He appeared to be staring off into the distance, rather than simply across a table. When he spoke, his voice was restrained. "It's been a long day," he said.

"But the list proved useful?"

"Yes."

"Then that's good," Hollis said with a smile.

"Yeah," Butch said, but remained distracted. A prolonged silence followed, in which both men drank from their water glasses and wiped their lips with their crisp white napkins. They busied themselves with the formalities of dining to fill the awkward moments. Hollis considered a number of topics of conversation, but all died in his throat as he struggled to form phrases that would introduce the subjects without jarring his companion.

Then Butch leaned on the table and asked, "Do you believe in magic?"

Clearly Butch wasn't as concerned about making jarring statements.

Of course Hollis didn't believe in magic. He'd seen the local voodoo nonsense paraded in the faces of tourists and superstitious old women, but he no more believed a needle in a doll would make his neck hurt than he believed a potion would bring him love. He never said these things out loud, because he lived in a superstitious city, but Hollis considered himself a rational man, well grounded, and though his philosophies might not have been conservative or even moderately acceptable to America at large, magic played no part in them.

"You don't," Butch said.

"It's not that simple," Hollis said. "We believe the things we need to believe to get through the day. For some that means there's a god watching their every move, judging their behaviors and threatening punishment. Others believe they interact with their gods, believe they can influence their deities with rituals and gifts. I think it's all bunk, but that doesn't mean it doesn't have power. Believing a thing, *really* believing it, makes it real on some level."

It appeared that Butch didn't like this answer. His face sagged and he looked around the room. "I need a drink," he said.

"They only serve in the private rooms," said Hollis. "I couldn't get a table."

"It's okay," Butch said. "A belt would grease my tongue is all." He ran a finger under his collar and scratched at his jaw. "What I saw today, Hollis, it wasn't a trick or a vaudeville illusion. It couldn't have been. I see this thing and I realize I don't know a damn thing. I've been outmatched since this started, you know, and I pretty much figured I wasn't going to slip the hold. I knew that from day one, but now I don't even know what kind of game I'm playing, let alone the rules."

"What did you see?"

"I'd rather not go into it," Butch said.

"You can't tip that cart in the middle of the street and then just walk off. What did you see?"

"Hollis, you don't want to get involved, and I don't want you involved. It's better for us both if don't get mixed up in this."

"I'd say I am mixed up in this."

"And I wouldn't. I appreciate the hospitality, but the less you know the better."

Hollis thought that was horseshit, but he wasn't going to waste the whole evening trying to pry information from the man. Things had been awkward enough between them.

"But it's about the necklace?" he asked.

"Everything is," Butch said, "but it isn't. I mean, it's all connected."

"You're not making this easy. But let me see if I've got this straight. The bottom line is once you find out what the necklace is, what kind of value it has, you can use it to clear your name?"

"My name is never going to be clear, Hollis. Even if I get out from under the Musante rap, the life I had is over."

He was probably right about that. Once a scandal got stuck to you, guilty or not, you were pretty much sunk. You didn't get a second round.

"Even so, the necklace is key. If it's valuable you have leverage. If it isn't... Then what?"

"I lay low," Butch said. "There are a hundred towns I could disappear into if I had to. Even here I'm relatively safe, depending on that Lowery kid."

"So you're planning to stay on with us for a while?"

"We'll see," said Butch.

Their entrees arrived. Both had ordered the prime rib of beef, and they set into their steaks as the waiter refilled the water glasses and removed the ashtray from the table.

After dinner, over cigars, Butch said, "So how do you know Rory?"

Hollis coughed on smoke and reached for his water as Butch clapped him lightly on the back. "We actually met after a bout I had with Simm," Hollis said.

"You wrestled Simm?" Butch asked. His brows knit and his jaw went tight.

"Early in both of our careers," said Hollis. "That son of a bitch about took my head off."

"The stranglehold?"

"Yeah, he put that hold on me and I tried every which way to slip it. But I dozed off like a baby with a full tummy. Couldn't turn my head for a week after that."

"Did Rory teach you how to get out of that one?"

"Nope. He just brought me a drink and some BC Powder, told me to get a new trainer."

"Did you?" Butch drew on his cigar and held the smoke in his mouth.

Hollis shook his head. "I...did...not. Two weeks later, Rory dropped me with the same hold."

Butch laughed at this, sending a cloud of smoke over the table. Hollis hadn't heard the man laugh before and it was a rich, deep-down chuckle that boomed in the high-ceilinged room. Ashing his cigar in the crystal tray, Butch said, "I never got to wrestle the old guy."

"It was like trying to move a boulder. Rory was some kind of solid."

"By the time I saw him, he'd lost a lot of his speed," said Butch. "He still had the strength, but he moved slow and didn't have the flexibility. I'll bet he was something to see in his prime."

"He was that."

For a time the meal took on the tenor of the evening Hollis had wanted. They talked about the ring, about opponents they'd both faced and those they'd never had the chance to meet. Hollis warmed to the conversation, as did Butch, but the man's enjoyment seemed to come and go, perhaps replaced by thoughts of magic or a tenuous future over which he had little control. The oddest moment of the night came as they finished their cigars.

Across the room a waiter set light to the contents of a silver chafing dish, likely cherries jubilee or perhaps a bananas foster, and as the alcohol burned the flame rose high, much to the delight of the restaurant's patrons, most anyway. Hollis turned to Butch to note his reaction to the scene and was surprised by the look of dread and awe drawn across the man's face. His eyes were large and held fear, as if he thought the flames alive and predatory. The expression only lasted a moment and then passed, but Hollis thought there was something to it, something about the fire.

"Everything okay?" asked Hollis.

"Fine," said Butch. "Everything is fine."

• • •

THE umbrellas proved insufficient to their task during the return trip to Hollis's bungalow. By the time they reach the gate, both men were soaked from the waist down and their socks squished in their shoes. Butch, who had spent the better part of a week in one form of discomfort or another, hardly minded. Though he could not shake the sight of Delbert Keane erupting into flames, a scene he imagined would always be very near the surface of his thoughts, he was feeling considerably better physically. The fine meal had helped. So had the conversation as it allowed Butch to thumb through good memories, memories of the sport, of the ring, of the men he'd called friends before they'd uniformly turned their backs on him.

Beneath the balcony, both men shook out their umbrellas and laughed at the state of their drenched attire. Hollis told Butch he had a bottle of decent whiskey to help get the chill off. "I'm going up to change out of this soaking rag." Butch remained outside, listening to the marching rain and observing the big house across the courtyard. The building loomed, enormous and dark. Though he knew a teaming city went about its business beyond the high and shadow-drenched walls, Butch felt a sense of pleasant isolation. They were alone here. Anything that happened here would be between Butch and his host. Anything said need never leave these walls.

In his room, Butch stripped out of his wet clothes. He draped the trousers and his drawers over the back of a chair. He hung the jacket from one of the bed's posters. He wrung the socks out into the porcelain bowl on the nightstand and then laid them out on the windowsill. Butch took the silk robe from the armoire and draped it across the bed. At the mirror, he smoothed down his hair and checked his teeth for scraps of food. Once he felt sufficiently dry, he wrapped himself in the robe and left the room.

He hadn't heard Hollis coming down the stairs, so Butch was surprised to see the man in the parlor, already holding two glasses of whiskey. Hollis had changed into dove-gray pajamas and a thick crimson robe.

"Nights like this I wish I had a fireplace," Hollis said. He handed a glass toward Butch. "This should take the edge off, though."

Butch accepted the glass and touched it to Hollis's before downing the contents in a single slug. Hollis chuckled at the display and reached to take the glass back. "It's going to be an early night if you keep that up."

At the tall silver cart, which served as the bar, Hollis set down his drink and Butch's empty glass. Butch stepped forward with feet that felt as if they'd been dipped in lead. Hollis chatted as he poured another drink, but the words were lost on Butch. He could only hear the sound of blood rushing to his ears. The whiskey's warm trail led to a coal burning low in Butch's gut. At Hollis's back he laid a hand on his host's shoulder. Hollis turned, and Butch grabbed the lapels of his robe, squeezing the fabric tightly in his fists, wringing it. Surprise widened Hollis's eyes, but before the man could voice concern, Butch pressed forward and kissed him.

When their lips touched, the roaring in Butch's ears intensified, became deafening. His heart kicked hard behind his ribs, and it felt as though he couldn't breathe. Hollis's beard tickled the soft skin between Butch's lower lip and chin, and the feeling proved intensely sensual. Hollis's hand went around the back of his head, holding Butch tightly in the kiss. Butch kept his grip on the lapels of Hollis's robe, choking the material between his fingers and keeping a narrow gap between their bodies.

Then Butch shoved Hollis away, but he maintained his grasp of the man's robe. He held his host at a distance. His elbows were locked and his arms strained.

"What's wrong?" Hollis asked.

Butch felt his features tighten. Nothing was wrong. Not really. But he couldn't help but admit, "I don't really know how all this works."

The comment brought a soft smile to Hollis's lips. He nodded. "The first thing you might want to do is unlock your elbows and maybe take it easy. We aren't opponents here."

"Yeah," Butch said, releasing his grip and letting his hands hang at his sides.

They stood facing one another, and the pause unnerved Butch. It gave him time to think, and he didn't want to think. He wanted to feel and forget about the rules and judgments he carried like scars. The kiss had consumed him, silenced the rational thoughts, but they were creeping back in. Fears and justifications knotted and uncoiled and wormed behind his eyes. He didn't want to be a punk. He wasn't one. He wasn't like Lionel Lowery. Hell, he wasn't like Hollis. This was a moment, physical and hungry and necessary. It wasn't a way of life. He didn't want it to be a fucking way of life, but he wanted this moment. Why was Hollis just standing there? Why didn't he say something? Why didn't he *do* something?

"This won't end well," Hollis said.

"Who fucking cares?" Butch asked.

He tramped forward and backed Hollis to the wall. He placed his hands gently on Hollis's shoulders and squeezed lightly before he pushed in for a kiss, and this time he didn't pull away. Hollis slid his hands around Butch's back and embraced him. Butch moved in even closer, pressing Hollis hard to the wall, experiencing the density of the man's chest against his. He felt the rigid shaft of Hollis's cock through the fabric of his pajama trousers, and he ground his hips forward, rubbing his own erection, which had escaped the silk robe, against Hollis's. Butch stepped back and pulled open Hollis's robe, then he lunged forward to reattach his lips to the man's as his fingers worked the buttons of the pajamas free. Every breath brought the scent of shaving soap and salt.

Hollis shrugged out of his robe and then reached down to untie the sash at Butch's waist. Butch slid a hand over the soft hairs on Hollis's belly and then gripped the waistband of his pajamas and worked them over the man's hips. And when Hollis was completely exposed with only the lapels of his pajama shirt draping either side of his torso, Butch buried his face in the man's neck and wondered at the powerful sensation of having Hollis's body against his.

They made their way to the couch and Hollis reclined. Butch lay over the top of him and immediately returned to rubbing against the man. He felt Hollis's hands on his buttocks, holding firmly and pulling to encourage the aggressive massage, and when Butch felt himself nearing climax, he rolled to the side for fear of bringing the encounter to an end. Hollis rolled too so that they were face to face. Butch took in the man's face, its strength and kindness, and he experienced a moment of complete peace. His passion had ebbed only a fraction, but his concerns were absolutely gone. His thoughts were clear. His body felt light, yet sensitive to every fiber of the sofa, every hair on Hollis's chest. Butch closed his eyes. A moment later, he felt Hollis's lips pressing softly against his.

Later, after both men had climaxed, they lay on the sofa with Butch on his side and Hollis on his back. Propped up on his elbow, Butch rested his hand on Hollis's chest.

(*And now,* Hollis thought, *he'll make his excuses and go to bed and in the morning, he'll be angry or deny the act outright, maybe he'll manage to figure out a way to blame me for what happened. He'll pull some shit. That much is for sure. Men's opinions changed about three seconds after their sacks emptied.*)

Butch scooted and adjusted his frame on the sofa, but he found the two of them only fit on the furniture together if they were stacked or laid out on their sides. He threw a leg over Hollis and did his best to reach the floor without disturbing the man. At the bar cart, he lifted the glasses of whiskey Hollis had poured and carried them back to the reclining man. He offered Hollis the glass. Hollis thanked him and raised himself to a sitting position.

"Thank you," Butch said, clicking his glass against Hollis's.

"Sure," Hollis said. (*This is it. Now, he escapes to build his excuses.*)

After taking a sip of the drink, Butch rubbed the back of his head. He yawned. He said, "I'm going to head into bed."

"Okay," Hollis said.

Butch couldn't help but notice a flash of emotion—What was it? Anger? Sadness?—skipping across Hollis's face. The expression came and went too quickly for Butch to identify. It was probably nothing. Butch couldn't think of a thing to be angry or sad about.

"You coming with me?" Butch asked.

Now Hollis looked surprised. Again, Butch couldn't figure the why of it, but it wasn't as if he were in familiar territory right now. In fact he'd rarely been in territory this strange. The brief moments with his cousin and the longer, though admittedly one-sided, exchanges with the Weeping Clown bore little resemblance to what he and Hollis had shared. He wondered if he was meant to retire on his own. Is that how this worked?

"Or are you going upstairs?" Butch said.

"No," Hollis said. He lifted himself from the sofa. He went to the cart and grabbed the bottle of whiskey.

In bed and propped against pillows they enjoyed their drinks in silence. Butch rested his hand on Hollis's thigh, tracing patterns in the hair with his fingers. Aware that the curtains were open, Butch climbed from the bed and crossed to the window. Before he tugged the drapes together he asked, "Who owns this place? I haven't seen a soul in the big house since I arrived."

"And you probably won't," Hollis said. "A kid named Travis Brugier owns the property. And when I say kid, I mean it. He can't be but about seventeen years old, if that. He used to frequent my club. He liked it. He liked me and he offered me this place a couple of years back once he'd had it refurbished. I've seen him half a dozen times since then. He's always traveling. Even when he's home, you wouldn't know it."

Butch closed the curtains and returned to the bed.

"You have to realize how surprising all of this is," Hollis said. "I mean I didn't think you—"

"Didn't think I was a sissy?" Butch asked. He rolled his head along the wall and looked at Hollis. "Me either."

"You think we're sissies?"

"Doesn't matter what I think. Right here…right now…in this bed, we're two men who've found a good way to get along. But we get out of this bed and leave this house and we're a couple of fruits, and there's no arguing out of it."

"So what happens when you get out of this bed and leave this house?"

"You're the one that said this wouldn't end well."

"You got me there."

"So why don't we worry about how this ends when it's over?"

"And you're okay with this?"

"Hollis, I'm not drunk, at least not yet. I'm not insane. I made a choice and acted on it, and right now it feels like the best choice I could have made, but I'm not that Lionel kid. I don't know much of anything—not about this. I'm supposed to believe it's wrong, but right now I don't. Tomorrow I might. I have no idea. But when I said thank you, I meant it. It's the only thing I'm certain of right now. I'm grateful for everything you've done for me, and I'm happy you're in this bed. So thank you."

"That may be the smartest thing you've said since you got here."

"Don't get used to it," Butch said. "Smart isn't really in my wheelhouse."

"I'm glad it happened," Hollis said, "and I'm glad Lionel is gone."

"Yeah, about that. I feel like a horse's ass about what I said that first morning, considering how we just spent the last hour. I don't really know how this happened... It's not like... I mean, I don't think I was jealous of the kid. I wasn't thinking about any of this when we spoke, but I know I was insulting to you, and I'm sorry."

"I expected you to hightail it out of the parlor when we finished up."

"I've done that before." He read the surprised expression on Hollis's face and said, "Those were very different circumstances."

"I'm looking forward to hearing about them."

"Maybe after another whiskey."

He finished his drink and handed it over to Hollis for a refill. When Hollis handed him the refreshed glass, Butch tipped some of the whiskey onto the man's chest. Hollis flinched. He moved to wipe the booze off of himself, but Butch stopped him. "I'll get it," he said and leaned over to lap the alcohol up, allowing his lips to press deeply against the brush of hair and the firm muscle beneath.

Chapter 33
Like Postcards from a Snake Pit

1

Beneath a cone of brilliant light from the surgeon's lamp, Paul Rabin stands with a knife lifted over his head. The doctor, Somerville, is on the table now, and his chest and belly are opened. Shreds of skin and shirt cotton hang from shattered ribs and drape into the glistening scarlet cavity below his neck. The red matches that leaking through the white pads of gauze affixed to Rabin's abdomen and lower back. The expression on Rabin's face is one of curious wonder.

2

On the second floor of a mansion, miles from the crowded snowy streets of Chicago, Marco Impelliteri sits on the edge of a bed. On the floor at his feet, a lavender duvet lies wadded on the carpet; the discarded coverlet resembles the corpse of a bulky man. Marco's head is down and he rests his face in his palms. He wears a dressing gown that is cinched tightly at the waist but has fallen open, draping one leg as if his knee were pushing aside a curtain to make a grand entrance. Behind him on the bed, his daughter lies on her back, staring at the ceiling. A trail of tears glistens, running from the corner of her eye to the tip of her ear. Her nightgown is gathered at her thighs.

3

A hospital room. Molly Sullivan stands in the doorway, facing away from the bed and leaning against the jamb. Her head is down. Shoulders slumped. The spill of her thick red hair arcs across her shoulder blades like a smile. Rory Sullivan lies on his back. His eyelids are parted, but only enough to reveal a vacant stare. His mouth is open and his upper lip has pulled back, receded to reveal a glimpse of teeth and gums, and it looks nothing like a smile at all.

4

Police Captain Wenders is seated in his chair. Two government agents dressed in charcoal gray suits, neither youthful in countenance, sit across from him. Between them is Wenders' walnut desk, the top of which is buried beneath files and papers. The Captain appears frustrated with the two men; one hand has formed a fist and is planted on the littered desk; the other is extended and points to the office door; his flabby jowls are tinged red; a spray of saliva hangs between his contorted mouth and a heap of documentation, on which sits a file bearing a name: *McGavin.* A yellow triangle of paper, the edge of an envelope, juts from the lip of the desk drawer beside his knee

5

Mr. Hayes and Mr. Brand stand inside Delbert Keane's house, gazing out through the beating rain. The furniture on the patio is tipped and scattered, except for a single chair, which remains upright, positioned very near the center of the flagstone court. A familiar dagger lies on the seat of the chair amid a black stain. Mr. Hayes appears calm, as if he's taking in a familiar and expected scene. Beside him, Mr. Brand is frowning with rage.

Chapter 34
Char

Hayes and Brand had arrived on an early train and after checking into a hotel three blocks from the station, they hired a taxi to take them to the address provided by 437 House in Jackson, Mississippi.

Delbert Keane didn't answer the bell. Hayes tried again and waited, and then used his pick to unlock the front door. Brand barreled into the house, shouting for Delbert Keane. He soon discovered the open back door and the suspicious scene on the patio. Though Brand had been struck silent, Hayes knew what his colleague was thinking—that Cardinal had murdered another member, albeit a tangential one, of the Alchemi. Keane hadn't reported back to 437 House after his initial call the previous day, he hadn't answered the door; those things in combination with the presence of the Promethean Blade and the charred chair made a strong case. Keane was dead, and it was a tragedy both Hayes and Brand felt deep within, but though Keane was most likely a victim in this matter, he was not precisely innocent.

"Keane must have stolen the Promethean Blade when he left the order," Hayes said, stepping into the downpour. Rain tapped on his hat and slid down the nape of his neck. "Cardinal wasn't responsible for that. The knife has been on the Lost Item list for years."

"That is what strikes you as important just now?" Brand asked.

Hayes stepped onto the patio and crossed to the knife. He lifted it, tested its weight, and felt a profusion of emotions pouring into his palm from the handle. Images and phantom voices filled his head, and Hayes closed his eyes. This was a powerful artifact, perhaps not as great as the Galenus Rose, but a truly valuable piece nonetheless. It didn't belong in Delbert Keane's possession. As he witnessed the blade's history amid short bursts of flame and smoke, he caught a vision of the weapon's last duty: Delbert Keane, his face carved with misery and regret, launching himself at the blade.

"Show me again," he whispered to the weapon. But his head cleared, leaving only traces of Keane's last moments and a newfound doubt. He handed the Promethean Blade to Brand. "You are better with these things." Then he told his colleague to focus on the knife's final impression.

Brand did as he was asked. With eyes open he moved his head up and down as if listening to music, noting each piece of information that passed from the knife's handle to his hand. Eventually his brow knit in perplexity. Brand shrugged and handed the weapon back to Hayes. "Keane sacrificed himself. Cardinal had him trapped and wanted information. Rather than telling Cardinal anything, he killed himself. Seems simple enough and quite brave on Keane's part."

The explanation was sound, and the images Hayes had seen supported the series of events Brand proposed, but he didn't believe it. Maybe it was the look on Keane's face or some other, intangible element, that had passed from the weapon into his hand, but Hayes felt certain that Cardinal had not murdered the owner of this house.

Inside out of the rain, Hayes asked that Brand call 437 House and inform them of Keane's likely passing and that they had recovered the Promethean Blade. Further he asked that Brand coordinate with their colleagues and build a list of Keane's known acquaintances in the city and any other persons of interest. Cardinal hadn't stumbled on the man by accident. Somebody had pointed him in Keane's direction. Brand, whose rage moved like roiling larvae in his eyes, nodded and went to the phone while Hayes began a search of Delbert Keane's home.

Items besides the Promethean Blade might have found their way into Keane's possession, so Hayes walked up the back staircase with the intent of beginning his search in the enormous house's attic. He would work his way down from there. Of course, searching the entire house thoroughly would take days, and that wasn't his intent. He needed to be away from Brand, wanted distance between himself and his colleague's searing temper. The man's emotions were valid, Hayes knew, but they were also upsetting and distracting. It was too easy to get caught up in them and ride the tide of fury, rather than examine the facts.

For Hayes, the facts didn't mesh. Lonnie Musante had been shot, and though the details of that night remained a mystery to him, the man's death had appeared to be quick and efficient. Whoever had murdered Humphrey Bell had taken joy in the execution. The duration of the torture and the carefully staged room suggested a killer who reveled in the art of murder, one who savored pain the way that others might savor a child's laughter.

What he knew of Delbert Keane's death showed him something wholly different, and though Keane might have ended his own life at the first sign of torture, Hayes did not think that was the case. When he examined these three disparate crimes against the backdrop of what he'd gathered about Butch Cardinal, he came away with doubts, doubts he would certainly voice to Brand once his colleague's emotions had calmed.

At the top of the house, he pushed open a door and began to climb the final flight of stairs to the attic. There he found a single trunk, a single rack of clothes. Though there were no vows made to poverty or moderation, the Alchemi did promote a simple existence, free from the weight of possessions. Hayes was glad to see Keane had taken this life view to heart. It would make his search considerably easier.

Chapter 35
Funeral Weather

The rain stopped for the afternoon, but charcoal clouds tumbled in the sky, rolling toward the south like a pack of dogs wrestling over scraps. Butch waited on the porch of Dauphine Marcoux's house for the second time, but neither the woman nor her secretary, the acerbic Asian woman, answered. Next door, a screen door slammed shut, and Butch turned to find a stooped woman with cotton-white hair and a dress the color of dishwater peering at him from beneath the eaves of her porch. She waved. Butch lumbered across Mrs. Marcoux's porch to speak with the woman, whose face was as wrinkled as a crumpled newspaper.

She made chewing motions with her toothless mouth, her lips mushing together softly, reminding him of Lonnie Musante and the conversation they'd shared, a conversation that had marked the end of Butch's life in Chicago. "Not home, that one," the woman said. She pointed a boney finger over his shoulder.

"I know," Butch replied.

"Then why you standing around on her porch? Ain't you got nothing better to do with your time?"

Not really, Butch thought. Hollis was at the club. The bungalow was too quiet without him.

"Ma'am, do you know when Mrs. Marcoux plans to return?"

She chewed for a moment. "Nah." Her face pinched, exploded with wrinkles. More chewing and she said, "I think that Oriental girl told me they was going to Baton Rouge. That was a few days back now, and she said it would be a few days. Hope it's soon. Got no one to play rummy with when that Oriental girl goes away. I don't suppose you play rummy, young man?"

"No, ma'am. I never learned."

After smashing her lips together like she was working through a steak, she put her hands on her hips and looked up at the sky. "Funeral weather," she said, and then turned and yanked open the screen door; its hinges squealed like an injured cat before it crashed closed.

"Thank you," Butch called, wondering on her hasty departure.

Instead of walking back to Hollis's place, Butch took advantage of the break in the weather and after returning to the Quarter he followed Burgundy Street to St. Anne, where he made a left and walked toward the river. The city's residents had emerged from their homes and shops to enjoy the respite. A fat man in an A-shirt stood on a balcony across the street and leaned on the wrought-iron railing, smoking a cigarette and looking at the sky. A plump black woman swept the sidewalk, for no purpose Butch could see but to move the wet around. At the corner of Chartres Street he stopped and glanced over his shoulder, thinking he might return the way he'd come, but the sight of two men who had stopped midway along the block behind him changed his mind. Both men, who now faced one another with their chins down as if in secretive conversation, were slender and wore good suits and hats. They carried umbrellas. One of the men nodded in Butch's direction and the other shook his head. Hollis's comments about the corruption in New Orleans, the way it tied back to Chicago's syndicates, skittered into his thoughts and began to gnaw. What if Lowery had put it together? What if he'd sniffed out the kind of men who would take interest in Butch's story? The chatting men could have been nothing more than a couple of businessmen out for a late afternoon stroll, or a couple of tourists. They could also be syndicate men or cops—not that there was much difference between the two. Whatever the case, they were putting on a good show, not looking his way, even though they'd clearly been headed toward him only moments ago. Butch faced forward and set off toward the river, walking at a brisk pace until he reached Decatur. The train station stood a short ways down the street. He didn't have enough cash to go far, but he had enough to get out of town. Should he run, again? Hide? Start all over even if it meant sharing a Hooverville tent for the next ten years? Eventually, he might be able to learn a trade and practice it in some small burg off the syndicate's map.

All of these thoughts came at once like a swarm of worked-up bees. His paranoia had disturbed the hive, sent the ideas to buzzing. But when the two men came around the corner only a minute after Butch, they were laughing, clapping one another on the back. They tossed glances Butch's way but the sight of him caused no reaction, not so much as a twitch of recognition. Chattering happily, the two men walked through the doors of a diner, never giving him a second look.

Butch exhaled. He hadn't even realized he'd been holding his breath until it blew from him in a noisy *shush*. Rubbing the back of his neck, a nervous gesture he'd employed since childhood, he shook his head.

He needed to get Rory on the phone, needed to know if his friend had found the money in Butch's apartment, needed to get a read on what was happening back in Chicago.

Beneath the roiling black sky, Butch strolled to the end of the block and turned back into the heart of the Quarter. When the rain resumed, he opened his umbrella, but he kept his pace slow and steady, even as the men and women around him dashed here and there, scurrying through gates and doorways to get out of the rain.

• • •

EARLY the next morning with sweat drying on his belly, Butch slid up on the bed and propped against the headboard. Next to him, Hollis sipped a drink. Butch reached over and took the glass from his friend and emptied the whiskey into his mouth. Then he handed it back for a refill.

"You've certainly made yourself comfortable," Hollis said.

"I am comfortable," Butch replied. "I wish it could last a while."

"But it won't."

"It might, but the odds aren't in our favor."

"The odds brought us together," Hollis said.

"Rory brought us together because he knew I didn't have anyplace else to go."

"I still find it strange you didn't have any friends or family who'd take you in." Hollis reached over to put his hand on Butch's cock. "You're not such a bad guy."

Butch chuckled. "Unfortunately, my friends are employed by the people who want me dead, and my family...well, that's not an option anymore."

"Something happen there?"

"Something," Butch said. Having the subject broached made him uneasy. He shifted against the headboard, trying to relieve the pressure on his neck. "I have a sister. We were close as kids."

"But not anymore?"

"After my career went south because of that Simm business, I found I had a little time off, so I went to visit her. She'd married this guy from town, a kid I went to school with: Myron Huckabee."

"There's a winner's name," Hollis said.

"Myron was a scrawny kid, and he grew into a scrawny man, but I never thought he was a bad guy. He worked hard. Had himself a job at a lumber mill and seemed to do well by Clara. I'd only seen them a few times since their wedding, and usually it was only for a day or so before I had to get back on the road.

"That last trip, I was there for more than a week, and I still hadn't figured out where I was going next. Clara seemed to like having me around, and Myron didn't put up a fuss. We went to the tavern together a few times so he could shoot pool with his buddies and he made it sound like I was a real big shot, even though those days were over.

"That last night, he drank a little too much and when I got him home he started yelling at Clara to make him eggs. I told him to settle down and I'd scramble some up. No reason to bother my sister, waking her and all. But there was nothing rational in that scrawny man. I don't know if it was the booze or if something had been building up, but he was just nuts. He wanted eggs and Clara had to fix them.

"When she didn't move fast enough, he hit her. He slapped her across the cheek, and I just stood there. Our father used to beat up on us, but mostly Clara. I think she took a lot of his hate so I wouldn't have to, and I couldn't believe she'd gone off and found another man like our dad to marry. But she did. After Myron slapped her, Clara lowered her head and closed her eyes, all calm and resolved, and I realized this was not a rare thing. It was a…I don't know, a ritual or something. Then Myron hauls off and punches her in the mouth.

"Clara didn't make a sound."

Hollis rubbed his palm in a gentle circle over Butch's stomach. His eyes, saddened but hungry for more of the story, locked on Butch's face. "What did you do?"

"A few times in my life I've lost control. What do they call it? Seeing red? You know, when everything just becomes a blur and you want to know that someone else is hurting. The thing about wrestling is, what I loved about it, was that you couldn't lose control. You had to stay focused no matter what the other fella was throwing at you. I liked that. I needed it. But with Myron, I saw red. I hurt him real bad.

"When my mind cleared some, I went to Clara, who was still on the floor from Myron's punch and I held her and told her to pack a bag. I'd take her with me. She didn't have to stay in that house. But…"

Butch looked at the ceiling.

"She didn't want your help," Hollis said, finishing his thought.

"No," Butch said. "In fact, she slapped me, and she started screaming, telling me I had no right to treat her husband that way. Said I'd abandoned her in Burlington and I had no right to come back and mess with her life. She crawled across the floor to Myron and sobbed over that scrawny little prick like he was a heroic prince who'd nearly died protecting her honor. I didn't know what was happening. How could she want that kind of life?"

"Sometimes there's no figuring it," Hollis said. "There are folks who get pain and love mixed up. Can't separate them out."

"Well, she gave me another good slap when I went over to help Myron up. I didn't say anything else to her. I drove her and her husband to the doctor's and then I kept driving. Haven't heard a word from her since."

"You miss her?" Hollis asked. He slid his massaging hand up to Butch's chest.

"Yeah," Butch said.

She had been the last, the *best* remnant of his childhood. Without her and his wrestling career, he'd felt wholly adrift from his past—*alone*, ice-cold empty and alone for the first time in his life. He'd felt that way before he and Hollis had become friends. Now he didn't feel as though he were drifting. Instead he felt as if he had washed up on an unfamiliar shore in a place where fear was as much a part of the landscape as comfort.

He rolled over and kissed Hollis, hard and insistent. Intimacy served to occupy his thoughts. It shielded him from past and present traumas with physical exertion and narcotic sensation. When he was with Hollis the ugly, hard-edged world receded. Joy helped him forget. More and more, Butch needed to forget.

Chapter 36
Two for the Show

Roger Lennon had no idea he'd shared a train from Chicago to New Orleans with Hayes and Brand. He'd spent most of the trip in his sleeper compartment reading Hammett's *The Glass Key*, which he found intriguing, though his thoughts wandered too often to allow any real immersion in the story. The gloom and rain greeting his train in New Orleans came as a surprise. He'd expected sunshine and warm temperatures, but he imagined a lot of things in this city would surprise him. Other than whispers about depravity and the entertainments a soft morality could offer, headlines about Huey Long, and frequent references to jazz music, Lennon had been all but oblivious to New Orleans. He'd prepared as best he could with maps and a tattered guide book. In his notebook he'd written two addresses: one for Hollis Rossington's home, and the other for the Hotel St. Pierre on Burgundy Street, the closest accommodations he could find to Butch Cardinal's hideaway.

In a small room that smelled of mold and jasmine, Lennon lay stretched on the bed, the Hammett novel open across his chest. When the rain began to let up, Lennon stood and stretched his back. At the front desk he asked where he might buy an umbrella, and the enthusiastic gentleman with the sparkling grin who had checked him in told him to wait, "Just a quick sec."

A quick sec after disappearing into the office behind the counter, the clerk reappeared, holding a large black umbrella in his bony fingers.

"One guest's misfortune is another guest's boon," he said happily, handing the thing to Lennon.

He thanked the clerk and left the hotel. By the time he reached the near corner, the rainfall had ended, but dampness hung in the air dense and heavy.

Lennon had a fine sense of direction and he'd memorized the map he'd carried with him from Chicago, so in less than ten minutes he was standing before the gate to Hollis Rossington's home, peering in through the wrought ironwork at the lush foliage blanketing the walls and spilling from pots. The layout of the property struck him as strange, with the main entrance to the residence being the narrow gate. It was isolating, prison-like.

Before he rang the bell, Lennon had some decisions to make. He'd come to New Orleans to warn Butch, to give the wrestler the lowdown on where he stood in the world—which was pretty damn low—but he could muck up the works if he didn't handle this thing right. Rossington had to know something about what was going on, and he wasn't likely to welcome a stranger in, not if that stranger was asking for Butch Cardinal. He could strong-arm his way through the door, using his police credentials, but that might make matters worse. He didn't want a ruckus, and he didn't want to spook Cardinal into running off. Lennon stepped away from the gate and observed his surroundings. Two-story buildings. A lot of these courtyard jobbies. Narrow streets. He might be able to loiter on the corner and keep an eye on things, but there was no place to blend into the scenery, making an extended surveillance of the property a bust. If he were in Chicago he could park a car at the curb and pretend to read the paper, but he didn't have a car. In no time flat, anyone exiting that gate or coming down one of the intersecting streets would spot him and have plenty of time to turn tail.

Rethinking his plan, Lennon turned and walked back to his hotel. He used the phone in the lobby and asked the operator to connect him with Hollis Rossington's home. The bell rang a dozen times before he hung up.

Instead of returning to his room, Lennon wandered back into the street. The damp air felt heavier. Soon enough, the rain would return to batter the city in violent sheets, but he felt restless and needed to be in motion. He walked the streets, marveling at the low buildings of the French Quarter and thinking they looked somehow false, like the sets of a play, particularly against the grim, charcoal-gray sky. After an hour he decided he should eat something, and he asked a shopkeeper where he might get some supper. The clerk sent him to an oyster house a block off Bourbon Street. The inside of the restaurant was dark with beams and pillars painted black. It didn't look particularly clean, and the menu seemed to have been written, at least partially, in code with a number of dishes he'd never heard of before.

Since Lennon had never formed a taste for oysters, he questioned the waiter, who recommended a shrimp dish that Lennon couldn't pronounce. Lennon agreed that that sounded fine. Just before his meal was served a jazz trio began to play in another part of the restaurant. The music had a peppy tempo, but it still managed to sound melancholy. Lennon, who had never heard much New Orleans jazz, found himself lost in the music and enjoying it far more than he would have expected.

He finished his meal and ordered a coffee. He lit a cigarette and leaned back on his chair. The rain marched in, following a roar of thunder that rolled down the street. Hissing and rapping, the rain sounded good with the music, sounded right.

He liked this place. Unlike the joints he frequented in Chicago, the restaurant didn't make him feel like he was on a stage, being watched, being judged.

Following his third cup of coffee, Lennon decided he had to leave the restaurant. He hadn't come all the way to New Orleans to eat shrimp and listen to music. He paid his bill, visited the men's room, and then smoked a last cigarette, standing in the doorway beneath a broad awning that shielded him from the rain.

That was when he saw the two men, men he recognized from Lonnie Musante's house, men who had questioned him and threatened the lives of his family. Their names were Hayes and Brand.

The two men had just turned onto the street when Lennon flicked his cigarette butt into the gutter. The sight of them was startling to be sure, but Lennon had assumed they would cross paths again, and he was grateful that he'd seen them first. Hayes and Brand shared an umbrella and walked shoulder to shoulder toward him. Engrossed in conversation, neither man noticed Lennon in the restaurant doorway. He slipped back into the restaurant and waited for Hayes and Brand to pass. Once they did, he gave a thirty-second lead and then he followed them through the rain.

Chapter 37
Monsters with Eyes of Blue or Green

If someone had asked Hollis in that moment whether he was happy or not, he would have certainly said, "Yes," but he didn't know if it was the contentment of a satisfied man or the bliss of a desperate wanderer seeing the promise of a mirage on the horizon. Butch continued to surprise him, and while most of the surprises had been good ones, they also put Hollis off his balance. At first Butch had condemned the intimacies of men and had done so vehemently. Then he'd thrown himself into the very affections he'd denounced. He seemed insatiable for them. Hollis could understand how this might happen, but the ease with which Butch had adjusted to this change in attitude was unquestionably odd. Hollis had been with enough men—warriors against their own needs—that almost no reaction, not even outright violence, would have surprised him. What had surprised him was Butch's acceptance of the situation. No excuses or accusations. No denial. It was as if he'd lived his life believing the sky was green, arguing it to anyone who might listen, and then one morning rising to discover it was blue and having no discernible conflict over the discovery.

Hollis closed the ledger on his desk. The club would open in thirty minutes. He would shake hands and smile, but he wanted to be at home. He wanted to be in bed with the wrestler. He hated leaving the man for even a handful of hours. Part of this was his fear that Butch's moral calibration might revert to the conservative in the hours of Hollis's absence, but mostly it was the feeling—a feeling he hadn't had in ages—of sharing a bed with a man with whom he genuinely wanted to spend time. He'd never felt that with Lionel Lowery. The kid had been eager and convenient, but never prized, at least not by Hollis.

That wasn't to say he saw nothing but a pot of gold in Butch. He couldn't even say their relationship was a good idea. The physical attraction couldn't be denied. Even for an athlete, Butch's physique was exceptional. Having a handsome face on top of all the muscle didn't hurt things either. Granted, Butch's mind wasn't as open as some. He constantly needed to know the rules, but his mind obviously wasn't a tin drum, sealed with welds and rust. When he spoke about the life he'd lost, Hollis felt nothing but misery for him, because Butch had been ground down undeservingly. Of course, this was the epoch of battered humanity. Millions of people around the world had been unfairly diminished. Still Hollis found Butch's fall from grace heartbreaking, perhaps because it had closely resembled Hollis's own descent. He felt a unity with the man, but he wasn't blinded by it. Butch had popped off about magic, and then had shut down tight as a clam. Was that sane behavior? It certainly wasn't stable. Plus there was the bounty on Butch's head, not to mention the murder rap. By sheltering the man, Hollis was making himself an accessory to murder and a target. None of which made Butch Cardinal the trophy many would claim for their own.

The bartender, Michael, poked his head in the office and said, "Remy is outside with our shipment. He wants to talk to you."

Great, thought Hollis. What kind of nonsense was the thug going to be dishing out today?

"Fine," Hollis said, pushing himself away from the desk.

Remy Long was a short, round man with a scarred face and eyes as blue as a summer sky, like two pristine ponds surrounded by a war-torn landscape. Though the acne scars covered more surface than the knife scars, the ragged, ugly lines running from Remy's nose to his jaw, shining and broad like snail trails, did far more to destroy his appearance. He would have been an ugly man even without the horrible welts; with them, he appeared monstrous.

Hollis held out his hand and Remy shook it. Behind the gangster, two down-and-outs hoisted boxes from the back of Remy's Ford and hauled them across the alley to Michael's waiting hands.

"Got a break in the rain," Remy said.

"Won't last," Hollis told him.

"I can see you're shitting sunshine today," Remy said. He removed a box of matches from his coat and a stub of cigar. Once he had it lit, he pointed the butt at Hollis. "Had to dip into your shipment this time around," Remy said. "Some of our whiskey got hung up in Biloxi, and we've got to spread what we've got out."

"Keep it all," Hollis said. Relieved to have some good news. "We're doing fine on stock."

"You sure?" Remy asked. "Won't be back for another week, you know."

"Not a problem."

"There's still a delivery fee to consider."

"Naturally," Hollis said.

"Let's go inside and have a drink. We can discuss it."

The request was uncommon and put Hollis on edge. Remy was one of the few people associated with his business to whom he didn't owe money, and the thug had made his distaste for Hollis and his club clear on more than one occasion. More times than not, he didn't even accompany his men on deliveries to the club, and when he did he kept his ass parked in the car. So what was the sudden interest in a drink? In conversation?

Whatever the motivation for the uncharacteristic request, Hollis knew better than to speak up about it. Hollis instructed Michael to help Remy's men haul the crates of liquor back to the man's Ford. Then he took a bottle from behind the bar and led Remy Long down the L-shaped hall, past the sketches of performers that decorated the walls. The women and the boys in gowns had been caricatured by a local artist who had used to frequent Lady Victoria's.

"All these cunts are men?" Remy asked, tapping his cigar against one of the frames and sending a shower of ash to the floor.

Hollis flinched at the disgusting comment but said, "Only about half."

"I think I'd have to gut any guy that made my dick hard," Remy replied.

Hollis chuckled dryly and pushed open the door to his office. Hollis couldn't remember a single time they'd met that Remy hadn't made some similarly offensive remark, as if the grotesque man thought himself alluring and needed to draw a line.

He retrieved glasses from his desk drawer and poured two fingers of whiskey into each of them.

"To your health," Hollis said.

"Good enough," the gangster replied. He took a slug of the whiskey and then puffed heavily on his cigar, creating a blue fog around his damaged face. "We got something to talk about."

"Do we?" Hollis said.

"We've got a ruckus going on up in Chicago. Well, fuck, there's always a ruckus going on up there. A bunch of shit-for-brains hotheads, if you ask me. I heard they had a street war, but it didn't sound like much more than a girlie slap fight. It got shut down pretty fast, so now they're just killing each other casual-like, same as always. But there's been word that the guy who created that ruckus might be crawling around New Orleans."

Hollis sipped from his glass. He shrugged, trying to mask his nervousness. "I don't really have any connections to Chicago. You got a picture or something? You want me to keep an eye out for this guy?"

"I heard there was a wrestler involved. Didn't you used to be in that game?"

"Yeah," Hollis said. "Long time ago."

"So maybe you know this guy."

"Could be. You got a name?"

"He goes by Cardinal. They used to call him the Butcher. You still know people in that racket?"

"A few," Hollis said.

"Well, if you hear anything, you give me a call. We might both find ourselves with a nice Christmas bonus." Eyes still slit, Remy returned to puffing on his stogie and stared at Hollis intently through the fog.

"You don't hear about those kinds of things down here," Hollis said. "The killings, I mean. You read the papers, and you think every corner in Chicago must have a corpse on it."

"Louisiana boys keep things quieter," Remy said. "They're discreet, and they got the Mississippi toilet out there to flush their shit away. A body hits that current and it's like the guy never existed. If they got the time, they take a trip to the bayou to feed the gators. Chicago's one big pissing match between the Irish and the Italians. They're always *making examples* and *sending messages*, but down here, boys just want to get their business done and slide into something warm at the end of the day. Now before I forget, I'm gonna need that delivery charge."

The gangster quoted his price, exorbitant of course, but still a relief compared to what a full shipment would have set him back. Hollis went to his safe and retrieved the cash, handed it to the ugly man, who counted it before sliding the bills into his jacket pocket. The conversation waned quickly after the transaction was completed. Neither man was particularly interested in the other's opinions about politics or picture shows, and they'd already discussed the weather. Remy emptied his glass for the third time and then clamped the cigar between his teeth. He stood from the chair, wobbled a bit, and then slapped on his hat.

"You hear anything about Cardinal and you give me a call," Remy said, before making his exit.

Hollis assured the scarred man he would, and then he showed him out. Back in his chair, he poured another drink. Remy had backed him to the edge of a cliff on that one, but he'd kept from falling off. He picked up the phone and called to warn Butch, but the bell just rang and rang. Butch was out searching for answers, trying to get the skinny on his necklace.

Today might be the day he finally got his answers. If so, Butch could leave at any time. Hollis closed his eyes and fought the sad ache in his gut. What had been inevitable was now imminent, and Hollis found he wasn't ready for it. He didn't want Butch to leave. Or more accurately, he didn't want Butch out of his life.

• • •

AFTER completing the delivery at the sissy's bar, Remy Long drove through the Central Business District and then followed Tchoupitoulas Street into the Irish Channel. The warehouse rolled up on his left and he raced the Ford through the open gate. The brakes squealed to a stop in front of the door to the building's business office. Remy climbed out. He surveyed the sky, and wondered when the next big wet would start. A few minutes? An hour? Whatever the case, the shit would be coming down hard by nightfall. That was good. Thunder and a good rain could cover a multitude of sins, including shouting and gunfire.

He walked into a gloomy corridor. Half a dozen doors opened onto it. Remy went to the last door on the left and bustled in, already removing his hat and shrugging the raincoat from his shoulders. Colin Welch, one of his longest standing buddies, sat in a chair by the door. He nodded when Remy entered. In the chair at the center of the room, sat a blond kid with a smooth face and big arms. This Lowery kid, Lionel Lowery, had tracked Remy down, spouting some shit about knowing where Butch Cardinal was holed up. How the kid knew Cardinal had a price on his head was beyond Remy. He'd only gotten word from Chicago the day before, but Lowery seemed to have hit the mark. Rossington had acted cool as a dead fish, but his color gave him away. He'd gone pale after Remy dropped Cardinal's name. A guy could control a lot of things in a conversation, but he couldn't force the color to stay in his cheeks.

"I was right, wasn't I?" Lowery asked, leaping from the chair.

"Sit your ass down, snowflake," Remy said. He crossed to the corner and draped his coat over a hook in the wall. His hat went on its neighbor. "But yeah, it looks like you called it." He turned to Colin by the door and asked, "We know where Rossington lives?"

Colin nodded and patted his chest. "All written down. It's in the Quarter. Easy to find."

"You done good, kid," Remy said.

Lowery smiled. The kid was already counting his money, already laying it out for the things he considered precious. "Told you, pal," he said to Colin Welch.

Remy pulled his Smith & Wesson from its holster and put a bullet behind Lionel Lowery's ear. The kid toppled over and hit the concrete with a *thwack*. "Fucking faggot," Remy said, shaking his head. He replaced the gun in its holster and retrieved a silver cigarette case from his pocket. After lighting up, he kicked Lowery's foot. "Get a couple of the boys to drive this punk to the swamp. Then have them meet you at Rossington's. Impelliteri wants Cardinal alive. If you can blow out his kneecap and keep him breathing, fine. If not, sometimes shit fucks up. We'll still get paid."

Colin nodded and stood from his chair. "What if he's not alone?"

"Don't ask stupid questions, Col. Just bring me the wrestler."

Chapter 38
The Galenus Rose

For the third afternoon in a row, Butch stood on Dauphine Marcoux's porch, knocking on the door. The woman he had met the previous afternoon sat in a rocking chair on her own porch across the way. Butch waved to the woman, who stood from her rocker, bent forward as if staring off into a great distance, and then, apparently recognizing him, she waved back before returning to her chair.

The door to the Marcoux home opened and the plump Asian woman stuck her face in the gap. Another cigarette burned between her lips. It took her a moment to recognize Butch from his earlier visit, but when she did, her put-upon expression brightened into one of interest.

"It's you," she said, sounding surprised. Again, Butch found her accent, that Brooklyn growl, surprising. "I figured you'd sober up and we'd never see you again."

"I wasn't drunk, and I'm here now, so may I please see Mrs. Marcoux?"

"Your appointment was days ago, and we've just returned from a trip."

Butch didn't consider a drive from Baton Rouge a particularly taxing journey, but he kept quiet. "I understand, and I'm sorry, but it is very important that I speak with Mrs. Marcoux."

The door closed in his face. Butch punched his thigh in frustration, wondering what was so god damn important about Mrs. Dauphine Marcoux that every moment of her life had to be scheduled. He just needed five minutes of her time, unless she decided to open him up in the way Keane had attempted.

When the door opened again, the Asian woman had put out her cigarette. She eyed him, doing nothing to mask the fact she found his existence an annoyance.

"Come in," she said. "Mrs. Marcoux will see you."

She stepped back and pulled the door with her, revealing a narrow hall ahead. Off to Butch's left stood a magnificent living room, lit by numerous electric wall fixtures and an ornate crystal chandelier. The walls above the chair rail wore a pale yellow paint. Below the rail, the walls were stark white.

"Wipe your feet on the mat," she said. "My name is Sadie. I am Mrs. Marcoux's secretary, her ambassador to the outside world."

Sadie held the door, looking at him expectantly. She was waiting for him to introduce himself. He fumbled for a moment and then said, "I'm William Cardinal."

With a dip of her head, Sadie stepped aside and Butch walked over the threshold. He closed his umbrella and dropped it into an empty stand beside the door. Sadie closed the door muffling the roar of the marching rain.

"This way," she said, leading him through the opulent living room.

Crystal vases, porcelain knickknacks, tiny metal sculptures, and framed photographs crowded the flat surfaces. Butch had trouble identifying the scents in the room. There were the obvious odors of cigarette smoke and wood polish, but beneath these a rich perfume of spices and paraffin and a scent that reminded Butch of blood flavored the air. Sadie led Butch through a doorway and into a chamber with far less ornamentation.

The study was dimmer than the living room, and the single table at the center of the room was bare, except for a small rectangular box that had been fashioned of old, splintering boards. The furnishings were spartan. Besides the table, there were a single chaise lounge and a short, narrow stool with a single spindle running up the back as a rest. To his left, the wall was ornamented with a dozen photographs in golden frames. The images drew him and he stepped closer to see the faces of men and women propped at tables or in armchairs or in coffins. They all wore their Sunday best: men in suits; women in frilly dresses, their hair swept back and pinned up. They were all dead, Butch knew. He'd heard about the practice of photographing the dead, capturing a final expression for grief-stricken loved ones to paste in an album, but he'd never known anyone who'd made a habit of collecting such images.

He reached out and grasped the corner of a photograph. In it, a little girl with black hair and a pale ribbon tied in a neat bow above her brow sat at a toy table set for tea. Unlike the other photographs, this little girl's eyes were partially opened. They reflected the glare of the photographer's flash, which had erased the irises, the pupils. Between the silken lashes, there was nothing but white, and Butch felt his skin shrivel at the sight.

"Will you take a seat, Mr. Cardinal?"

Butch turned away from the photograph. He assumed the chaise was for the lady of the house, so he squatted down on the odd little stool, which proved to be even less comfortable than it had appeared.

"And why have you come to see Mrs. Marcoux?" Sadie asked.

"Is she here?"

"You speak with me first. If I feel your inquiry is worthy, she will see you."

"Yeah," Butch said. He told her about the necklace in vague terms, said he needed to know what it was.

Sadie nodded. She lit another cigarette and held it between her lips. The smoke wafted around her round face. With stubby fingers she withdrew the cigarette, turned her head and spit a flake of tobacco on the floor. "I'd imagine a jeweler would be more helpful in this matter than my employer."

"I thought so too, but I was told that this wasn't a normal piece of jewelry. A friend thought Dau…thought Mrs. Marcoux would know more about such things."

"I see," Sadie said. "And who sent you here?"

"Andersen Seward."

After hearing the name, Sadie nodded her head with approval. "A good friend to have," she said. "And not one to waste Mrs. Marcoux's time. One moment."

Sadie exited, leaving Butch alone in the parlor. He didn't like this room, hated it, in fact. The place was a tribute to death. He felt the photographs on the wall behind him. Their presence unnerved him as if the dead themselves and not just their images had been pinned to the wall.

Mrs. Marcoux appeared in the doorway and the sight of her surprised him. He hadn't expected her to be black. Her coffee-with-cream skin was tight and shone as if recently scrubbed, and she was much younger than he would have expected.

But more to the point, Butch had never seen a woman this beautiful in his life. None of the arena dolls or mob molls even came close. Her skin appeared free of make-up and her hair was slicked back, drawing away from her high, narrow cheekbones to arc over her petite ears. A white dress clung to her curves like a second skin from shoulder to ankle, hugging her hips and her breasts. She held the kind of beauty men fought over; the kind they died over. From reflex he stood and folded his hands in front of him.

"If you'll take a seat, Mr. Cardinal," Mrs. Marcoux said. She crossed to the chaise and stood behind it, one hand placed delicately on the raised back of the furnishing. "Andersen is a dear friend. If he sent you here, I imagine the reason is quite sound. Now then, you have an item?"

"Yeah," he said.

"I'd like to see it now."

Butch fumbled for the bauble. It came free in his hand and Mrs. Marcoux's eyes grew wide. She smiled and knelt down so that her face was even with his.

"The Galenus Rose," she whispered in deference. "Where did you find this?"

The Rose. The Galenus Rose. Finally, he had a name for the piece, and the expression on Mrs. Marcoux's face clearly showed she knew a great deal about it.

"It was given to me," he said.

"May I touch it?"

"Yes."

Her long fingers wrapped around the Rose and stroked its metal surface. She closed her eyes as she petted it, cooed a soft sound, rubbed the charm with a thumb, bit her lower lip. When she opened her eyes she appeared disappointed. She frowned and released the necklace.

"It doesn't breathe for me," she said.

He remembered a similar comment from Keane, something about his knife not dancing for him. And though he knew that the knife was uncommon, had felt a union with the handle and the blade, he still didn't understand what either comment had meant.

"Can you tell me what it's supposed to do?"

Dauphine raised herself from the floor. She moved sinuously like an ascending pillar of smoke. Her body seemed unrestricted by muscle and bone. Only the lowest hem of the white dressed rippled; the rest of the fabric followed the movement of her body.

"Does it breathe for you?" she asked.

"I don't think so. I don't know what that means."

"There are items, Mr. Cardinal—ropes of copper and brass, toys and icons, weapons, the charm around your neck—and they are ancient. They were forged centuries ago from deposits of living metal. When they are held by one attuned to their energies, their power is magnificent." Mrs. Marcoux lifted the rough wooden case from the table and held it out before her as if offering Butch a cigarette. "Many practitioners of the local religion believe that dolls carry the power to curse or save. But they're wrong. It is these, the Vodun Pins, that have the real power. Come, Mr. Cardinal. See if they breathe for you."

Butch leaned forward and peered in the case. A row of eight needles rested on a velvet lining. Each was the color of burnished steel; they jutted from squared hilts of shining onyx. He placed his palm over the pins and electricity shot through his hand and up his arm. Screams filled his head. Laughter ran beneath the shrieks in a thick basso melody. Faces appeared, some in agony and others in bliss, and then they vanished as the energy continued to pour into him, throbbing at the base of his skull and along his extremities. His cock grew hard instantaneously and phantom sensations, not quite pain but something echoing pain, came and went rapidly over his body. He yanked his hand away.

"They breathe for you," Dauphine said. She smiled warmly at him as if he were a favored brother. "But not the Galenus?"

"I guess not," Butch said.

"Oh, what that must feel like," she said. "The power of the Galenus Rose in your fingers, your hands."

"But what does it do?"

"It is said to be a protective icon," Dauphine said. "The Galenus Rose was named for a prominent physician of Ancient Greece. He was revered in his time for the advances he made in anatomy and physiology. Like myself, he tenaciously pursued knowledge of his given field but his concern was for the physical and emotional state of man, not the preternatural forces surrounding him, as mine is. In the simplest terms, the Rose is supposed to cure and to heal."

Butch considered all that he'd been through since having received the thing—the nick in his ear, the sickness, the fresh burns on his chest and arm—and it became clear that whatever power the Galenus Rose possessed, it was being more than stingy with it. Maybe there had been a mistake—a similar icon with different properties.

"Well, it's not working," Butch said. He stood up and began to pace the room. His legs ached from his time on the low seat, and he needed to stretch out the muscles.

"The only real experts in such matters are the Alchemi," Dauphine said. "The man who explained all of this to me was one of their scholars, and he knows far more about the metals than I do."

Butch thought of Delbert Keane and his anxiety returned. Dauphine wasn't likely to take kindly to the fact he'd all but murdered the man—if indeed she was talking about Keane—so he kept his eyes on the floor and asked, "What is the Alchemi?"

"The Alchemi are the collectors and the keepers of the metals," Dauphine said. "I would imagine they are very eager to have the Galenus Rose returned."

"A lot of people want this thing."

"But it *belongs* to them. They will pursue you to the ends of the earth to retrieve it. They are obsessed. The friend I mentioned certainly was. Night after night he'd speak about this object or that object—a knife, a ring, a child's toy, a woman's hatpin—and he described them with a loving detail that bordered on mania. He spoke freely because he knew he could trust me, though I felt certain I could not trust him."

"Why is that?"

"I have a piece or two he would very much like to get his hands on. Even though he abandoned the order, due to personal failings, he remains devout, and given the chance, he would loot my treasures and send them off to one of the Alchemi's vaults."

"You said personal failings," Butch noted. "What do you mean?"

"The men of power in that organization don't just collect and protect the metals, they are also united with them, attuned to their energies. Keane believed that with study and practice, he would one day attune himself, but it never happened. It couldn't. Like a talentless singer who practices for hours a day only to hear her voice degrade rather than improve, Keane had no innate facility, so his efforts proved futile. It wasn't his fault. From what I've gathered, communion with the metals is rare and extremely random. It may pass down a family line, but it does so sporadically. A father may be wholly connected to the ore and his children may be completely deaf to its calling. Still, within the Alchemi there is a universal belief that one either carries the talent within them, or they don't."

"And your friend didn't."

"Exactly," said Mrs. Marcoux. "But he has spent his life serving the order, so that's where his loyalties lie. I knew I couldn't trust him with the few items I'd gathered over the years. Without question he would have called his brethren and my treasures would have been confiscated."

Mrs. Marcoux's assessment of Keane seemed right on the money, but Butch couldn't figure the emotional connection, if there was one, between this stunning woman and the man who had tried to kill him. As such Butch remained quiet about Keane's death. The information wasn't necessary.

"What about the Rose?" Butch asked.

"What do you feel when you hold it?"

"Nothing."

"And yet I clearly saw you react to my special needles."

"Maybe certain pieces only work for certain people," Butch offered. "It may just not work for me."

"That's like saying a violin can only make sound for a talented musician. Certainly anyone can make the strings screech. Mr. Keane had a knife that could set items ablaze, and yet he didn't possess an iota of talent for the metals. I can make my pins work, but I can't feel them working."

"What difference does it make, then?" Butch asked. "If these things work the same for everyone..."

"You misunderstand," she said, "they work for everyone, but they don't work the same way. Those that are attuned can create wonders beyond the basic capabilities of the metals. They are the prodigies and the maestros. They possess true talent."

"So you're saying I'm like one of these Alchemi guys?" Butch asked.

"Indeed," Mrs. Marcoux said. "You have a talent for the metals. The Alchemi would be very interested in a man like you."

"Terrific," Butch said. "All of the people who take an interest in me lately are people who want me dead."

"They aren't likely to kill you if they know of your talent. There are far too few men and women so attuned."

"Maybe so," Butch said though he figured the Alchemi were the least of his problems right now. He was far more concerned with the men who carried guns. "I still don't understand about the Galenus Rose."

"Really?" Mrs. Marcoux asked. She seemed genuinely surprised. "I would have thought you'd have figured that out by now."

"Figured *what* out?"

Mrs. Marcoux looked squarely in Butch's eyes. "Mr. Cardinal, what you have is not the Galenus Rose. It's a fake with no more value than a button or a marble or a half-penny nail."

Chapter 39
Convergence

Butch followed a winding route back to Hollis's. Rain pummeled the umbrella and soaked his trousers below the knees, but he was oblivious to the noise and discomfort. Even before Dauphine Marcoux had exposed the Rose as a fake, Butch had suspected it. And with this knowledge came Butch's sense of total defeat. He couldn't sell the Rose, couldn't bargain with it. It was as disposable as he was.

Hollis had been right: trying to play life straight was a sucker's game. The world was being run by liars and cheats who sold other men's lives as easily as a baker sold his loaves of bread. Laws were bent, broken, and ignored because these men had power, because they had money. Humanity meant nothing. Logic and honor and compassion were cheap commodities, easily traded for petty comforts and distractions. The only things that mattered were guns and knives, silver and gold. A human being didn't stand a chance in a world that worshipped metals.

Worse still, Butch knew he'd been no better than Powell or Impelliteri and this understanding only added to his desolation. He'd tried to play fair but it had failed him. So he'd allowed himself to bend in order to fit into the crooked world, but he'd botched that, too. Maybe there was no place for him, or his experiences had not properly prepared him to find it. What he knew was that he was done hiding. He knew he would not passively walk into a bullet the way Lonnie Musante had. Butch had been a fighter his entire life. If he was going to hit the mats he was going to break some heads on his way down.

Distracted by his thoughts, he walked past the street that would have taken him to Hollis's house. He paused in the middle of the next block and searched the neighborhood, which was familiar, but still felt strange to him. The roads were empty. He was the only pedestrian on the walks. Homes and shops blurred and dulled by the downpour appeared sinister and vacant.

He crossed the road and headed back to the intersection. At the corner he turned right. Two men in black trousers and white shirts stood beneath an umbrella on the distant corner, and the sight of other men sharing this storm brought a momentary whisper of relief. Approaching the gate of Hollis's home, Butch reached into his pocket for the key. As he did so, he threw another glance at the men and saw they were heading for him.

The guy in the lead, a tall, distinguished looking man, held an iron bar two feet long. The second man, a short and burly fireplug with his sleeves rolled up to reveal one muscular forearm and another that looked as if it belonged to a child, clutched a knife. Both men began to run when they saw him.

Butch spun on his heels and broke into a sprint. He released the handle of the umbrella and let it drift off behind him. Rain beat on his face, fouled his vision as drop after drop splashed against his eyes, but Butch didn't slow. He made the corner and raced to the left. Behind him, he heard the slapping of shoes on the wet pavement, but he didn't turn to check on his pursuers until he reached the next corner. There he was grateful to see he'd put distance between himself and the men. He continued running for two more blocks and then, after checking on the position of the men again, he made another left turn.

But then he stopped. He'd promised himself an end to the running. He'd promised himself a fight.

Butch pressed his shoulders to the side of a house and waited. When he heard the slap-slap, slap-slap, of approaching feet he inhaled deeply and spun away from the wall, swinging his arm like a bat.

The fireplug with the knife bolted around the corner. Butch hit him across the bridge of his nose with a forearm. The nose popped at impact. The shorter man's feet went out from under him, kicking comically high into the air before the guy came down hard on his back. Butch drove his foot into the man's side with two vicious kicks before stepping over him and meeting his taller pursuer at the corner.

Butch threw a punch to the distinguished man's sternum. It stopped the guy cold. Butch followed this initial attack with three sharp jabs to the man's cheek and jaw, which sent him crumpling to the ground. The length of steel in his hand clanked against the wet sidewalk before rolling into the gutter. Butch returned his attention to the shorter man, who had climbed onto his knees. Butch kicked him in the face, sending him back against the building. The shorter man grunted, but used the wall to support himself and rose to standing.

Under other circumstances, Butch might have admired the man's constitution, but right now all he wanted was for the fucker to lie down and stay down. The guy still held his knife and he lifted it high. Butch saw the blades undulating, and realized it was Keane's knife—the blade that had produced fire. The edges rippled and waved. It danced for the stocky man. These guys weren't thugs, working for Impelliteri's crew. These were members of the Alchemi.

The stocky man lunged forward with the knife, and Butch grabbed his wrist. At first his palm slipped and a flare of dread fired in Butch's chest as the tip of the blade came within half an inch of his cheek, but he secured the grip and shoved the man back. The man threw his left fist, which was attached to the withered, child-sized arm, and Butch grasped that wrist as well, and for a moment the two men looked as if they were awkwardly working out dance steps. Butch secured the man's left wrist, and his palm encountered a cold metallic surface, which quickly sent familiar energy up Butch's arm. He turned his head and observed a copper-colored strip that wrapped around the scrawny arm like a pet snake. Butch clamped down as hard as he could on the metal and the wrist beneath it.

Then the copper ribbon began to unwind. It whipped away from the skin and bone, coming alive in Butch's hand. The stocky man gasped, and his struggle weakened. Butch pushed him into the side of the house and stepped back. In his hand Butch held a narrow rod, longer than his arm. He waved it in the air and found that instead of bending with the motion, the copper had become rigid like a spear shaft.

Butch cocked his arm back and swung. The stocky man's eyes grew wide, and he threw himself away from the building, hitting the ground in a roll that took him across the sidewalk. The copper staff tore through wood and stone, cutting a deep trench in the materials as easily as a sword would cut through a paper screen.

The power of the weapon amazed Butch; it thrilled him. He spun to finish his attack on the squat man and encountered the distinguished companion standing several feet away.

"Wait. Wait. Wait," the man insisted, holding up his hands in surrender. His hair lay pasted across his brow and his jaw was already beginning to swell from the punches he'd received. "There's been a misunderstanding."

"Stay away from me," Butch said.

"Mr. Cardinal—"

"I haven't got what you're looking for," Butch said. "So stay the fuck back."

"I don't think you understand," the distinguished man said. "My name is Hayes. This is my colleague, Mr. Brand. We just want to speak with you."

Dauphine Marcoux had said that the Alchemi would find value in a man like him. Maybe it was true, but he was too worn to believe in the beneficence of strangers. He backed away, holding the copper staff above his shoulder, ready to swing.

"There's been a misunderstanding," Hayes said. "If you'll just give me a second to explain."

Adding to Butch's confusion, a third man appeared from around the corner. He was a handsome guy with a black mustache, who bounded gracefully into the scene. Rain coursed over his fedora and raincoat in great sluicing sheets. He held a gun, and it was aimed at Hayes's head.

"Don't move," he said, pressing the muzzle of the gun to the man's temple. "I'm still feeling a little upset about the shit you pulled in Chicago."

"An unavoidable situation, Detective Lennon," said Hayes.

"My ass," the man named Lennon replied.

Butch backed up another step, gripping the copper rod as tightly as he could.

Lennon looked at him and said, "Hey, Butch, some weather we got, huh?" He looked back at Hayes. "You and your buddy should take a walk, now. I need to speak with Mr. Cardinal, and it's a private conversation."

"Who are you?" Butch asked.

"Believe it or not, I'm a friend. But I need you to drop that stick."

Appearing in the windows across the street, Butch noticed faces like pale, bland masks. Sheets of rain added a hoary quality like a shimmering shroud settling over a mass grave. He took a step back, looking at Hayes and the gun at his temple and then at Lennon, who had lost the expression of amusement he'd carried into the fight.

Then Butch turned to the shorter, stocky man, with the withered arm the guy his buddy had introduced as Mr. Brand. He saw determination in the eyes, and even before the man took his first step, Butch read Brand's face, and the message there was one of pure violence.

Brand gamboled gracefully from the side, drawing Lennon's attention. Hayes spun away as Lennon repositioned his gun, taking aim at the shorter man.

"Don't!" Lennon called.

But it was too late. Brand barreled forward, shoulder down in a ramming posture. Lennon fired into the man's chest at point blank range and Brand dropped to the walk.

"Son of a bitch," Lennon shouted. He repositioned his aim toward Hayes. "What the hell is wrong with you people?"

Hayes didn't answer. He dropped to his knees to tend to his friend, though Butch imagined the man was long past care. You didn't take a bullet to the chest at that range and shake it off.

Cheeks burning red, Lennon stomped away from the men and headed for Butch. "Drop the fucking stick, Butch. I feel bad enough as it is. Don't make me feel worse."

Butch did as he was told. The staff couldn't outreach a bullet. He dropped the copper rod on the sidewalk, where it clinked and rocked before coming to a stop.

"Turn around and walk," Lennon said. "And walk fast."

• • •

BUTCH expected to be directed into an alley, where the man would put a bullet in his head. Hayes had addressed the man as "Detective Lennon," which meant the guy was probably one of Impelliteri's cop puppets sent to clean up the problem of Butch Cardinal.

Instead, the man walked him onto Royal Street and down several blocks. When they reached a glass-faced restaurant, the man with the gun said, "This'll do. Just don't cause any trouble." Then he holstered his gun.

Inside they took a table away from the window, in a dark corner by a cart that held dirty plates and glasses. Butch used the napkin on the table to wipe his face and hands.

"Who do you work for?" he asked.

"Not sure," Lennon replied. "I'm a detective with the Chicago Police Department, let's just go with that."

"I didn't kill Musante," he said.

"Yeah, I know," Lennon replied, "but that doesn't change your situation."

"Come again?"

"Give me a minute. I just shot a guy."

"Wouldn't surprise me if you'd shot a lot of guys over the years."

"Well, I haven't. I figure he deserved it, but that doesn't make it easy."

They sat quietly and then a waiter arrived to take their orders—coffee for both. Lennon removed his hat and stared at it before setting it on the floor.

"I need you to keep your lid on when I tell you this," Lennon said. "You've tossed me once before, and I'd rather not have it happen again."

Butch looked at the man and tried to decipher what he meant. Had they met? When? Where? He searched Lennon's face and remembered the mustache, of all things. This was the guy he'd bowled over at Musante's, the guy he'd mistaken for a shooter coming through the back door.

"So you know I had nothing to do with gunning Musante down, because you were one of the guys hired to do it."

"Not exactly," Lennon said. "But I was there."

Butch listened as Lennon laid it out for him: Curt Conrad's guilt in Musante's death; Terry McGavin's involvement; the conversation he'd had with his captain, who'd told Lennon that Butch was taking the fall regardless of what the evidence said. As he listened he felt his anger ticking up by degrees until he found himself barely suppressing the urge to flip the table over in Lennon's face.

"Now just settle down," Lennon said, noticing Butch's ire.

"Are you serious? Settle down? I'm supposed to drink this up like lemonade?"

"This doesn't have to be the end of the line. I came down here to warn you, to keep you from trying to work a deal with anyone involved in this shit, because there is no deal. I figured you might be looking to put things together, maybe trying to exonerate yourself, but it doesn't matter what you find. You need to know that. As for whatever it is you have that Impelliteri wants, hold on to it or sell it or throw it away. If you ask me, you should get your ass on a train to Florida, change your name, and then find a rich widow or get a job on a fishing boat."

Lennon lit a cigarette and looked at Butch.

So that was it? Some miserable little thug like Terry McGavin has a beef—nothing real, nothing deserved—and with a single phone call, he destroys Butch's life? It could have been any guy in Musante's rundown house, any punk off the street. All of this misery and death because a petty man with a bit of power decided Butch was an annoyance, not even a threat, but an irritation he intended to scratch out of existence.

"Of course the guys this afternoon are a different matter. I've met them before, and they have some interesting and dangerous toys. I don't know who they work for though."

"They work for themselves," Butch said. "Did you follow them down here?"

"I thought they followed me."

"How'd you know I was here?"

Lennon flinched at the question. He drew on his cigarette and looked over his shoulder. With his thumb and index finger, he picked a bit of tobacco off of his tongue and dropped it in the ashtray.

"Something happened to Rory," Butch said. That was the only answer. Rory had sent him to Hollis Rossington, and Rory wouldn't have talked unless he'd had no choice. No one else in Chicago knew where to find him. "He's dead."

Lennon nodded. "The doctors said he probably wouldn't have made it another month anyway."

"What does that mean? What happened to him?"

"There's another player in all of this," Lennon said. "I think he's on Impelliteri's payroll but I can't get any confirmation of that. I spent a couple of days up north trying to ID the guy, but came up with nothing. What I know is he killed my partner, and he tried to kill Rory Sullivan and his daughter."

"Molly?"

"She's okay. The killer got a shiv into her father's shoulder. It wouldn't have been a big deal, except Sullivan's heart gave out. He made it through the day, but he had a second attack a couple of nights later. I'm sorry. I know he was your friend."

Butch's anger collapsed. It dropped through him, tearing a path from his throat to his belly. He began to cry. He hadn't cried since childhood, but the tears welled hot in his eyes and his chest hitched and before he even understood what had overcome him, he was sobbing. Lennon looked away and finished his cigarette, and Butch shoved the napkin against his eyes, and he fought against the miserable expression of weakness, but he had no power over it.

"Pull yourself together," Lennon whispered.

"Fuck you," Butch managed between sobs.

"Then listen," the detective said. "This other player, the mystery hitter, he also knows you're down here. On the bright side, Molly Sullivan shot him in the gut, and that might lay him up for a while. You might even be really lucky and the fucker is already cold, but he knows what I knew: that you're staying in New Orleans with a guy named Rossington. It took me all of five minutes to find the address. So he's going to need to be warned before you take off."

"I'm not going anywhere," Butch said. He sniffed loudly and wiped the last of the tears from his eyes.

"Let me be clear, Butch. It's all coming down on you, and it's coming down *here and now*. Those men, Hayes and Brand, followed me to Rossington's place, and they saw you standing at the gate. Brand is gone, but Hayes probably has friends. Then you've got this hitter from up north, and if he is working for Impelliteri then all it's going to take is a phone call to a local boss, and this whole place turns into a war zone."

And it's all for nothing, Butch thought. It should have been funny; all of this fuss and energy wasted on a useless chunk of metal. But there was nothing funny here. How many people were about to die pointlessly? He knew he'd never be able to convince Impelliteri or anyone on his crew of the Rose's uselessness, and what were the chances the men he sent would spare Hollis? No. He couldn't leave. He had no choice, at least no choice he could live with.

"Are you listening to me?" Lennon asked.

"I think I'm ready for a fight," Butch said. "What about you?"

Lennon closed his eyes in apparent frustration. "I have a wife and two daughters to think about, so I'm not looking to play cowboy. I took a big enough chance just coming down here."

"Then you should go," Butch said. "Thanks for your help."

"You can't win."

"I was never meant to win, Lennon." Butch stood from the table. "Thanks again," he said, and then he walked out of the restaurant into the persistent thunderstorm.

Chapter 40
The Last Night in New Orleans

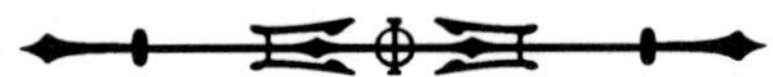

At the gate to Hollis's house, Butch paused and checked his surroundings. Seeing no one on the streets, he opened the gate.

Hollis was home. He hugged Butch when he stepped through the door.

"I thought you were at the club," Butch said.

"I was. I had a visitor."

Butch listened as Hollis related the exchange he'd had with a gangster named Remy Long. Though Hollis didn't know how the thug had come across his information, Butch figured the Lowery kid had finally put it together and sought out a syndicate man to set his revenge in motion. Considering the direction of his luck, Butch shouldn't have been surprised.

Lennon had been right. It was all coming down on his head. Right here. Right now.

He needed to get Hollis out of the house, had to keep him away until this mess was handled. Looking into Hollis's concerned face, a face he wanted to hold close, the lie formed easily.

"We can't stick around here," Butch said. "I have one more guy to see about the necklace. He's Uptown so it'll take me a couple of hours."

"Can't it wait?" Hollis asked.

"Wait for what?" Butch asked. "The longer I'm in town, the more dangerous it gets."

"Then let's leave," Hollis said. He stepped forward and rested his hands on Butch's shoulders. "I can scrape some money together, enough to get us by for a couple of months until all of this quiets down."

Butch pretended to think it over, though his mind was already made up. "Then you should start scraping. Get the money together. But I have to see this man. He's the only one who knows exactly what this necklace is, and I need to know. Once I do, I'll meet you at the club and we can decide where to go from there."

"I think it would be better if we stuck together."

"There's no time. Look, if they know I'm here, then the longer we stand around talking the more trouble we've got. Get your ass back to the club. I need to change into something dry, and then I'm leaving too. They aren't likely to spot me on the street, especially once I get out of the Quarter. When I get the information I need, I'll meet you at the club. Do not leave the club until I get there, because we're going to need to leave fast, and I can't be looking all over town for you."

"You shouldn't be alone."

Butch moved in and kissed Hollis on the lips, but he couldn't enjoy the intimacy. He felt the outside world encroaching on this place, felt eyes on him. Shame and uncertainty rushed in, and he pulled away. He patted Hollis's chest.

"Go," Butch said. "I'll see you in a couple of hours."

Concern pinched Hollis's lips, but he gave a quick nod. "Okay. Sure. You know where the club is?"

He couldn't even remember the club's name. "Yeah. I'll be there as soon as I can."

Hollis leaned in and kissed him again. Butch felt uneasy but refused to pull away this time. He wrapped his arms around the man and held him tightly. Once the kiss was broken, he whispered, "Thank you," into Hollis's ear, and then he said, "You have to go now."

And Hollis left. Butch watched him pause at the door. He lifted his hand in a half wave and waited for the door to close behind his friend. The *click* of the door securing triggered a dull pain in the center of his chest.

He never expected to see the man again.

In his room, he closed the drapes and peeled off his wet clothes and then stood at the foot of the bed. The ceiling fan made slow revolutions above, sending a chill breeze over his scalp and shoulders, and Butch closed his eyes and breathed deeply. He imagined the house on good land, his oldest dream, only now he pictured Hollis there with him. His friend stoked the wood stove, stirred the contents of a pot on its scalding surface. He poured beer into glasses and carried them out to the porch where Butch waited, staring at a sunset woven of purple and crimson and orange. Hollis took a seat next to him. They said nothing. Nothing needed to be said.

Butch opened his eyes. After his skin had dried, he dressed in a pair of Hollis's gray trousers, a white undershirt, and a pair of warm woolen socks. Then he left his room.

In the kitchen he put on a percolator of coffee, knowing it could be a long night. It could also be a very short night. There was no way for him to know. A killer might already be aiming a rifle at him through the kitchen window or a gang of thugs might be converging in the courtyard, having walked through the gate only seconds after Hollis had left the property.

Just leave, he thought. *Walk into the rain.* Let Hollis believe the mobs had fed him to the gators so the man could get on with his life. He couldn't let his friend give up everything for him, no matter how much he wanted it.

He could disappear the way Detective Lennon had suggested—a long, uneventful life on a Florida beach, tanning his skin and fishing and drinking rum until the sound of the ocean lulled him to sleep.

Butch decided that if he lived through the night, he'd consider it again. For the moment, he poured himself a cup of coffee and returned to his room. There he set the cup on the nightstand and performed a series of stretches to loosen his muscles. Feeling limber enough, he drank more of the coffee, sat on the edge of the bed, and thought the evening through.

• • •

THEY came for him at eight o'clock. The rain persisted, beating hard on the flagstones and the leaves of the succulent plants. Butch stood against the ivy-draped wall of the slave quarters, pushed deep into the shadows. He'd waited there for two hours, his mind numb to the downpour and the chill, ears adjusted to the marching rain, listening for the soft squeal of the hinges on the courtyard gate.

When it came, Butch tensed and made himself stand as motionless as a statue. A shadow appeared to his left and he saw the silhouette of a gun. Only a few steps into the courtyard, the man paused, turned back. For a second, he looked directly at Butch but must have only seen the camouflage of bushes and gloom. The man tested the door to Hollis's bungalow and then leaned in close to peer through the window.

Satisfied that the building was empty, he turned to the big house and began creeping across the courtyard.

Butch launched himself away from the wall of ivy and hit the flagstones in a run. He was grateful to the rain for covering the sounds of his footsteps. He was only a few steps from the shooter when the man heard his approach. He looked up and swung in Butch's direction. But Butch was already diving at the man. They landed hard on the flagstones. Butch leapt to his feet and brought his foot down hard on the man's wrist, stomping again and again until the gun fell from his fingers. Butch retrieved the weapon and aimed it at the man's face, which was still little more than a smear of pale skin.

The man on the ground kicked Butch in the stomach and tried to get to his feet, but the kick had been poorly delivered, ineffective. Butch kept the man in the gun's sights.

"Did you come alone?" Butch asked.

"Fuck off," the man said.

Butch fired the gun into the wall beside the killer's head. The man squealed and covered his face with his arms.

"Did you come alone?"

"Two waiting in the car. If I don't come out, they come in."

He could handle two more. With the gun it would be easy enough. He wasn't much of a shot, but he wouldn't need to be if he could keep the element of surprise on his side.

"Let me go, buddy, and I'll tell them I got the job done. You'll be free and clear."

"I'm finding it hard to trust you."

"You better think this through. We don't show after the job, and Remy'll send a fucking army over here. You run and he'll find you. He'll hunt you till the day you die."

"There's a line already formed for that one. Get up," he told the man.

After the man stood, Butch ordered him across the courtyard. He put his hand in the center of the man's back and walked him toward the corridor beside the bungalow. The shooter wobbled on his feet, stumbling ahead like a drunk on sand. He paused and lurched and dipped to the side. Butch thought he might topple over.

It was a ruse, and the shooter, whipped around, knocking the gun aside. Butch recovered quickly and threw an elbow to the man's jaw, sending him to the wall. The shooter pushed himself from the brick wall. Butch took two awkward steps backward.

Gunfire erupted. The cracking reports cut through the rain's clatter in a staccato thunder. It came from the gate at the end of the corridor.

Butch scurried to the center of the courtyard out of the line of fire, but the shooter danced back and forth as a barrage of bullets entered his chest and face. The man collapsed. The glass of the French doors along the ground floor of the main house shattered. Butch raced toward the big house and took up a position behind a potted plant in the corner of the portico.

All of this happened in seconds. Reflex guided his actions more than rational thought, but he was still breathing. Through pure dumb luck, his would-be killer had saved his life. Butch just hoped the luck would hold. The gunfire quieted, leaving only the sound of the beating rain. He looked through the leaves of the plant and saw movement, but it was the motion of shadows on shadows. He could not place where the men were standing with any certainty.

"I think we shot Colin," a man said.

"Son of a bitch. Remy ain't gonna like hearing that."

"We'll tell him the wrestler done it."

Butch tried to get a bead on the voices. It should have been easy enough as the mouth of the corridor that opened onto the courtyard wasn't that wide, but he didn't want to waste the bullets he had. The other men weren't so worried about conserving their ammunition. They opened fire a second time, strafing the French doors and windows behind Butch as if they found glass offensive. One bullet passed through the lip of the pot giving him cover, and fragments of ceramic flew in the air amid a puff of mud. Butch lay down flat on the ground until the second wave of gunfire ended.

From what Butch could tell, the men had positioned themselves against the wall of the corridor, using the corner for cover. He might get lucky with a shot, but he had no faith in his marksmanship, and as it stood the men seemed uncertain of his exact location in the courtyard. A few bad shots would give him away and do more harm than good.

Even so, he couldn't stay where he sat. Eventually the men would dare the courtyard. They would find him.

He got his feet under him and duck-walked backward into the house, wincing at the sound of the glass crunching under his feet. He made it halfway across the foyer before the men caught sight of him and the barrage of gunfire resumed. Butch bolted, making for the stairs on his right. Bullets followed him across the room, never quite reaching him, and he threw himself over the banister. He hung in the air for a moment, feeling the dread of exposure. Then he dropped hard. One of the stairs dug deep into his ribs. He didn't stop to entertain the pain, but rather got to his feet and raced up the stairs. He went to the window on the landing and looked out.

The men had moved into the center of the courtyard, surveying the destroyed wall of glass. Butch carefully aimed the pistol at the man on the left, and he took a deep breath before he began to pull the trigger.

Before he could fire, a blur caught his eye. The pale smudge came from the corridor the men had recently vacated, and it moved swiftly to their backs like an eager phantom. It took a moment for Butch to realize the smudge was a man. Butch squinted to make out the details of the scene through the rain, but his eyes never quite caught up with the action. One moment the two gunmen were facing the house, holding their weapons at the ready, and the next, they were in pieces on the ground. Their torsos had been cleaved in half and blood poured into the puddles of rainwater. Their severed arms still clutched their guns.

Butch struggled to keep his eyes on the scene below.

Though he told himself it wasn't possible, Mr. Brand, the man Detective Lennon had shot that afternoon, stared up at Butch. In his hand he held the copper staff. With a flick of his wrist, the staff drooped like a ribbon and then climbed up the man's skinny arm, wrapping itself like a snake as it rose to his bicep. Mr. Brand saluted Butch and then made his way into the house.

Light blossomed from the crystal chandelier hanging over the foyer. Butch blinked away the sudden glare. A moment later Brand appeared in the foyer. He walked to the bottom of the stairs and looked up.

"Mr. Cardinal," he said.

"You should stay down there," Butch replied.

"I intend to," Mr. Brand said. "And you'll come and join me."

Butch aimed the gun. "I don't think so."

"You'd better be a good shot," Mr. Brand said. "Better than your friend at any rate."

"So you're invincible?"

Mr. Brand laughed. He parted the lapels of his shirt, revealing a bib of golden metal beneath. "No, Mr. Cardinal, just very well prepared."

Was he supposed to believe that a thin mesh of metal had stopped Lennon's bullet? And then he did believe it, because there was no other explanation. After the things he'd seen, was this really so miraculous?

"Where's your pal?"

"He's crossing the courtyard now. Would you rather speak with him?"

"I'd rather you both left."

Hayes stepped into the foyer and surveyed the house with a slow, sweeping glance. Though not as badly injured as his friend, Hayes's jaw was swollen and the color of a plum.

"We should talk first," Mr. Brand said. He cocked his head to the side and continued smiling, eyeing Butch as he might a dog doing tricks. "It's become clear that we're on the same side."

"I suppose you attacking me with a knife this afternoon kind of threw me off."

"That's when we realized we were on the same side, Mr. Cardinal," Mr. Hayes said, stepping up to the side of his companion. "The metals live for you, the way they live for us."

"And that automatically makes me a good guy?" Butch asked.

"Not in and of itself," said Hayes. "But we tracked down your detective friend after he left you this afternoon. He clarified several issues for us."

"He's okay?" Butch asked.

"We didn't harm him, if that's what you're asking. We had a pleasant chat. He seemed extremely relieved and grateful to find Mr. Brand in such good health."

"Okay, so you're the Alchemi," Butch said.

"We belong to the Alchemi, yes," Hayes said. "I imagine Mr. Keane told you about us."

"Not really. He didn't say much of anything useful."

"Well, we'd be glad to answer any questions you might have. If you'd rather not chat, we would be happy to take the Galenus Rose and be on our way. We have no interest in harming you, unless you interfere."

"The Rose is a fake," Butch said.

"I can assure you it's not," Hayes replied.

Butch kept his aim on Hayes and fished beneath his shirt until he had the worthless piece of metal in his fist. He yanked, snapping the chain, and tossed the necklace down the stairs. Hayes caught it. His eyes lit with excitement and then dimmed. Hayes frowned.

"You've made a replica," he said as if it were the most obvious thing in the world.

"No," Butch said, "I didn't. That is the same piece that Musante gave me in Chicago. I didn't even know what it was supposed to do until this afternoon."

The men at the bottom of the stairs exchanged a glance. Neither looked happy. Hayes turned his attention back to Butch. "Then I suppose we can guess what's become of the original."

"I think so," Butch said. "Lonnie Musante. He didn't die in Chicago, or if he did, he didn't stay that way."

• • •

THE standoff on the staircase lasted only another minute. Butch lowered the gun. He didn't exactly trust the men, but he knew they believed his story. Killing him wouldn't get them what they wanted, and if Dauphine Marcoux was right, they'd want him on their side. Butch put the gun in his waistband and walked down the stairs. He remained tense through the introductions, shaking the men's hands, but they made no suspicious moves. They followed him into the parlor on the far side of the foyer. Both men stood as Butch sat on the red velvet settee. He'd been on his feet for hours, and fatigue was setting in hard.

"You understand it is difficult for us to believe Mr. Musante succeeded in keeping the Rose for himself?" Hayes asked. "The idea presents a number of questions."

"I think he screwed his boss, too," Butch said, ignoring Hayes as he tried to put things together. "The way Musante set this up, it wasn't just to throw your people off his tail. My guess is Impelliteri paid a good deal of money for the Galenus Rose. That's why I've got every hood in the country looking for me. He doesn't know I've got a fake." Butch noted the frustration on the men's faces and found it insulting. They'd lost their bauble and a bit of their time; he'd lost his entire life because of Musante's game. He was further aggravated to realize he'd played the game exactly as Musante had intended. "The whole time I was in Musante's place he was warning me about what was going to happen. He told me there was a shooter outside, told me we were both about to die. He kept on about it, and I couldn't figure out why, and the simple answer was, he wanted me to escape. Musante knew I'd be framed for the crime because he had a cop execute the hit, and the cop had to blame someone. He also knew that would mean my name would be in the papers fast so Impelliteri had himself a target. He wanted all eyes on me—cops, Impelliteri, you guys—so he could do whatever was necessary to vanish forever. It didn't matter if I got caught a day later or a year later or never got caught at all. He just needed a window of time and a decoy."

"But Mr. Musante was cremated," Hayes said. "We have witnesses who can account for him at every point between his house and the furnace. Believe me, we considered this possibility from the beginning."

"Then someone made a mistake or was paid off," Butch said. "Unless whoever sold the thing to Musante sold him a phony."

"We believe he had the original."

"Could he have used it to fake his own death? Would it have brought him back from two bullets to the chest?"

"Very possibly," Hayes admitted. "Long before it came under our protection it was used by religious zealots and high courts as an instrument of torture. During interrogation prisoners would be abused to the point of death, and if they managed to maintain their secrets, then the Galenus Rose was used to heal them, so the torture could start over again."

"Why wasn't the Rose found on Musante?" Butch said. "The police would have collected any personal items on him. Hell, the cop who murdered him would have had plenty of time to grab it, if he knew what he was looking for."

"They wouldn't have seen it," Hayes said. "By the time your authorities reached Mr. Musante, the Galenus Rose was already at work. On an injured body, The Rose dissolves and takes on a consistency not unlike mercury before fragmenting into microscopic motes. For a moment a mist is visible above the skin, and then nothing. It makes its way to the wounds and it repairs the damage. With wounds as serious as those Mr. Musante incurred, it might take days for the Rose to complete its mending. His body could be searched inside and out and the icon wouldn't have been found."

"Then I think you have your answer," Butch said. "And since he has a serious head start, he could be about anywhere in the world by now, laughing it up at all the feeblos he had dancing for him."

"That's disappointing," Hayes said.

"Yeah," Butch agreed. Disappointing was one way of putting it.

Hayes sighed and checked over his shoulder, eyeing Mr. Brand. The burly man stood with his hands clasped behind his back. He nodded at Hayes, telegraphing agreement to whatever silent question Hayes had asked.

"Mr. Cardinal," Hayes said, "would you be interested in helping us find Mr. Musante?"

Yes, Butch thought.

He would be very interested in tracking down that son of a bitch.

Chapter 41
Blood Loss

Paul Rabin leaned against the wall of the corridor and peered into the courtyard. He observed the men standing in the house and the corpses on the flagstones. One man had been shot multiple times. That was interesting but it was the pieces of men near the portico that genuinely intrigued him. He admired the skill of those murders. The bodies looked as if they'd been run across a buzz-saw blade, and he wondered what kind of weapon could produce such thorough and efficient cuts. A sword? A scythe? He'd like to have it, whatever it was.

Again a crowded street scene unfolded in his mind, men and women and children lined up like daisies to be messily felled by the sword or axe that had disassembled the two men, and as the fantasy began to take hold, each death of the faceless mob drawing him farther from reality, a bolt of fear startled Rabin out of his reverie. Such fugues had become too common. Irene's confession (*or maybe it was that Irish bitch's bullet*) had broken some manner of vessel, releasing these occupying thoughts at every turn like pleasant, yet distracting, toxins. He pressed a hand to his wound and increased the pressure until he winced from the pain. The sharp ache cleared his head.

He recognized the wrestler standing inside and studied his heavy expression. When he'd begun this job, Rabin had hoped to go toe to toe with the big man, tear the fucker apart with his bare hands just to see if he could, but that plan had leaked out of his side onto the table of Dr. Somerville. He didn't have the strength for a brawl just now. A gun would do. All he needed was the necklace. The Galenus Rose. He would take it back to Chicago and cure Irene, and when she was feeling better and in her right mind, he would be cured, too. They would go back to their happy life, and she would do her needlepoint and ask about his day, and he would lie to her, and she would let the lie settle like a mote of dust among all of the other motes he'd brought her over the years. And he could put the monster back in its closet and maybe he wouldn't feel the pulsing desire to kill every fucking thing he set his eyes on.

Rabin suppressed a growl deep in his throat. He needed to keep his focus. No one had to die here, no matter how badly he wanted it. It would be far easier to demand the charm at gunpoint, and once he had it in his hand, he could turn around and leave. He wasn't working for Impelliteri now and he didn't give a damn about the wop's revenge game. The wrestler was nothing but smoke, quickly dissipating. Soon enough he'd be in a cell or dead and there was no reason for Rabin to do anything foolish with so many witnesses (*victims*) on hand.

The wrestler and the two men in black trousers walked to the patio door. The larger of these men pointed at the bodies on the flagstones. He was speaking but Rabin couldn't hear what was being said. Like a silent film etched with scratches, the scene played out beneath the rain. The shorter man, the thickly built one with the strangely underdeveloped arm, nodded and pointed at the bodies himself. The wrestler watched the exchange but added nothing to it. His face remained heavy and sorrowful as if he'd been recently widowed.

Then Cardinal turned away and walked into the house. One of the black-trousered men, the taller one, followed, leaving the stocky deformed man alone in the rain.

With so many distractions and the swelling anticipation of a kill, Rabin had forgotten about the listening device he'd taken from the boy Humphrey. He felt foolish for having ignored such an asset, and he quickly retrieved the device from his pocket and affixed it to his head. The rain amplified, sounding like a thousand hammers falling on a field of tin, and voices overwhelmed him, coalesced in a nonsensical chorus until the individual conversations came clear.

A dart of pain ran through his wound and Rabin grit his teeth against it. He relinquished his view of the courtyard and pressed against the wall to ride out the misery. A wave of nausea passed through him and his head swam. Rabin removed his hat and turned his face into the rain in the hope that the cold splashes would keep him from passing out in the corridor. He'd lost consciousness on the train ride to New Orleans and twice more in his hotel room, and though those episodes had proved harmless he couldn't risk incapacitation. Not now. Not when he was so close.

He inhaled cold wet air and felt a weakness in his legs. Silently he cursed and began to pant for air. The world toppled to the side for a moment and then righted and the spell passed, leaving Rabin shaken, but awake, against the wall.

"When the others come—"

"We won't be here when the others come. How long is it going to take to clean up those bodies?"

"Mr. Cardinal, if these men know about the Rose, they present a danger to the Alchemi and we must meet them head on."

"They're hired thugs. They don't know anything, and they don't care about anything except whatever piece of a reward they're going to get."

Rabin struggled with another flash of pain. All of the noises, the voices, and the sounds were confusing him, so he pulled the device from his ear and deposited it in his pocket.

When he again looked into the courtyard he was surprised to see a fire guttering near the portico. The stocky man was burning the bodies.

How? Rabin wondered.

With all of the rain, a match would never have stayed lit long enough to ignite the remains, even if they'd been doused in kerosene. Dragging the last body, the gunshot victim, away from the shattered doors, the stocky man stumbled on the flagstones but managed to right himself with hardly a break in his step. He hoisted the dead man in the air and dropped him on the low pyre in the courtyard, and then the man did something wholly surprising to Rabin. He removed a knife from a sheath at his back and plunged it into the corpse's belly.

A moment later, the body erupted in flames. Rabin gasped at the sight as the fire consumed the pile of bodies in only a handful of minutes. The rain did not diminish the flames, but it seemed to act as a hindrance to the smoke, which hovered in a low cloud over the sizzling bodies.

After the corpses were reduced to sticky black ash, the stocky man retrieved his knife and returned it to the sheath in his belt. Then he gathered up two tommy guns before making his way into the house. As he walked inside, Rabin's gaze was locked on the handle of the wonderful weapon. Oh, the things he could do with a blade like that. The marvels he could perform. And again he was in the street amid a horde of humanity—cutting, slicing, and now burning his way through the neighborhood, leaving atrocity in his wake as he tore a path all the way home.

Chapter 42
Enter, Monster

Butch stood with Hayes and Brand in the foyer of the big house. Light bathed the tiled floors, revealing footprints and streaks of mud brought in on the men's shoes. Outside, the blackened remains of the shooters glistened like heaps of polished onyx.

"Let's get out of here," Butch said.

"No reason for us to remain," said Hayes.

Butch uncrossed his arms. "I've got a couple of things to get out of my room. It won't take a minute."

He led them outside, skirting the black stain on the flagstones. The insistent rain rapped on his head and shoulders, cooling him after the heat of exertion. At the bungalow, he unlocked the door and ushered the two men inside. He didn't bother closing the door. He wouldn't be long.

He left the two men and walked to the guest room. Memories overwhelmed him here, and he struggled against them. Amid all of the pain, the sickness, and the fear, this room had proven a sanctuary, but only because Hollis had shared it with him. Now he was leaving the man behind. He couldn't decide whether it was more selfish to abandon Hollis or to keep him involved in this bloody business. In the end, it was clear he couldn't ask Hollis to give up his life, a good life from what Butch had seen, just because he was tired of being alone. Even without the ever-present possibility of violence, Butch had no right to ask that of the man.

He took his money clip and wallet from the nightstand, and immediately left the room behind.

As he walked through the parlor, he said, "That's it. Let's…"

Except the kitchen was empty. Butch threw a glance at the spiral staircase and the landing above. No sign of the men. He turned to the open door and peered into the courtyard.

Hayes stood with his hands up; his weapon, the metal rod, lay on the flagstones at his feet. Brand stood rigid, arms at his sides. An older man, perhaps the age of Hayes, stood behind Brand, holding the ornate blade of Keane's dagger to the stocky man's throat and pointing a gun at Hayes. The intruder's mouth was open and the corners turned up, though the expression was not a smile. When combined with the dark, stone-hard eyes, Butch could not say the expression reflected anything more than the man's insanity.

"At last we meet, Mr. Cardinal," the intruder said. His voice was as dry as the shed skin of a snake.

"Who are you?" Butch asked, his voice raised to be heard through the downpour.

"Rabin. But what's in a name?" The old man's head canted to the side and his eyes widened. A sigh hissed through his open mouth.

But *who* was he? A local hitter who'd gotten wind of an easy bounty? It wasn't likely. Butch remembered something that detective, Lennon, had said, something about a wild card, an employee of Impelliteri's who had attacked Rory and Molly Sullivan. Yes, he could see how a man like this could get Rory to talk, especially if Molly were at stake.

"You want the necklace," Butch said.

"Indeed, yes," Rabin said. "Yes and yes and yes."

"You take it and leave," Butch said, taking a step forward. He reached a hand into his pocket to grasp the pendant. "No one has to get hurt."

"Of course not," Rabin said. "No one *has* to get hurt, although it would liven up the evening."

"We've had a very lively evening," Butch said, forcing his voice to remain steady. Though he continued to walk forward, he had no intention of attempting to trick the well-armed lunatic. The necklace wasn't worth a nickel, let alone anyone's life. He withdrew the imitation of the Galenus Rose from his pocket and dangled the piece in the air. "We'd be happy enough to keep things uneventful. Just take this and go."

Rabin's head eased back to the side, eyeing Butch like a lizard waiting for a butterfly to come within range of its tongue. His knuckles gripped the handle of the knife so tightly white horseshoes of bone were visible through the skin, but his hands were steady, absolutely motionless as if he'd been designed to hold weapons. Over the years, Butch had seen a number of fighters who had adopted façades of lunacy to get inside his head, to intimidate; not one of them had come anywhere near conveying the genuine ice-cold madness of the man before him.

"That's far enough," Rabin said. He waved his gun in the air. "I want you standing right there, and I want the old man facing the wall. We'll move things along once I'm not having to keep an eye on everyone."

"Fine," Hayes said, stepping backward, keeping his hands even with his ears.

Brand glared at Butch. Butch didn't like what he saw there. He didn't like it one bit. The guy was brave, but Brand's impulsive nature was going to result in bloodshed if he didn't keep a handle on it.

"Just do as he says," Butch told Brand, through a tight jaw. To his left, Hayes had reached the courtyard wall. "Two minutes and everyone gets what they want."

"Indeed," Rabin said. "You seem very accommodating, Mr. Cardinal. I can't help but wonder why, when you must know the value of what you're holding in your hand."

"I know what it's worth." *Nothing.* "And I know I've spent all I intend to on it."

Once Hayes had taken his place at the wall, Rabin waved Butch forward with the gun before leveling it at his brow. "You hand the Rose to your friend here, and then you back your ass up. If you get too close, I start carving."

Butch intended to do exactly as Rabin suggested. He was more than happy to be free of the useless bit of metal, and by the time the lunatic discovered it held no more magic than a crust of bread, Butch and the Alchemi would be long gone. It wasn't complicated.

But as with so many recent events, Luck had found Butch unworthy and turned her head away.

"What is all of this?" Hollis asked.

The man emerged from the corridor beside the bungalow, holding an umbrella. His expression slowly melted into one of understanding and fear.

Why didn't you stay at the club? Butch wondered. *Why the hell didn't you listen to me?*

Rabin's face erupted: his grin broadened; his eyes widened. Butch could see he'd been waiting for an excuse to kill, and the sudden appearance of Hollis had provided it. Brand must have realized this himself. He threw his elbow back, driving it into Rabin's side, but instead of sending the killer off balance and giving himself a chance to escape, he only drew the madman's attention, and with a whisper that crackled like the voice of a consumptive, the ornate blade slid through Brand's throat, cutting and scorching a black trail. Brand looked at Butch, offering a perplexed glance before dropping to the wet courtyard floor.

"Hollis, run!" Butch called.

Hollis opened his mouth to respond, but a crimson dot appeared on the chest of his suit. Without so much as a gasp, Rossington collapsed. Butch didn't hear, couldn't even acknowledge the gunshot until Hollis lay crumpled on the ground. He stared at his body and felt a slash of despair.

"Now we're cooking with gas," Rabin shouted, merrily.

Butch whipped around to the source of the voice.

The lunatic stood with his legs bent. He swept the gun around the courtyard, hoping to find another moving target. With his left hand, he drew the knife through the air in sinuous waves. It all looked like a bizarre dance, the hypnotic shimmy of a cobra before it sank its fangs into meat. On the ground at his side, Brand, who was not yet dead, clutched the wound on his neck and moved his mouth, pointlessly and silently, a fish in the bough of a boat.

Then Rabin fired again. Butch followed the angle of the gun and saw Hayes slam into the wall. Though the hole in Hayes' shirt was right over his heart, a precise and deadly shot, the madman decided to shoot the man a second time and a third. Hayes dropped.

"And then there was us," Rabin said.

Every nerve in Butch's body resonated, thrumming madly and creating a confusing static that filled his brain and broke apart his thoughts. He brought his hands to the sides of his head and grasped tightly as if a strong enough grip could quell the noise, and after a time, though he did not believe the silence had anything to do with his fingers or palms, the static did clear. In its wake was a thought that might save his life.

"You're falling apart, Mr. Cardinal," Rabin said. He appeared curious, narrowed eyes observing Butch intently. "I think I expected more from you."

Butch held up the necklace and let the charm dangle from his hand. "You know how this works," he said. "If you try to kill me it goes to work, and you won't be able to get your hands on it."

"You're trying to bluff me?" Rabin said, shaking his head. "Are you really so pathetic?"

"I thought you knew how this worked?" Butch challenged. He allowed his eyes to dart to the side, where he saw Brand weakly rolling on the stones. Already the brass band unraveled from his arm, snaking into the air at Rabin's back. "You don't though, do you?"

Rabin aimed his gun at Butch's brow. "I've got time to figure it out."

In his weakened state, Brand nearly dropped the staff. He managed to keep it grasped in his palm, though its hilt hit the flagstone with a startling crack. Rabin leapt to the side and pivoted on his foot, swinging the gun wide as Brand's staff came down. The copper pole sliced through Rabin's fingers and sheered away the muzzle of the gun. The pole fell to the floor and curled in on itself, rolling up like a Christmas ribbon.

Rabin stared at his wounded hand in awe. He gasped in air and squeezed his eyes closed for a moment before sighing out a ragged breath. Rabin pulled back his foot and kicked Brand's head, burying the toe of his shoe into the man's temple with ugly force. Something in Brand's neck popped, and he lay motionless as Rabin, still armed with the knife, returned his attention to Butch.

But Butch was already in motion, covering the distance between himself and the madman in a few long strides. He collided with Rabin's chest, feeling the satisfying puff of air on his throat as he tackled the man and drove his head back on the hard stones. The older man's eyes rolled up and closed, but they didn't stay that way. When they sprang open, they were sharp and focused and they burned with rage. Butch had hoped the brutal concussion of bodies would knock the knife out of Rabin's hand, but the older man had kept his grip, and before Butch could secure his arm, the blade drove in from the side. Butch deflected the knife, and then he scurried off the madman and rolled before the metal returned for him. Twisting his legs in the air, he spun himself over and landed in a crouch, ready for the next attack.

Rabin didn't keep him waiting. The man rolled the other direction and climbed to his feet, holding the blade out in front of him with one hand as what remained of the other clutched his side. Rabin winced. Wobbling badly, like a drunk about to tumble, Rabin swept his arm as he'd done before, only this time, it was clearly to help him balance. He growled deep in his throat and charged forward in a shuffling gait.

Butch darted to the center of the courtyard, and Rabin followed, all but dragging his right leg as he shambled after him.

"I wa-want to see what this knife can really do," Rabin said.

"You won't," Butch said. He stopped and squared off on Rabin, who was still three steps away. "You're done now."

The growl returned and Rabin brought the knife up, its point aimed at Butch's gut, but the man was so weak Butch had more than enough time to step away, and before Rabin could recalculate his position, Butch was there, gripping the madman's forearm tightly and twisting it until the cartilage in his elbow ground and snapped. The knife fell. Rabin regarded Butch with an expression of reverence, as if he'd been wholly unable to imagine a force strong enough to bring him down. Butch drove a fist into Rabin's mouth, and the man stumbled two steps and then dropped on his ass. Butch walked behind him and crouched down and wrapped his hand around the killer's face. Then he snapped Rabin's neck.

He stood and let the body slap against the wet flagstones. Without pausing, he retrieved Keane's knife from the floor and drove the ornate blades into the center of Rabin's chest. And he stood there, momentarily empty, thoroughly numb, until the madman was reduced to a mound of char, slowly dispersing with the rain.

"Thank you," Mr. Hayes said at his back.

Butch turned. The older Alchemi had untucked his shirt and was brushing the bullets from his chain mail vest. One of the slugs bounced on the ground and landed on the back of Hollis's outstretched hand, and the sight of it hit Butch in the stomach like brass knuckles. He crossed to Hollis and bent down, lifting the body from the wet ground. The bullet dropped from his hand and clacked away. He carried his friend to the bungalow and carefully made his way to the room they had shared. As gently as he could, he laid Hollis on the bed and positioned his arms at his side. He closed his eyes with a sweep of his palm, and he stepped away.

Then he left Hollis in the room and he stepped to the door. Outside he removed the knife from the mound of ash that had been Paul Rabin. Amid the oily char he noticed a bit of metal that had survived the blaze. When he touched it, he heard the fleeting echoes of conversations and knew the metallic device had value. He put the thing in his pocket and secured the knife in his belt, and several steps away he reached down and grasped Mr. Brand's brass ribbon. It came alive and tested the air. Then its end slipped beneath the cuff of Butch's shirt. It slid up his arm, wrapping itself around his skin and muscle and massaging his arm with pulsing energy, feeling more like the warm touch of a lover than a length of metal.

"Mr. Brand deserves better than this," Hayes said at his back.

"We can't take him."

"I know. But I can't leave the metals with him. I'll need your help."

Together they managed to get Brand's shirt off and Hayes removed the bulletproof bib, sliding it gently over his friend's head. He retrieved a small dagger from a sheath at Mr. Brand's ankle. He muttered a few words, and Butch looked away, unable to deal with the misery on the older man's face. He had his own sorrow to carry.

"Rest now, friend," Hayes said. He arranged Brand's arms neatly at his sides and then stood. "Nothing more to do."

Butch nodded. Then he led Hayes to the gate and then to the street, leaving the house behind forever.

Chapter 43
Back from the Dead

Butch lay on the bed of a comfortable hotel room in Madison, Wisconsin, reading the paper. Through the window, he could see, when he looked up from the pages, fat flakes of snow drifting lazily and decorating the limbs of an ancient oak. The shouts and cries of happy children, playing in the snow, floated up to his room and made him smile as he licked a thumb and turned a page. Mr. Hayes had taken an early walk to observe the city before it truly woke. After finishing the sports reports, Butch set the paper on the edge of the bed, and he stood to loosen his muscles. He did a series of pushups, and those felt so good, he set into a lively round of squat thrusts. Butch paused in mid crouch upon hearing Hayes's key in the lock. The Alchemi opened the door, eyed Butch and his odd pose with humor, and closed the door behind him.

"Get dressed," Hayes said. He turned from the door with a half-smile on his lips. "You were right. We found him."

"Are you sure?" Butch asked.

"The message was waiting for me when I returned from my walk," Hayes said. "My associate, Mr. Ross, discovered the location and confirmed Mr. Musante's identity. Once we knew where to look, Mr. Musante wasn't particularly difficult to track down. Thank you for that."

Lonnie had talked about a lot of things the night Butch had made his acquaintance, and among his various comments had been the description of a small vacation house on the shores of Lake Wisconsin, a place he'd bought because he'd met a lady up that way. Musante's mention of his dream house had resonated with Butch, tickled him with envy. He'd imagined a similar future for himself, away from the squabbles of his species, living quietly and honestly in a small house on a good piece of land.

"He's outside a town called Merrimac about forty miles north of here. We'll meet Mr. Ross at ten and proceed directly to Mr. Musante's home."

"You think he'll give us a fight?" Butch asked.

"No. Nothing in his past suggests even remote competence in the art of violence. He's a manipulator and a thief. I could be wrong, but I think he'll surrender quietly."

"That's a shame," Butch said.

He completed his set of squat thrusts and then made his way to the bathroom to splash his face with cold water before dressing for the drive.

• • •

As they drove north through the wintry landscape, the chassis of the Ford bucking and swaying over the uneven road, Butch found it difficult not to fidget, not to flex his fingers and tap his feet. Against a line of white pine and scotch pine, on the far side of a stretch of unbroken snowy field, he saw an old barn, boards made gray with age as time had sapped all remnants of life from the wood. The roof had caved in and several boards had released their grasps on the side of the building. He observed the countryside but saw no fencing in the area, saw no old farmhouse that might have once been the barn's companion. It was such an ugly, lonely thing to find amid the beautiful terrain.

He'd spent days trying to manage his feelings about Hollis, not only his loss, but the influence he'd had on Butch's life while alive. Labels he'd once so easily affixed to this kind of man or that kind of man had smeared and become illegible. Was Butch a sissy now? A punk? Or had it been a situational passion? Would he ever feel the depth of connection he'd felt for Hollis with another man? Another *person*? He couldn't imagine it, and considering the pain that had burned cruelly and persistently in his belly since Hollis's murder, Butch wasn't sure he wanted to imagine it. It might have been love. It might have been panic. He wasn't sure which explanation he preferred.

"Lost in thought, Mr. Cardinal?" Hayes asked.

"Sightseeing," Butch said. "I like the snow."

"Too cold for my old bones."

The wheel fell into a pit in the road, casting a spray of slush over the window beside Butch, smearing the landscape with a dirty brown film. Ahead, two narrow, parallel trenches in the snow, the trails of cars that had travelled before them, were the only indication of the road.

"What'll you do with him?" Butch asked.

"Mr. Musante? We'll take him with us back to New York and he'll face a tribunal."

"Yes, you told me that. But what will you *do* with him?"

"He will be detained."

"Will you execute him?"

"It rarely comes to that."

Butch accepted the answer and returned his gaze to the window beside him. Dirty snow slid down the glass.

"You never answered my question."

"What question?" Butch asked.

"Last night, I asked if you'd consider joining us. Even without the recent losses of Mr. Bell and Mr. Brand, we could use you and your skills."

"I don't know. Let's get through this first."

"Once we have the Rose, and whatever other items Mr. Musante might have acquired, this will be finished. If all goes well, we'll be on our way back to New York this evening."

"When has *all* ever gone *well*?" Butch asked. "Besides, there's still Impelliteri to consider."

"He's not our concern. He doesn't have any of the metals, nor does he have access to them any longer. Fortunately, Mr. Musante proved a less than reliable go-between, and the man has no other connection to our group."

So, Impelliteri gets away with murder because he suddenly wasn't the Alchemi's problem? No. That wasn't right. If anything, that was at the core of the world's problem. How many men rose to power on a pile of corpses because those with the power to stop them turned away, closed their eyes, indulged in distractions, simply because they were not directly affected by the atrocities? How many people stood by to watch men and women die in gutters, indifferent because these were not their friends, not their families? Butch knew he could go to New York with Hayes, join the Alchemi, and likely live the rest of his life in comfort, never again having to think about Marco Impelliteri, or Angus Powell, or the City of Chicago, but who else would suffer for his sanctuary? He'd considered all of this since the night he'd carried Hollis's body to the guest room bed, but now he was resolved.

"After Musante," Butch said, "I'm going back for Impelliteri."

Hayes didn't reply. He navigated a bend in the road. He remained silent, and Butch joined him in that silence until they reached the outskirts of Merrimac, where a rotund man with a baby face lifted his pudgy hand in a wave.

Mr. Ross looked like the comedian Oliver Hardy, only with a smooth upper lip. He grinned when Butch and Mr. Hayes climbed out of the car, but as he rushed forward, eager and jovial, it was Butch who had clearly drawn his attention.

"Big fan," Ross said, pumping Butch's hand forcefully. "I saw you grapple Zbyszko, and I had tickets to your bout with Simm. Damn shame about what happened there. Damn shame. I heard rumors Simm rigged it up, had that Hungarian hobble you. Is that true? Did he have that Hungarian hobble you? I saw him, the Hungarian, not Simm mind you, in a bout with Jesse Petersen, and he wasn't nothing much to see, and I couldn't imagine him hobbling you, but who can say?"

"Mr. Ross," Hayes said dryly.

"Sure, yeah, sorry," Ross said, releasing Butch's hand. "I hope we get a chance to talk later. Big fan."

"Thanks," Butch said. He couldn't help but smile.

Ross's demeanor changed instantly, though. His smile vanished and the star struck glimmer in his eyes faded. He cleared his throat and stood rigidly, facing Hayes. "Mr. Musante owns a small house on the lake. Six rooms total. No basement. There is a crawl space beneath the house, but I found no means of egress around the foundation. Two doors: front and back. Windows at points around the perimeter, eight total. He owns a small rowboat, which has been removed from the water through the winter. The lake has a frame of ice, which would make escape via water unlikely. As such, his means of transportation are limited to one car, a Ford Model T in working if not pristine condition, which he keeps parked in a detached garage."

Ross completed his report and folded his hands behind his back, appearing quite pleased with himself.

"Thank you, Mr. Ross," Hayes said. "You and I will enter the house and apprehend Mr. Musante. Mr. Cardinal will wait in the car and be prepared should Mr. Musante escape."

"Wait a minute," Butch said. "I'm not just going to sit on my ass."

"Alchemi protocol dictates that Mr. Ross and I go in alone." Hayes delivered the information dryly, like a beleaguered schoolmaster. "We can't guarantee your safety in this matter."

"Is that a joke?" Butch asked.

"Mr. Cardinal—"

"Stop calling me that," Butch said. "And stop with the protocol horseshit. Unless you intend to tie me up, knock me out, or kill me, I'm going in."

Mr. Ross struggled to suppress his amusement and surprise. Mr. Hayes simply looked frustrated.

"This must be done with absolute precision," said Hayes. "If Mr. Musante incurs any injury, any at all, the Rose will absorb into his system."

"Fine, I don't clock the guy," Butch said.

"It's more delicate than that, Mr.…" Hayes shook his head. "Mr. Musante may injure himself to keep us from the Galenus Rose in the hope of escaping or perhaps negotiation."

"If he's wearing it," Butch said.

"If you were in Mr. Musante's position, would you ever take it off?"

Butch thought this over and decided Hayes was right. If he possessed the Galenus Rose, he'd wear it day and night. Musante might well feel that he'd succeeded and his old friends—mobster and Alchemi alike—were no longer a threat, but accidents happened.

"So what's your strategy?" he asked.

• • •

HAYES and Ross circled the tree line, leaving Butch positioned behind a balsam at the back of the house. On Musante's front stoop, Hayes tested the knob and found the door unlocked. He waved Mr. Ross to the side, on the off chance the house was protected by traps, and then he pushed open the door. No explosion of gunfire followed. No surprise or shouts from Mr. Musante. Hayes stepped into the house and Ross followed. The rotund man shut the door behind them.

Compared to the hovel Mr. Musante had kept in Chicago, this house had a cleanliness and warmth to it. Though sparsely decorated, with a simple sofa, table, console radio, and rocking chair, the home appeared comfortable. A fire burned on the hearth, sending waves of heat over them. The adjoining room, visible through a plain archway was apparently the dining room, though it remained unfurnished. Anyone might have lived in this place. No trinkets or photographs of a particular life adorned the walls or ornamented the table or mantle.

Hayes took a step into the living room and then paused when he heard a board creak at the back of the house. He lifted the iron rod to his side, ready to throw it if Musante leapt out with a weapon, but when Lonnie Musante appeared, it was clear he had not seen their approach, nor had he expected anything of this sort to happen.

Musante walked into the dining room space, rubbing a towel over his head. He wore a clean white sleeveless undershirt over tan trousers, and as he scrubbed his head, the trinket around his neck jostled noticeably. He'd bought a new chain for the Galenus Rose, a short length of gold that kept the pendant tight to his skin, just below his throat. Musante finished drying his hair and lowered the towel. Then he saw Hayes and Ross and gasped, startled. He stumbled back a step, eyes wide and mouth absently open.

"Mr. Musante," Hayes said. "Please remain where you are."

Except for the photographs from the Chicago morgue, Hayes had not seen Lonnie Musante in decades. His hair was black and lustrous with streaks of gray at the temples. His full face, never a handsome face nor even a pleasing one, was cocked to the side. His surprise faded, leaving behind an expression both relaxed and smug. Musante grinned, revealing rows of perfect, white teeth; he dropped his towel on the floor; and he faced off on Hayes and Ross.

"So what brings you by?" Musante asked. He drew a small knife from his belt and held it over his forearm, a move Hayes had feared from the start. "And you could have wiped your feet. For the love of fuck, look what you're doing to my floor. That's bad manners, right there. Your mother would have something to say about that."

"Mr. Ross, please remain at the door," Hayes said, ignoring Musante's rambling. He left his colleague and crossed to the center of the room, pausing only when Musante made a show of placing the blade of his knife against the exposed skin of his arm. "Mr. Musante, we are representatives of the Alchemi. You are in possession of an item which is our responsibility, and we've come to—"

"Yeah. Yeah," Musante snapped. "But you know what? You…can't…have it."

"It is the property of the Alchemi."

"People help themselves," Musante said. "Keeps the world turning. Ol' Marco Impelliteri taught me that." He looked up at Hayes. "Now there's a sick fuck for you. You know why he wants the Rose? You have any idea what sickness he's trying to cure?"

"It's not our concern," said Hayes.

"Me, I had the cancer real bad, not to mention a laundry list of other aches and pains and problems that needed fixing. I only had one tooth left in my mouth before I got my hands on the Rose, now look at my choppers." Musante curled back his lips in a grotesque smile to expose his large white teeth. "But Impelliteri, his sickness goes deeper than any cancer, worms its way clean through his body and into his soul."

"Is that so?"

"That is most certainly *so*," Musante said, his tone mocking. He rocked the knife back and forth over his arm. "Impelliteri is a wonder, he is. He never goes for the whores, keeps himself away from all those flapper sows with their clap and syph. Keeps himself clean. He's got himself a lovely wife and a beautiful daughter. Problem is, he gets them confused every now and then, if you see where I'm going with this? Treats his daughter like he treats his wife. Keeps his cock in the family, you know?"

Hayes nodded, disgusted by the information.

"As a Catholic boy, there's little worse, 'less he had a son instead of a daughter." This made Musante chuckle. "He thinks the Rose will cure him of his urges, will wipe them clean away. Oh, he's also interested in staying alive, no doubt, but it's this other, this living sickness inside of him, that makes him want the Rose."

"Why are you telling me this?" Hayes asked.

"I talk," Musante said. "It's what I do. I wonder on things, and I talk."

"You're responsible for the deaths of a number of people."

"No, I am *not*! I never killed nobody but myself," Musante said. "Wasn't me who told McGavin to use Cardinal for the hit. Wasn't me telling Cardinal he needed to quit his strongman act and start busting heads for Powell. No, sir. My plan was that everyone else walk out of that house alive. I wanted Cardinal alive, needed him to get away, and he did. After that, folks did what folks always do when they want what they want."

"I see," Hayes said. Musante's denial sickened him. It was like a man accusing his bullets of bad behavior. He turned to Ross who stood rigid and attentive by the front door. The man shook his head all but imperceptibly.

"And you want to make this my fault. It's not right what you're planning to do," Musante said, his voice quiet and earnest. "Not right at all. You're blaming me for what other people done, and you're going to murder me for it."

"You should know that's not how we do things," Hayes said.

"Right, you just stick a pin in my head and I go numb and blank for a few years, unless I get lucky and the petrification kills me."

"If you injure yourself, we will take you into custody," Hayes said. "We can be patient."

"You'll have to be," Musante said, "because I will bite my fucking tongue off once a week to keep you from getting it. I'd rather turn it over to naughty papa Impelliteri than you smug fucks."

He resents us, Hayes realized. *He's jealous.*

Mr. Musante wanted to punish the group, wanted to shame it, because they'd once shown the good sense to keep Lonnie Musante away from the objects of power.

"What if I just give you the Rose?" Musante said. He lifted the knife to his throat and scratched beneath his chin with the blade. "No foul. You take it and leave and I go about my business."

"If I agreed to that, you'd know I was lying," Hayes said. "Even if we took the Galenus Rose and left, others would return. You can't trick us again, and you know that, which makes your bargain somewhat empty."

"You're a smart one," Musante said, still scraping the blade over his neck. "I know you're right. I know how this goes. Just wasn't quite ready to put holes in myself. Guess I'm about there now, though."

"It won't change anything," Hayes said.

"His pocket," Mr. Ross said from behind him.

Hayes had noticed Musante's hand sliding into the pocket of his trousers, but his attention was fixed on the blade, knowing that once it opened the man's neck the Galenus Rose would be, if only for a brief time, out of their reach. Apparently, that was exactly what Musante had been hoping for.

From the pocket, Mr. Musante drew a familiar object, a disk only slightly larger than a half-dollar piece, intricately etched and weathered by time. Hayes cocked his arm to launch the iron rod at the man, but Musante moved too fast. With a snap of his wrist, Musante threw the disk into the air. It shattered, broke into thousands of tiny, glittering flecks. Light blinded Hayes momentarily and then it soothed him. At turns brilliant and then grim, the flickering chiaroscuro stunned him and then it entranced him. Moments of absolute serenity gave way to hard-edged dread and then returned again, lulling him as he stood transfixed and unable to move before the shimmering display.

• • •

LONNIE Musante sighed with relief and stepped away from the scene in his living room. Mr. Hayes and his lard-assed buddy wouldn't be bothering him again anytime soon. In fact, the Mesmer Coin could keep those ass-wipes occupied for hours, days even if the circumstances were favorable. They could die on their feet. Dehydrate and starve while watching the pretty metal twinkle before their eyes.

No skin off his ass.

That wasn't likely to happen though. No doubt they'd cleared their little plan with 213 House, so if Hayes didn't check back in soon enough another squad of Alchemi bastards would drop on his head like a weak ceiling. Lonnie considered the knife in his hand, thought about running it ear-to-ear on Hayes and then the fat one, but Lonnie didn't have the belly for wet work. Never had. No doubt he would have gone a lot further in the Chicago syndicate if he could have stomached a hit or two, but that wasn't his way. He didn't care if people died. He just didn't need to see it.

Besides, what he'd accomplished was so much better. Sweeter. It was the bee's fucking knees. He'd made fools of them all: Marco Impelliteri's gang, the Chicago death machine; and the Alchemi with their pompous, ridiculous devotion to squirreling away tools and weapons, instead of using those things the way they'd been intended. Marco had the right idea. He sure did, but Lonnie had learned to hate the piece of shit. He'd rather melt everything down than let the gangster get his hands on a single piece of the living steel.

Musante slid his knife back into the belt of his trousers. He went to the window and peered at the unbroken snow behind his house, searched the tree line for signs of additional Alchemi intruders. Normally, the Alchemi travelled in packs of two, so he'd likely covered his ass by mesmerizing the two in his living room, but maybe he'd warranted more attention. The Galenus Rose wasn't some prop in a parlor trick.

He squinted through the glass, thinking he saw a shape hiding behind a balsam tree. He leaned in close.

Then an arm wrapped around his throat, and another slid around his side and quickly yanked upward, immobilizing Lonnie's right arm. In seconds he felt the pressure of a stone-solid biceps pressing against the side of his neck. He struggled, but the man behind him had too much strength. The arm around his neck tightened, and the snowy field and the tree line began to pulse as if in respiration. The edges of his vision lost focus. His chest heaved for breath until it felt like a pair of fists beat at his ribcage from the inside. Then the white field raced toward him, filled his vision until it blinded him, leaving the world black and silent and motionless.

Chapter 44
Never Meant to Win

During the two weeks following his return from New Orleans, Roger Lennon's life had returned to normal, which was to say, the tedium had returned. Edie and the girls were home, and Edie was already pressing him to follow through on his promise of a Florida vacation. The talk around the station had moved away from Curt Conrad, except for the occasional idiot who tried to engage Lennon in an inspirational story about his late partner, as if Lennon might actively want to keep the man's memory alive instead of forgetting him like a bad meal. His current caseload was light. It kept him busy during office hours, but it left him plenty of time to wonder about Butch Cardinal.

He hoped the wrestler was taking his advice, moving on and starting a new life in a town where they'd never be able to dredge up his past. The guy deserved a little peace and quiet.

At his desk in the station, Lennon sipped from his coffee and gazed across the room, where Sally, one of the switchboard operators, was delivering a telegram to Officer Evanston. Sally wore a bright red dress with a sprig of pine pinned to the lapel.

The holidays had snuck up on Lennon. With everything else on his mind, he'd forgotten about Christmas until that morning, when Edie had insisted he bring home a "Nice, full tree." Of course, he'd seen the decorations in the windows of the downtown stores and the radio played little but cheerful holiday tunes, but for some reason he'd taken none of it personally, as if it were a festival for strangers, a holy night for a religion he didn't practice. Edie had bought the girls' gifts. She'd managed the wrapping and decorating the house, which she'd been frantic over when Lennon had left for work that morning. None of it had felt quite real until Edie's request for a tree, soon followed by the sudden, shocking realization that he hadn't bought his wife's gift yet. He knew he could take a long lunch to fight similar procrastinators at Marshall Field's, but he had no idea what Edie might want. Surely she'd dropped hints, but Lennon hadn't been of the mind to catch them.

He thought about jewelry, clothing, and appliances—ran a list through his head to see if he could remember Edie having mentioned any specific want, but there was nothing but a hole where that kind of information should have resided.

Sally appeared in his doorway. She wasn't a beautiful woman, hardly pretty at all. Her face was severe, with thin lips and razor sharp cheekbones that made her seem always in a state of disapproval. Today she'd gone heavy on the rouge and the slashes of red on her cheeks looked like wounds. But despite her harsh appearance she was a good gal. Pleasant. Quiet. Quick with a laugh.

Lennon experienced a brief dislocation. Suddenly, Molly Sullivan was on his mind; Molly who looked soft and sweet, but was as hard as nails. He wondered how she was holding up since her father's death and even thought to pay her a visit, perhaps before the new year. This notion was easy enough to dismiss. He couldn't even pretend that she'd welcome his company; he was part of the machine, and her father's blood had helped grease its gears.

"A letter for you," Sally said. Her voice was bright and cheerful, a good switchboard voice. She handed him an envelope with his name scrawled in large letters across its face. Lennon didn't recognize the handwriting, but notes and cards came in droves during the holidays. "Merry Christmas," she said, giving him a little wave and spinning on her heels.

He thanked her and returned the sentiment. Then Lennon opened the envelope and withdrew a stiff sheet of paper:

Detective Lennon,

Thank you for what you tried to do for me in New Orleans, but I can't take your advice. I'm back in Chicago to finish this business. I have a request, and I suggest you carry it out and then remove yourself from this matter. Stay in your home tonight and enjoy the fire. I can't ask any more of you.

As for me, I've come for a fight. Too many people sit it out. They turn away and pretend nothing is happening because it isn't happening to them, and men like Impelliteri feed on the things others refuse to protect. He grew strong not because people were afraid of him, but because no one cared enough to stop him. Or because they were getting just deep enough into his wallet to buy whatever toys or spirits provided their chosen distraction.

You've done it. I've done it.

We both know diplomacy is pointless. The men in power laugh negotiation off as weakness, and the only thing that gets their attention is pain: hurting their wallets or breaking their necks, and I don't want his money.

I know you are associated with Marco Impelliteri. I want you to let him know I'm coming for him. I'm coming for him tonight. If he values his family, he will send them away. I don't want innocent lives on my conscience.

In New Orleans, I told you I was never meant to win this fight. I still believe that. But there are ways to lose that are easier to stomach than others.

Regards,
Butch Cardinal.

"Idiot," Lennon muttered.

If he warned Impelliteri, the bastard would call his entire crew in. Butch would walk into a chorus of tommy guns singing his requiem. But he had to know that. He couldn't expect Impelliteri to send his family away and then wait in his house alone. So what was Butch's angle? Lennon really wanted to know, because right now it sounded like the wrestler was looking for a quick and cheap suicide. And what was Lennon supposed to do about it? If he reported Cardinal to his colleagues on the force, then there'd be twice as many guns at Impelliteri's house, twice as many men who wanted Cardinal cold and quiet. Impelliteri might even make that call himself, knowing he had nothing to fear from Chicago's finest.

Lennon stood from his desk and then sat again. What was that horse's ass thinking? Had he lost his fucking mind?

Chapter 45
Steel to Blood

At ten P.M. on Christmas Eve, Butch pressed tightly to the brick wall that surrounded Marco Impelliteri's home. The mansion was set back from the road and guarded by two men at the gate. He needed to find a clear area to hop the barrier without being seen. Snow fell and the accumulation had risen to his ankles. Wind gusted. He noted the cold but it didn't get inside of him. He was too anxious. Too aware of his own fear.

He set off along the wall away from the road, deeper into the wooded area adjacent to the Impelliteri estate. He would approach the house from the side. Less yard there. Like Musante's place in Wisconsin, the perimeter of the house was wide open, with no good cover save for the occasional decorative trees and shrubs about the property.

He built up his courage, thinking about Hollis and Rory and the faceless men and women the gangster had allowed to be murdered for his pitiful wants. In Impelliteri he saw Jerry Simm, and Lonnie Musante, and Paul Rabin, and Lionel Lowery. That singular guise encompassed every gangster, every rotten cop, every crooked promoter. He pulled the strings. He soured the world.

When Butch came to the point at the wall that was closest to the house, he turned and put his palms on the cold brick. A hand grabbed his wrist and Butch spun, ready for a fight.

John Hayes stood beside him in the snow, eyes wide and hands in the air, palms, gloved in black leather, out in a passive display. The Alchemi was bundled in a thick coat and a long gray scarf that matched his hat.

"What are you doing here?"

"I was sent to Chicago to retrieve the Galenus Rose," Hayes said. "I haven't done that yet."

"How'd you find me?"

"You'd made your plans clear enough in Wisconsin, though it would have saved me three nights in the blistering cold if I'd known you were planning to attack Mr. Impelliteri on a holiday."

"It's the day before a holiday," Butch corrected. He lifted his head and scanned the woods behind Hayes. "Where's your buddy?"

"Mr. Ross is escorting Mr. Musante back to New York."

"Well, there, you got something out of the deal."

"True. But you could have disengaged the Mesmer Disk before you stole our car. Mr. Musante could have murdered us where we stood. Fortunately, the disk disengaged on its own before he woke."

"Good to hear," Butch said, throwing a quick glance at the top of the wall. "Maybe we could get caught up another time?"

"How did you get the Rose from him, Mr. Cardinal?"

"Stranglehold," Butch said, distractedly. He eyed the woods and the fence line. Neither he nor Hayes were speaking loudly, but they shouldn't have been speaking at all. If Impelliteri had guards roaming the grounds, any conversation would eventually be heard. "Cuts off the blood flow to the brain but causes no tissue damage. I figured the Rose wouldn't go to work if nothing was broken or bleeding."

"Do you have the Rose, Mr. Cardinal?" Hayes asked. His expression was earnest, a father demanding the truth from his child.

"Don't be feeble. Of course, I have it," Butch said. He patted his chest with three light raps. "I also have that bullet-stopping bib Mr. Brand wore and his arm band. You can have them all back when I'm done here. Now, you need to get moving."

"What if I came to help, Mr. Cardinal?"

"Then I'd say you're a damn fool. And I'd thank you."

"We should get started then." Hayes dug in a pocket and produced two small items. They looked like thumbtacks with gnarled heads and long rough pins. "Take one of these."

"What's it do?" Butch asked, reaching for one of the tacks.

"It's a petrification thorn. Lodge it in a man's skin and he'll be paralyzed until it's removed. We found a trove of items at Musante's, but the bulk of them were taken back to New York with Mr. Ross. I kept a few things, anticipating a night like this."

Butch clapped Hayes lightly on the shoulder and then turned back to the brick barrier. He pulled himself up until his sightline was even with the top of the wall. Snow fell in fat wet flakes, giving the grounds and the house at their center a pristine, idyllic appearance. Ground-mounted floodlights bathed the exterior of the house in illumination, making the gangster's palace appear flat and unreal. In the yard a dozen paces from the edge of the drive, a sixteen-foot pine fell beneath a similar bath of lights. Shining ornaments hung from the boughs in acknowledgement of the holiday. Dull light showed in two of the windows, but the remainder of the interior was dark. A row of parked cars, eight in all, drew a line from the front drive to the garage on the side, yet there was no sign of movement in or around the house. Lennon had delivered Butch's message, and Impelliteri had responded with a clear show of strength, a dare, a taunt.

Butch lowered himself and turned to Hayes. The man was affixing the hearing device they'd taken from Rabin's ashes to the side of his head. He held up a finger to Butch, requesting silence as he adjusted the metal strip over his ear. After a moment, he closed his eyes and leaned against the brick and maintained this pose for more than a minute, occasionally bobbing his head lightly as if listening to music. When he opened his eyes, he mouthed, "They're inside," to Butch and again lifted his finger for silence.

Finally, Hayes removed the device and returned it to the pocket of his black overcoat.

"What have we got?"

"Trouble," Hayes said. "Based on the number of conversations and a number of sounds I can positively attribute to human activity, we're looking at no less than twelve men. Taking into account the likelihood that not everyone involved is speaking or moving around, we could be looking at significantly more."

"I expected that."

"And you still want to go in?"

"Do you want to wait here?"

"Not even a little," Hayes said. He removed the iron rod from his coat lining and held it tightly. "There are four men walking the perimeter." With a startling swing, he rapped the bar against the brick wall and the metal trembled; it separated lengthwise until he held two narrow lengths of the rod. With a bar in each hand, he said, "I'll take the two in the back. Yours are on either side of the gate. One just lit a cigarette and the other is humming Christmas carols."

Butch put his hands on the top of the wall and launched over. On the other side, he dropped into a snowdrift that rose halfway up his calf. He crouched low and set off along the fence line, grateful the electric bulbs pointed at the house and left the bulk of the yard in shadow. Clouds blotted out the stars and moon, but the snow made its own kind of light as if each flake had captured a bit of star shine before falling to earth.

He ducked behind a thick shrub and moved forward, wincing every time one of his feet crunched through the packed snow even though the gusting wind erased the noises within moments. In fact, the howling gusts were so vociferous he found himself only a few steps from the humming gunman before he'd even realized the man was ahead of him. Fortunately, the man's back was to him, otherwise the evening might have ended far earlier than Butch would have liked.

The guy was tall and slender. His coat was too big for him, and it hung from his shoulders like an adult garment being modeled by a child. Butch noted the barrel of the tommy gun jutting out from the crook of his elbow.

He took two quick steps forward. The tall man must have heard him, because he spun and tried to change his grip on the gun, but before he could get off a shot, Butch yanked the machine gun out of his hands and tossed it in the snow. Then he slapped a palm over the man's face to keep him from calling his buddy. Butch stepped forward and pivoted, so that he faced the wall, and with another step, he put all of his weight into a forward thrust that crushed the man's skull against the bricks. The guy's eyes rolled up in their sockets, and though it appeared clear the first blow had succeeded in incapacitating the man, Butch repeated the motion and then let the thug drop.

After retrieving the gun, he eased toward the gate. A brief summation of his situation made it clear that crossing the drive without being seen wasn't likely, even with the gloom and snowfall. He backed away. Once he was certain he was out of view of the second guard, he leapt over the wall and made a wide loop across the street from Impelliteri's house. When he jumped over the fence again he was on the west side of the property, thirty yards from where he'd left the body of the first guard. He snuck up on the second man and pressed the muzzle of the tommy gun into the guy's back.

"Toss it," Butch said.

The guard didn't need any explanation. He threw his weapon to the ground and raised his hands into the air. Butch knocked the man unconscious with the butt of his gun, driving the wooden stalk into the base of his skull with a crack that was muffled and quickly erased by the wind.

Hayes met him outside the wall where they'd first parted. The older man's lip quivered, either from the cold or in response to what he'd just done.

"Okay?" Butch asked.

Hayes nodded rapidly. "Easy as pie."

"These were kids," Butch said. "Impelliteri put his disposables outside. The guys in the house aren't going to be nearly this green."

"Indeed," Hayes replied. "I'd suggest we head along and meet them. I'm freezing out here."

The Impelliteri house had three doors: front, back, and another on the west side providing access to and from the garage. Butch wasn't interested in these; they would be the logical places for Impelliteri to station the most guards. The plan was to enter through one of the dozen windows on the ground floor, but the question remained, which window? Butch stood and looked over the fence, eyeing the layout through the falling snow. Impelliteri could have multiple guards at every window in the house; it was too dark to determine.

Butch wished he'd come with a better plan in his pocket. From where he stood, he could only see the edge of the garage, poking out from the far side of the house.

"If I could make a suggestion, Mr. Cardinal?" Hayes said at his side.

"I'd be grateful."

"Instead of rushing into the wolves' den, it might be best to flush them out."

"Come again?"

"Burn it to the ground," Hayes said. Butch looked at the man, whose lip continued to quiver, and now he believed it was merely a response to the bitter night. His eyes were solid and calm. "The garage is the natural point of attack here. I assume there are canisters of petrol inside, as a man like Impelliteri might find it necessary to flee the city without stopping at a gasoline-filling station along the way. Though not part of the house, the garage connects to the house via a narrow walkway covered by a wooden awning. Further, I believe there is only one man stationed inside. If we ignite the garage and the fire spreads, which it should despite the precipitation, Impelliteri and his men would be forced to come out, and we might better act against them."

"That's pretty good," Butch admitted. "I've got Keane's knife. That'll get a fire started."

"Or we could use the matches in my pocket," Hayes said wryly. "Whatever the case, we will know their numbers and they will be exposed. Unfortunately, it will require us to remain outdoors, and it really is unbearably cold."

"A burning house might take the edge off that," Butch noted.

They circled the fence line around the back of the house. At the corner, they encountered a stubby man with a cigar jutting from his lips; its end glowed orange in the otherwise black and white landscape. Hayes saw the guard first and instantly quieted him by impaling him with the iron rod, which passed through the man's clothes, his skin and muscle and bone, as easily as it would pass through a drift of snow. Surprised and already well on his way to death, the guard's jaw clamped down in pain, biting through the end of his cigar, a piece of which fell to the snow. Its burning end hissing as the wet accumulation snuffed out the lit tobacco.

Butch picked up the man's machine gun. In a few minutes, it wouldn't matter how much noise they made. Impelliteri would know they'd arrived.

At the garage, Butch worked his way around to the sliding doors. They were all open, revealing Impelliteri's three vehicles: a Chrysler Custom Imperial, a Lincoln Zephyr, and an Auburn Speedster.

Butch didn't immediately notice the guard. He sat on a stool behind the Chrysler. Butch crept into the structure. A rapid cracking, like a lit packet of firecrackers, filled the garage. He dropped to the hard floor and scooted close to the front bumper of the Lincoln. Peering beneath the carriage, Butch could not make out the legs or feet of the gunman, but he knew the shooter had to be standing somewhere behind the car. Instead of trying to aim, Butch swept his gun in a smooth arc across the floor, keeping a steady pressure on the trigger. The front tires popped and a man shouted amid another raucous spray of bullets. With his ammunition expelled, Butch lay quietly listening for his opponent's location. A series of high-pitched curses rose from the back of the building, followed by the ratcheting click of a new ammo cylinder being locked into place. Then there was an animal grunt, and Hayes softly called, "All clear."

Hayes had come in through the back door of the garage and finished the guard. Butch met him at the trunk of the Auburn. The man lay in the corner, a hole the size of a golf ball punched through the bridge of his nose.

"They had to have heard that," Butch said.

Hayes responded with a finger to his lips. They waited, but no shouting mob burst from the house. No fresh percussion of gunfire disturbed the night. Satisfied that Impelliteri's men had either not heard the gunfire—a highly unlikely prospect—or they were simply waiting to ascertain its meaning, Butch jabbed a finger at Hayes and then pointed to the back door. He needed the man to keep an eye on the walkway connecting the building to the house while he prepared the garage for a blaze.

He grasped the base of the copper band and it uncoiled from his arm. Though it was firmly in his grip, Butch felt oddly bereft, having come to take comfort in the metal's presence on his skin. His arm felt wrong without it, but he needed the staff. Using long, calculated slashes, Butch ripped through the sides of the cars, severing the steel and the fuel lines in the process. Along the east wall, he found three large cans for gasoline. One of them was empty, but the other two held liquid. He upended one can and let its contents run across the floor of the garage. The other he carried to the doorway where Hayes waited. Outside, Butch poured a line of gasoline around the base of the garage and tossed the can into the snow. Already prepared, Hayes held a wooden match between his fingers, but Butch raised his hand: *Not yet.*

Easing close to the back door, muscles coiled and ready for a fight, he brought his arms back and then swung the staff with only a whisper of effort and lodged the copper in the doorjamb about two feet above the threshold. Then he turned to Hayes and nodded.

The fire came on quickly, but it seemed hushed, even gentle as it spread out around the foundation of the garage and slithered through the open doorway. Certainly, it would do the trick, but Butch had expected a more dramatic blaze, perhaps even an explosion.

That came two minutes later, after he and Hayes were on the far side of the west wall.

Flames engulfed the base of the garage and smoke poured from the openings. The snowfall oppressed the rising smoke, keeping it low and tight and thick around the roof of the structure. Then the first of Marco Impelliteri's cars exploded, and then the second. By the time the third car went up, the side door of the house was thrown open and a man attempted to bolt onto the walkway. The copper staff did its job, severing his legs at the knees. The man flipped in the air, screaming until the concrete walk knocked the breath out of him. Butch had hoped the staff would cripple several of Impelliteri's men, bringing the numbers down to a more reasonable level, but it only claimed that single victim, whose blood gushed onto the snow like spilled oil. When the third car exploded, tearing through the roof of the garage with a deafening thunder, the other men had backed away from the side door. It closed a second later.

Butch waited at the wall. His heart beat heavily against his ribs while flames claimed the building. As Hayes had predicted, the flames ran along the awning and began to lap at the side of Impelliteri's house. One of the cars in the drive ignited and exploded and two more followed in a strange, incendiary domino effect.

Men began to pour out the kitchen door, and Butch crouched low, quickly counting five gunmen, all of whom swept their weapons randomly around the yard. Behind them walked another man, wearing a double-breasted brown suit and a crimson tie, who pushed his way through the group and proceeded to the corner. His angry face, with knit brows and a scowling mouth, emerged in the firelight. To Butch, the guy was an incarnation of Satan peering at the inferno.

"That's him," Hayes said at Butch's shoulder. "That's Impelliteri."

He had already figured that out. "Come on," he said. Impelliteri would have to call the fire brigade if he wanted to save his house, not that Butch intended to let him live to enjoy it. If this was going to end tonight, Butch wanted it to happen before any innocent civil servants drove blindly into the crossfire.

Leading Hayes again, Butch hurried around the back of the house and hopped into the yard. He raced to the east side of the structure and without pausing, drove the blade of Keane's knife through a window. He made quick work of the pane, scraping glass out of the frame and then found the latch. A few moments later, he was climbing inside. He checked the window and saw Hayes lumbering through the snow in the side yard. The old guy was doing his best, but the snow was working against his muscles and his stamina. Butch leaned over the sill and held out his hand, which Hayes took the moment fresh gunfire erupted from the front yard. Butch yanked with all of his strength, hauling the older man into the room before slamming what was left of the window closed. Together they slid to the floor, protected by the brick and lathe as bullets *chicked* against the side of the house. Glass shattered above them, rained down. Next to him Hayes groaned.

"Don't sweat," Butch said. "They're wasting their ammo."

"Not a complete waste," Hayes said.

The Alchemi bent his knee and in the gloom Butch noted the streak of glimmering fluid running down the man's pant leg from knee to ankle. One of the bullets had tagged the back of the older man's calf. The wound wasn't fatal, but Hayes's running was over for the night.

"You'll be okay," Butch said. "Use your scarf to tie around the wound. I'm going to see if that door locks."

Rising to his feet, he heard the first footfalls crashing in the hall. Hayes leaned back against the wall with a resolute look on his face and sighed, as if saying: that's it. Butch wasn't as committed to surrender. His mind sparked and snapped. Every moment was as clear as crystal and charged with possibility. Simultaneous to the door's being thrown open, Butch grabbed the metal bar from Hayes's hand, and with little that amounted to a true aim, he whipped the bar toward the doorway and fell back as the ratchet fast explosions of gunfire peeled through the room. Plaster popped from the wall, leaving dozens of divots in a line where a standing man's chest would be, but then the relatively uniform pattern shifted, drawing lines down the walls. Both Hayes and Butch himself would have been cut down had it not been for the mahogany desk between them and the gunmen. Slugs ripped through the top of the furniture and lodged in the thick, polished boards. Butch's ears rang, but all else was silent.

He slid on his back until he could peer around the desk. There he saw two men lying in a heap beyond the threshold with the iron bar jutting from the wall behind and above them. Though he couldn't imagine what magic the bar had performed to bring down both men, he accepted it as a blessing. A miracle. Butch leapt to his feet and sprinted to the hall. With a quick check of the corridor, he stepped over the dead men and pulled the iron bar free. Back in the room, he retrieved the dead men's guns, sliding them across the floor where they came to a stop against the edge of the carpet. He locked the door and removed the key. He carried it and the iron bar back to Hayes, who was wrapping his scarf around the bullet hole in his leg.

"That's a thick door. They won't be getting in here anytime soon."

"And you're telling me this, because you intend to leave me here?"

"I can't carry you."

"You do remember this house is burning, right?"

"I won't be long," Butch said. "If I don't come back, wait until you're certain the fire brigade has arrived. Stay close to them until you can get back to the car. It'll be your best chance."

Shouts and pounding footsteps rose in the hall as Impelliteri's men gathered outside the door. Butch stood and pressed against the wall beside the window. He checked the side yard. Two men stood in a crater of trampled snow. When they saw Butch, they opened fire, sending a barrage of bullets across the side of the house and through the open window. Leaving the wall, Butch crouched and duck-walked across the study to retrieve the machine guns he'd taken from the dead men in the hall. He gave one to Hayes, who looked at the weapon like it was a monstrous child. He kept the other and used it to send a short burst of fire through the window. The men fired back, but Butch had the advantage over the more experienced gunmen because they stood like arrogant statues in the middle of the open yard—dark targets amid a field of white. Butch's bullets ripped through the shoulder and neck of one man, who spun away and toppled into the snow. The other man received a slug in the biceps, which sent his arm back and down. He fired useless rounds into the snow and Butch took him out with another short burst of fire.

In the hall beyond the study door, voices were raised. The doorknob rattled. Someone called for Impelliteri to bring a key.

"I have to go," Butch said.

Hayes nodded, pulling the tommy gun into his lap.

It was a meager farewell for them both, but there was no time for sentiment or even well wishes. Butch climbed onto the windowsill and dropped into the snow. He ran toward the front of the house, hugging the siding.

After finding the front yard empty, he ran to the brick wall and climbed over it. Secure behind the barricade, his mind raced, clicked and hummed as he considered his next move.

Hayes might live through this, though Butch found it unlikely. His own chances of survival were next to zero. Even if their conservative estimate of a dozen men proved accurate, that meant three armed guards remained, and Impelliteri wasn't going to let them leave his side. On the other hand, Impelliteri's force might have only been halved, leaving a squad of ten gun-toting lunatics between Butch and his target.

He had not intended to walk away from this place. That was okay. As long as Impelliteri didn't see Christmas, that was okay.

Chapter 46
Seeing the Future

Hayes used the metal bar as a cane, pressing it hard against the floor as he slid up the wall. He balanced on one leg. Eventually he had to give up on the bar because it was too short to help him complete the task, but he managed to stand, using Impelliteri's desk for support. The pain from his leg came in waves, though the throbbing there was as consistent as a drum beat. Icy wind blew through the shattered window, working its way into his skin and bones. Snow danced in the opening; it frosted the sill and the edge of the desk. Men talked in the hall outside the study door. They'd given up on beating the wood with their fists and testing the knob. Instead, they waited for the master of the house to bring them the spare key. Hayes needed to get to the door and jam the lock before that key arrived, but getting to his feet had proved an uncommon effort, and Hayes took a moment to compose himself. He rested his hands on the desk and took deep breaths, which had the power to sporadically ease the pain below his knee. As he prepared to push on toward the door, a large photograph in the center of the desk caught his attention. His eyes had adjusted to the deep gloom in the study, and though he could not see the picture clearly from where he stood, something about its subject caught Hayes's eye. Before he could remind himself that the door's lock was his priority, Hayes slid the photograph across the desktop. A bullet had punched a hole in the upper left quadrant, but the image and what it represented was perfectly clear. His heart raced, momentarily eclipsing the pain and pulse in his leg.

"No," he whispered, feeling the kind of panic a parent endures when seeing their child toddling into a busy street.

Hayes squinted and pulled the picture closer to his face and then held it away, but distance didn't change the wholly familiar structure he saw there.

One of the men in the hallway laughed, startling Hayes out of his disturbance. Ignoring the pain, he hopped quickly to the door and pressed against it as he fished the Ever Key from his pocket. He slid the steel pin into the lock. A moment later, it had adapted to the mechanism and would serve as a perfect key, but Hayes needed something else from the object. With a flick of his finger, he tapped the blunt, dime-sized handle three times. The protruding metal shifted and melted, flattened out against the keyhole, forming a seal that was as impenetrable as if he had poured molten lead into the apparatus. Then he hopped back to the desk and lifted the photograph, hoping the image had changed, had proven itself nothing more than a figment of his panicked imagination.

But this was not the case. There on the paper, captured by a camera's lens was the exterior of 213 House—the home of the Alchemi and the metals they protected. Hayes had retrieved the photograph from a spray of papers at the center of Impelliteri's desk. He swept these together and took them to the corner, where he sank down on the floor. Using his matches for light Hayes read the telegrams and the notations, each one adding weight to his dread.

On one sheet, Impelliteri had written notes, which would have been all but nonsensical to most. *The rose and what else? How many men inside? No survivors/no backlash/no one to talk. I'll need a crew of ten maybe fifteen. Contact Larocca for local muscle. Come into my house? I'll tear yours to the fucking ground.*

Impelliteri was planning to attack 213 House. After acquiring the Galenus Rose, the mobster intended to visit Brooklyn with a squad of men, and wage war on the Alchemi, murdering every one of Hayes's associates. Nothing in the notes indicated that Impelliteri knew about the arsenal of metals in the chambers beneath the house, but Lonnie Musante had told his boss about the Rose. Was it so unlikely the man would offer up more information? Maybe even everything he knew about the Alchemi and the pieces they guarded?

It's my fault, Hayes thought. He shook out the match, which was dangerously close to burning his fingers, tossed it on the floor, and lit another. *Brand and I confirmed Musante's story. The mobster might have thought it all some ridiculous fairy tale, but the moment we stepped into his house we made it real like two elves stepping from the pages of a Hans Christian Andersen tale.*

Obscenities rose outside the door. Apparently the gunmen had found a second key, which would do them no more good with the lock than a chicken bone or a bowl of soup. Eventually, they'd give up and come around to the window. Hayes eyed the tommy gun on the floor and knew he could defend the study's one means of entry, but he couldn't stay here. The house was burning. If Mr. Cardinal failed, Hayes was as good as dead, and his home, the place he prized above all others, would come under attack.

Again he used the iron rod for a cane. This time he found it much easier to get to his feet. He slid along the wall and lifted the gun from the floor. Hayes poked his head out the window and found the side yard clear. After dropping his two weapons into the snow, he began the painful task of following them.

Chapter 47
Forfeit

"The punk jammed something in the lock," DeNardo said. "Key won't even go in."

Marco ground his teeth and closed his eyes, fighting the persistent urge to bellow his rage. The wrestler and his Alchemi stooge had invaded his home, had killed too many of his men; the cocksuckers had lit his house on fire, and it was coming down around Marco's ears. Though the fire had not spread beyond the west wing, smoke filled the hallway. The abrasive mist stung his eyes, worked on his throat like sandpaper.

"Shut it down," he said, quietly. "DeNardo take Robertson to the side of the house. Join up with Rudy and Theo and keep those two pinned down inside. If they try to slip out, kill the old man, but the wrestler has information I need. If he tries to run, take his legs off. He'll only need to talk for a minute."

DeNardo nodded his head and clapped Robertson on the back as he set off along the hallway. The other two men—Jake and Luke—remained in the hall, waiting for their orders. Marco would keep these two close. Both had hard, square faces with pencil-thin mustaches, and both had hands that looked like they could crush bowling balls if called to do so. They looked like twin statues carved from aggression. They weren't bright enough to question his orders, but they'd proven themselves time and again—riding shotgun on shipments of whiskey from Canada—to be smart enough in a pinch. Marco trusted them as much as he trusted any men.

"Let's get outside," he said. "You two stay in front of me in case those fuckers managed to get out of the house."

"Boss," the men said in unison. They nodded their heads in assent.

The foyer of Marco's home had grown oven hot, with smoke so heavy he couldn't see more than a foot in front of him, and his rage ticked up another notch when he realized the place wasn't going to be saved. The fire brigade would arrive in time to comb through charred and melted history, nothing more. Carmen would wail and sob and ask god, "Why?" on bended knees. His daughter, Sylvia, would be sorrowful and withdrawn, frightened to think that something so sturdy, so trusted, could be taken away with the striking of a match. At least they were safe. After the cop had called to pass along the wrestler's threat, Marco had ushered his family out of the house. They would have dinner with Carmen's parents and then go to Assumption for the Midnight Mass, where Marco had intended to meet them, but that wasn't going to happen now. Even after he watched Cardinal bleed out, he'd have to remain on the property to explain the bodies littering his yard. He'd have to explain the fire. He'd have to relive every fucking thing that had gone wrong. Outside he followed Jake and Luke into the middle of the snowy lawn and looked back to see orange flames feeding on the walls and roof of his house. A lesser man would mourn the little things, the mementoes collected over the years to remind him of travels and milestones, weddings and fatherhood, but Marco kept sentimentality out of it. The house had cost a fortune—two fortunes by current standards—and now it was in the process of being reduced to black shit, and if he could murder Cardinal a hundred times—each one slower than the last—it still wouldn't be enough to pay back this offense.

He thought only briefly about Paul Rabin. It seemed clear enough the man hadn't done his job. Whether that meant Rabin was dead or merely incompetent mattered little. In fact it was good news in its own way. The fewer people who knew about the Rose the better.

Heat from the inferno that had been his home broke the worst of the nighttime chill. It wrapped around Marco like a blanket, and he closed his eyes and steadied his breathing. For a moment, he imagined the near future, a calming trick that Lon had taught him years ago.

Tomorrow at this time the wrestler would be dead, he told himself. Marco would set his family up at the Drake and he'd head east, back to Brooklyn, to a house which stood only three miles from the dilapidated tenement his parents had called home. If Lonnie Musante hadn't been blowing hot air up his ass, Marco would find weapons there waiting like plagues to spread death and submission—weapons so powerful he'd never have to worry about Angus Powell or Bugs Moran again. For that matter, he wouldn't have to worry about Nitti or Ricca or anyone else in the rackets, either.

Twenty-four hours wasn't long. It was all in the way you looked at a thing.

He opened his eyes and immediately saw motion on the periphery of his vision. DeNardo was loping around the side of the house, making his way toward him.

"Yeah, Rudy and Theo are morgue ornaments," he said. "Looks like the wrestler got himself a heater and threw some lead. Our guys are tits to god."

"Are Cardinal and that other fuck still inside?"

"Yeah, can't tell," said DeNardo. "It was quiet over there, but I wasn't about to stick my head through the window to say, 'Hello,' if you know what I mean? I'm headed back over. Robertson and I will move in close and get the skinny, but I thought you'd want to know about Rudy and Theo."

"What I want is Butch Cardinal in pieces all over this front yard, so why don't you figure out a way to make that happen?"

"Yeah, sure," DeNardo said nervously. The man spun on his heels and headed off.

Flames had reached the midpoint of his house. They roared like dragons, that had conquered a castle and perched on the roof to celebrate the meat in their bellies. Marco studied them, lost himself in their dance as he thought through the evening, using what had already happened to form a logical conclusion about what would happen next. If Cardinal had gotten out of the study, then he was likely lurking along the fence line, watching Marco and his men and waiting for a new opportunity. He'd want to thin the ranks further, maybe take out DeNardo and Robertson, before moving on Jake, Luke and Marco.

Through the dragon song of his house's destruction, he imagined he heard his name, called softly or from a great distance. For the briefest of moments, he actually thought the fire was speaking to him, summoning him, but he recognized the impossibility of such a ridiculous idea. When his name again floated through the air, Marco turned away from the burning house.

"Boss," Jake said, jabbing the muzzle of his machine gun at the distant gate. "Company's coming."

Two men walked across the snowy yard. Their faces were masks of orange catching the flame light at Marco's back. The sight of them was part joy and part fury, like water hitting a pan of hot oil. His body sizzled and crackled.

Butch Cardinal trudged toward him, his hands clasped behind his lowered head. At his back was the cop—Lennon—who had his service piece wedged tightly behind the wrestler's ear. Marco pushed his way through Jake and Luke and waved for his men to follow.

"Merry Christmas," Lennon said. He kicked the back of Cardinal's knees, and the wrestler dropped to the snow, head still lowered. Defeated. "When we spoke on the phone earlier you said something about my present. Ten grand?"

Before Marco responded to Lennon he grasped either side of Cardinal's head and leaned in close. "They'll find pieces of you inside," he said, his voice barely audible through the wind and the roar of flames. "Give me the Rose and I'll put two behind your ears before we start sawing. Fuck me around, and you'll be wide awake when we take your arms."

Cardinal didn't respond, and his silence infuriated Marco. He wanted to hear excuses and pleading, and he wanted to hear the voice of the son of a bitch who had run him around the pole a hundred times. But apparently the wrestler had become resolved to his fate and saw no point in wasting his breath.

Marco turned to his guards. With a voice as serene as if he were asking a florist for a particular cut of flower, he said, "Jake, I want you to strip this guy down and check every pocket. Search him from tits to toes. Put your hands up his ass if you need to. If this guy is hiding anything, I want it found. Luke, you cover them. If Cardinal breathes wrong, blow out his knees."

As Jake stepped forward and Luke took a firing stance at Cardinal's side, Lennon lowered his gun and returned it to his holster. "Now how about you come across with that reward, so I can get back to my family?"

Marco eyed the detective with annoyance. The guy had nerve, Marco had to admit that, but he didn't have to appreciate it. He pointed over his shoulder at the burning house, "Access to my funds is a little complicated right now. I know where to find you. You'll be paid."

"I hope you've got a fireproof safe," said Lennon.

Why was the cop needling him? Did he honestly think now was the time to play it cute? When Marco's house was about ten minutes from collapsing? He checked on the progress with Cardinal. Jake had the man's overcoat in his hands and was searching the pockets.

"Check the lining as well," Marco said. Then he turned back to Lennon. "You'd better be on your way, detective. I'll be sure there isn't enough of Cardinal left to warrant an investigation."

"Actually, you'd be doing me a greater favor if you left him intact," Lennon said. "We get a clean identification and we can close Musante's case and everyone gets back to a normal life. Carve as many pieces out of him as you want, I'm just saying leave the face alone and have one of these saps drop the body someplace public. Or just shoot him as a trespasser and let us clean up the mess."

Though it didn't play into his need to hear Butch Cardinal's screams, the detective's suggestions were logical enough. Marco wasn't completely swayed—there was a lot to be said for watching a rival bleed—but he had time to think it over.

"It's no sweat off my brow one way or the other," Lennon continued.

"You can go now, detective," Marco replied.

"Boss," Jake said, drawing everyone's attention to where he stood beside Cardinal. "You wanna tell me what the hell that is?"

What looked like a wide, flat bib made of golden chain draped Cardinal's shoulders; it lay across his chest and stopped at mid-belly. Though he couldn't be certain, Marco wanted to believe it was another artifact from the Alchemi's vaults, another bit of magical metal. Maybe Cardinal had several more pieces on him—a fine start to Marco's collection.

"Take it off of him," Marco said. "Toss it over here."

"You're a fancy dresser," Jake told Cardinal. He lifted the odd garment over the wrestler's head and flung it to the snow at Marco's feet.

But Marco barely noticed the metallic bib. Once it was removed, he saw the necklace dangling from a chain at Cardinal's throat. He recognized the ugly blob of metal from a sketch Lonnie had drawn him. It was the Galenus Rose. Anticipation suffused his system like a drink of water after a long dry spell. His nerves tingled and his head went light. All of this happened in a second, the length of time it took for the Rose to settle against Butch Cardinal's chest.

"Stay back," he told Jake. Marco walked toward Cardinal, extending his hand for the treasure hanging from the man's throat. It was a beacon guiding him to peace. It was salvation.

Chapter 48
Flashes Before Your Eyes

Butch tensed as Impelliteri prowled forward. Snow melted beneath his shins, soaking his pants and affixing to his legs like frozen steel plates. Instinct insisted he lunge at the son of a bitch before Impelliteri wrapped his fat hand around the Rose. A mental picture show played in which Butch found his footing and drove his shoulder into Impelliteri's gut, taking the filthy punk down, and then grasping his head and snapping the gangster's neck with a satisfying crack, the way he'd done to that mad dog, Rabin. But Butch resisted any such dramatic display. A gun pointed at his head, and more could be drawn in seconds. He stood no more chance of outmaneuvering bullets than he did of sprouting wings and flapping his way into the snowy night.

How many seconds left before he died? How many thoughts? Would any of them be worth spit on a griddle? Where was the epiphany, the moral? His entire life had been one long rigged bout. He couldn't beat it. No one could. You were either in on the rig or you got taken by it.

The crooked cop kept his hand on the butt of his gun. He wanted to draw the weapon, Butch could see the eagerness in his eyes, like a kid eyeing a plate of his mama's chicken. Each of Impelliteri's steps cracked like applause from a distant crowd. His eyes sparked pure longing for the bauble dangling from Butch's throat. As he planted his feet in front of Butch's kneeling form he peered down and released a smirk of scalding disdain. *Bum,* that face said. *Just another speck of human shit needing to be wiped from the earth.*

Where is Hayes? Butch wondered. Had the old man escaped? Had he collected the copper staff and the Alchemi's other precious articles and limped off into the night? Or had a different squad of Impelliteri's men broken through the door of the study, chased him across a side yard or through the house, only to shoot the injured man down like a lame horse? He'd liked Hayes. He hoped the man found his way far from this place and managed to leave the infected city.

Impelliteri yanked off a glove and reached for the Galenus Rose. His warm hand brushed over the cold-pimpled flesh on Butch's chest. Grasping the pendant tightly in his fist, Impelliteri yanked it away from Butch and lifted his hand close to his face to better inspect his prize. He turned in the snow and set off toward the cop's side. The thug named Jake sidled up to his boss and leaned in close to get a better look at the Rose, and like a child who refuses to share the joys of a special toy, Impelliteri shoved the man away. Jake stumbled in the snow.

With the two men distracted, Butch knew his only opportunity had been presented. He rolled the thorn Hayes had given him on his tongue and pushed it out over his lips. Turning himself for a better angle, he spit the thorn at Luke, who had turned his head to grin like an idiot at his stumbling counterpart. The thing struck the distracted gunman in the cheek, and his expression of amusement froze. His body stiffened and he teetered for a moment before crashing back into the snow, like a statue that had been pushed from its pedestal.

Butch reached for Keane's knife, which had been lashed to the side of his ankle with a strip of shirt. His fingers grazed the hilt, and then a sudden punch at his shoulder knocked his hand away. Warmth ran over his skin, emanated from a place beneath his collarbone that pulsed with ache.

He lifted his head and saw the crooked cop, Lennon, aiming down the barrel of his revolver. Smoke rose from the gun's muzzle. Steam lifted from the barrel. Light flashed. The second bullet punched into Butch's chest just above his left nipple. Another shot. Another punch. More warmth. The pain erupted across his body. His chest constricted as if pinched between two train cars. He struggled to breathe.

This is how it was always going to end.

A final shot.

Butch experienced no flood of emotion, no parade of memories from a life that had proved misspent. He saw no welcoming light, nor felt the overwhelming caress of peace he'd often heard men experienced in their last moments.

His thoughts emptied and his senses closed down. All but for sight.

Before him stood a static tableau, like a photograph that filled his vision with motionless figures. Fire raged through the Impelliteri house, but the guttering dance of flames had stopped as if frozen by the unforgiving cold. The smoke was similarly captured, no longer drifting skyward, but rather casting an unmoving haze over the decimated home. In front of these was the tree decorated for Christmas, and each ornament, each shining piece of cheap metal, was vivid and etched with the finest detail. To the left of the tree, Detective Lennon, wearing a rigid, inscrutable face, pointed his gun. And there was Jake staring dumbly with the barrel of his tommy gun planted in the snow. Two other men were frozen in mid step as they ran around the side of Impelliteri's house, machine guns at the ready. And there in front of him, Marco Impelliteri threw a glance over his shoulder at Butch. He wore an expression of surprise that had been captured in the moment it was transitioning to amusement. From his hand, barely visible beneath the cuff of his expensive overcoat was a chain, and at the end of the chain, an ugly wad of metal dangled like the pendulum of a melted clock.

Chapter 49
Common Valor

On the third day of 1933, Detective Roger Lennon stood on stage next to Police Commissioner Allman. Before him his colleagues, wearing dress blues and faces of sedate admiration, listened to a tale of Lennon' bravery in his apprehension of wanted killer William "Butch" Cardinal. If they knew the commissioner's words were nothing more than fabrication, as Lennon did, the knowledge was absent from their expressions.

As for Lennon, his back and feet hurt from standing at attention for so long. He'd already listened to the same horseshit falling from Wenders' fat, wet lips, and had endured poorly worded accolades from two other detectives on the subject. The steam heat clutched his uniform and soaked into the fibers, pushing through his shirt and skin like burrowing insects. Perspiration saturated his collar and cuffs, and he experienced moments of light headedness so profound he felt certain he would topple over.

But he stood there. He heard the lies, though they hit his eardrums in a hum as if the organs refused to translate any further deceit. The voices he heard in his head belonged to the man he'd killed and to himself.

On Christmas Eve, he'd stood outside the gate to Marco Impelliteri's home, watching the blaze from a distance and hearing the occasional pop of gunfire. He'd spent a long time debating the situation, wondering if there was anything left to be done. And then Butch Cardinal emerged from the shadows, holding a tommy gun on him. Two minutes later, Butch explained the situation.

Then he told Lennon he had a plan:

"You may have to shoot me," Butch said. "I don't want Impelliteri to have the satisfaction. Things go bad and you do the shooting yourself. It may be the only thing that saves your skin."

"I've got more than enough rounds for Impelliteri and his men," said Lennon.

"You can't count on that," Butch said. "I made a mistake letting Hayes get involved in all of this. He's trapped in the house, and he's got himself a bum peg. We need to give him some time to get clear."

"We can all get clear."

"No, we can't." Resolution hardened the frown on Butch's lips, tightened the line of his jaw. "Too many men. Too many questions to answer. If Hayes gets away he can fix this. He'll bring men. They can retrieve what was lost. You have to take me in there and give me a chance at Impelliteri, but if it goes bad, you do the shooting."

Then Butch managed to take out Luke Chalice, but he wasn't going to be fast enough to get a drop on Impelliteri. More men were racing through the snow. Jake would see, and he'd get his gun up plenty quick, and though Lennon might have been able to thin out the crowd, he'd put his neck on the block in the process. If even one of Impelliteri's men escaped to tell the tale, Lennon and his family might as well cut their own throats because no amount of talk or scratch would save their asses. So Lennon had taken his shot. He'd wanted to get a clean shot to the heart, but his hands were shaking and his aim went foul. Realizing he'd only wounded the big man, Lennon took a second shot, and this one had hit the mark, just above the lower arc of the pectoral, but Butch had reacted as if he hadn't noticed, so Lennon had shot again and again, wanting nothing more than to put the wrestler down, put him out of his misery, and bring the whole mess of a night to an end.

Eventually Butch had toppled in the snow, but not after what struck Lennon as interminable minutes. Sadness and perplexity cast shadows over the man's eyes, even as the light from Impelliteri's burning house reflected on the glassy lenses.

Regret seized Lennon's chest and head before Butch crashed into the snow. How could he have done it? Why had it been so easy to shoot the wrestler? Lennon would have taken longer to bring down a rabid dog. Had he wanted to murder the man who'd brought so much turmoil to his life? Was he that kind of man? He didn't want to believe it, but killing Butch Cardinal had been the easy thing, the smart thing. Now, normality could return to Lennon's life. The balance was restored.

Standing on the stage in front of his equally corrupt brothers, Lennon felt as if wishing for normality in this city was like praying for the clap, begging for a tumor. He knelt before the throne of a diseased king and ate grapes from his shit-smeared fingers and he considered himself blessed.

Another wave of dizziness overwhelmed him, and Lennon adjusted his stance. He breathed deeply, enduring one spike of shame after another. Even telling himself that he'd only done as the wrestler had asked achieved nothing but greater levels of grief and self loathing, and there was no way to make this crime right, no way to cleanse his soul of this shame.

When the commissioner said Roger Lennon's name and then pulled away to lead the applause, Lennon stepped forward to accept his commendation.

Chapter 50
The Last Violent Business

On the sixth day of the new year John Hayes organized his men outside of a squat office building in Chicago's Southside. The sun shone, but an icy wind cut down the streets, blowing past pedestrians whose brows were chafed red by the cruel air. Men and women spotted the group of well-dressed men congregated before the building and crossed the street to avoid involvement in what was likely violent business.

They weren't wrong.

After his house had been reduced to condemned cinders on Christmas Eve, Marco Impelliteri had moved his family into the Drake Hotel, where they were pampered to assuage their grief and frustration, but he spent little time in their company. Hayes' men had reported that with the exception of New Year's Eve Impelliteri had slept elsewhere. His men had tracked Impelliteri constantly in the days following the gangster's acquisition of the Galenus Rose and several other items of interest to the Alchemi. *Butch Cardinal's* ill-conceived attack on Impelliteri's home had resulted in the loss of not only the Rose, but also a Petrification Thorn, a bullet-resistant tunic, Brand's copper arm band, and the Promethean Blade. It had been a dreadful night for everyone involved, if not a complete failure. Mr. Cardinal had managed to send Impelliteri's gang into disarray. With so many men dead and injured, the gangster had been forced to begin rebuilding his mob, starting mostly from scratch, which had slowed his plans to mount an attack on 213 House. For that, Cardinal had Hayes' gratitude. But while his family enjoyed the comforts and the services at the Drake Hotel, Impelliteri spent most of his time, day and night, in an office on the second floor of the Southside building.

As with their capture of Musante (Butch Cardinal's capture of Musante, Hayes noted to himself), they had to tread lightly. If injured while wearing the Galenus Rose, Impelliteri would have to be taken into custody and observed until the Rose emerged. Hayes didn't want that. He wanted a clean operation that put the Rose in his hand and put Impelliteri in the ground. Once he had regained possession of the Alchemi's property, Hayes intended to leave Chicago and never return, and that could not happen fast enough for him. He associated the city with misery, like the wind, all but constant with only subtle lulls to make the next gust all the more dreadful.

He reiterated caution to his men. Impelliteri's guards would be armed and ready to kill. They were not the sort to question or bargain. "Immobilize on sight," Hayes said. "Do not hesitate."

Limping to the door, Hayes held it open and ushered his men over the threshold into the shadowed foyer of the building. A click at the end of the hall announced a door being latched shut. Another door, this one on Hayes' right, opened a crack to reveal a curious eye before slamming closed.

With his injured leg, Hayes could lead his men only in strategy. As they raced up the stairs to the office where Marco Impelliteri had spent the last several nights, Hayes hobbled up the stairs, clutching the rail tightly and occasionally wincing when his weight came down wrong and sent a flare of pain from ankle to groin.

At the landing he paused to give his leg a moment to recover. From the end of the hall, came a great racket of voices and shuffling feet. He was surprised to hear nothing in the way of gunshots or cries of pain. Soon enough all sounds hushed. He limped down the hall and entered an office lobby that held a small cherry-wood secretary's desk and chair. Sun streamed through the wooden blinds in harsh planes that stung his eyes. He observed the small space, and was again surprised. There should have been bodies here: Impelliteri's guards.

Hayes continued into the main office and found his men lining the perimeter of the room, all of their eyes focused on the same spot. The office décor consisted of half a dozen filing cabinets along the back wall, a small radio, a steel fan, a large black safe with its door open, and Impelliteri's desk and chair. Impelliteri sat in the chair, holding a gun in one hand and the Galenus Rose in the other. His eyes were moist from tears and his cheeks burned crimson. He raised his gun and pointed it at Hayes' chest.

"Tell me how it works," the gangster said, his voice cracking with misery. "You have to tell me."

Hayes recalled his conversation with Mr. Musante, who had been more than generous with his information about Marco Impelliteri's personal deviations. He had wanted the Rose for a number of reasons, but the primary of those was the hope that it would cure him of a sickness that was not the result of virus or bacterium. He lusted after his own child and Hayes knew of no ameliorative agent for such a thing.

"It only mends the body's tissues," Hayes said. "Flesh and blood and bone. It can't heal a diseased soul."

"Liar!" Impelliteri cried, shaking his gun in Hayes' direction. "Lonnie told me it would cure me. Now tell me how it works or I'll start putting holes in your friends."

Though disgusted with the man and wholly impatient with his irrational sense of entitlement, Hayes still found the expediency with which he killed Marco Impelliteri shocking. He hadn't thought to cock his arm back, nor had he thought to launch the iron bar in the gangster's direction. It happened so quickly, Hayes hadn't given himself time to consider these things, but they happened nonetheless.

Impelliteri had his head turned, his gun pointed at Mr. Ross, who stood before the window. "How about fat boy?" Impelliteri said. "If I open him up, you think you might change your mind?"

Then the bar was rocketing through the air. Hayes had never put such force behind a throw in his life. The rod broke apart into dozens of needle-sharp spears, and they hit the gangster in the head. Impelliteri's face and skull vaporized, broken and shredded and dragged away on the surfaces of the projectiles. Like the aftermath of a shotgun blast at close range, nothing but tattered flesh remained above Marco Impelliteri's neck.

Hayes wondered how long it would take the Galenus Rose to repair that level of damage, or if it even could. He stepped forward, eyeing the pendant still grasped in Impelliteri's motionless palm. Any second it would become liquid and then vapor, vanishing into the man's pores to begin its reconstruction of him.

But that didn't happen.

With his men still in position around the edges of the room, waiting for his instruction, Hayes approached the desk. He tossed a glance toward Ross, who showed his understanding of Hayes' concern with a cocking of his head.

Hayes reached over the desk and lifted the Galenus Rose from Impelliteri's hand.

He felt nothing.

At contact, he should have been accosted by a thousand memories of healing. Further, with his leg so damaged, the Rose should have begun its curative work on him, but there was nothing. The Galenus Rose rested in his palm, a hunk of red-tinged metal, with no more power than a wad of chewing gum.

Hayes turned to observe his men as he thought this development through. When his eyes fell on Mr. Ross, he noticed the man was fighting against a grin. His eyes sparkled with amusement.

And Hayes knew why. Ross had already figured what was just now occurring to Hayes: he was holding the copy of the Galenus Rose. For a time, Butch Cardinal had possessed both. He had gone to Impelliteri's with a clear plan of dying, of being murdered, so that no one, not the syndicate men nor the police, would ever look for him again. Around his neck, the most obvious place a man like Impelliteri would look, he'd worn the fake Rose. As for the real icon, the one with power, Mr. Cardinal had likely hidden it lower on his body, in a region that a man like Impelliteri would only search as a last resort.

It was so simple. So obvious. But only obvious to those who had been part of the chase.

Hayes returned Mr. Ross's smile and nodded his head. Then he ordered his colleagues to search the safe and the desk and the closet and Impelliteri's person. He left them to their work and returned to the landing and the stairs.

Outside he limped to the car and opened the door.

It was there. Returned.

On the passenger side of the front seat laid the real Galenus Rose.

Hayes' breath caught in his throat. Even without touching the pendant he could feel its authenticity. He pulled away and straightened up and looked over the top of the car at the sunlit streets, searching hopefully for a familiar face amid the harried pedestrians.

They moved as if in unison, a single herd. Wrapped in hats, scarves, and heavy coats, some so threadbare they seemed more like the garments of the long dead. Men and women made their ways to their homes, or their offices, or to shops where every purchase was the result of agonizing debate—every penny paid a sacrifice. Irretrievable. For some their destinations would prove dull, familiar, and colorless. Others would find joy. Others would find misery. But they carried on, moving forward, bundled and hunched, walking swiftly with their heads down to survive the cold.

Acknowledgments

My thanks to those talented writers who took the time to read and critique this work, either in whole or in part: Nate Southard, Connie May Fowler, Richard McCann, Abby Frucht, and Domenic Stansberry. Along those lines, I send additional thanks to the students and faculty of the Vermont College of Fine Arts Masters Program in Writing. I've enjoyed little in life as much as I enjoyed my time amongst them. May the circle be unbroken.

On the home front, thanks to my ever-enduring partner, John, and our "kids," Mina and Buster. Much thanks to Ken Ingram and Don Denham for their friendship.

Continued thanks to Steve, Kip, Toby, and Alex at Lethe Press, and a special thanks to Matt Cresswell for his stunning cover design.

LEE THOMAS is the Bram Stoker Award and two-time Lambda Literary Award-winning author of *The German*, *Ash Street*, *Torn*, *The Dust of Wonderland*, *In the Closet, Under the Bed*, *Like Light for Flies*, and many other books. He lives in Austin, TX with his partner, John, his cat, Buster, and his dog, Mina. Find him on the web at leethomasauthor.com

CPSIA information can be obtained at www.ICGtesting.com
Printed in the USA
BVOW01s0813010514

352270BV00002B/5/P